Maive S. H Stokes

Indian fairy Tales

Maive S. H Stokes

Indian fairy Tales

ISBN/EAN: 9783337024352

Printed in Europe, USA, Canada, Australia, Japan

Cover: Foto ©Andreas Hilbeck / pixelio.de

More available books at **www.hansebooks.com**

INDIAN FAIRY TALES

COLLECTED AND TRANSLATED

BY

MAIVE STOKES.

WITH NOTES BY MARY STOKES,

AND AN INTRODUCTION BY W. R. S. RALSTON, M.A.

London :

ELLIS & WHITE, NEW BOND STREET.

1880.

To my dear Grannie, Susan Bazely.

PREFACE.

THE first twenty-five stories in this book were told me at Calcutta and Simla by two Ayahs, Dunkní and Múniyá, and by Karím, a Khidmatgar. The last five were told Mother by Múniyá. At first the servants would only tell their stories to me, because I was a child and would not laugh at them, but afterwards the Ayahs lost their shyness and told almost all their stories over again to Mother when they were passing through the press. Karím would never tell his to her or before her. The stories were all told in Hindústání, which is the only language that these servants know.

Dunkní is a young woman, and was born and brought up in Calcutta. She got the stories, she told me, from her husband, Mochí, who was born in Calcutta and brought up at Benares.

Múniyá is a very old, white-haired woman. She has great-grandchildren. She was born at Patna, but when she was seven years old she was taken to Calcutta, where she was brought up and married. She and Dunkní are both Hindús.

Karím is a Muhammadan and was born at Lucknow. He says that "The Mouse" and "The Wonderful Story" are both Lucknow tales.

The notes to this book were written by Mother, and Father helped her to spell the Native names and words. He also made the Index.

Dr. George King helped us in the Botany; Mr. Tawney and Mr. Campbell of Islay, who saw many of the stories in manuscript, have given us several remarks. So has my uncle, John Boxwell.

M. S. H. STOKES.

CALCUTTA,
March 24th, 1879.

INTRODUCTION.

IN almost every part of Europe the tales current among the common people have been of late years diligently sought out, and carefully collected. Variants of them pour in profusely every year. But it does not seem probable that any entirely new stories will be discovered in any European land. Nor is it likely that in fresh variants of the longer and apparently more artificial tales, any quite new incidents, or even any unquestionably novel features, will be found. The harvest has been abundant, its chief fruits are now stored, and the work which is still going on among the gleaners, although in itself good and praiseworthy, may be regarded without the excitement of eager hope. The task of the present seems to be, not so much the garnering of European folk-tales, as their comparison and elucidation, and, so far as possible, their explanation. But in many cases they do not appear to contain in themselves the ingredients which are necessary for their resolution into their primary elements. Nor do the records of the lands in which they exist always supply what is wanted. The "fairy tales" of Europe throw very little light upon, are but slightly illuminated by, the histories of the widely differing lands in which they so closely resemble each other. And the most interesting among them, those which appear most clearly to bear witness to their being embodiments of mythological ideas, or expansions of moral precepts, seem

to be but little in keeping with what we know of the senti-
ments and beliefs of the heathen ancestors of the villagers
in whose memories they have been for so many centuries
retained. Among such tales of this kind, for instance, as
linger on in our own islands, there is but little to be found
which can be looked upon as a specially characteristic
deposit left by the waves of Iberian, Celtic, and Teutonic
population which have successively passed over the face of
the land. This statement does not, of course, hold good in
the case of such legends about national heroes as Mr. J. F.
Campbell has found thriving in Ireland and the West Highlands of Scotland, and which he justly believes to be "bardic
recitations, fast disappearing, and changing into prose."
They belong to a different section of popular fiction from
that to which reference is now made. It is often difficult
to draw the line between these two classes of folk-tales.
But there is a striking difference between the typical repre-
sentatives of the two divisions, between cosmopolitan
novelettes like Cinderella or the Sleeping Beauty, on the
one hand, and pseudo-historic legends about local heroes
on the other. It is unfortunate that we do not possess a
sufficiency of accurate designations for the numerous species
of the genus folk-tale. Their existence would prevent much
misapprehension. But in their absence, a discusser of
popular tales should take pains to define precisely to what
tribe, family, or group of stories his remarks are intended to
apply.

There are to be found, in all European lands, certain tales
which are of a more complex structure than the rest, which
appear to have been constructed by a skilled workman, to
be artificial productions rather than natural growths. It is
only with such stories as these that we have at present to
deal. These novelettes or comediettas, as they may be
called, of the European common people, differ but little in

their essential parts, whether they are recited in the cold north or the balmy south, the rude east or the cultured west.   Their openings, it is true, vary with their localities ; but in the main body of the tale, not only does the same leading idea pervade all the variants, but also the same sequence of events leads up in almost every case to the same termination.   To this class of stories belong nearly all the tales which, under considerably modified forms, have naturalized themselves in the nurseries of Europe.   In it are comprised many popular fictions, on the obscurer parts of which a quite insufficient light is thrown by researches among the manners and mythologies of old European heathenism.

It is upon such stories as these that a kindly light beams with the greatest advantage from Asia.   Very similar stories have been preserved in the memories of the common people in many parts of Asia, but especially in India.   And their leading ideas are perfectly in accordance with the mythology or the moral teaching of the Asiatics who, age after age, have delighted in telling or hearing them.   In such cases as these it seems to be not very unreasonable to suppose that the story was originally, if not created, at all events shaped and trimmed in Asia, and thence was afterwards conveyed from lip to lip into Europe. Such universal favourites as Beauty and the Beast and Puss in Boots may be confidently cited as oriental fictions which have taken possession of European minds.   There is a rich store of other popular fictions, which may be left to be accounted for according to the two principal methods of interpretation in vogue.   They may be explained as independent developments of mythological germs common to the ancestors of the various Aryan peoples of Europe.   Or they may be regarded as embodiments of certain ideas common to savages of all races.   It will be sufficient to deal at present with the more limited, but better known class, to which special attention has been called.

Among the Asiatic folk-tales which seem likely to assist in their explanation, none are more copious or more useful than those of India. There the old religion has maintained itself with which so many of these stories are linked, and there the moral teaching still prevails which made its voice heard in other tales of the far-off time when they first became current. Any collection of genuine Indian Fairy Tales is therefore certain to be, not only of interest to the general reader, but also of real value to the specialist who devotes himself to the comparison of folk-tales. The collection now before us has great merits of its own. The stories have been told in Hindústáni to the very young collector by two ayahs, who are both Hindús, and by a Muhammadan man-servant. In this respect Miss Stokes's contribution to our knowledge of India differs from the very similar, and very charming, work by Miss Frere, "Old Deccan Days," the stories in which were told by an ayah who was, as her father and grandfather had been, a native Christian. The two books ought to be compared with each other. No possessor of the one ought to be without the other. All the stories contained in the present volume, as we learn from the notes, have been read back by the young collector to the tellers in Hindústáni after they were told, and a second time by the annotator before they were printed. "I never saw people more anxious to have their tales retold exactly, than are Dunkní and Múniyá," the two story-telling ayahs. Not till each tale was pronounced by them to be exact was it sent to the press. The stories may be taken then as faithful transcripts of Indian thought. The merits of the copious Notes contributed by the late Mrs. Whitley Stokes, bearing witness to a very wide range of reading, and to a most intelligent use of the authorities referred to, will be fully acknowledged by all who have had occasion to explore the regions from which she has gathered so much valuable information. Throughout the whole of the work thus conscientiously compiled and intelligently annotated, there will be found scattered, in addition to its other merits, many a parallel with our own popular tales, many an illustration or explanation of their meaning—a ray of light shot here or there which illumines their dark places, and may enable the explorers of their mystic domains to avoid stumbles which are often somewhat mortifying. It remains only to point out a few of the most important passages.

Some of the stories in this volume are so thoroughly oriental, so little in accordance with western thought or feeling, that they have not found an echo among ourselves ; their counterparts are not to be found naturalized in European lands. Of such a kind are the legends, taken from literary sources, of " The Upright King," and of " Rájá Harichand's Punishment," in which the patience of a religious monarch is tried as was that of Job, and comes out from the trial equally victorious. The sorrows of Patient Grissel have met with sympathy in many lands, for meekness has ever been considered a womanly virtue. But the heroism of a husband and father who sells his wife to a merchant, and his son to a cowherd, in order that he may be able to keep his promise to a holy mendicant, and bestow upon him two pounds and a half of gold, can scarcely be expected to invest itself, to western eyes, with the air of a manly virtue. In the same way, the great sitting powers displayed by King Burtal, who never once moves from his seat in the jungle for twelve whole years, during which space of time he neither eats nor drinks, and thereby elevates himself to the dignity of a fakír, are not of a kind to elicit the sympathies or command the admiration of nations addicted to active exercise.

The explanation of Nánaksá's thrice repeated laugh, also,

could retain its vitality only in an atmosphere pervaded by a belief in the transmigration of souls. Buddhistic apologues have sometimes passed into legends of Christian Saints. But it would be difficult to perform the operation in the case of an account of how a woman, who had tormented to death her husband's sister, was justly punished by the reappearance in the world of the ill-used sister-in-law, in the form of that unkind woman's exceedingly peevish baby daughter. Numerous, also, as are European stories about ogres, vampires, and other demoniacal cannibals, we shall not readily find a western counterpart of the terrible tale, in No. 24, of the " Rakshas " which sometimes appears as a goat, and sometimes as a most beautiful young girl, dressed in grand clothes and rich jewels, but at midnight turns into a devouring demon with a craving for human flesh.

Just as some of the themes of these stories do not seem to have European counterparts, so portions of their machinery appear to be without exact western equivalents. The stupendous transformations which now and then take place (see pp. 5, 148, 244) can reconcile themselves only to an oriental imagination. However much the occidental mind may attempt to " make believe," it cannot credit such a statement as that when the Bél-Princess died, her eyes turned into two birds, her heart into "a great tank," and her body into "a splendid palace and garden," her arms and legs becoming "the pillars that supported the verandah roof," and her head "the dome on the top of the palace." In almost all countries, when a fairy hero has been slain by a demoniacal or otherwise villainous personage, he is recalled to life by magic means. In European folk-lore the resuscitating remedy is usually a Water of Life, or a Balsam, or some similar fluid. In these Indian tales, it is blood streaming from the resuscitator's little finger. Thus when Loving Lailí (p. 83) found her husband dead and headless, she put his head back on his shoulders, and smeared his neck with the blood which flowed

" like healing medicine," when " she cut her little finger inside her hand straight down from the top of her nail to her palm." A power of becoming at will invisible is everywhere often attributed to heroes of romance. But it is generally connected with "a cap of darkness," or some similar magic article. But the Prince of No. 21, when he seeks the Bél-Princess, becomes invisible to the "demons and fairies" who surround her, when he blows from the palm of his hand, "all along his fingers," the earth which a friendly fakír has given him for that purpose. A " sleep-thorn," or other somniferous piece of wood, is commonly employed in our fairy tales, in order to throw a hero or heroine into a magic slumber. In these Indian stories a state of catalepsy, or of death, is produced or relieved by a peculiar application of a magic stick. Thus the Princess who was called the Golden Rání, "because her teeth and her hair were made of gold," and who was stolen by a demon, informed the Prince who found her, motionless but not sleeping, that "the Rakshas who had carried her off, and whom she called papa, had a great thick stick, and when he laid this stick at her feet she could not stir, but when he laid it at her head she could move again." In " The Demon and the King's Son" (No. 24), the hero opens a " forbidden chamber," and there finds the demon's daughter lying on a bed, apparently lifeless ; for " every day, before her father went out he used to make the girl lie on her bed, and cover her with a sheet, and he placed a thick stick at her head, and another at her feet ; then she died, till he came home in the evening and changed the sticks, putting the one at her head at her feet, and the one at her feet at her head. This brought her to life again." An interesting parallel to the " sleep-thorn " is afforded by the pin which, while it remains in the head of the bird which had been the wife of the Pomegranate King (No. 2), prevents her from resuming her human shape.

When the Rájá pulled out the pin, "his own dear wife, the Pomegranate Rání, stood before him." Magic boxes are common in fairy land. But there is something new in at least the name of the "sun-jewel box," which was sent by the "Red Fairy," who lived at the bottom of the well, to "The Princess who loved her father like salt" (No. 23), and which contained "seven little dolls, who were all little fairies."

Of more general interest than the few peculiarities of these tales are the many points in which they resemble and illustrate some of the familiar features of European folklore. As an example of the latter may be taken a "husk-myth," which is a valuable contribution to the literature of the "Beauty and the Beast" cycle. In all the stories belonging to that group, the action turns upon the union of the human hero or heroine with a spouse who is really or apparently an inferior animal. In the modified version of the story with which our nurseries have become acquainted through a French literary medium, the species of Beast to which the Beauty is wedded is not stated, and its transformation into a princely husband is attributed to her unaided love. But in by far the greater part of the variants of the folk-tale on which it seems to have been founded, as well as of the other stories in which a similar transformation is the principal feature—variants which have been gathered in abundance from all parts of Europe, not to speak of Asia— the animal nature of the mysterious spouse is clearly defined. In them the husband whom the Beauty is induced by filial affection, fear, or compassion to wed, is an unmistakable Beast—a pig in Sicily, a bear in Norway, a hedgehog in Germany, a goat in Russia. Sometimes he is even of a lower type, often a frog or a snake. And once, in Wallachia, he has been transferred from the animal to the vegetable world, and figures as a pumpkin. In every instance he is represented as being able to change at times his repulsive appearance for one of beauty, and this he generally does by doffing a kind of husk which when donned conceals his real form, and invests him with that of an inferior being. If this husk be destroyed during the temporary absence of its owner, he loses his transforming power. The destruction of the husk is generally the work of the wife, who is sometimes rewarded, her husband remaining with her constant to his true nature ; at other times she is punished, he being lost to her for a time or for ever. These stories about a monster husband have their exact counterparts in tales about a monster wife, the leading idea being the same in both groups ; the only difference being that it is the wife who appears at times as a frog or other inferior creature, and who continues to do so until her transforming power terminates with the destruction of her disguising husk.

Now these temporary transformations, though common to the folk-tales of all parts of Europe, are not in accordance with the European superstitions of the present day, nor with those, so far as we are acquainted with them, of old European heathenism. The nearest approach to them is afforded by the wehr-wolf superstition, but that is an isolated belief, and appears to be based upon altogether different ideas. As to the metamorphoses of classical literature, they are of a nature quite alien to that of the voluntary eclipse, under a degrading form, of a Frog Princess or a Pig Prince. It may be said with confidence that European "husk-myths" do not explain themselves ; the peasants among whom they are current, cannot explain them ; and the knowledge we have of ancient European paganism throws no light on their meaning. But in India, where countless variants of such tales exist—many of them preserved in ancient as well as in modern literature, but by far the greater part still current among the common people—the transformations in question are frequently, if not generally, explained in the stories themselves, and explained in a manner perfectly in accordance with the Indian thought of the present as well as of the past. To Indian minds there is nothing monstrous in the belief that a celestial being may have been condemned, in consequence of the wrath of a superior divinity, or even of the magic words pronounced by an offended sage, to assume for a time the inferior form of a mere man or woman, or even to wear the shape of an inferior animal—a monkey or a frog; and that this transformation is to continue chronic, though not constant, until the destruction of the disguising skin or husk, by the donning of which it is from time to time brought about, deprives the curse of its power, and enables earth's celestial visitor to return to heaven. The whole story is closely connected with Indian religious beliefs, and may fairly be looked upon, when found in India, as an expansion of a Hindu myth. Its existence in other parts of Asia may, at least frequently, be attributed to the natural spread of Hindu tales among the various tribes and nations which accepted Buddhism from India.

If all this be true, and the "husk-myth" stories which are current all over Europe may justly be supposed to have drifted westwards from India, then all Indian variants of these tales naturally become invested with special importance. The specimen in the present volume, the "Monkey Prince" (No. 10), belongs to a remarkably interesting class—that in which the story-teller gives an explanation of the hero's transformation. A childless king is told by a fakír to give some mangoes to his seven wives. Six of them eat up the fruit, and each of the six gives birth to a prince of the usual kind. But the seventh wife, who has been able to obtain as her share only the stone of one of the mangoes, "had a monkey, who was

called in consequence Bandarsábásá, or Prince Monkey."
In reality, the story-teller goes on to explain, " he was a boy,
but no one knew it, for he had a monkey-skin covering him."
And this monkey-skin he takes off when he wishes to appear
in true princely form, as when he woos and wins the Princess
Jahúran. Finding out what his real nature is, she insists
upon marrying him, in spite of her vexed father's natural
question : "Who ever heard of any one marrying a nasty
monkey ? " When he is alone with his wife he takes off his
monkey-skin, and reveals himself in all his beauty, reply-
ing to her questions as to its use, " I wear it as a protection, because my brothers are naughty, and would kill
me if they knew what I really am." On one occasion, when
he has gone in state to a nautch, after taking off his monkey
skin, folding it up, and laying it under his wife's pillow,
she reveals her husband's secret to his mother, who,
"though she was very glad her monkey-son had such a
wife, could never understand how it was that her daughter-
in-law was so happy with him." Taking the monkey-skin
from under her pillow, " See," she says, " when your son
puts this on, then he is a monkey; when he takes it off he
is a beautiful man. And now I think I will burn this
skin, and then he must always be a man." So she throws it
into the fire. Prince Monkey's heart instantly tells him his
wife has burnt his skin, and he returns home in a rage.
It passes off, however, and all goes well. He now appears
always as a beautiful prince, " with his hair all gold." " Why
did you wear that monkey-skin ? " naturally asks his father.
" Because," he replies, " my mother ate the mango-stone
instead of eating the mango, and so I was born with this
skin, and God ordered me to wear it till I had found a
wife." The story has evidently been considerably altered in the
course of time from its original form, but it still keeps true
to its ancient lines. In it, as in many other specimens of the

same class, the idea of the degradation of a divine or semi-divine being has been lost, and the sufferer is merely a human being cased in a disfiguring hide. It is note-worthy that, as we are informed at p. 259, Dunkní, the narrator of the tale, "in telling this husk-story, just as often called the monkey-skin a husk, as she called it a skin."

Another of the apparently mythological European folk-tales, instructive parallels to which are contained in the present volume, is that which may be designated as the Golden-locks myth. It relates the fortunes of a brilliant being, usually a radiant prince, who, often without any apparent reason, submits himself to a voluntary eclipse, hides from sight his grandeur and his good looks, and assumes an appearance of squalor and misery. Like Cinderella, whose male counterpart he is, he at times arises from his low estate, becomes again a brilliant prince, but always capriciously eludes those who wish to retain him in that shape. At last he is always detected, and then he has to remain constant to his true and magnificent form. His temporary eclipse is somewhat similar to that of the hero of a husk-myth; but no special power is attached to the wrappings under which his brilliance is concealed, nor is his change of form imposed upon him against his will. The meaning of the Golden-locks story, in its original form, still remains to be discovered, as also does that of the sister tale of Cinderella. That they both refer to the temporary eclipse, seclusion, or obscuration of a brilliant being, is evident. But what that brilliant being represents is a problem of which several solutions have been confidently offered, but which does not seem to have been as yet certainly solved. In the story of "The Boy who had a Moon on his forehead and a Star on his chin" (No. 20), the self-eclipsing process is brought about by a twist of his right ear; "when the boy had twisted it, he was no longer a handsome prince, but a poor, common-looking, ugly man; and his moon and star were hidden." And so, after he has been chosen out of a number of suitors by a princess whose heart he has won by the beauty of his singing, he restores himself to his true form by twisting his left ear; after which operation "he stood no longer a poor, common, ugly man, but a grand young prince, with a moon on his forehead and a star on his chin."

A third class of stories for which an Asiatic origin may fairly be claimed, contains those in which figures a monster or demon who cannot be killed until some external object with which his life is mysteriously linked has been destroyed. Such a being occurs at times in European folk-tales, especially in those of the east and north of Europe. The most familiar instance is that of "The Giant who had no Heart in his body" of the "Tales from the Norse." Some of the best specimens of this kind of monster are to be found in the Russian tales about Koshchei the Deathless. But these remarkably abnormal beings scarcely seem at home in western folk-lore. They are but little in keeping with their European surroundings, and never seem to divest themselves of their alien air. In oriental stories, on the other hand, they figure frequently, and they seem to occupy a familiar and an appropriate place. The oldest of the world's tales of wonder, the Egyptian story of the Two Brothers, contains an heroic being whose life comes to an end when his heart falls to the ground from the tree upon which he has hung it. And in the modern folk-tales of India, demons of this kind play their part without exciting any more than usual surprise. Miss Frere's Deccan stories make us well acquainted with one of these personages, "a wicked magician named Punchkin," whose name serves as a convenient designation for the long-lived monsters in question.

The present collection contains several specimens. In " Brave Hírálálbásá " (No. 11) we meet with a Rakshas, who is induced, as usual by female wiles, to reveal the secret of his life. "Sixteen miles away from this place," he says, " is a tree. Round the tree are tigers, and bears, and scorpions, and snakes; on the top of the tree is a very great flat snake; on his head is a little cage; in the cage is a bird; and my soul is in that bird." When the bird is seized by the hero of the story, the Rakshas feels that something terrible has occurred. When the bird's legs and wings are pulled off, the Rakshas becomes a mere head and torso; and when the bird's neck is wrung, down falls the Rakshas dead. In like manner, in the tale of "The Demon and the King's Son " (No. 24), the demon dies when the prince has killed a certain bird, the lives of the bird and of the demon being conterminable. According to the narrator Dunkní, " all Rakshases keep their souls in birds;" but another authority asserts (p. 261) that " a whole tribe of Rakshases, dwelling in Ceylon, kept theirs in one and the same lemon."

The tale of " The Voracious Frog " (No. 6) is a valuable contribution to the store we already possess of what appear to be myths relating to apparent destruction, but ultimate resuscitation. To this class seem to belong the stories on which Little Red Riding Hood was probably based, describing how a wolf or other monster swallowed various innocent beings, but was at last forced to restore them uninjured to the light of day. In its original form the tale may have been a nature myth, illustrating the apparent annihilation brought about by the darkness of night or the cold of winter, and the revival which accompanies the return of the day or of spring; or, perhaps, a moral apologue, intended to suggest that death may not be a lasting annihilation. In its modern forms, whether in the east or the west, it often assumes a grotesque air. A good illustration of this fact is afforded by the well-known Norse tale of " The Greedy Cat," of which " The Voracious Frog " (No. 6) is an Indian counterpart. The cat, after devouring all that comes in its way, is at last split in half by a goat, whereupon all its victims come forth unhurt. The frog, after similar feats of gluttony, is cut open by a barber, who, while shaving it, thinks that it looks very fat ; and its victims also emerge uninjured.

There are many tales now current in different parts of Europe, but chiefly in the south and east, which turn upon the relations existing between human beings and their fates : each person being supposed to have a special fate or fortune, a species of guardian demon, upon whose good will all his or her success in life depends. It is very doubtful whether such stories are products of European fancy, their leading ideas seeming to be little in keeping with the religious beliefs—whether of classic times, or of Teutonic, Slavic, or Celtic antiquity—respecting either an overruling destiny, or a triad of Fates or Norns. But in India a belief in a personal " luck " has prevailed from very early times ; and such stories as " The Man who went to seek his Fate " (No. 12), appear there to be as indigenous as in Europe they seem to be exotic. The Servian story, for instance, of the man who sets out to look for his fate, and the Sicilian account of how the unfortunate Caterina is persecuted by hers until she discovers its hiding-place, and propitiates it by cakes (see Notes, p. 263), have a foreign air about them, which does not manifest itself in the Indian tale. The likeness between the Servian and the Indian variants of the narrative, especially as regards the questions which the fate-seeker is requested by the beings he meets on the way to ask when he arrives at his destination, is too great to allow it to be supposed that they have been independently developed from a common germ. They are manifestly, so far as the journey is concerned, copies of the same model, differing but slightly from each other. But the embodiment of the wayfarer's destiny is quite differently represented in the two stories. The Servian pilgrim first discovers his fortune, or rather misfortune, in the person of a hag, who tells him she has been given to him as his luck by Fate. Then he seeks out Fate, who appears in human form. But in the Indian tale, "the fates are stones, some standing, and others lying on the ground." One of the prostrate stones, the traveller felt sure, must belong to him. "This must be mine," he said; "it is lying on the ground, that's why I am so poor." Whereupon he took to beating it, and continued to do so all day. When night came, " God sent a soul into the poor man's fate, and it became a man," who satisfied the wanderer's own wishes, and also answered the questions which he had been requested to ask. Then " God withdrew the soul, and the fate became a stone again, which stood up on the ground."

There are two stories which enjoy a world-wide popularity in peasant circles, but which have not been made familiar by modern literature to cultured children. One of them may for the sake of convenience be known by the name of the Substituted Bride, and the other by that of the Calumniated Wife. The first relates the sorrows of a maiden who is compelled to see an impostor seated in the place which she was intended to fill, by the side of the princely husband whom she was meant to wed. The second describes the sufferings long undergone by a faithful wife and tender mother, who is falsely accused of some crime by an envious rival, and is hastily punished by her angry lord. In both of them the supernatural usually plays a part, but their main interests are always human, and it is easier to sympathize with their heroines than with most of the similar characters of popular fiction. Yet those ill-used but patient princesses are but little known to the thousands of story-readers who are familiar with the adventures of Cinderella and the Sleeping Beauty, Little Red Riding Hood, and the wives of Bluebeard and of the Beast. They have at various times entered into literature, but not into that section of it which has supplied our nursery fiction. They figure in most of the now so numerous collections of folk-tales, but they have not been introduced into society by the novelists or playwrights who have made their sister-sufferers undying favourites. They are essentially moral tales, their good characters bearing their unmerited misfortunes with unvarying meekness and patience, and being ultimately rewarded, while the envious and malicious rivals who have supplanted or slandered them are punished in the end. But they have not taken a firm hold on the west, where they are probably destined to become forgotten when the progress of education has replaced folk-lore by literature, while they are likely to go on living for ages in the east, which seems to have been their original home.

In the present collection the story of the Substituted Princess occurs several times. In " Phúlmati Rání " the heroine is a wife instead of a bride, which makes the substitution more than usually improbable. As she and her husband are resting beside a tank, a shoemaker's wife comes up, and pushes her into the water, in which she is drowned. The shoemaker's wife takes her place, though she is " very black and ugly," one-eyed, and exceedingly wicked. It may be remarked that the substitution in question generally takes place by the side of water. In the " Bél-Princess," the beautiful maiden who has come out of the fruit which the prince opened by the side of a well, is pushed into the water, while the prince is asleep, by a wicked woman, very ugly, and with " something wrong with one of her eyes," who then assumes her place. In tales like the story of

"The Princess who loved her Father like Salt," the trans-formation scene is of a different nature, though the leading idea of the change is the same. It is not an ordinary bride or wife who is supplanted, and the substitution need not take place beside water. The heroine is a stranger who, gene-rally after long wanderings, finds a prince really or apparently dead, by patient watching all but effects his cure, but is at the last moment supplanted by a servant, who gives the final touch to the work, claims its entire merit, and is made the wife of the grateful patient. In the Indian tale the prince lies motionless, his body "stuck full of needles." The heroine sits down by the side of his couch, and there remains for a whole week "without eating, or drinking, or sleeping, pulling out the needles." At the end of two weeks more the needles are all extracted, except those in the eyes. She then goes away to bathe; and while she is absent, a servant maid whom she has left in charge of the body pulls out the remaining needles. The prince opens his eyes, thanks God for bringing him to life again, and makes the servant maid his wife. The substitution is similar to that which takes place in such stories as the Norse "Bushy Bride;" but closer parallels are supplied by some of the stories of southern Europe. Mrs. Stokes refers in her Notes to the dead prince in one of Gonzenbach's Sicilian tales, who is brought to life by a wandering princess, who for more than seven years rubs his body with grass from Mount Calvary. Pitre's great collection of Sicilian *Fiabe* also offers several variants of the substitution story, in some of which occurs the singular incident, known also to Swedish and Finnish folk-tales, of the imprisonment of the heroine, after she has been flung into the sea, by a submarine supernatural being. In some instances it is not water which the heroine has to dread, but light. The true bride must be conveyed to the bridegroom's palace in a darkened vehicle. Her supplanter draws aside a curtain. The sunlight shines in. The princess turns into a lizard or some other animal, and the false bride takes her place.

The Calumniated Wife story which occurs in No. 20 of the present collection, closely resembles many European variants. A king hears a girl say that when she is married she will have a son with a moon on his forehead and a star on his chin. So he marries her. She gives birth to a boy who really is thus decorated. But the king's other wives, naturally jealous of her, put a stone in her bed, and pretend that it is the object which she has brought into the world, upon which she is disgraced and turned into a servant maid. In other variants of the story she is often accused of having murdered her children, and even eaten them. In one instance her mortified husband is represented as twice forgiving her, after remonstrating with her on her inordinate appetite, but as thinking it necessary to take some precautions when the possibility of her committing the crime for the third time makes itself manifest. Sometimes all the innocent wives of a king are accused of murderous habits by a guilty wife, who is in reality a destroying and devouring demon. Such is the case in No. 20 of the present collection, which ends with the restoration of the seven calumniated wives, and the death by burning of the demon spouse.

Besides illustrating the themes or leading ideas of many groups of European tales, these Indian stories frequently serve to throw light upon some of their obscurer features, or at least to offer such parallels to them as are useful contributions to our stock of materials for a systematic classification. Among the strange characters who figure in European folk tales, there are few more puzzling than the fair maidens who are at times discovered inside fruits, and who must be provided with water to drink the moment they emerge into the light, or else they will die. They seem properly to belong to the south and east of Europe, to such countries, for instance, as Greece, Sicily, and Wallachia. When they are found elsewhere, as in the Norse tale of "The Three Lemons," the very name of which speaks of the sunny south, they seem out of keeping with their surroundings. In these Indian stories, the enclosure of a heroine in a fruit is an incident which does not appear to be more than usually amazing. The need of immediate water drinking is not referred to. But the hero is warned (p. 81) that he must not open the fruit in public, because the enclosed maiden will be quite destitute of clothes. In another story which is widely spread over Europe—but which we know best in the form of the tale of "The Blue Bird," founded upon the theme of "The Lay of Ywonec," by Marie de France—the murderous means by which the bird-lover is all but done to death by jealous hands, which set sharp knives in the narrow opening through which he has to fly, or beset his path with some other instruments of ill, find their counterpart in the powdered glass employed to injure the hero of the "The Fan Prince" (No. 25). His wife's six sisters, who " were angry at their youngest sister being married, while they who were older were not married,". insist upon making his bed, and cover the spot on which he is to lie with the powder into which they have ground a glass bottle. Whereupon the prince becomes very ill, from the glass powder going into his flesh.

The ordinary opening of many familiar folk-tales, including the "Beauty and the Beast" story, finds a parallel in the same Indian tale (p. 195). In all of them a man, when starting on a journey, promises his youngest daughter that he will bring her back some object. This he forgets to obtain. On his homeward journey, his ship refuses to move until he has acquired the object in question.

The Indian parent promised to bring home Sabr to his daughter, having no idea what Sabr meant. Not having obtained it, he set out on his homeward journey. "But the boat would not move, because he had forgotten one thing— the thing his youngest daughter had asked for." Sabr turns out to be a fairy prince. It is a common incident in Indian tales for a hero or heroine to demand a spouse, generally of a more or less supernatural nature, whose name is known but nothing more. Just as the Fan Prince was demanded, under the apparently meaningless name of Sabr, so is the hand of the Princess Labám longed for by the Rájá's son in No. 22, although her existence was unknown to him till he heard a parrot pronounce her name one day; and so is the acquisition of a Bél-Princess resolved upon by the prince in No. 21, because his sisters-in-law say to him, in a disagreeable manner, "We think that you will marry a Bél-Princess." Múniyá, the narrator of the story, "says that telling the prince he would marry a Bél-Princess was equivalent to saying he would not marry at all; for these brothers' wives knew she lived in the fairy country, and that it would be very difficult, if not impossible, for the prince to find her, and take her from it." But this seems to be merely a rationalistic view of the matter. Some mystery seems to underlie these suggestions of, or desires for, unions with unfamiliar beings. They occur not unfrequently in Russian tales. In one of Afanasief's skazkas (vol. vii., No. 6) a baby prince cries, and refuses to go to sleep, till his royal father rocks his cradle, crooning the while, "Sleep, beloved one! When you grow up you shall marry Never-enough-to-be-gazed-at Beauty, daughter of three mothers, sister of nine brothers." Having slept vigorously, the baby awakes, asks for the king's blessing, and sets out in search of the unknown Beauty in question. In another (vol. i., No. 14), Prince Ivan, having married his three sisters to the Wind, the Hail, and the Thunder,

wanders forth in search of a bride. Finding the remains of
two slaughtered armies, and discovering that their slaugh-
terer was named Anastasia the Fair, he resolves, though
knowing nothing else about her, to make her his wife.
Among the numerous minor incidents which are common
to eastern and western folk-tales, may be mentioned the
aid lent to heroes in difficulties by Magic Instruments, as
in No. 22, or by Grateful Beasts, as in No. 24. A belief in
magic is of course world-wide, but the particular instruments referred to seem to have good reasons for claiming an
oriental extraction. The stories in which stress is laid
upon the gratitude of the inferior animals are almost always
derivable from the east; especially if, as in the correct
versions of the tale on which Puss in Boots is founded, their
gratitude is contrasted with the ingratitude of that superior
animal, man. When we meet with so close a resemblance
as exists between the miracle wrought by Shekh Faríd
(p. 97), who turns the lying carter's sugar into ashes, and that
attributed to St. Brigit, who turns the liar's salt into stones,
we need have little scruple about referring both stories to
the same source and, considering how much monastic
legend-writers were indebted to oriental fancy, in locating
that source in the east.

The comic elements of eastern and western folk-lore are
closely akin, and the Lie-stories, or *Lügenmärchen*, in Nos.
4, 8, and 17 of these Indian Tales find their parallels in most
European collections. As an example of the close kinship
which prevails among the jests which make merry the hearts
of men far apart from each other, we may take the Indian
story of " Foolish Sachúlí," and compare it with the Russian
tale of " The Fool and the Birch Tree " (Afanasief, vol. v.,
No. 22). Sachúlí kills a woman; his Russian counterpart kills
a man. The corpse of the woman is hidden away in a well,
that of the man in a cellar. In each case the fool's sensible
relatives, knowing that he will be sure to tell the truth if

he is asked, withdraw the body during his absence, and substitute for it that of an animal killed for the purpose. When the seekers after the victim arrive at Sachúli's home, he at once conducts them to the well. Being let down into it, he asks, "Has she got eyes?" "Of course, every one has eyes," is the reply. "Has she a nose?" "Yes, she has a nose." But at last he inquires if she has four feet; and the seekers after the dead woman find that the body in the well is that of a sheep. In the same way, when the Russian fool has confessed his guilt, and has gone into the cellar to look for his victim's remains, he finds there the body of a goat. So he calls out to the anxious inquirers, "Was your man dark-haired?" "He was." "And had he a beard?" "Yes, he had a beard." "And had he horns?" "What horns are you talking about, fool?" they reply. So he hands up the goat's head, and the Russian tale comes to the same conclusion as the Indian. The likeness here is too strong to be attributed to an accidental coincidence.

It does not, of course, follow that, because a story is found both in Europe and Asia, therefore the western version has been borrowed from the east. Europe has, doubtless, sometimes lent a fancy to Asia. Greek fables are supposed to have exercised an influence upon the Indian mind. European missionaries may have sometimes rendered a Christian legend current among Hindus. Professor Monier Williams was assured by an intelligent native that the spread of railways had materially diminished the number of malignant ghosts in India. Still, as a general rule, the east is stubbornly conservative. The Japanese, it is true, are abandoning their own costume and art for ours, not entirely to their advantage. But the various peoples of India have never shown any such tendencies towards change. In their popular fiction, at all events, they have never shown an inclination to import foreign manufactures in order to replace their home products. In their thoughts and feelings they are now very much what they have been for periods of time which it would be difficult to define. When we find stories now current in all parts of India, which we know from their occurrence in Sanskrit literature must have existed there very long ago, and we see that the mythological element in those stories is in accordance with religious ideas that have prevailed there for countless centuries, we can have no doubt that these stories were framed there at a very early period. Then if we find almost identical stories current in all parts of Europe, many of their at least apparently mythological features offering difficulties which cannot be removed by a reference to the mythologies of the heathen ancestors of the peasants who now repeat them, it seems not unreasonable to come to the conclusion that such stories have been borrowed by the west from the east. From mythological germs common to European and Asiatic Aryans, it is quite true that legends might arise in Europe and in Asia, independent of each other, but similar in their general tenour. But it is not likely that out of any common germ could be independently developed in several different countries as many variants of the same tale, in each of which there is a similar sequence of scenes or acts, and the dramatic action is brought to a close by a termination that scarcely ever varies. Far more difficult is it to believe in such a triumph of independent development, than to place reliance upon a statement to the effect that the wave of story-telling, as well as of empire, has wended its westward.

W. R. S. RALSTON.

CONTENTS.

INDIAN FAIRY TALES.

I.

PHÚLMATI RÁNÍ.

HERE were once a Rájá and a Rání who had an only daughter called the Phúlmati Rání, or the Pink-rose Queen. She was so beautiful that if she went into a very dark room it was all lighted up by her beauty. On her head was the sun; on her hands, moons; and her face was covered with stars. She had hair that reached to the ground, and it was made of pure gold.

Every day after she had had her bath, her father and mother used to weigh her in a pair of scales. She only weighed one flower. She ate very, very little food. This made her father most unhappy, and he said, "I cannot let my daughter marry any one who weighs more than one flower." Now, God loved this girl dearly, so he went down under the ground to see if any of the fairy Rájás was fit to be the Phúlmati Rání's husband, and he thought none of them good enough. So he went in the form of a Fakír to see the great Indrásan Rájá who ruled over all the other fairy Rájás. This Rájá was exceedingly beautiful. On his head was the sun; and on his hands, moons; and on his face, stars. God made him weigh very little. Then he said to the Rájá, " Come up with me, and we will go to the palace of the Phúlmati Ráni." God had told the Rájá that he was God and not a Fakír, for he loved the Indrásan Rájá. "Very well," said the Indrásan Rájá. So they travelled on until they came to the Phúlmati Ráni's palace. When they arrived there they pitched a tent in her compound, and they used to walk about, and whenever they saw the Phúlmati Ráni they looked at her. One day they saw her having her hair combed, so God said to the Indrásan Rájá, "Get a horse and ride where the Phúlmati Ráni can see you, and if any one asks you who you are, say, 'Oh, it's only a poor Fakír, and I am his son. We have come to stay here a little while just to see the country. We will go away very soon.'" Well, he got a horse and rode about, and Phúlmati Ráni, who was having her hair combed in the verandah, said, "I am sure that must be some Rájá ; only see how beautiful he is." And she sent one of her servants to ask him who he was. So the servant said to the Indrásan Rájá, "Who are you? why are you here? what do you want?" "Oh, it's only a poor Fakír, and I am his son. We have just come here for a little while to see the country. We will go away very soon." So the servants returned to the Phúlmati Ráni and told her what the Indrásan Rájá had said. The Phúlmati Ráni told her father about this. The next day, when the Phúlmati Ráni and her father were standing in the verandah, God took a pair of scales and weighed the Indrásan Rájá in them. His weight was only that of one flower! "Oh," said the Rájá, when he saw that, "here is the husband for the Phúlmati Ráni!" The next day, after the Phúlmati Ráni had had her bath, her father took her and weighed her, and he also weighed the Indrásan Rájá. And they were each the same weight. Each weighed one flower, although the Indrásan Rájá was fat and the Phúlmati Ráni thin. The next day they were married, and there was a grand wedding. God said he was too poor-looking to appear, so he bought a quantity of elephants, and camels, and horses, and cows, and sheep, and goats, and made a procession, and came to the wedding. Then he went back to heaven, but before he went he said to the Indrásan Rájá " You must stay here one whole year; then go back to your father and to your kingdom. As long as you put flowers on your ears no danger will come near you." (This was in order that the fairies might know that he was a very great Rájá and not hurt him.) " All right," said the Indrásan Rájá. And God went back to heaven.

So the Indrásan Rájá stayed for a whole year. Then he told the Rájá, the Phúlmati Rání's father, that he wished to go back to his own kingdom. "All right," said the Rájá, and he wanted to give him horses, and camels, and elephants. But the Indrásan Rájá and the Phúlmati Rání said they wanted nothing but a tent and a cooly. Well, they set out ; but the Indrásan Rájá forgot to put flowers on his ears, and after some days the Indrásan Rájá was very, very tired, so he said, " We will sit down under these big trees and rest awhile. Our baggage will soon be here ; it is only a little way behind." So they sat down, and the Rájá said he felt so tired he must sleep. " Very well," said the Rání ; " lay your head in my lap and sleep." After a while a shoemaker's wife came by to get some water from a tank which was close to the spot where the Rájá and Rání were resting. Now, the shoemaker's wife was very black and ugly, and she had only one eye, and she was exceedingly wicked. The Rání was very thirsty and she said to the woman, " Please give me some water, I am so thirsty." " If you want any," said the shoemaker's wife, " come to the tank and get it yourself.' " But I cannot," said the Rání, "for the Rájá is sleeping in my lap." At last the poor Rání got so very, very thirsty, she said she must have some water; so laying the Rájá's head very gently on the ground she went to the tank. Then the wicked shoemaker's wife, instead of giving her to drink, gave her a push and sent the beautiful Ráni into the water, where she was drowned.   The shoemaker's wife then went back to the Rájá, and, taking his head on her knee, sat still until he woke.   When the Rájá woke he was much frightened, and he said, " This is not my wife.   My wife was not black, and she had two eyes."   The poor Rájá felt very unhappy.   He said, " I am sure something has happened to my wife."   He went to the tank, and he saw flowers floating on the water and he caught them, and as he caught them his own true wife stood before him.

They travelled on till they came to a little house.   The shoemaker's wife went with them.   They went into the house and laid themselves down to sleep, and the Rájá laid beside him the flowers he had found floating in the tank.   The Ráni's life was in the flowers.   As soon as the Rájá and Ráni were asleep, the shoemaker's wife took the flowers, broke them into little bits, and burnt them.   The Ráni died immediately, for the second time.   Then the poor Rájá, feeling very lonely and unhappy, travelled on to his kingdom, and the shoemaker's wife went after him.   God brought the Phúlmati Ráni to life a second time, and led her to the Indrásan Rájá's gardener.

One day as the Indrásan Rájá was going out hunting, he passed by the gardener's house, and saw a beautiful girl sitting in it.   He thought she looked very like his wife, the Phúlmati Ráni.   So he went home to his father and said, " Father, I should like to be married to the girl who lives in our gardener's house."   "All right," said the father; "you can be married at once."   So they were married the next day.

One night the shoemaker's wife took a ram, killed it, and put some of its blood on the Phúlmati Ráni's mouth while the Ráni slept.   The next morning she went to the Indrásan Rájá and said, " Whom have you married ?   You have mar-

ried a Rakshas. Just see. She has been eating cows, and
sheep, and chickens. Just come and see." The Rájá went,
and when he saw the blood on his wife's mouth he was
frightened, and he thought she was really a Rakshas. The
shoemaker's wife said to him, "If you do not cut this
woman in pieces, some harm will happen to you." So the
Rájá took a knife and cut his beautiful wife into pieces.
He then went away very sorrowful. The Phúlmati Ráni's
arms and legs grew into four houses ; her chest became a
tank, and her head a house in the middle of the tank ; her
eyes turned into two little doves ; and these five houses, the
tank and the doves, were transported to the jungle. No one
knew this. The little doves lived in the house that stood in
the middle of the tank. The other four houses stood round
the tank.

One day when the Indrásan Rájá was hunting by himself
in the jungle he was very tired, and he saw the house in the
tank. So he said, " I will go into that house to rest a little
while, and to-morrow I will return home to my father." So,
tying his horse outside, he went into the house and lay down
to sleep. By and by, the two little birds came and perched
on the roof above his head. They began to talk, and the
Rájá listened. The little husband-dove said to his wife,
"This is the man who cut his wife to pieces." And then he
told her how the Indrásan Rájá had married the beautiful
Phúlmati Ráni, who weighed only one flower, and how the
shoemaker's wife had drowned her ; how God had brought
her to life again ; how the shoemaker's wife had burned her ;
and last of all, how the Rájá himself had cut her to pieces.
" And cannot the Rájá find her again ? " said the little wife-
dove. " Oh, yes, he can," said her husband, " but he does
not know how to do so." " But do tell me how he can find
her," said the little wife-dove. " Well," said her husband,
every night, at twelve o'clock, the Ráni and her servants

come to bathe in the tank. Her servants wear yellow dresses, but she wears a red one. Now, if the Rájá could get all their dresses, every one, when they lay them down and go into the tank to bathe, and throw away all the yellow dresses one by one, keeping only the red one, he would recover his wife."

The Rájá heard all these things, and at midnight the Rání and her servants came to bathe. The Rájá lay very quiet, and after they all had taken off their dresses and gone into the tank, he jumped up and seized every one of the dresses,— he did not leave one of them,—and ran away as hard as he could. Then each of the servants, who were only fairies, screamed out, "Give me my dress! What are you doing? why do you take it away?" Then the Rájá dropped one by one the yellow dresses and kept the red one. The fairy servants picked up the dresses, and forsook the Phúlmati Rání and ran away. The Rájá came back to her with her dress in his hand, and she said, "Oh, give me back my dress. If you keep it I shall die. Three times has God brought me to life, but he will bring me to life no more." The Rájá fell at her feet and begged her pardon, and they were reconciled. And he gave her back her dress. Then they went home, and Indrásan Rájá had the shoemaker's wife cut to pieces, and buried in the jungle. And they lived happily ever after.

Told by Dunkní at Simla, July 25th, 1876.

II.

THE POMEGRANATE KING.

HERE was once a Mahárájá, called the Anárbása, or Pomegranate King ; and a Mahárání called the Gulianár, or Pomegranate-flower. The Mahárání died leaving two children : a little girl of four or five years old, and a little boy of three. The Mahárájá was very sorry when she died, for he loved her dearly. He was exceedingly fond of his two children, and got for them two servants : a man to cook their dinner, and an ayah to take care of them. He also had them taught to read and write. Soon after his wife's death the neighbouring Rájá's daughter's husband died, and she said if any other Rájá would marry her, she would be quite willing to marry him, and she also said she would like very much to marry the Pomegranate Rájá. So her father went to see the Pomegranate Rájá, and told him that his daughter wished to marry him. "Oh," said the Pomegranate Rájá, "I do not want to marry again, for if I do, the woman I marry will be sure to be unkind to my two children. She will not take care of them. She will not pet them and comfort them when they are unhappy." "Oh," said the other Rájá, "my daughter will be very good to them, I assure you." "Very well," said the Mahárájá, "I will marry her." So they were married.

For two or three months everything went on well, but then the new Rání, who was called the Sunkasi Mahárání, began to beat the poor children, and to scold their servants.

One day she gave the boy such a hard blow on his cheek that it swelled. When the Mahárájá came out of his office to get his tiffin, he saw the boy's swollen face, and, calling the two servants, he said, " Who did this? how did my boy get hurt?" They said, " The Rání gave him such a hard blow on his cheek that it swelled, and she gets very angry with us if we say anything about her ill-treatment of the children, or how she scolds us." The Mahárájá was exceedingly angry with his wife for this, and said to her, " I never beat my children. Why should you beat them? If you beat them I will send you away." And he went off to his office in a great rage. The Rání was very angry. So she told the little girl to go with the ayah to the bazar. The ayah and the little girl set off, never suspecting any evil. As soon as they had gone, the Rání took the little boy and told him she would kill him. The boy went down on his knees and begged her to spare his life. But she said, " No; your father is always quarrelling with me, beating me, and scolding me, all through your fault." The boy begged and prayed again, saying he would never be naughty any more. The Rání shook her head, and taking a large knife she cut off his head. She then cut him up and made him into a curry. She then buried his head, and his nails, and his feet in the ground, and she covered them well with earth, and stamped the ground well down so that no one should notice it had been disturbed. When the Pomegranate Rájá came home to his dinner, she put the curry and some rice on the table before him ; but the Rájá, seeing his boy was not there, would not eat. He went and looked everywhere for his son, crying very much, and the little girl cried very much too, for she loved her brother dearly. After they had hunted for him for some time, the little boy appeared. His father embraced him. " Where have you been?" said he. " I cannot eat my dinner without you." The little boy said, " Oh, I was in

the jungle playing with other boys." They then sat down
to dinner, and the curry changed into a kid curry. The
Ráni was greatly astonished when she saw the boy. She
said to herself, "I cut his head off; I cut him into little
pieces, and I made him into a curry, and yet he is alive!"
She then went into the garden to see if his head, and nails,
and feet were in the hole where she had buried them.
But they were not there; it was quite empty. She then
called a sepoy, and said to him, "If you will take two children into the jungle and kill them, I will give you as much
money as you like." "All right," said the sepoy. She
then brought the children, and told him to take them to
the jungle. So he took them away to the jungle, but he
had not the heart to kill them, for they were exceedingly
beautiful, and he left them in the jungle near their dead
mother's grave. Then he returned to the Ráni, saying he
had done as she wished, and she gave him as much money
as he wanted.

The poor Pomegranate Rájá was very unhappy when he
saw his children were not in the palace, and that they could
not be found. He asked his Ráni where they were, but
she said she did not know; they had gone out to play and
had never returned. From the day he lost his children the
Pomegranate Rájá became melancholy. He did not love
the Ráni any more; he hated her.

Meanwhile the children lived in a little house built close
to their mother's grave. God had given her life again that
she might take care of them. But they did not know she
was their mother; they thought she was another woman
sent to take care of them. God sent also a man to teach
them. Somehow or other the Ráni Sunkasí heard they
were still alive in the jungle. She did not know how she
could kill them. So at last she pretended she was very ill,
and she said to the Rájá, "The doctor says that in the
jungle there are two children, and he says if you will have

them killed, and will bring their livers for me to stand on when I bathe, then I shall get well." The Rájá sent a second sepoy to kill the children, and this man killed them and brought their livers to the Rání. She stood on them while bathing, and then said she was quite well. She then threw the livers into the garden, and during the night a tree grew up there with two large beautiful flowers on it. Next morning the Rání looked out and said, "I will gather those flowers to-day." Every day she said she would gather them, and every day she forgot. At last one day she said, "Every day I forget to gather those flowers, but to-day I really will do so," and she sent her servant to pluck them. So he went out, and, just as he was going to gather them, the flowers flew up just out of his reach. Then the Rání went down, and when she was going to pick them they flew up so high that they could not be seen. Every day she tried to gather them, and every day they went high up, and came back again to the tree as soon as she had gone. Then the flowers disappeared and two large fruits came in their stead. The Rání looked out of her window: "Oh, what delicious fruits! I'll eat them all myself. I won't give a bit to anybody, and I'll eat them by myself quite quietly." She went down to the garden, but they flew high up into the sky, and then they came down again. So this went on, day after day, until she got so cross she ordered the tree to be cut down. But it was of no use. The tree was cut down, but the fruits flew high up into the sky, and in the night the tree grew up again and the fruits came back again to it. And so this went on for many days. Every day she cut down the tree, and every night it grew up again, but she could never get the fruits. At last she became very angry, and had the tree hewn into tiny bits and all the bits thrown away, but still the tree grew again in the night, and in the morning the fruits were hanging on it. So she went to the Rájá and told him that in the garden was a tree with two fruits, and every time she tried to get them, the fruits went up into the air. She had had the tree cut down ever so many times, and it always grew up again in the night and the fruits returned to it. " Why cannot you leave the tree alone ? " said the Rájá. " But I should like to see if what you say is true." So the Rájá and the Rání went down to the garden, and the Rání tried to get the fruits, but she could not, for they went right up into the air.

That evening the Rájá went alone to the garden to gather the fruits, and the fruits of themselves fell into his hand. He took them into his room, and putting them on a little table close to his bed, he lay down to sleep. As soon as he was in bed a little voice inside one of the fruits said, " Brother ; " and a little voice in the other fruit said, "Sister, speak more gently. To-morrow the Rájá will break open the fruits, and if the Rání finds us she will kill us. Three times has God made us alive again, but if we die a fourth time he will bring us to life no more." The Rájá listened and said, " I will break them open in a little while." Then he went to sleep, and after a little he woke and said, " A little while longer," and went to sleep again. Several times he woke up and said, " I will break the fruits open in a little while," and went to sleep. At last he took a knife and began cutting the fruits open very fast, and the little boy cried, " Gently, gently, father ; you hurt us ! " So then the Rájá cut more gently, and he stopped to ask, " Are you hurt ? " and they said, " No." And then he cut again and asked, " Are you hurt ? " and they said, " No." And a third time he asked, " Are you hurt ? " and they answered, " No." Then the fruits broke open and his two children jumped out. They rushed into their father's arms, and he clasped them tight, and they cried softly, that the Rání might not hear.

He shut his room up close, and fed and dressed his

children, and then went out of the room, locking the door behind him. He had a little wooden house built that could easily catch fire, and as soon as it was ready he went to the Rání and said, "Will you go into a little house I have made ready for you while your room is getting repaired?" "All right," said the Rání; so she went into the little house, and that night a man set it on fire, and the Rání and everything in it was burnt up. Then the Pomegranate Rájá took her bones, put them into a tin box, and sent them as a present to her mother. "Oh," said the mother, "my daughter has married the Pomegranate Mahárájá, and so she sends me some delicious food." When she opened the box, to her horror she found only bones! Then she wrote to the Mahárájá, "Of what use are bones?" The Mahárájá wrote back, "They are your bones; they belong to you, for they are your daughter's bones. She ill-treated and killed my children, and so I had her burnt."

The Pomegranate Rájá and his children lived very happily for some time, and their dead mother, the Gulianár Rání, having a wish to see her husband and her children, prayed to God to let her go and visit them. God said she could go, but not in her human shape, so he changed her into a beautiful bird, and put a pin in her head, and said, "As soon as the pin is pulled out you will become a woman again." She flew to the palace where the Mahárájá lived, and there were great trees about the palace. On one of these she perched at night. The doorkeeper was lying near it. She called out, "Doorkeeper! doorkeeper!" and he answered, "What is it? Who is it?" And she asked, "Is the Rájá well?" and the doorkeeper said, "Yes." "Are the children well?" and he said, "Yes." "And all the servants, and camels, and horses?" "Yes." "Are you well?" "Yes." "Have you had plenty of food?" "Yes." "What a great donkey your Mahárájá is!" And then she began to cry very much, and pearls fell from her eyes as she cried. Then she began to laugh very much, and great big rubies fell from her beak as she laughed. The next morning the door-keeper got up and felt about, and said, " What is all this?" meaning the pearls and the rubies, for he did not know what they were. " I will keep them." So he picked them all up and put them into a corner of his house. Every night the bird came and asked after the Mahárájá and the children and the servants, and left a great many pearls and rubies behind her. At last the doorkeeper had a whole heap of pearls and rubies.

One day a Fakír came and begged, and as the doorkeeper had no pice, or flour, or rice to give, he gave him a handful of pearls and rubies. " Well," said the Fakír to himself, " I am sure these are pearls and rubies." So he tied them up in his cloth. Then he went to the Rájá to beg, and the Rájá gave him a handful of rice. " What !" said the Fakír, " the great Mahárája only gives me a handful of rice when his doorkeeper gives me pearls and rubies !" and he turned to walk away. But the Mahárájá stopped him. " What did you say?" said he, " that my doorkeeper gave you pearls and rubies?" " Yes," said the Fakír, " your door-keeper gave me pearls and rubies." So the Mahárájá went to the doorkeeper's house, and when he saw all the pearls and rubies that were there, he thought the man had stolen them from his treasury. The Mahárájá had not as many pearls and rubies as his doorkeeper had. Then turning to the doorkeeper he asked him to tell him truly where and how he had got them. " Yes, I will," said the doorkeeper. " Every night a beautiful bird comes and asks after you, after your children, after all your elephants, horses, and servants ; and then it cries, and when it cries pearls drop from its eyes ; and then it laughs, and rubies fall from its beak. If you come to-night I dare say you will see it." " All right," said the Pomegranate Rájá.

So that night the Mahárájá pulled his bed out under the

tree on which the bird always perched. At night the bird
came and called out, "Doorkeeper! doorkeeper!" and the
doorkeeper answered, "Yes, lord." And the bird said, "Is
your Mahárájá well?" "Yes." "Are the children well?"
"Yes." "And all his servants, horses, and camels and
elephants—are they well?" "Yes." "Are you well?"
"Yes." "Have you had plenty of food?" "Yes."
"What a fool your Mahárájá is!" And then she cried, and
the pearls came tumbling down on the Mahárájá's eyes, and
the Mahárájá opened one eye and saw what a beautiful
bird it was. And then it laughed, and rubies fell from its
beak on to the Mahárájá.

Next morning the Mahárájá said he would give any one
who would catch the bird as much money as he wanted. So
he called a fisherman, and asked him to bring his net and
catch the bird when it came that night. The fisherman said
he would for one thousand rupees. That night the fisherman, the Mahárájá, and the doorkeeper, all waited under
the tree. Soon the bird came, and asked after the Mahárájá,
after his children, and all his servants and elephants, and
camels and horses, and then after the doorkeeper, and then
it called the Mahárájá a fool. Then it cried, and then it
laughed, and just as it laughed the fisherman threw the net
over the bird and caught it. Then they shut it up in an
iron cage, and the next morning the Mahárájá took it out
and stroked it, and said, "What a sweet little bird! what a
lovely little bird!" And the Mahárájá felt something like a
pin in its head, and he gave a pull, and out came the pin,
and then his own dear wife, the Pomegranate-flower Rání,
stood before him. The Rájá was exceedingly glad, and so
were his two children. And there were great rejoicings,
and they lived happily ever after.

Told by Dunkní at Simla, 26th July, 1876.

III.

THE CAT AND THE DOG.

Introduction.

NOW all cats are aunts to the tigers, and the cat in this story was the aunt of the tiger in this story. She was his mother's sister. When the tiger's mother was dying, she called the cat to her, and taking her paw she said, "When I am dead you must take care of my child." The cat answered, "Very well," and then the tiger's mother died. The tiger said to the cat, "Aunt, I am very hungry. Go and fetch some fire. When I go to ask men for fire they are afraid of me, and run away from me, and won't give me any. But you are such a little creature that men are not afraid of you, and so they will give you fire, and then you must bring it to me." So the cat said, "Very good," and off she started, and went into a house where some men were eating their dinner : they had thrown away the bones, and the cat began to eat them. This house was very near the place where the tiger lived, and on peeping round the corner he saw his aunt eating the bones. "Oh," said he, "I sent my aunt to fetch fire that I might cook my dinner as I am very hungry, and there she sits eating the bones, and never thinks of me." So the tiger called out, "Aunt, I sent you to fetch fire, and there you sit eating bones and leave me hungry ! If ever you come near me again, I will kill you at once." So the cat ran away screaming, "I will never go near the tiger again, for he will kill me !" This is why all cats are so afraid of tigers, or of anything like a tiger. And this is why, when the cat in the story saw the tiger, her nephew, fighting with the man, she ran away as hard as she could.

The Story.

There were once a dog and a cat. It was a very rainy day, and some men were eating their dinner inside their house. The cat sat inside too, eating her dinner, and the dog sat on the door-step. The cat called out to the dog, "I am a high-caste person, and you are a very low-caste person." "Oh," said the dog, "not at all. I am the high-caste person and you are of very low caste. You eat all the men's dinner up, and snatch the food from their hands just as they are putting it into their mouths. And you scratch them, and they beat you ; while I sit away from them, and so they don't beat me. And if they *give* me any dinner I'll eat it; but if they don't, I won't." "Oh," says the cat, "not a bit of it. I eat nice clean food ; but you eat nasty, dirty food, which the men have thrown away." "No," said the dog, "I am high caste and you are very low caste, for if I gave you a slap you would tumble down directly." "No, no !" said the cat. And they went on disputing and began to fight, till the dog said, "Very well, let us go to the wise jackal and ask him which of us is the better." "Good," said the cat. So they went to the jackal and asked him. Said the cat, " I am of the higher caste, and the dog is of the lower caste." "No," said the jackal, "the dog is of the higher caste." The cat said, "No," and the jackal said, "Yes," and they began to fight. Then the jackal and the dog proposed to go and ask a great big beast who lived in the jungle and was like a tiger. But the cat said, "I cannot go near a tiger or anything like one." So then they said, "When we come near the beast, you can remain behind, and we will go on and speak to him." So they ran into the jungle, where there was a tiger who had been lying on the ground with a great thorn sticking in his foot. When his aunt, the cat, saw him, she scampered off, for she was dreadfully frightened.

The thorn had given the tiger great pain ; for a long while he could get no one to take it out, so had lain there for days. At last he had seen a man passing by, to whom he called and said, "Take out this thorn, and I promise I won't eat you." But the man refused through fear, saying, " No, I won't, for you will eat me." Three times the tiger had promised not to eat him ; so at last the man took out the thorn. Then the tiger sprang up and said, " Now I will eat you, for I am very hungry." " Oh, no, no ! " said the man. " What a liar you are ! You promised not to eat me if I would take the thorn out of your foot, and now that I have done so you say you will eat me." And they began to fight, and the man said, " If you won't eat me, I will bring you a cow and a goat." But the tiger refused, saying, " No, I won't eat them ; I will eat you."

At this moment the jackal and the dog came up. And the jackal asked, " What is the matter ? why are you fighting ? " So then the man told him why they were fighting ; and the jackal said to the tiger, " I will tell you a good way of eating the man. Go and fetch a big bag. So the tiger went and fetched the bag, and brought it to the jackal. Then the jackal said, " Get inside the bag, and leave its mouth open and I'll throw the man in to you." So the tiger got inside the bag, and the jackal, the dog and the man quickly tied it up as tight as they could. Then they began to beat the tiger with all their might until at last they killed him. Then the man went home, and the jackal went home, and the dog went home.

IV.

THE CAT WHICH COULD NOT BE KILLED.

THERE were once a dog and a cat, who were always quarrelling. The dog used to beat the cat, but he never could hurt her. She would only dance about and cry, "You never hurt me, you never hurt me! I *had* a pain in my shoulder, but now it is all gone away." So the dog went to a *mainá*[1] and said, "What shall I do to hurt this cat? I beat her and I bite her, and yet I can't hurt her. I am such a big dog and she is rather a big cat, yet if I beat her I don't hurt her, but if she beats me she hurts me so much." The *mainá* said, "Bite her mouth very, very hard, and then you'll hurt her." "Oh, no," said the cat, who had just come up, laughing; "you won't hurt me at all." The dog bit her mouth as hard as he could. "Oh, you don't hurt me," said the cat, dancing about. So the dog went again to the *mainá* and said, "What shall I do?" "Bite her ears," said the *mainá*. So the dog bit the cat's ears, but she danced about and said, "Oh, you did not hurt me; now I can put earrings in my ears." So she put in earrings.

The dog went to the elephant. "Can you kill this cat? she worries me so every day." "Oh, yes," said the elephant, "of course I can kill her. She is so little and I am so big." Then the elephant came and took her up with his trunk, and threw her a long way. Up she jumped at once and danced

---

[1] A kind of starling.

about, saying, "You did not hurt me one bit. I *had* a pain, but now I am quite well." Then the elephant got cross and said, "I'll teach you to dance in another way than that," and he took the cat and laid her on the ground and put his great foot on her. But she was not hurt at all. She danced about and said, "You did not hurt me one bit, not one bit," and she dug her claws into the elephant's trunk. The elephant ran away screaming, and he told the dog, "You had better beware of that cat. She belongs to the tiger tribe." The dog felt very angry with the cat. "What shall I do," said he, "to kill this cat?" And he bit her nose so hard that it bled. But she laughed at him. "Now I can put a ring in my nose," said she. He got furious. "I'll bite her tail in half," said he. So he bit her tail in half, and yet he did not hurt her.

He then went to a leopard. "If you can kill this cat I will give you anything you want." "Very well, I'll kill her," said the leopard. And they went together to the cat. "Stop," said the cat to the leopard; "I want to speak to you first. I'll give you something to eat, and then I'll tell you what I want to say." And then she ran off ever so far, and after she had run a mile she stopped and danced, calling out, "Oh! I'll give you nothing to eat; you could not kill me." The leopard went away very cross, and saying, "What a clever cat that is."

The dog next went to a man, and said, "Can you kill this cat, she worries me so?" "Of course I can," said the man; "I'll stick this knife into her stomach." And he stuck his knife into the cat's stomach, but the cat jumped up, and her stomach closed, and the man went home.

And the dog went to a bear. Can *you* kill this cat? I can't." "I'll kill her," said the bear; so he stuck all his claws into the cat, but he didn't hurt her; and she stuck her claws into the bear's nose so deep that he died immediately.

Then the poor dog felt very unhappy, and went and threw himself into a hole, and there he died, while the cat went away to her friends.

Told by Dunkní at Simla, July 26th, 1876.

V.

THE JACKAL AND THE KITE.

HERE was once a she-jackal and a she-kite. They lived in the same tree; the jackal at the bottom of the tree, and the kite at the top. Neither had any children. One day the kite said to the jackal, "Let us go and worship God, and fast, and then he will give us children." So the jackal said, "Very good." That day the kite ate nothing, nor that night; but the jackal at night brought a dead animal, and was sitting eating it quietly under the tree. By-and-by the kite heard her crunching the bones, instead of fasting. "What have you got there," said the kite, "that you are making such a noise?" "Nothing," said the jackal; "it is only my own bones that rattle inside my body whenever I move." The kite went to sleep again, and took no more notice of the jackal. Next morning the kite ate some food in the name of God. That night again the jackal brought a dead animal. The kite called out, "What are you crunching there? Why are you making that noise? I am sure you have something to eat." The jackal said, "Oh, no! It is only my own bones rattling in my body." So the kite went to sleep again.

Some time after, the kite had seven little boys—real little boys—but the jackal had none, because she had not fasted. A year after that the kite went and worshipped God, asking Him to take care of her children. One day—it was their great day—the kite set out seven plates. On one she put

cocoa-nuts, on another cucumbers, on a third rice, on a fourth
plantains, and so on.   Then she gave a plate to each of her
seven sons, and told them to take the plates to their aunt the
jackal.   So they took the seven plates, and carried them to
their aunt, crying out, "Aunty, aunty, look here!   Mamma
has sent you these things."   The jackal took the plates, and
cut off the heads of the seven boys, and their hands, and
their feet, and their noses, and their ears, and took out their
eyes.   Then she laid their heads in one plate, and their eyes
in another, and their noses in a third, and their ears in a
fourth, and their hands in a fifth, and their feet in a sixth,
and their trunks in the seventh, and then she covered all the
plates over.   Then she took the plates to the kite, and called
out, "Here! I have brought you something in return.   You
sent me a present, and I bring you a present."   Now the
poor kite thought the jackal had killed all her seven children,
so she cried out, "Oh, it's too dark now to see what you
have brought.   Put the plates down in my tree."   The
jackal put the plates down and went home.   Then God
made the boys alive again, and they came running to their
mother, quite well.   And instead of the heads and eyes, and
noses and ears, and hands and feet, and trunks, there were
again on the plates cocoa-nuts and cucumbers, and plantains
and rice, and so on.

Now the jackal got hold of the boys again.   And this
time she killed them, and cooked them and ate them ; and
again God brought them to life.   Well, the jackal was very
much astonished to see the boys alive, and she got angry,
and said to the kite, "I will take your seven sons and throw
them into the water, and they will be drowned."   "Very
well," said the kite, "take them.   I don't mind.   God will
take care of them."   The jackal took them and threw them
into the water, and left them to die, while the kite looked
on without crying.   And again God made them alive, and

the jackal was so surprised. " Why," said she, " I put these children into the water, and left them to drown. And here they are alive ! " Then God got very angry with the jackal, and said to her, " Go out of this village. And wherever you go, men will try to shoot you, and you shall always be afraid of them." So the jackal had to go away ; and the kite and her children lived very happily ever afterwards.

Told by Dunkní.

VI.

THE VORACIOUS FROG.

THERE were a rat and a frog. And the rat said to the frog, "Go and get me some sticks, while I go and get some flour and milk." So the frog went out far into the jungle and brought home plenty of sticks, and the rat went out and brought home flour and milk for their dinner. Then she cooked the dinner, and when it was cooked she said to the frog, "Now, you sit here while I go to bathe, and take care of the food so that no one may come and eat it up." Then the rat went to take her bath, and as soon as she had gone the frog made haste and ate up the dinner quickly, and went away.

When the rat came back she found no dinner, and she could not find the frog. So she went out to look for him, calling to him as loudly as she could, and she saw him in the distance, and overtook him. "Why have you eaten my dinner? Why did you go away?" said the rat. Said the frog, "Oh, dear! it was not I that ate your dinner, but a huge dog that came; and I was only a tiny, tiny thing, and he was a great big dog, and so he frightened me, and I ran away." "Very well," said the rat; "go and fetch me more sticks while I go for flour and milk." So the frog went out far into the jungle and brought back plenty of sticks. And the rat went to fetch flour and milk. Then she lit the fire and cooked the dinner, and told the frog to take care of · the dinner while she went to bathe. As soon as she had gone, the frog ate up all the dinner, and went away and hid himself. When the rat came back she saw no frog, no dinner. She went away into the jungle and called to him, and the frog answered from behind a tree, " Here I am, here I am." The rat went to him and said, " Why did you eat my dinner ? " " I didn't," said the frog. " It was a great big dog ate the dinner, and he wanted to eat me too, and so I ran away." The rat said, " Very well. Go and fetch me some more sticks, and I will go for flour and milk." Then she cooked the dinner again and went to bathe. The frog ate up all the dinner, and went away and hid himself. When the rat returned she saw no dinner, no frog. So she went far into the jungle, found the frog, and told him that it was he that had eaten the dinner. And the frog said, " No," and the rat said, " Yes." And the frog said, " If you say that again, I will eat you up." " All right," says the rat, " eat me up." So he ate her up and sat behind a tree, and the baker came past. The frog called out, " Baker, come here ! come here ! Give me some bread." The baker looked about everywhere, could not see anybody, could not think who was calling him. At last he saw the frog sitting behind a tree. " Give me some bread," says the frog. The man said, " No, I won't give you any bread. I am a great big man, and you are only a little frog, and you have no money." " Yes, I have money. I will give you some pice, and you will give me some bread." But the man said, " No, I won't." " Well," said the frog, " if you won't give me bread, I will eat you up first, and then I will eat up your bread." So he ate up the man, and then ate up his bread. Presently a man with oranges and lemons passed by. The frog called to him, " Come here ! come here ! " The man was very much afraid. He didn't know who had called him. Then he saw the frog, and the frog said, " Give me some lemons." The man wouldn't, and said, " No." " Very well," says the ·

frog, " if you won't, I'll eat you up." So he ate up the man with his lemons and oranges. Presently a horse and his groom went by. The frog says, " Please give me a ride, and I will give you some money." " No," said the horse, " I won't let you ride on me. You are like a monkey,—very little—I won't let you ride on my back." The frog said, " If you won't, I'll eat you up." Then the frog ate him up, and his groom too. Then a barber passed by. " Come and shave me," says the frog. " Good," says the barber, " I'll come and shave you." So he shaved him, and he thought the frog looked *very* fat, and so as he was shaving him he suddenly made a cut in his stomach. Out jumped the rat with her flour and milk—the baker with his bread— the lemon-seller with his oranges and lemons—the horse and his groom. And the barber ran away home. And the frog died.

VII.

THE STORY OF FOOLISH SACHÚLÍ.

HERE once lived a poor old widow woman named Hungní, who had a little idiot son called Sachúlí. She used to beg every day. One day when the son had grown up, he said to his mother. "What makes women laugh?" "If you throw a tiny stone at them," answered she, "they will laugh." So one day Sachúlí went and sat by a well, and three women came to it to fill their water-jars. "Now," said Sachúlí "I will make one of these women laugh." Two of the women filled their water-jars and went away home, and he threw no stones at them; but as the last, who also had on the most jewels, passed him, he threw a great big stone at her, and she fell down dead, with her mouth set as if she were smiling. "Oh, look! look! how she is laughing!" said Sachúlí, and he ran off to call his mother.

"Come, come, mother," said he, "and see how I have made this woman laugh."

His mother came, and when she saw the woman lying dead, she was much frightened, for the dead woman belonged to a great and very rich family, and she wore jewels worth a thousand rupees. Hungní took off all her jewels, and threw her body into the well.

After some days the dead woman's father and mother and all her people sent round a crier with a drum to try and find her. "Whoever brings back a young woman who wears a great many gold necklaces and bracelets and rings shall get a great deal of money," cried the crier. Sachúli heard him. "I know where she is," said he. "My mother took off all her jewels, and threw her into the well."

The crier said, "Can you go down into the well and bring her up?"

"If you will tie a rope round my waist and let me down the well, I shall be able to bring her up."

So they set off towards the well, which was near Hungní's house; and when she saw them coming, she guessed what they came for, and she ran out and killed a sheep, threw it into the well, and took out the dead woman and hid her.

The crier got some men to come with him, and they let Sachúli down the well. "Has she got eyes?" said Sachúli. "Of course, every one has eyes," answered the men. "Has she a nose?" asked Sachúli. "Yes, she has a nose," said the men. "Has she got a mouth?" asked Sachúli. "Yes," said the men. "Has she a long face?"

"What does he mean?" said the men, who were getting cross. "No one has a long face; perhaps she has, though. Yes, she has a long face," cried the men.

"Has she a tail?"

"A tail! Why no one has a tail. Perhaps, though, she has long hair. No doubt that is what he calls a tail. Yes, she has a tail."

"Has she ears?"

"Of course, every one has ears."

"Has she four feet?"

"Four feet!" said the men. "Why, no one has four feet. Perhaps you call her hands feet. Yes, she has four feet. Bring her up quickly."

Then Sachúli brought up the sheep.

The men were very angry when they saw the sheep, and they beat Sachúli, and called him a very stupid fellow and a great liar, and they went away feeling very cross.

Sachúlí went home to his mother, who, as soon as she saw him coming, ran out and put the woman's body back in the well, and when he got home she beat him. " Mother," said he, " give me some bread, and I will go away and die." His mother cooked him some bread, and he went away.

He walked on, and on, and on, a long way.

Now, some Rájá's ten camels had been travelling along the road on which Sachúlí went, each carrying sacks of gold mohurs and rupees, and one of these camels broke loose from the string and strayed away, and the camel-drivers could not find it again. But Sachúlí met it, and caught it and took it home.

" See, mother! see what a quantity of money I have brought you ! " cried Sachúlí. Hungní rushed out, and was delighted to see so much money. She took off the sacks at once and sent the camel away. Then she hid the rupees and the gold with the jewels she had taken from the dead woman. And, as she was a cunning woman, she went and bought a great many comfits and scattered them all about her house, when Sachúlí was out of the way. " Oh, look ! look ! " cried Sachúlí, " at all these comfits." " God has rained them from heaven," said his mother. Sachúlí began to pick them up and eat them, and he told all the people in the village how God had rained down comfits from heaven on his mother's house. " What nonsense ! " cried they. " Yes, he has," said Sachúlí, " and I have been eating them." " No comfits have fallen on our houses," said they. " Yes, yes," cried he, " the day my mother got all those rupees, God rained comfits on our house." " What lies ! " cried the people ; " as if it ever rained comfits. Why did not the comfits rain down on our houses ? Why did they fall only on your house ? And what's all this about rupees ? " And then they came to see if there were any rupees or comfits in Hungní's house, and they found none at all, for Hungní had hidden the rupees and thrown away the comfits. "There," said they to Sachúlí, "where are your rupees? where are your comfits? What a liar you are! as if it ever rained comfits. How can you tell such stories?" And they beat him. "But it did rain comfits," said Sachúlí, "for I ate them. It rained comfits the day my mother got the rupees."

Now the Rájá who had lost his camel sent round the crier with his drum to find his camel and his money-bags. "Whoever has found a camel carrying money-bags and brings it and the money back to the Rájá, will get a great many rupees," cried the crier. "Oh!" says Sachúlí, "I know where the money is. One day I went out and I found a stray camel, and he had sacks of rupees on his back, and I took him home to my mother, and she took the sacks off his back and sent the camel away." So the crier went to find the rupees, and the people in the bazar went with him, But Hungní had hidden the rupees so carefully that, though they hunted all over her house, they could find none, and they beat Sachúlí, and told him he was a liar. "I am not telling lies," said Sachúlí. "My mother took the rupees the day it rained comfits on our house." So they beat him again, and they went away. Then Hungní beat Sachúlí, and said, "What a bad boy you are! trying to get me beaten and put into prison, telling every one about the rupees. Go away; I don't want you any more, such a bad boy as you are! go away and die." He said, "Very well, mother; give me some bread, and I'll go."

Sachúlí set off and took an axe with him. "How shall I kill myself?" said he. So he climbed up a tree and sat out on a long branch, and began cutting off the branch between himself and the tree on which he was sitting. "What are you doing up there?" said a man who came by. "You'll die if you cut that branch off." "What do you say?" cries Sachuli, jumping down on the man, and seizing his hand.

" When shall I die ? " " How can I tell ? Let me go." " I won't let you go till you tell me when I shall die." And at last the man said, " When you find a scarlet thread on your jacket, then you will die."

Sachúlí went off to the bazar, and sat down by some tailors, and one of the tailors, in throwing away their shreds of cloth, threw a scarlet thread on Sachúlí's coat. " Oh," said Sachúlí, when he saw the thread, " now I shall die ! " " How do you know that ? " said the tailors. " A man told me that when I found a scarlet thread on my jacket, I should die," said Sachúlí ; and the tailors all laughed at him and made fun of him, but he went off into the jungle and dug his grave with his axe, and lay down in it. In the night a sepoy came by with a large jar of ghee on his head. " How heavy this jar is," said the sepoy. " Is there no cooly that will come and carry my ghee home for me ? I would give him four pice for his trouble." Up jumped Sachúlí out of his grave. " I'll carry it for you," said he. " Who are you?" said the sepoy, much frightened. " Oh, I am a man who is dead," said Sachúlí, " and I am tired of lying here. I can't lie here any more." " Well," said the sepoy, very much frightened, " you may carry my ghee." So Sachúlí put the jar on his head, and he went on, with the sepoy following. " Now," said Sachúlí, " with these four pice I will buy a hen, and I will sell the hen and her eggs, and with the money I get for them I will buy a goat ; and then I will sell the goat and her milk and her hide and buy a cow, and I will sell her milk ; and then I will marry a wife, and then I shall have some children, and they will say to me, ' Father, will you have some rice ? ' and I will say, ' No, I won't have any rice.' " And as he said, " No, I won't have any rice," he shook his head, and down came the jar of ghee, and the jar was smashed, and the ghee spilled. " Oh, dear ! what have you done ? " cried the sepoy. " Why did you shake your head ? "

" Because my children asked me to have some rice, and I
did not want any, so I shook my head," said Sachúlí. " Oh,"
said the sepoy, " he is an utter idiot." And the sepoy went
home, and Sachúlí went back to his mother. " Why have
you come back ? " said she. " I have been dead twelve years,"
said Sachúlí. " What lies you tell ! " said she. " You have only
been away a few days. Be off ! I don't want any liars here."

Sachúlí asked her to give him two flour-cakes, which she
did, and he went off to the jungle, and it was night. Five
fairies lived in this jungle, and as Sachuli went along, he
broke his flour-cakes into five pieces, and said, " Now I'll eat
one, then the second, then the third, then the fourth, and then
the fifth." And the fairies heard him and were afraid, and
said to each other, " What shall we do ? Here is this man,
and he is going to eat us all up. What shall we do to save
ourselves ? We will give him something." So they went out
all five, and said to Sachúlí, " If only you won't eat us, we
will give you a present." Now Sachúlí did not know there
were fairies in this jungle. " What will you give me ? " said
Sachúlí. " We will give you a cooking-pot. When you want
anything to eat, all you have to do is to ask the pot for it,
and you will get it. Sachúlí took the pot and went off to
the bazar. He stopped at a cook-shop, and asked for some
pilau. " Pilau ? There's no pilau here," said the shopman.
" Well," said Sachúlí, " I have a cooking-pot here, and I
have only to ask it for any dish I want, and I get it at once."
" What nonsense ! " said the man. " Just see," said Sachúlí ;
and he said to the cooking-pot, " I want some pilau," and
immediately the pot was full of pilau, and all the people in
the shop set to work to help him to eat it up, it was so good.
" Oh," thought the cook, " I must have that pot," so he gave
Sachúlí a sleepy drink. Then Sachúlí went to sleep, and
while he slept the cook stole the fairy cooking-pot, and put
a common cooking-pot in its place. Sachúlí went home

with the cook's pot, and said, " Mother, I have brought home a cooking-pot. If you ask it for any food you want, you will get it." " Nonsense," said Hungní ; " what lies you are telling ! " " It is quite true, mother ; only see," and he asked the pot for different dishes, but none came. Hungní was furious. " Go away," she said. " Why do you come back to me ? I want no liars here." " Give me five flour-cakes and I will go," said her son. So she baked the bread for him, and he set off for the jungle where he had met the five fairies, and as he went along he said, " I will eat one, and I will eat two, and I will eat three, and I will eat four, and I will eat five." The five fairies heard him, and were terrified. " Here is this bad man again," said they, " and he will eat us all five. Oh, what shall we do? Let us give him a present." So they went to Sachúlí, and said, " Here is a box for you. Whenever you want any clothes you have only to tell this box, and it will give them to you ; take it, and don't eat us." So he took the box and went to the bazar, and he stopped at the cook-shop again, and asked the cook for a red silk dress, and a pair of long black silk trousers, and a blue silk turban, and a pair of red shoes, and the cook laughed and asked how he should have such beautiful things. " Well," said Sachúlí, " here is a box ; when I ask it for the dress and trousers, and turban and shoes, I shall get them." So the cook laughed at him. " Just see," said Sachúlí, and he said, " Box, give me a red silk dress and a pair of long black silk trousers, and a blue silk turban, and red shoes," and there they were at once. And the cook was delighted, and said to himself, " I will have that box," and he gave Sachúlí a good dinner and a sleepy drink, and Sachúlí fell fast asleep. While he slept the cook came and stole the fairy box, and put a common box in its place. In the morn-ing Sachúlí went home to his mother and said, " Mother, I've brought you a box. You have only to ask it for any clothes

D

you may want, and you will get them." " Nonsense," said
his mother, " don't tell me such lies." " Only see, mother ;
I am telling you truth," said he. He asked the box for coats
and all sorts of things—no ; he got nothing. His mother
was very angry, and said, " You liar ! you naughty boy ! Go
away and don't come back any more." And she broke the
box to pieces, and threw the bits away. " Well, mother, bake
me some flour-cakes." So she baked him the cakes and
gave them to him, and sent him away. He went off to the
fairies' jungle, and as he went he said, " Now I'll eat one,
then two, then three, then four, then five." The five fairies
were very frightened. " Here is this man come back to eat
us all five. Let us give him a present." So they went to
him and gave him a rope and stick, and said, " Only say to
this rope, ' Bind that man,' and he will be tied up at once ;
and to this stick, ' Beat that man,' and the stick will beat
him." Sachúlí was very glad to get these things, for he
guessed what had happened to his cooking-pot and box.
So he went to the bazar, and at the cook-shop he said, " Rope,
bind all these men that are here ! " and the cook and every
one in the shop were tied up instantly. Then Sachúlí said,
" Stick, beat these men ! " and the stick began to beat them.
" Oh, stop, stop beating us, and untie, and I'll give you
your pot and your box ! " cried the cook. " No, I won't
stop beating you, and I won't untie you till I have my pot
and my box." And the cook gave them both to him, and he
untied the rope. Then Sachúlí went home, and when his
mother saw him, she was very angry, but he showed her the
box and the cooking-pot, and she saw he had told her the
truth. So she sent for the doctor, and he declared Sachúlí
was wise and not silly, and he and Hungní found a wife for
Sachúlí, and made a grand wedding for him, and they lived
happily ever after.

Told by Dunkní.

VIII.

BARBER HÍM AND THE TIGERS.

NCE there lived a barber called Hím, who was very poor indeed. He had a wife and twelve children, five boys and seven girls : now and then he got a few pice. One day he went away from his home feeling very cross, and left his wife and children to get on as best they could. "What can I do?" said he. "I have not enough money to buy food for my family, and they are crying for it." And so he walked on till he came to a jungle. It was night when he got there. This jungle was called the "tigers' jungle," because only tigers lived in it ; no birds, no insects, no other animals, and there were four hundred tigers in it altogether. As soon as Barber Hím reached the jungle he saw a great tiger walking about. "What shall I do?" cried he. "This tiger is sure to eat me." And he took his razor and his razor-strap, and began to sharpen his razor. Then he went close up to the tiger, still sharpening his razor. The tiger was much frightened. "What shall I do?" said the tiger ; "this man will certainly gash me." "I have come," said the barber, "to catch twenty tigers by order of Mahárájá Káns. You are one, and I want nineteen more. The tiger, greatly alarmed, answered, "If you won't catch us, I will give you as much gold and as many jewels as you can carry." For these tigers used to go out and carry off the men and women from the villages, and some of these people had rupees, and some had jewels, all of which the tigers used to

collect together. " Good," said Hím, " then I won't catch
you." The tiger led him to the spot where all the tigers
used to eat their dinners, and the barber took as much gold
and as many jewels as he could carry, and set off home
with them.

Then he built a house, and bought his children pretty
clothes and good food, and necklaces, and they all lived very
happily for some time. But at last he wanted more rupees,
so he set off to the tigers' jungle. There he met the tiger as
he did before, and he told him the Mahárájá Káns had sent
him to catch twenty tigers. The tiger was terrified and said,
" If you will only not catch us, I will give you more gold
and jewels." To this the barber agreed, and the tiger led
him to the old spot, and the barber took as many jewels and
rupees as he could carry. Then he returned home.

One day a very poor man, a fakír, said to him, " How did
you manage to become so rich ? In old days you were so
poor you could hardly support your family."

" I will tell you," said Hím. And he told him all about
his visits to the tigers' jungle. " But don't you go there for
gold to-night," continued the barber. " Let me go and listen
to the tigers talking. If you like, you can come with me.
Only you must not be frightened if the tigers roar."

" I'll not be frightened," said the fakír.

So that evening at eight o'clock they went to the tigers'
jungle. There the barber and the fakír climbed into a tall
thick tree, and its leaves came all about them and sheltered
them as if they were in a house. The tigers used to hold
their councils under this tree. Very soon all the tigers in
the jungle assembled together under it, and their Rájá—
a great, huge beast, with only one eye—came too. " Brothers,"
said the tiger who had given the barber the rupees and
jewels, " a man has come here twice to catch twenty of us for
the Mahárájá Káns ; now we are only four hundred in num-

ber, and if twenty of us were taken away we should be only
a small number, so I gave him each time as many rupees
and jewels as he could carry and he went away again. What
shall we do if he returns?" The tigers said they would meet
again on the morrow, and then they would settle the matter.
Then the tigers went off, and the barber and the fakír came
down from the tree. They took a quantity of rupees and
jewels and returned to their homes.

"To-morrow," said they, "we will come again and hear
what the tigers say."

The next day the barber went alone to the tigers' jungle,
and there he met his tiger again. "This time," said he, "I
am come to cut off the ears of all the four hundred tigers
who live in this jungle; for Mahárájá Káns wants them to
make into medicine."

The tiger was greatly frightened, much more so than at the
other times. "Don't cut off our ears; pray don't," said he,
"for then we could not hear, and it would hurt so horribly.
Go and cut off all the dogs' ears instead, and I will give
you rupees and jewels as much as two men can carry."
"Good," said the barber, and he made two journeys with
the rupees and jewels from the jungle to the borders of his
village, and there he got a cooly to help him to carry them
to his house.

At night he and the fakír went again to the great tree under
which the tigers held their councils. Now the tiger who had
given the barber so many rupees and jewels had made ready
a great quantity of meat, fowls, chickens, geese, men the tigers
had killed—everything he had been able to get hold of—and
he made them into a heap under the tree, for he said that
after the tigers had settled the matter they would dine. Soon
the tigers arrived with their Rájá, and the barber's tiger said,
"Brothers, what are we to do? This man came again to-day
to cut off all our ears to make medicine for Mahárájá Káns.

I told him this would be a bad business for us, and that he must go and cut off all the dogs' ears instead ; and I gave him as much money and jewels as two men could carry. So he went home. Now what shall we do ? We must leave this jungle, and where shall we go ?" The other tigers said, " We will not leave the jungle. If this man comes again we will eat him up." So they dined and went away, saying they would meet again to-morrow.

After the tigers had gone, the barber and fakír came down from the tree and went off to their homes, without taking any rupees or jewels with them. They agreed to return the next evening.

Next evening back they came and climbed into the great tree. The tigers came too, and the barber's tiger told his story all over again. The tiger Rájá sat up and said, fiercely, " We will not leave this jungle. Should the man come again, I will eat him myself." When the fakír heard this he was so frightened that he tumbled down out of the tree into the midst of the tigers. The barber instantly cried out with a loud voice, " Now cut off their ears ! cut off their ears ! " and the tigers, terrified, ran away as fast as they could. Then the barber took the fakír home, but the poor man was so much hurt by his fall that he died.

The barber lived happily ever after, but he took good care never to go to the tigers' jungle again.

Told by Dunkní.

IX.

THE BULBUL AND THE COTTON-TREE.

HERE was once a bulbul, and one day as he was flying about, he saw a tree on which was a little fruit. The bulbul was much pleased and said, " I will sit here till this fruit is ripe, and then I will eat it." So he deserted his nest and his wife, and sat there for twelve years without eating anything, and every day he said, " To-morrow I will eat this fruit." During these twelve years a great many birds tried to sit on the tree, and wished to build their nests in it, but whenever they came the bulbul sent them away, saying, " This fruit is not good. Don't come here." One day a cuckoo came and said, " Why do you send us away? Why should we not come and sit here too? All the trees here are not yours." " Never mind," said the bulbul, ." I am going to sit here, and when this fruit is ripe, I shall eat it." Now the cuckoo knew that this tree was the cotton-tree, but the bulbul did not. First comes the bud, which the bulbul thought a fruit, then the flower, and the flower becomes a big pod, and the pod bursts and all the cotton flies away. The bulbul was delighted when he saw the beautiful red flower, which he still thought a fruit, and said, " When it is ripe, it will be a delicious fruit." The flower became a pod, and the pod burst. " What is all this that is flying about? " said the bulbul. " The fruit must be ripe now." So he looked into the pod, and it was empty; all the cotton had fallen out.   Then the cuckoo came and said to the angry bulbul, "You see if you had allowed us to come and sit on the tree, you would have had something good to eat ; but as you were selfish, and would not let any one share with you, God is angry and has punished you by giving you a hollow fruit."   Then the cuckoo called all the other birds, and they came and mocked the bulbul.   "Ah ! you see God has punished you for your selfishness," they said.   The bulbul got very angry and all the birds went away. After they had gone, the bulbul said to the tree, "You are a bad tree.   You are of use to no one.   You give food to no one."   The tree said, "You are mistaken.   God made me what I am.   My flower is given to sheep to eat.   My cotton makes pillows and mattresses for man."

Since that day no bulbul goes near a cotton-tree.

Told by Dunkni.

X.

THE MONKEY PRINCE.

NCE upon a time there was a Rájá called Jabhú Rájá, and he had a great many wives; at least he had seven wives, but he had no children. Although he had married seven wives, not one of them had given him a child. At this he was greatly vexed and said, " I have married seven wives, and not one of them has given me a child." And he got very angry with God : he said, " Why does not God give me any children ? I will go into the jungle and die by myself." The Ránís coaxed him to stay, but he wouldn't; he would go out into the jungle.

So he went out into the jungle very far, and God sent him an old fakír leaning on a stick. The Rájá met him, and the fakír said, "Why do you come into the jungle? If you go far into the jungle you will meet plenty of tigers, and they will eat you. Tell me what you want. Whatever you want I will give you." " No, I won't tell you," said the Rájá. But at last the Rájá told him, " I have seven wives, and none of them has given me any children, and so here I will die by myself." Then the fakír said, " Take this stick, and a little way off you will find a mango-tree with some mangoes on it. Throw the stick at the mangoes with one hand, and catch them as they fall with the other, and when you have caught them all, take them home and give one to each of your seven wives." So the Rájá went and knocked the mangoes off the tree and caught them as the fakír had told him. Then he looked about for the fakír, but he could not find him, for he had gone away into another part of the jungle. So he went home and gave the seven mangoes to his wives. But the fruit was so good that six of the wives ate it up, and would not give the youngest wife any. She cried very much, and went into the compound and picked up one of the mango stones which one of the six wives had thrown away, and ate it. By and by each of the six wives had a son; but the one who had eaten the stone had a monkey, who was called in consequence Bandarsábásá, or Prince Monkey. He was really a boy, but no one knew it, for he had a monkey-skin covering him. His six brothers hated him. They went to school every day; and the monkey went under the ground, and was taught by the fairies. His mother did not know this; she thought, as he was a monkey, he went to the jungle and swung in the trees. He was the best and the cleverest of all the boys.

Now, in a kingdom a three months' journey off by land from Jabhú Rájá's country, there lived a king called King Jamársá. He had a very beautiful daughter whose name was Princess Jahúran, and as her father wanted a very strong son-in-law, he had a large heavy iron ball made, and he sent letters to all the Rájás and Rájás' sons far and near to say that whoever wished to marry his daughter, the Princess Jahúran, must be able to throw this heavy ball at her and hit her. So many Rájás went to try, but none of them could even lift the ball. Now, one of these letters had come to Jabhú Rájá, and his six elder sons determined they would go to King Jamársá's country, for each of them was sure he could throw the ball, and win the princess.

Prince Monkey laughed softly and said to himself, "I will go and try too. I know I shall succeed."

Off, therefore, the six brothers set on their long journey, and the monkey followed them; but before he did so, he went into the jungle and took off his monkey-skin, and God

sent him a beautiful horse and beautiful clothes. Then he
followed his brothers and overtook them, and gave them
betel-leaf and lovely flowers. "What a beautiful boy!"
they said. "Who is it owns such a beautiful boy? He
must be some Rájá's son." Then he galloped quickly away,
took off his grand clothes and put them on his horse, and
the horse rose into the air. He put on his monkey-skin an
followed his brothers.

When they reached King Jamársá's palace they pitched
their tents in his compound, which was very big. Every
evening the princess used to stand in her verandah and let
down her long golden hair so that it fell all round her, and
then the Rájás who wished to marry her had to try to hit her
with the great heavy ball that lay on the ground just in front
of where she stood.

King Jamársá's house had more than one storey, and
you had to go upstairs to get to the Princess Jahúran's
rooms which led into the verandah in which she used to
stand.

Well, Prince Monkey's six elder brothers all got ready to
go up to the palace and throw the ball. They were quite
sure they would throw it without any trouble. Before they
went they told their monkey brother to take care of their
tents, and to have a good dinner ready for them when they
returned. "If the dinner is not ready, we will beat you."

As soon as they were gone, Prince Monkey took some
gold mohurs he had, and he went to a traveller's resting-
house, which was a little way outside King Jamársá's compound, and gave them to the man who owned it, and bade
him give him a grand dinner for his six brothers. Then he
took the dinner to the tents, went into the jungle, and took
off his monkey-skin. And God sent him a grand horse from
heaven, and splendid clothes. These he put on, mounted
his horse, and rode to King Jamársá's compound. There he

took no notice of either the king, or his daughter, or of the ball, or of the Rájás who were there to try and lift it. He spoke only to his brothers, and gave them lovely flowers and betel-leaf. Meanwhile, everybody was looking at him and talking about him. "Who can he be? Did you ever see any one so lovely? Where does he come from? Just look at his clothes! In our countries we cannot get any like them!" As for the Princess Jahúran she thought to herself, "That Rájá shall be my husband, whether he lifts the ball or not." When he had given his brothers the flowers and betel-leaf, Prince Monkey rode straight to the jungle, took off his clothes, laid them on his horse (which instantly went up to heaven), put on his monkey-skin, went back to the tents, and lay down to sleep.

When his brothers came home they were talking eagerly about the unknown beautiful Rájá. All the time they were eating their dinner they could speak of nothing else.

Well, every evening for about ten evenings it was just the same story. Only every evening Prince Monkey appeared in a different dress. The princess always thought, "That is the man I will marry, whether he can throw the ball or not." Then about the eleventh evening, after he had given his brothers the flowers and betel-leaf, he said to all the Rájás who were standing there, and to King Jamársá and to all the servants, "Now every one of you go and stand far away, for I am going to throw the ball." "No, no!" they all cried, "we will stand here and see you." "You must go far away. You can look on at a distance," said the Monkey Prince; "the ball might fall back among you and hurt you." So they all went off and stood round him at a distance.

"Now," said Prince Monkey to himself, "I won't hit the princess this time; but I will hit the verandah railing." Then he took up the ball with one hand, just as if it were quite light, and threw it on the verandah railing, and then he rode off fast to the jungle.

The next evening it was the same thing over again, only this time he threw the ball into the Princess Jahúran's clothes.

The next evening the ball fell on one of her feet, and hurt her little toe-nail. Now, Princess Jahúran was very angry that this unknown beautiful prince should have thrown the ball three times, and hit her twice, and hurt her the third time, and yet had never spoken to her father, or let any one know who he was, and had always, on the contrary, ridden away as hard as he could, no one knew where. She was very much in love with him, and was very anxious to find this Rájá who had hit her twice, so she ordered a bow and arrow to be brought to her, and said she would shoot the Rájá the next time he hit her. She would not kill him ; she would only shoot the arrow at him. Well, the next evening Prince Monkey threw the ball, and it fell on her other foot and hurt her great toe-nail. When he saw she was hurt, he was very sorry in his heart, and said, " Did I hurt you ? " " Yes," she said, " very much." " Oh, I am so sorry," said the prince. " I would not have thrown the ball so hard had I thought it would hurt you." Then she shot the arrow, and hit him in the leg, and a great deal of blood came out of the wound ; but he rode hard away to the jungle all the same, only this time he did not take off his fine clothes, but he drew the monkey-skin over them, and his horse went up to heaven, and he went back to the tents. Then the princess sent a servant into the town, and said, whoever or whatever he should hear crying with pain, he should bring to her—were it a man, or a jackal, or a dog, or a wild beast. So the servant went round the town. The six brothers had gone to sleep, but the poor monkey brother could not sleep, but sat up crying from pain. He could not help it, do what he would, and the servant, as he went round the town, heard him crying. So he took him and brought him to the princess, and the princess said she would marry him.

" What ! " cried her father, " marry that monkey ? Never !

Who ever heard of any one marrying a monkey, a nasty
monkey ? "   But in spite of all the king said, the princess
declared marry that monkey she would. " I like that monkey
very, very much," she said.   " I will marry him.   It is my
pleasure to marry him."   " Well," said the Rájá at last, "if
it is your pleasure to marry him, you must marry him ; but
who ever heard of any one marrying a nasty monkey?"

So they were married at once ; and the Monkey Prince
wore his monkey-skin for a wedding garment.

That night when they went to bed, the young prince drew
off his skin and lay down by Jahúran, and when she saw
her beautiful husband she was so glad, so glad.   " Why do
you wear a monkey-skin?" she asked.   He answered, "I
wear it as a protection, because my brothers are naughty,
and would kill me if they knew what I really am."

They lived very happily with King Jamársá for six months,
and the six elder brothers went on living there too, and hating him more and more for having such a beautiful wife.

But one night Prince Monkey thought of his mother, and
he said to his wife, " My mother perhaps is crying for me.
Let us go to my father's kingdom, and see her."   Princess
Jahúran agreed; so next morning they spoke to King
Jamársá, who said they might go.

The six brothers at once said, "We will go with you;"
and they also said, " Let us get two big boats, one for you
and the princess, and one for ourselves, and let us go by
water, and not by land."   Now by water it took only six
days to get to Jabhú Rájá's kingdom, by land it took three
months.   The Monkey Prince agreed to all his brothers
said.

Princess Jahúran heard them planning to throw the monkey into the water on the journey, and then to take her home
to their father as the wife of one of them ; so as she was very
wise she went to her father and begged him to have six large
beautiful mattresses, well stuffed with cotton, made for her.

" What can you want with six mattresses ? " said the king.
" I want my bed to be very comfortable on board the boat,"
said his daughter. Her father loved her dearly, so he had
her mattresses made, beautiful mattresses and well stuffed
with cotton. The princess had them all carried to her
boat.

When everything was ready they went on board the boats
with the monkey's six brothers. Now, the princess had
warned her husband of his brothers' wicked plans, and she
said to him, " Never go near your brothers ; never speak to
your brothers ; for they want to kill you." The first day the
six brothers said to the monkey, " Please bring us a little
salt." But the monkey said, " No ; my wife will take you
some." " No," said the brothers, " your wife cannot bring us
any. She is a princess. Do you bring us some." So they
threw a rope from one boat to another, and the monkey went
on the rope, and the brothers untied it, and the monkey fell
into the water. Then the princess cried out, " My husband
will be drowned ! My husband will be drowned ! " And
she threw out one of the mattresses ; the monkey sat on it ;
it floated back to his boat, and the crew drew him up.

The next day the six brothers begged Prince Monkey to
bring them water, and they threw a plank from their boat to
his for him to cross on. The prince set off with the water, in
spite of all his wife's entreaties, and his brothers tilted the
plank into the water. The prince would have been drowned
had not the Princess Jahúran thrown him a mattress. And
the same thing happened during the next four days. The
brothers wanted something to eat or drink, and their monkey-
brother brought it them across a rope or plank, which they
cut or dropped into the water, and he would have died but
for the mattresses which his wife threw to him one by one.

When they reached Jabhú Rájá's kingdom, the eldest son
went on shore up to his father's palace. Each of the Rájá's
seven wives had a house to herself in his compound. He

went to his mother's house and said, " Give me your palanquin, mother, for I have brought home a most lovely wife,
and want to bring her to the palace."

At this news his mother was delighted, and she told it to
the other Ránís, and said, " My son has brought home such
a lovely wife ! I am so glad ! oh, I am so glad !" The
youngest Rání began to cry bitterly.   " My son," she said,
" is nothing but a monkey ; he will never be married ; he
will never have a wife at all."

Then the palanquin was got ready, and the seven Ránís and
the prince went with it to the boat. The Princess Jahúran came
on land with her monkey, and when the Ránís saw her, they
all cried, " How lovely she is ! how beautiful !" And the eldest
Rání was gladder than ever, and the youngest cried still more.
The princess got into the palanquin with her monkey.
" What are you doing with that horrid monkey ?" said the
eldest prince. " Put him out of the palanquin directly." " Indeed I will not," said the princess. " He is my husband, and
I love him." " What !" cried all the Ránís, " are you married
to that monkey ?" " Yes," said the princess. " Then get out
of my palanquin at once," said the eldest Rání. " You shall
not ride in my palanquin with that nasty monkey." The
youngest Rání was very glad her son had such a beautiful wife.
So the princess got out, and took her monkey in her arms and
walked with him to the youngest Rání's house, and there they
all lived for some time.   Now the little Rání did not know
her son was really a beautiful man, for the princess never
told her, as her husband had forbidden her to tell any one.

One evening Jabhú Rájá's servants had a grand nautch in
the Rájá's compound, and the Rájá and his sons and the
neighbouring Rájás all came to see it.   Prince Monkey said
to his wife, " I, too, will go and see this nautch." So he took
off his monkey-skin, folded it up and laid it under her pillow.
Then he put on the clothes God had sent him from heaven

the last time he threw the ball, and which he had not laid on his horse's back when he put his monkey-skin on again, and when he came among all the Rájás and people who were looking on at the nautch, they all exclaimed, "Who is that? Who can it be?" He was very handsome, and he had beautiful hair all gold. When he had stayed some time, Prince Monkey went quickly back to his wife, and in the morning he put on his monkey-skin again.

Now the little Rání, his mother, though she was very glad her monkey son had such a wife, could never understand how it was that her daughter-in-law was so happy with him. "How could you marry him?" she used to say to her. "Because it pleased me to marry him," the princess used to answer. "How can you be so happy with him?" said the mother. "I love him," said the princess; and the poor Rání used to wonder at this more and more.

Well, one day there was another nautch, and Prince Monkey went to it; but he left his skin under his wife's pillow. As soon as he had gone, she called the little Rání, and said, "See, you think my husband is a monkey; he is no monkey, but a very handsome man. There is no one like him, he is so beautiful." The Rání did not believe her. Then the princess took the skin from under her pillow. "See," she said, "when your son puts this on, then he is a monkey; when he takes it off he is a beautiful man. And now, I think I will burn this skin, and then he must always be a man. What do you say?" "Are you sure it won't hurt him if you burn his skin?" said his mother. "Perhaps he may die if it is burnt." "Oh, no, he won't die," said the princess. "Shall I burn it?" "Burn it," said the little Rání. Then the princess threw the skin on the fire and burnt it quite up.

Prince Monkey was sitting looking on at the nautch when suddenly his heart told him his wife had burnt his skin. He jumped up directly and went home, and when he found

E

his heart had told him true, he was so angry with his wife, that he would say nothing to her but "Why did you burn my skin?" and he was in such a rage that he went straight to bed and went to sleep.

In the morning, while he slept, the princess went to the little Ráni, and said, "Come and see your beautiful son." "I am ashamed to do so," said the Ráni. "Ashamed to look at your own son? What nonsense! Come directly," said Princess Jahúran. Then the little Ráni went with her, and when she saw her beautiful son she was indeed glad, and the prince opened his eyes and saw her, and then he kissed her, and they were very happy.

The news spread through the compound, and Jabhú Rájá and his sons and everybody came at once to see if it were true. When they saw the beautiful young prince, with his hair all gold, they could not stand, but fell down. Prince Monkey lifted his father and loved him, and put his arms round him, and said, "I am your son, your own son; you must not fall down before me." "Why did you wear that monkey-skin?" asked his father. "Because," he said, "my mother ate the mango stone instead of eating the mango, and so I was born with this skin, and God ordered me to wear it till I had found a wife." His brothers said, "Who could have guessed there was such a beautiful man inside that monkey-skin? God's decrees are good! And they left off hating their brother, Prince Monkey.

There were great rejoicings and feasts now, and all were very happy. The six elder brothers lived always with their father and Prince Monkey, but none of them ever married.

Told by Dunkní.

XI.

BRAVE HÍRÁLÁLBÁSÁ.

NCE there was a Rájá called Mánikbásá Rájá, or the Ruby King, who had seven wives and seven children. One day he told his wives he would go out hunting, and he rode on and on, a long, long way from his palace. A Rakshas was sitting by the wayside, who, seeing the Rájá coming, quickly turned herself into a beautiful Rání, and sat there crying. The Rájá asked her, "Why do you cry?" And the Rakshas answered, "My husband has gone away. He has been away many days, and I think he will never come back again. If some Rájá will take me to his house and marry me, I shall be very glad." So the Rájá said, "Will you come with me?" And the Rakshas answered, "Very well, I will come." And then the Rájá took the pretended Rání home with him and married her. He gave her a room to live in. Every night at twelve o'clock the Rakshas got up and devoured an elephant, or a horse, or some other animal. The Rájá said, "What can become of my elephants and horses? Every day either an elephant or a horse disappears. Who can take them away?" The Rakshas-Rání said to him, "Your seven Ránís are Rakshases, and every night at twelve o'clock they devour a horse, or an elephant, or some other creature."

So the Rájá believed her, and had a great hole dug just outside his kingdom, into which he put the seven Ránís with their children, and then he sent a sepoy to them and bade him take out all the Ránís' eyes, and bring them to him. This

the sepoy did. After a time the poor Ránís grew so hungry
that six of them ate their children, but the seventh Rání, who
was the youngest of them all, declared she would never eat
her child though she might die of hunger, "for," she said, "I
love him a great deal too much." God was very pleased with
the seventh Rání for this, and so every day he sent her a little
food, which she divided with the other Ránís. And every
day her little boy grew bigger, and bigger, and bigger, until
he had become a strong lad, when, as he thought it was very
dark in the hole, he climbed out of it and looked all about.
Then he came back to his mothers (for he called all the
seven Ránís " Mother" now), who told him he was not to
clamber up out of the hole any more, for if he did, some
one might kill him. " Still, if you will go," they added,
" do not go to your father's kingdom, but stay near this
place." The boy said, " Very well," and every day he climbed
out of the hole and only went where his seven mothers told
him he might go, and he used to beg the people about to
give him a little rice, and flour and bread, which they did.

One day he said to his mothers, " If you let me go now to
my father's kingdom, I will go." " Well, you may go," they
said ; " but come back again soon." This he promised to do,
and he went to his father's kingdom. For some time he stood
daily at the door of his father's palace and then returned to
the hole. One day the Rakshas-Rání was standing in the
verandah, and she thought, "I am sure that is the Rájá's
son." The servants every day asked the boy, " Why do you
always stand at the door of the palace?" " I want service
with the Rájá," he would reply. " If the Rájá has any place
he can give me, I will take it."

The Rakshas-Rání said to the Rájá, " The boy standing
out there wants service. May I take him into mine?"
The Rájá answered, " Very well, send for him." So all the
servants ran and fetched the boy. The Rakshas-Rání asked

him, "Are you willing to do anything I tell you?" The boy said, "Yes." "Then you shall be my servant," she said, and first she told him he must go to the Rakshas country to fetch some rose-water for her. "I will give you a letter," she said, "so that no harm may happen to you." The lad answered, "Very well, only you must give me three shields full of money." She gave him the three shields full of money, and he took them and went home to his mothers. Then he got two servants for them, one to take care of them, and one to go to the bazar. His mothers gave him food for the journey, and he left them the remainder of his money, telling them to take great care of it. He then returned to the Rakshas-Rání for his letter. She told the Rájá she was feeling ill, and would not be quite well until she got some rose-water from the Rakshas country. The Rájá said, "Then you had better send this boy for it." So she gave him a letter, in which she had written, "When this boy arrives among you, kill him and eat him instantly," and he set out at once.

He went on and on till he came to a great river in which lived a huge water-snake. When the water-snake saw him it began to weep very much, and cried out to the boy, "If you go to the Rakshas country you will be eaten up." The lad whose name was Hírálálbásá, said, "I cannot help it; I am the Rání's servant, so I must do what she tells me." "Well," said the water-snake, "get on my back, and I will take you across this river." So he got on the water-snake's back, and it took him over the river. Then Hírálálbásá went on and on until he came to a house in which a Rakshas lived. A Rání lived there too that the Rakshas had carried off from her father and mother when she was a little girl. She was playing in her father the Sondarbásá Rájá's garden, which was full of delicious fruits, which the Rakshas came to eat, and when he saw Sonahrí Rání he seized her in his mouth and ran off with her. Only she was so beautiful he could never find it in his heart to eat her, but brought her up as his own child. Her name was Sonahrí Ráni, that is, the Golden Rání, because her teeth and her hair were made of gold. Now the Rakshas who had carried her off, and whom she called Papa, had a great thick stick, and when he laid this stick at her feet she could not stir, but when he laid it at her head, she could move again.

When the Rájá's son came up, Sonahrí Ráni was lying on her bed with the thick stick at her feet, and as soon as she saw the Rájá's son she began to cry very much. "Oh, why have you come here? You will surely be killed," she said. The Rájá's son answered, "I cannot help that. I am the Ráni's servant, so I must do what she tells me." "Of course," said Sonahrí Ráni; "but put this stick at my head, and then I shall be able to move." The Rájá's son laid the stick at her head, and she got up and gave him some food, and then asked him if he had a letter. "Yes," he answered. "Let me see it," said the Sonahrí Ráni. So he gave her the letter, and when she had read it she cried, "Oh, this is a very wicked letter. It will bring you no good; for if the Rakshases see it, they will kill you." "Indeed," said Hírálálbásá. And the Sonahrí Ráni tore up the letter and wrote another in which she said, "Make much of this boy. Send him home quickly, and give him a jug of rose-water to bring back with him, and see that he gets no hurt." Then the Rájá's son set out again for the Rakshas-Rání's mother's house. He had not gone very far when he met a very big Rakshas, and he cried out to him, "Uncle." "Who is this boy," said the Rakshas, "who calls me uncle?" And he was just going to kill him when Hírálálbásá showed his letter, and the Rakshas let him pass on. He went a little further until he met another Rakshas, bigger than the first, and the Rakshas screamed at him and was just going to fall on him and kill him, but the Rájá's son showed the letter, and the Rakshas let

him pass unhurt. When Hírálálbásá came to the Rakshas-Rání's mother he showed her the letter, and she gave
him the rose-water at once and sent him off. All the Rakshases were very good to him, and some carried him part of
the way home. When he came to Sonahrí Rání's house she
was lying on her bed with the stick at her feet, and as soon
as she saw Hírálálbásá she laughed and said, " Oh, you have
come back again? Put this stick at my head." ." Yes," said
the Rájá's son, " I've come back again, but I was dreadfully
frightened very often." Then he put the stick at her head,
and she gave him some food to eat. After he had eaten it
he went on again, and when he came to the river the water-
snake carried him across to the other side, and he travelled
to his father's kingdom. There he went to the Rakshas-
Rání and gave her the rose-water. She was very angry at
seeing him, and said, " I'm sure my father and my mother,
my brothers and my sisters, don't love me one bit."

And she said to Hírálálbásá, " You must go to-morrow to
the Rakshas kingdom to fetch me flowers." " I will go,"
said Hírálál, " but this time I must have four shields full of
rupees." The Rakshas-Rání gave him the four shields full
of rupees ; and the Rájá's son went to his mother's hole and
bought a quantity of food for them, enough to last them all
the time he should be away, and he hired two servants for
them, and said good-bye to his seven mothers and returned
to Mánikbásá's palace for his letter. This the Rakshas-Rání
gave him, and in it she wrote, " Kill him and eat him at once.
If you do not, and you send him back to me, I will never
see your faces again." Hírálál took his letters and went on
his way. When he reached the river the water-snake took
him across to the other side, and he walked on till he came,
to Sonahrí Rání's house. She was lying on the bed with
the stick at her feet. " Oh, why have you come here again?"
she said. " How can I help coming?" said the Rájá's son.

"I must do what my mistress bids me." "So you must," said the Sonahrí Rání; "but put this stick at my head." This he did, and she got up and gave him food, and asked him to let her see his letter, and when she had read it she cried, "This is a very wicked letter. If you take it with you, you will surely die." Then she tore up the letter and burnt it, and wrote another in which she said, "You must all be very good to this boy. Show him all the gardens and see that he is not hurt in any way." She gave it to Hírálál, and he begged her to ask the Rakshas, her father, where he kept his soul. Sonahrí Rání promised she would. She then turned Hírálál into a little fly, and put him into a tiny box, and put the box under her pillow. When the Rakshas came home he began sniffing about and said, "Surely there is a man here," "Oh, no," said Sonahrí Rání; "no one is here but me." The Rakshas was satisfied. When Sonahrí Rání and her father were in bed she asked, "Papa, where is your soul?" "Why do you want to know?" said the Rakshas. "I will tell you another day."

The next day at nine in the morning the Rakshas went away, andSonahrí Rání took Hírálál and restored him to his human shape, and gave him some food. and he travelled on till he reached the Rakshas-Rání's mother, whom he called Grannie. She welcomed him very kindly and showed him the garden, which was very large. The Rájá's son noticed a number of jugs and water-jars. So he said, "Grannie, what is there in all these jars and jugs?" She answered, showing them to him one by one, "In this is such and such a thing," and so on, telling him the contents of each, till she came to the water-jar in which were his mothers' eyes. "In this jar," said the Rakshas, "are your seven mothers' eyes." "Oh, grannie dear!" said Hírálál, "give me my mothers' eyes." "Very well, dear boy," said the old Rakshas, "you shall have them." She gave him, too,

some ointment, and told him to rub the eyes with it when
he put them into his mothers' heads, and that then they
would see quite well; and he took the eyes and tied them
up in a corner of his cloth. His grannie gave him the
flowers, and he went back to Sonahrí Rání. She was lying
on her bed with the stick at her feet, and when she saw
him she laughed and said, "Oh, so you have come back
again?" "Yes, I have," said Hírálál; "and I have got
the flowers, and my seven mothers' eyes too." "Have you
indeed?" said Sonahrí Rání. "Put this stick at my head."
He did so, and she got up and gave him some food, and he
told her to ask her father the Rakshas where his soul was.
She promised she would, and she changed him into a little
fly, and shut him up in a tiny box, and put the tiny box
under her pillow. By and by home came the Rakshas, and
began to sniff about crying, "A man is here!" "Oh, no,"
said Sonahrí Rání; and she gave him some dinner, and when
they were in bed she asked him, "Papa, where is your soul?"
"I'll tell you another day," said the Rakshas. The next day,
when he had gone out to find food, Sonahrí Rání took the
little fly, Hírálál, and restored him to his human shape, and
gave him some food and sent him on his way. When he
reached the river, the water-snake took him over to the other
side, and he journeyed on till he came to his father's kingdom. First he went to his mothers' hole and gave them their
fourteen eyes, and he put them into their heads with the
ointment which the Rakshas-grannie had given him. Then
he went to Mánikbásá Rájá's palace, and when the Rakshas-
Rání saw him she was furious. "I am sure my father and
my mother, my sisters and my brothers, do not love me one
bit. I will never see their faces again. But I'll send him to
them once more."

This is what she thought, but she took the flowers and
said, "You must go a third time to the Rakshas country."

"I will," said the boy : " only I'll not go till the fourth day from to-day, for I am very tired. And you must give me four shields full of rupees." "Good," said the Rakshas-Ráni. "This time you must get me a sárí."[1] And she gave him the four shields full of money. Then he went to his mothers, and bought them a house and got food for them, and stayed with them four days.

At the end of the four days he went to the Rakshas-Ráni, who gave him a letter in which she had written, " If you do not kill and eat this boy as soon as he arrives, I will never see your faces again." The Rájá's son took the letter and set out on his journey.

When he came to the river, the water-snake took him across ; and when he arrived at Sonahrí Ráni's house, there she was lying on her bed with the thick stick at her feet. She said, "Oh, you have come here again, have you ?" "Yes," he said, "I have come for the last time." "Put the stick at my head," said she. So he laid the stick at her head. Then she gave him some food, and just before the Rakshas came home, he bade her ask him where he kept his soul. When she saw him coming, Sonahrí Ráni turned Hírálálbásá into a little fly, put him in a tiny box, and put the box under her pillow. As soon as she and the Rakshas had gone to bed, she asked him, " Papa, where do you keep your soul?" "Sixteen miles away from this place," said he, "is a tree. Round the tree are tigers, and bears, and scorpions, and snakes ; on the top of the tree is a very great fat snake ; on his head is a little cage ; in the cage is a bird ; and my soul is in that bird." The little fly listened all the time. The next morning, when the Rakshas had gone, Sonahri Ráni took the fly and gave him back his human form, gave him some food, and then asked to see his letter. When she had read it she

[1] A long piece of stuff which Hindu women wind round the body as a petticoat, passing one end over the head, like a veil.

screamed aud said, " Oh ! if you go with this letter you will surely die." So she tore it up into little bits and threw it into the fire. And she wrote another in which she said, " Make a great deal of this boy; see that he gets no hurt ; give him the sárí for me ; show him the garden ; and be very kind to him." She then gave Hírálál the letter, and he journeyed on in safety till he reached his Rakshas-grannie's house.

The Rakshas-grannie was very good to him; showed him the garden, and gave him the sárí ; and he then said his mother, the Rakshas-Ráni, was in great trouble about her soul, and wanted very much to have it. So the Rakshas-grannie gave him a bird in which was the Rakshas-Ráni's soul, charging him to take the greatest care of it. Then he said, " My mother, the Rakshas-Ráni, also wants a stone such that, if you lay it on the ground, or if you put it in your clothes, it will become gold, and also your long heavy gold necklace that hangs down to the waist." Both these things the Rakshas-grannie gave to Hírálál. Then he returned to Sonahrí Ráni's house, where he found her lying on her bed with the thick stick at her feet. "Oh, there you are," said Sonahrí Ráni, laughing. " Yes," he said, " I have come." And he put the stick at her head, and she got up and gave him some food.

He told her he was going to fetch her Rakshas-father's soul, but that he did not quite know how to pass through the tigers and bears, and scorpions and snakes, that guarded it. So she gave him a feather, and said, " As long as you hold this feather straight, you can come to no harm, for you will be invisible. You will see everything, but nothing will see you."

He carried the feather straight as she had bidden him and reached the tree in safety. Then he climbed up it, took the little cage, and came down again Though the Rakshas was far off, he knew at once something had happened to his bird. Hírálál pulled off the bird's right leg, and the Rakshas' right leg fell off, but on he hopped on one leg. Then the

Rájá's son pulled off the bird's left leg, and off fell the Rakshas' left leg, but still he went on towards his house on his hands. Then Hírálál pulled off the bird's wings, and the Rakshas' two arms fell off. And then, just as the Rakshas reached the door of his house, Hírálál wrung the bird's neck, and the Rakshas fell dead. Sonahrí Rání was greatly frightened when she heard such a heavy thing fall thump on the ground so close to the house, but she could not move, for the thick stick lay at her feet. Hírálál ran as fast as he could to Sonahrí Rání. When he arrived at the door of her house he saw the Rakshas lying dead, and he went in and told Sonahrí Rání that her Rakshas-father was killed. "Nonsense," she said. "It is true," said Hírálál; "come and see." So he put the stick at her head. "I am sure you are telling a lie," said Sonahrí Rání. "I should be very glad if he were dead, for I do not like living with him, I am so afraid of him." "Indeed he's dead. Do come and see," said Hírálál. Then they went outside, and when Sonahrí Rání saw her Rakshas-father lying there dead, she was exceedingly happy, and said to Hírálál, "I will go home with you, and be your wife." So they were married, and then they went into Sonahrí Rání's Rakshas-father's house and took all the money and jewels they could find. And Hírálál gave the sárí, the stone, and the necklace to Sonahrí Rání, and he took some flowers for the Rakshas-Rání.

When they came to the river, the water-snake carried them across to the other side, and they travelled on till they came to Mánikbásá Rájá's kingdom. There Hírálál went first of all to his mothers, and when they saw Sonahrí Rání they wondered who the beautiful woman could be that their son had brought home. He said to them, "This is Sonahri Rání, my wife. But for her I should have died." Then he bought a grand house for Sonahrí Rání and his seven mothers to live in, and he got four servants for Sonahrí Rání, two

to cook, and two to wait on her. The seven mothers and
Sonahrí used all to sit on a beautiful, clean quilted cushion,
as big as a carpet, Sonahrí Rání in the middle and the seven
mothers round her, while they sewed, or wrote, and talked.
Hírálál then went to the Rakshas-Rání and said, " I could
not get the sárí you sent me for, so I brought you these
flowers instead." When she saw the flowers she was frantic.
She said, " My father, my mother, my sisters, my brothers,
don't care for me, not one bit ! not one scrap ! I will never
see their faces again—never ! never ! I will send sóme
other messenger to them."

One day the Rájá's son came to Mánikbásá and said,
" Would you like to see a grand sight ? " Mánikbásá Rájá
said, " What sight ? " Hírálál said, " If you would like to see
a really grand sight you must do what I tell you." " Good,"
answered Mánikbásá, " I will do whatever you tell me."
" Well, then," said his son, " you must build a very strong
iron house, and round it you must lay heaps of wood. In that
house you must put your present Rání." So Mánikbásá Rájá
had a very strong iron house built, round which he set walls
of wood. Then he went to his Rakshas-Rání and said,
" Will you go inside that iron house, and see what it is like ? "
" Yes, I will," answered she. The Rájá had had great venetians made for the house, and only one door. As soon as
the Rakshas-Rání had gone in, he locked the door. Then
Hírálál took the little bird, a cockatoo, in which was the
Rakshas-Rání's soul, and showed it to the Rakshas-Rání
from afar off. When she saw it she turned herself into a
huge Rakshas as big as a house. She could not turn in the
iron house because she was so huge. Mánikbásá was dreadfully frightened when he saw his Rání was a horrible Rakshas. Then Hírálál pulled off the bird's legs, and as the
Rakshas was breaking through the iron house to seize
Hírálál, he wrung the cockatoo's neck, and the Rakshas

died instantly. They set fire to the walls of wood, and the body of the wicked Rakshas was burnt to fine ashes.

The Rájá's Wazír turned to the Rájá and said, " What a fool you were to marry this Rakshas, and at her bidding to send your seven wives and your seven sons away into the jungle, taking out your seven wives' eyes, and being altogether so cruel to them ! You are a great, great fool ! " The poor Rájá wept, and then the Wazír, pointing to Hírálál, said, " This is your seventh and youngest Rání's son." The Rájá then embraced Hírálálbásá and asked his forgiveness. And Hírálál told him his story, how he and his mothers had lived a long, long time in the hole ; how six of the Ránís had eaten their children ; how his mother had not had the heart to eat him ; how he had got his seven mothers' eyes from the Rakshas-grannie ; and lastly, how he had married Sonahrí Rání. Then the Rájá ordered seven litters for his seven Ránís, and a beautiful litter with rich cloth for Sonahrí Rání. The Rájá and his Wazír and his attendants, and his son, all went with the litters to Hírálál's house ; and when the Rájá saw Sonahrí Rání he fell flat on his face, he was so struck by her beauty. For she had a fair, fair skin, rosy cheeks, blue eyes, rosy lips, golden eyelashes, and golden eyebrows, and golden hair. When she combed her hair, she used to put the hair she combed out in paper and to lay the paper on the river, and it floated down to where the poor people caught it, and sold it, and got heaps of money for it. Her sárí was of gold, her shoes were of gold, for God loved her dearly. Then the Rájá rose and embraced all his wives and Sonahrí Rání, and the seven Ránís walked into the seven litters; but Sonahrí Rání was carried to hers, for fear she should soil her feet, or get hurt. Then Mánikbásá Rájá gave Hírálál's house to his Wazír, while his seven Ránís and Hírálál and Sonahrí Rání lived with him in his palace. And they lived happily for ever after.

Told by Dunkní at Simla, 26th July and 1st August, 1876.

XII.

THE MAN WHO WENT TO SEEK HIS FATE.

ONCE there was a very poor man who had a wife and twelve children, and not a single rupee. The poor children used to cry with hunger, and the man and his wife did not know what to do. At last he got furious with God and said, " How wicked God is ! He gives me a great many children, but no money." So he set out to find his fate. In the jungle he met a camel with two heavy sacks of gold on its back. This camel belonged to a Rájá, and once it was travelling with other camels and with the Rájá's servants to another country, and carrying the sacks of gold. Every night they encamped and started again early in the morning; one morning the servants forgot to take this camel with them, and the camel forgot the road home, and the sacks were too tightly strapped for it to get rid of them. So it wandered about the jungle with the sacks on its back for twelve years. The camel asked the poor man where he was going. " I am going to seek my fate, to ask it why I am so poor," he answered. The camel said, " Ask it, too, why for twelve years I have had to carry these two sacks of gold. All this time I have not been able to lie down, or to eat, or to drink." " Very well," said the man, and he went on.

Then he came to a river in which he saw an alligator. The alligator took him across, and when he got to the other side it asked him where he was going. The man said,

"I am going to seek my fate, to ask it why I am so poor."
"Then," said the alligator, "ask it also why for twelve years
I have a great burning in my stomach." "I will," said the
man.

Then he went on and on till he came to a tiger, who was
lying on the ground with a great thorn sticking in his foot.
This tiger had gone out one day to hunt for food, and not
looking where he was going, he put his foot on the thorn,
and the thorn ran into his foot. And so God grew very
angry and said, "Because you are such a careless, stupid
fellow, and don't look where you are going, for twelve years
this thorn shall remain in your foot." "Where are you
going?" the tiger asked the man. "I am going to seek my
fate, to ask it why I am so poor. Some one told me that my
fate was far, far away, a twelve years' journey from my own
country, and that it was lying down, and that I must take a
thick stick and beat it with all my might." "Ask it, too,"
said the tiger, "why for twelve years I have had this thorn in
my foot and cannot get it out, though I have tried hard to
do so." "Yes, I will," said the man.

Then he came to the place where every one's fate lives.
The fates are stones, some standing and others lying on the
ground. "This must be mine," he said; "it is lying on the
ground, that's why I am so poor." So he took the thick
stick he had in his hand, and beat it, and beat it, and beat
it, but still it would not stir. As night was approaching he
left off beating it, and God sent a soul into the poor man's
fate, and it became a man, who stood looking at the poor
man and said, "Why have you beaten me so much?"
"Because you were lying down, and I am very poor, and
at home my wife and my children are starving." "Oh, things
will go well with you now," said the fate, and the man was
satisfied. He said to his fate, "While coming here I met a
camel who for twelve years has had to wander about with two

heavy sacks of gold on its back, and it wants to know why it must carry them." "Oh," said the fate, "just take the sacks off its back and then it will be free." "I will," said the poor man. "Then I met an alligator who for twelve years has had a great burning in its stomach." The fate said, "In its stomach is a very large ruby, as big as your hand. If the alligator will only throw up the ruby, it will be quite well." "Next I met a tiger who has had for twelve years a great thorn in his foot which he cannot take out." "Pull it out with your teeth," said the fate; and then God withdrew the soul, and the fate became a stone again which stood up on the ground.

Then the man set out on his journey home, and he came to the tiger. "What did your fate say?" said the tiger. "Give me your foot and I will take out the thorn," said the poor man. The tiger stretched out the foot with the thorn in it, and the man pulled out the thorn with his teeth. It was a very large thorn, as big as the man's hand. The tiger felt grateful to the poor man, and as he was very rich, for he had eaten a great many Rájás and people, and had all their money, he said to the man, "I will give you some gold in return for your kindness." "You have no money," said the man. "I have," said the tiger, and he went into his den, and the poor man followed. "Give me your cloth," said the tiger. The man laid it on the ground. Then the tiger took quantities of gold and jewels and filled the cloth with them. And the poor man took up his cloth, thanked the tiger, and went his way. Then he met the alligator who took him across the river. The alligator said, "Did you ask your fate why there is such burning in my stomach?" "I did," said the man. "It is because you have a very large ruby in your stomach. If you will only throw it up, you will be quite well." Then the alligator threw the ruby up out of its mouth, and that very instant the burning in its stomach

F

ceased. "Ah," said the alligator, looking at the ruby, "I swallowed that one day when I was drinking." And he gave the ruby to the man, saying, "In return for your kindness I will give you this ruby. It is a very precious stone." (In old days every Rájá possessed such a ruby; now very few Rájás, if any, have one.) The poor man thanked the alligator, put the ruby into his cloth, and went on his way till he came to the camel, who said, "Did you ask your fate why I have to carry these two sacks of gold?" "I did," said the man, and he took the sacks off the camel's back. How happy and grateful the camel felt! "How kind of you," he said to the man, "to take the sacks off. Now I can eat, now I can drink, and now I can lie down. Because you have been so kind to me, I give you the two sacks of gold, and I will carry them and your bundle home to your house for you, and then I will come back and live here in the jungle." Then the poor man put the two sacks of gold and his bundle on the camel, who carried them to his house. When he got there, he took the sacks and his bundle off the camel, who thanked him again for his kindness and went back to his jungle, feeling very glad at having got rid of his heavy burthen.

When the poor man's wife and children saw the gold and jewels and the ruby, they cried, "Where did you get these?" And the man told them his whole story. And he bought food for his wife and children, and gave them a beautiful house, and got them clothes, for now he was very rich.

Another poor man who was not quite, but nearly, as poor as this man had been, asked him where he had got his riches. "I got them out of a river," answered the man. "I drew the water with a bucket, and in every bucketful there was gold." The other man started off to the river and began drawing up water in a bucket. "Stop, stop!" cried an alligator, who was the king of the fishes; "you are taking all the water out of the river and my fishes will die." "I want money," said the man, " and I can find none, so I am taking the water out of the river in order to get some." "You shall have some in a minute," said the alligator, "only do stop drawing the water." Then a great wave of water dashed on to the land and dashed back into the river, leaving behind it a great heap of gold, which the man picked up joyfully. The next day he came again, and night and day he drew water out of the river. At last the alligator got very angry, and said, "My fishes will all die for want of water. Once I gave the man a heap of gold, and yet he wants more. I won't give him any," and the alligator thrust up his head out of the river, and swallowed the man whole. For four days and four nights the man lived in the alligator's stomach. At the end of the fourth night the king of the fishes said to him, "I will let you get out of my stomach on condition that you tell no man what has happened to you. If you do, you will die instantly." The man jumped out of the alligator's mouth and walked towards his house. On his way he met some men and told them what had happened to him, and as soon as he got home he told his wife and children, and the moment he had done so he became mad and dumb and blood came out of his mouth, and he fell down dead.

Told by Dunkní.

XIII.

THE UPRIGHT KING.

HERE was a great Mahárájá whose name was Harchand Rájá, and he had an only son called Mánikchand. He was very rich and had a great deal of money, and he also had a very large garden full of lovely flowers and fruits which he prized greatly. Every morning before he bathed he used to give some poor fakír two pounds and a half of gold. Now Harchand Mahárájá used to pray a great deal to God, and God was very fond of him, so he said one day, " To see if Harchand Mahárájá really loves me, I will make him very poor for twelve years." And at night God came down in the shape of a great boar, and ate up everything that was in Harchand Mahárájá's garden. The boar then ran away into the jungle. Next morning the gardener got up and looked out into the garden, and what was his astonishment when he saw it was all spoilt. Nothing was left in it; it was not a garden any more. He went quickly to the Mahárájá and said, " Oh, master ! oh, Mahárájá ! your garden is quite spoilt. Last night a boar came and ate up everything in it." " Nonsense," said the Mahárájá, who would not believe him. " It is quite true," said the gardener; " you can come and see for yourself." So the Rájá got up at once and put on his clothes, and went into the garden, and found it all empty. He went back to the house very melancholy. Then as usual he gave a fakír his two pounds and a half of gold. After breakfast he went out hunting. The boar which had run away into the wood changed himself into a very old fakír, who shook from old age. As Harchand Mahárájá passed, the old fakír held out his hand, saying, "Please give me a few pice, I am so poor and hungry." The Mahárájá said, "Come to my palace and I will give you two pounds and a half of gold." "Oh, no," said the fakír, "surely you would never give me so much as that." "Yes, I will," said the Mahárájá. "Every morning before I bathe I give a fakír two pounds and a half of gold." "Nonsense," said the fakír, "you don't give away your money in that way." "Really, I do," said the Mahárájá, "and I promise to give you two pounds and a half of gold." So the fakír followed Harchand Mahárájá home, and when they reached the palace, the Mahárájá told his treasurer to give the old fakír two pounds and a half of gold. The treasurer went into the treasury, but all the Mahárájá's gold and silver and jewels had become charcoal! The treasurer came out again to the Mahárájá saying, "Oh, Mahárájá, all your gold and silver and jewels are turned into charcoal!" "Oh, nonsense," said the Mahárájá. "Come and see, Mahárájá," said the treasurer, who was in a great fright. The Mahárájá went into his treasury, and was quite sad at the sight of the charcoal. "Alas!" he said, "God has made me very poor, but still I must give this fakír his money." So he went to the fakír and said, "All my gold and silver and jewels are turned into charcoal; but I will sell my wife, and my boy, and myself, and then I will give you the money I promised you." And he went and fetched his wife and son, and left his palace, his houses, servants, and possessions.

He then went to a merchant, who bought from him his Mahárání, who was called Hírálí, that is, the diamond lady, for she was very beautiful, and her face shone like a diamond. Her hands were very small, and so were her feet. The mer-

chant gave the Mahárájá a pound of gold for the Mahárání.
Next, Harchand Mahárájá went to a cowherd and sold him his
son Mánikchand. The cowherd gave him for the boy half a
pound of gold. Then he went to a dom, that is, a man of a
very low caste, who kept a tank into which it was his business
to throw the bodies of those who died. If it was a dead man or
woman, the dom took one rupee, if it was a dead child he was
only paid eight annas. To this dom Harchand sold himself for
a pound of gold, and he gave the two pounds and a half of gold
to the fakír, who then went home. The dom said, "Will,
you stay by the tank for a few days while I go home and do
my other work, which is weaving baskets? If any one brings
you a dead body you must throw it into the water. If it
is the body of a man or woman, take one rupee in payment ;
if it is a dead child, take eight annas ; and if the bearers have
got no money, take a bit of cloth. Don't forget." And the
dom went away, leaving Harchand sitting by the tank.

Well, Harchand Mahárájá sat for some days by the tank,
and when any one brought him dead bodies he threw them
into it. For a dead man or woman he took one rupee, for
a dead child eight annas, and if the bearers had no money
to give him, he took some cloth. Some time had passed, and
Mánikchand, the Mahárájá's son, died ; so Hírálí Rání went
to the cowherd to ask him for her dead child. The cowherd
gave him to her, and she took him to the tank. Harchand
Mahárájá was sitting by the tank, and when Hírálí Mahárání
saw him she said, "I know that man is my husband, so he
will not take any money for throwing his child into the water."
So she went up to him and said, ' Will you throw this child
into the tank for me?" "Yes, I will," said Harchand Mahárájá ; only first give me eight annas." "You surely wont
take any money for throwing your own son into the tank ? "
said the Mahárání. "You must pay me," said Harchand
Mahárájá, "for I must obey the dom's orders. If you have

no money, give me a piece of cloth." So the Mahárání tore off a great piece of her sárí and gave it him, and the Mahárájá took his son and threw him into the tank. As he threw him in he cried out to the king of the fishes, who was an alligator, " Take great care of this body." The king of fishes said, "I will." Then the Mahárání went back to the merchant.

And the Mahárájá caught a fish, and cooked it, and laid it by the tank, saying, "I will go and bathe and then I will eat it." So he took off his clothes and went into the tank to bathe, and when he had bathed he put on fresh clothes, and as he took hold of his fish to eat it, it slipped back alive into the water, although it had been dead and cooked. The Mahárájá sat down by the tank again, very sad. He said, " For twelve years I have found it hard to get anything to eat ; how long will God keep me without food ? " God was very pleased with Harchand for being so patient, for he had never complained.

Some days later God came down to earth in the shape of a man, and with him he took an angel to be his Wazir. The Wazir said to God, "Come this way and let us see who it is sitting by the tank." "No," said God, " I am too tired, I can go no further." " Do come," said the Wazir ; " I want so much to go." God said, " Well, let us go." Then they walked on till they came to the place where Harchand Mahárájá was sitting, and God said to him, " Would you like to have your wife, and your son, and your kingdom back again." "Yes, I should," said the Mahárájá ; " but how can I get them ? " " Tell me truly," said God, " would you like to have your kingdom back again ? " " Indeed I should," said the Mahárájá. Then Mánikchand's body, which had never sunk to the bottom of the tank like the other bodies, but had always floated on the water, rose up out of the water, and Mánikchand was alive once more.

The father and son embraced each other. "Now," said God, "let us go to the dom." Harchand Mahárájá agreed, and they went to the dom and asked him how much he would take for Harchand Mahárájá. The dom said, " I gave one pound of gold for him, and I will take two pounds." So they paid down the two pounds of gold. Then they went to the merchant and said to him, " How much will you take for Hírálí Rání?" The merchant said, "I gave a pound of gold for her ; I will take four pounds." So they paid down the four pounds of gold, took Hírálí Rání, and went to the cowherd. " How much will you take for Mánikchand?" said they to him. "I gave half a pound of gold for him," answered the cowherd; " I will take one pound." So they paid down the pound of gold, and Harchand Mahárájá went home to his palace, taking with him Hírálí Rání and Mánik-chand, after thanking the strange man for his goodness to them. When they reached the palace, the garden was in splendid beauty ; the charcoal was turned back into gold, and silver, and jewels ; the servants were in waiting as usual, and they went into the palace and lived happily for evermore.

Told by Dunkní.

XIV

LOVING LAILÍ.

ONCE there was a king called King Dantál, who had a great many rupees and soldiers and horses. He had also an only son called Prince Majnún, who was a handsome boy with white teeth, red lips, blue eyes, red cheeks, red hair, and a white skin. This boy was very fond of playing with the Wazír's son, Husain Mahámat, in King Dantál's garden, which was very large and full of delicious fruits, and flowers, and trees. They used to take their little knives there and cut the fruits and eat them. King Dantál had a teacher for them to teach them to read and write.

One day, when they were grown two fine young men, Prince Majnún said to his father, " Husain Mahámat and I should like to go and hunt," His father said they might go, so they got ready their horses and all else they wanted for their hunting, and went to the Phaláná country, hunting all the way, but they only found jackals and birds.

The Rájá of the Phaláná country was called Munsúk Rájá, and he had a daughter named Lailí, who was very beautiful ; she had brown eyes and black hair.

One night, some time before Prince Majnún came to her father's kingdom, as she slept, God sent to her an angel in the form of a man who told her that she should marry Prince Majnún and no one else, and that this was God's command to her. When Lailí woke she told her father of the angel's visit to her as she slept ; but her father paid no attention to

her story.   From that time she began repeating, " Majnún,
Majnún; I want Majnún," and would say nothing else.   Even
as she sat and ate her food she kept saying, "Majnún, Majnún;
I want Majnún."   Her father used to get quite vexed with
her.   "Who is this Majnún? who ever heard of this Majnún?" he would say.   "He is the man I am to marry,"
said Lailí.   "God has ordered me to marry no one but
Majnún."   And she was half mad.   Meanwhile, Majnún and
Husain Mahámat came to hunt in the Phálaná country; and
as they were riding about, Lailí came out on her horse to
eat the air, and rode behind them.   All the time she kept
saying, "Majnún, Majnún; I want Majnún."   The prince
heard her, and turned round.   "Who is calling me?" he
asked.   At this Lailí looked at him, and the moment she
saw him she fell deeply in love with him, and she said to
herself, "I am sure that is the Prince Majnún that God says
I am to marry."   And she went home to her father and said,
"Father, I wish to marry the prince who has come to your
kingdom; for I know he is the Prince Majnún I am to marry."
"Very well, you shall have him for your husband," said Múnsúk
Rájá.   "We will ask him to-morrow."   Lailí consented to wait,
although she was very impatient.   As it happened, the prince
left the Phálaná kingdom that night, and when Lailí heard he
was gone, she went quite mad.   She would not listen to a word
her father, or her mother, or her servants said to her, but
went off into the jungle, and wandered from jungle to jungle,
till she got farther and farther away from her own country.
All the time she kept saying, "Majnún, Majnún; I want
Majnún; and so she wandered about for twelve years.

At the end of the twelve years she met a fakír—he was
really an angel, but she did not know this—who asked her,
"Why do you always say, 'Majnún, Majnún; I want Majnún'?" She answered, "I am the daughter of the king of
the Phálaná country, and I want to find Prince Majnún; tell

me where his kingdom is." "I think you will never get there," said the fakír, " for it is very far from hence, and you have to cross many rivers to reach it." But Lailí said she did not care ; she must see Prince Majnún. "Well," said the fakír, "when you come to the Bhágírathí river you will see a big fish, a Rohú ; and you must get him to carry you to Prince Majnún's country, or you will never reach it."

She went on and on, and at last she came to the Bhágírathí river. There there was a great big fish called the Rohú fish. It was yawning just as she got up to it, and she instantly jumped down its throat into its stomach. All the time she kept saying, " Majnún, Majnún." At this the Rohú fish was greatly alarmed and swam down the river as fast as he could. By degrees he got tired and went slower, and a crow came and perched on his back, and said, " Caw, caw." " Oh, Mr. Crow," said the poor fish, " do see what is in my stomach that makes such a noise." " Very well," said the crow, " open your mouth wide, and I'll fly down and see." So the Rohú opened his jaws and the crow flew down, but he came up again very quickly. " You have a Rakshas in your stomach," said the crow, and he flew away. This news did not comfort the poor Rohú, and he swam on and on till he came to Prince Majnún's country. There he stopped. And a jackal came down to the river to drink. " Oh, jackal," said the Rohú, " do tell me what I have inside me." " How can I tell ? " said the jackal. " I cannot see unless I go inside you." So the Rohú opened his mouth wide, and the jackal jumped down his throat; but he came up very quickly, looking much frightened and saying, " You have a Rakshas in your stomach, and if I don't run away quickly, I am afraid it will eat me." So off he ran. After the jackal came an enormous snake. " Oh," says the fish, " do tell me what I have in my stomach, for it rattles about so, and keeps saying, " Majnún, Majnún; I want Majnún." The snake said,

" Open your mouth wide, and I'll go down and see what it is." The snake went down : when he returned he said, " You have a Rakshas in your stomach ; but if you will let me cut you open, it will come out of you." " If you do that, I shall die," said the Rohú. " Oh, no," said the snake, " you will not, for I will give you a medicine that will make you quite well again." So the fish agreed, and the snake got a knife and cut him open, and out jumped Lailí.

She was now very old. Twelve years she had wandered about the jungle, and for twelve years she had lived inside her Rohú ; and she was no longer beautiful, and had lost her teeth. The snake took her on his back and carried her into the country, and there he put her down, and she wandered on and on till she got to Majnún's court-house, where King Majnún was sitting. There some men heard her crying, " Majnún, Majnún; I want Majnún," and they asked her what she wanted. " I want King Majnún," she said. So they went in and said to Prince Majnún, " An old woman outside says she wants you." " I cannot leave this place," said he ; "send her in here." They brought her in and the prince asked her what she wanted. " I want to marry you," she answered. " Twenty-four years ago you came to my father the Phaláná Rájá's country, and I wanted to marry you then; but you went away without marrying me. Then I went mad, and I have wandered about all these years looking for you." Prince Majnún said, " Very good." " Pray to God," said Lailí, " to make us both young again, and then we shall be married." " So the prince prayed to God, and God said to him, " Touch Lailí's clothes and they will catch fire, and when they are on fire, she and you will become young again." When he touched Lailí's clothes they caught fire, and she and he became young again. And there were great feasts, and they were married, and travelled to the Phaláná country to see her father and mother.

Now Laili's father and mother had wept so much for their daughter that they had become quite blind, and her father kept always repeating, " Laili, Laili, Laili." When Laili saw their blindness, she prayed to God to restore their sight to them, which he did. As soon as the father and mother saw Laili, they hugged her and kissed her, and then they had the wedding all over again amid great rejoicings. Prince Majnún and Laili stayed with Múnsúk Rájá and his wife for three years, and then they returned to King Dantál, and lived happily for some time with him.

They used to go out hunting, and they often went from country to country to eat the air and amuse themselves.

One day Prince Majnún said to Laili, " Let us go through this jungle." " No, no," said Laili ; " if we go through this jungle, some harm will happen to me." But Prince Majnún laughed, and went into the jungle. And as they were going through it, God thought, " I should like to know how much Prince Majnún loves his wife. Would he be very sorry if she died ? And would he marry another wife ? I will see." So he sent one of his angels in the form of a fakír into the jungle ; and the angel went up to Laili, and threw some powder in her face, and instantly she fell to the ground a heap of ashes.

Prince Majnún was in great sorrow and grief when he saw his dear Laili turn into a little heap of ashes ; and he went straight home to his father, and for a long, long time he would not be comforted. After a great many years he grew more cheerful and happy, and began to go again into his father's beautiful garden with Husain Mahámat. King Dantál wished his son to marry again. " I will only have Laili for my wife ; I will not marry any other woman," said Prince Majnún. " How can you marry Laili ? Laili is dead. She will never come back to you," said the father. " Then I'll not have any wife at all," said Prince Majnún.

Meanwhile Lailí was living in the jungle where her husband had left her a little heap of ashes. As soon as Majnún had gone, the fakír had taken her ashes and made them quite clean, and then he had mixed clay and water with the ashes, and made the figure of a woman with them, and so Lailí regained her human form, and God sent life into it. But Lailí had become once more a hideous old woman, with a long, long nose, and teeth like tusks ; just such an old woman, excepting her teeth, as she had been when she came out of the Rohú fish ; and she lived in the jungle, and neither ate nor drank, and she kept on saying, "Majnún, Majnún ; I want Majnún."

At last the angel who had come as a fakír and thrown the powder at her, said to God, "Of what use is it that this woman should sit in the jungle crying, crying for ever, ' Majnún, Majnún ; I want Majnún,' and eating and drinking nothing ? Let me take her to Prince Majnún." "Well," said God, "you may do so ; but tell her that she must not speak to Majnún if he is afraid of her when he sees her ; and that if he is afraid when he sees her, she will become a little white dog the next day. Then she must go to the palace, and she will only regain her human shape when Prince Majnún loves her, feeds her with his own food, and lets her sleep in his bed." So the angel came to Lailí again as a fakír and carried her to King Dantál's garden. "Now," he said, "it is God's command that you stay here till Prince Majnún comes to walk in the garden, and then you may show yourself to him. But you must not speak to him, if he is afraid of you ; and should he be afraid of you, you will the next day become a little white dog." He then told her what she must do as a little dog to regain her human form.

Lailí stayed in the garden, hidden in the tall grass, till Prince Majnún and Husain Mahámat came to walk in the garden. King Dantál was now a very old man, and Husain

Mahámat, though he was really only as old as Prince Majnún, looked a great deal older than the prince, who had been made quite young again when he married Lailí.

As Prince Majnún and the Wazír's son walked in the garden, they gathered the fruit as they had done as little children, only they bit the fruit with their teeth; they did not cut it. While Majnún was busy eating a fruit in this way, and was talking to Husain Mahámat, he turned towards him and saw Lailí walking behind the Wazír's son. "Oh, look, look!" he cried, "see what is following you; it is a Rakshas or a demon, and I am sure it is going to eat us." Lailí looked at him beseechingly with all her eyes, and trembled with age and eagerness; but this only frightened Majnún the more. "It is a Rakshas, a Rakshas!" he cried, and he ran quickly to the palace with the Wazír's son; and as they ran away, Lailí disappeared into the jungle. They ran to King Dantál, and Majnún told him there was a Rakshas or a demon in the garden that had come to eat them. "What nonsense," said his father. "Fancy two grown men being so frightened by an old ayah or a fakír! And if it had been a Rakshas, it would not have eaten you." Indeed King Dantál did not believe Majnún had seen anything at all, till Husain Mahámat said the prince was speaking the exact truth. They had the garden searched for the terrible old woman, but found nothing, and King Dantál told his son he was very silly to be so much frightened. However, Prince Majnún would not walk in the garden any more.

The next day Lailí turned into a pretty little dog; and in this shape she came into the palace, where Prince Majnún soon became very fond of her. She followed him everywhere, went with him when he was out hunting, and helped him to catch his game, and Prince Majnún fed her with milk, or bread, or anything else he was eating, and at night the little dog slept in his bed.

But one night the little dog disappeared, and in its stead there lay the little old woman who had frightened him so much in the garden; and now Prince Majnún was quite sure she was a Rakshas, or a demon, or some such horrible thing come to eat him; and in his terror he cried out, " What do you want? Oh, do not eat me; do not eat me!" Poor Lailí answered, " Don't you know me? I am your wife Lailí, and I want to marry you. Don't you remember how you would go through that jungle, though I begged and begged you not to go, for I told you that harm would happen to me, and then a fakír came and threw powder in my face, and I became a heap of ashes. But God gave me my life again, and brought me here, after I had stayed a long, long while in the jungle crying for you, and now I am obliged to be a little dog; but if you will marry. me, I shall not be a little dog any more." Majnún, however, said " How can I marry an old woman like you? how can you be Lailí? I am sure you are a Rakshas or a demon come to eat me," and he was in great terror.

In the morning the old woman had turned into the little dog, and the prince went to his father and told him all that had happened. " An old woman! an old woman! always an old woman!" said his father. "You do nothing but think of old women. How can a strong man like you be so easily frightened?" However, when he saw that his son was really in great terror, and that he really believed the old woman would come back at night, he advised him to say to her, " I will marry you if you can make yourself a young girl again. How can I marry such an old woman as you are?"

That night as he lay trembling in bed the little old woman lay there in place of the dog, crying, " Majnún, Majnún, I want to marry you. I have loved you all these long, long years. When I was in my father's kingdom a young girl, I knew of you, though you knew nothing of me, and we should have been married then if you had not gone away so suddenly, and for long, long years I followed you." "Well," said Majnún, "if you can make yourself a young girl again, I will marry you."

Lailí said, "Oh, that is quite easy. God will make me a young girl again. In two days' time you must go into the garden, and there you will see a beautiful fruit. You must gather it and bring it into your room and cut it open yourself very gently, and you must not open it when your father or anybody else is with you, but when you are quite alone ; for I shall be in the fruit quite naked, without any clothes at all on." In the morning Lailí took her little dog's form, and disappeared in the garden.

Prince Majnún told all this to his father, who told him to do all the old woman had bidden him. In two days' time he and the Wazír's son walked in the garden, and there they saw a large, lovely red fruit. "Oh !" said the Prince, "I wonder shall I find my wife in that fruit." Husain Mahámat wanted him to gather it and see, but he would not till he had told his father, who said, "That must be the fruit ; go and gather it." So Majnún went back and broke the fruit off its stalk ; and he said to his father, "Come with me to my room while I open it ; I am afraid to open it alone, for perhaps I shall find a Rakshas in it that will eat me." "No," said King Dantál ; "remember, Lailí will be naked ; you must go alone, and do not be afraid if, after all, a Rakshas is in the fruit, for I will stay outside the door, and you have only to call me with a loud voice, and I will come to you, so the Rakshas will not be able to eat you."

Then Majnún took the fruit and began to cut it open tremblingly, for he shook with fear ; and when he had cut it, out stepped Lailí, young and far more beautiful than she

G

had ever been. At the sight of her extreme beauty, Majnún fell backwards fainting on the floor.

Lailí took off his turban and wound it all round herself like a sárí (for she had no clothes at all on), and then she called King Dentál, and said to him sadly, " Why has Majnún fallen down like this? Why will he not speak to me? He never used to be afraid of me; and he has seen me so many, many times." King Dentál answered, " It is because you are so beautiful. You are far, far more beautiful than you ever were. But he will be very happy directly." Then the King got some water, and they bathed Majnún's face and gave him some to drink, and he sat up again. Then Lailí said, "Why did you faint? Did you not see I am Lailí?" " Oh!" said Prince Majnún, " I see you are Lailí come back to me, but your eyes have grown so wonderfully beautiful, that I fainted when I saw them." Then they were all very happy, and King Dentál had all the drums in the place beaten, and had all the musical instruments played on, and they made a grand wedding-feast, and gave presents to the servants, and rice and quantities of rupees to the fakírs.

After some time had passed very happily, Prince Majnún and his wife went out to eat the air. They rode on the same horse, and had only a groom with them. They came to another kingdom, to a beautiful garden. " We must go into that garden and see it." said Majnún. · " No, no," said Lailí; "it belongs to a bad Rájá, Chumman Básá, a very wicked man." But Majnún insisted on going in, and in spite of all Lailí could say, he got off the horse to look at the flowers. Now, as he was looking at the flowers, Lailí saw Chumman Básá coming towards them, and she read in his eyes that he meant to kill her husband and seize her. So she said to Majnún, " Come, come, let us go; do not go near that bad man. I see in his eyes, and I feel in my heart, that he will kill you to seize me." " What nonsense," said

Majnún. " I believe he is a very good Rájá. Anyhow, I
am so near to him that I could not get away." " Well," said
Lailí, " it is better that you should be killed than I, for if I
were to be killed a second time, God would not give me my
life again ; but I can bring you to life if you are killed."
Now Chumman Básá had come quite near, and seemed very
pleasant, so thought Prince Majnún; but when he was
speaking to Majnún, he drew his scimitar and cut off the
prince's head at one blow.

Lailí sat quite still on her horse, and as the Rájá came
towards her she said, " Why did you kill my husband ? "
" Because I want to take you," he answered. " You cannot,"
said Lailí. " Yes, I can," said the Rájá. " Take me, then,"
said Lailí to Chumman Básá; so he came quite close and
put out his hand to take hers to lift her off her horse. But
she put her hand in her pocket and pulled out a tiny knife,
only as long as her hand was broad, and this knife unfolded
itself in one instant till it was such a length ! and then Lailí
made a great sweep with her arm and her long, long knife,
and off came Chumman Básá's head at one touch.

Then Lailí slipped down off her horse, and she went to
Majnún's dead body, and she cut her little finger inside her
hand straight down from the top of her nail to her palm,
and out of this gushed blood like healing medicine. Then
she put Majnún's head on his shoulders, and smeared her
healing blood all over the wound, and Majnún woke up and
said, " What a delightful sleep I have had ! Why, I feel as
if I had slept for years ! " Then he got up and saw the Rájá's
dead body by Lailí's horse. " What's that ? " said Majnún.
" That is the wicked Rájá who killed you to seize me, just as I
said he would." " Who killed him ? " asked Majnún. " I did,"
answered Lailí, " and it was I who brought you to life." " Do
bring the poor man to life if you know how to do so," said
Majnún. " No," said Lailí, " for he is a wicked man, and will

try to do you harm." But Majnún asked her for such a long time, and so earnestly to bring the wicked Rájá to life, that at last she said, "Jump up on the horse, then, and go far away with the groom." "What will you do," said Majnún, "if I leave you? I cannot leave you." "I will take care of myself," said Lailí; "but this man is so wicked, he may kill you again if you are near him." So Majnún got up on the horse, and he and the groom went a long way off and waited for Lailí. Then she set the wicked Rájá's head straight on his shoulders, and she squeezed the wound in her finger till a little blood-medicine came out of it. Then she smeared this over the place where her knife had passed, and just as she saw the Rájá opening his eyes, she began to run, and she ran, and ran so fast, that she outran the Rájá, who tried to catch her; and she sprang up on the horse behind her husband, and they rode so fast, so fast, till they reached King Dentál's palace.

There Prince Majnún told everything to his father, who was horrified and angry. "How lucky for you that you have such a wife," he said. "Why did you not do what she told you? But for her, you would be now dead." Then he made a great feast out of gratitude for his son's safety, and gave many, many rupees to the fakírs. And he made so much of Lailí. He loved her dearly; he could not do enough for her. Then he built a splendid palace for her and his son, with a great deal of ground about it, and lovely gardens, and gave them great wealth, and heaps of servants to wait on them. But he would not allow any but their servants to enter their gardens and palace, and he would not allow Majnún to go out of them, nor Lailí; "for," said King Dentál, "Lailí is so beautiful, that perhaps some one may kill my son to take her away."

Told by Dunkní.

XV.

HOW KING BURTAL BECAME A FAKÍR.

ONCE there was a great king called Burtal, and he had a hundred and sixty wives, but he had no children, which made him sad. One day he said to his wives, " I am going to a very distant jungle which is full of antelopes, to hunt them." " Very well," they answered, " go." So he went. In that jungle lived neither tigers nor men, but only antelopes. When King Burtal reached the jungle, some of the antelopes came to him and said, " Pray don't kill the black antelope, for he is our Rájá, and we have no other antelope like him among us ; but try to kill any of the others—the brown or the yellow antelopes—that you choose. Now, the king was not a kind man, and he said, " I will kill your black antelope, and no other." So he shot him dead. When the other antelopes saw this they began to scream and cry with sorrow. But the dead antelope's wife said to them, " There is a holy man, a fakír, in the jungle. Let us take the dead body to him and ask him to bring our Rájá to life." And King Burtal laughed at them and said, " How can any man bring a dead antelope to life ? " But the antelopes took the body of their dead Rájá on their backs, and the dead antelope's wife went at their head ; and King Burtal went too ; and they carried it to the fakír, who was called Goraknáth, and who was resting in the jungle, and they said to him, " Bring our Rájá to life again.

for what can we do without a Rájá? and he has left no son to succeed him." And the queen antelope said, "I have no other husband. I had only this one husband. Do bring him to life for me." King Burtal laughed and mocked them, and said to the fakír, "I never heard of any man being able to bring a dead antelope to life. I don't believe you can do it." At this Goraknáth got angry, and he knelt down and asked God to bring the antelope to life; and God told him to take a wand and beat the dead antelope with it, and then the antelope would be alive again. So Goraknáth took a wand and beat the dead antelope, and it was alive once more, and then it instantly sprang up into heaven. The antelopes were delighted to see their Rájá alive again, and they said, "We do not mind his going up to heaven, for he will come down again to us."

King Burtal had stood by all the time, and he said to Goraknáth, "Make me a fakír like yourself," for he thought it would be fine to do such wonderful things. But Goraknáth would not, and King Burtal stayed in the jungle with Goraknáth for twelve years, and all that time he never ceased begging and praying to be made a fakír, till at last Goraknáth said, "I cannot make you a fakír unless you go home and address your wives as 'Mamma,' and ask them to give you money and food." Now, it is a very shameful thing to call one's wife 'Mamma,' for if a wife is called 'Mamma' she has to leave her husband. Then Goraknáth took off the king's clothes, and dressed him only in a cloth and a tiger's skin; and the king went to his palace and began begging for rice and food, and he would not take any from the palace servants: he said he must and would see the Ránís, and that they themselves should give him food. The servants told the Ránís about this fakír who said he must and would see them himself, and that they should give him food and rice with their own hands, and one of their ayahs, who had recognized King Burtal, told them the fakír was their husband who had been away twelve years. The Ránís cried out, " Do not talk nonsense. That fakír can never be our husband." " Go and see for yourselves," answered the ayah. They went, and the fakír said to them, " Mamma, give me rice." " Why do you call us ' Mamma ' ? " they said, " We have no sons. You are not our son." But at last they saw he was indeed their husband, and they wrung their hands and wept bitterly, and threw themselves on the ground before him and said, " Why have you called us ' Mamma ' ? Why do you ask for bread? We must now leave you." " Don't go away," said the king. " Take my kingdom, my money, my houses, and stay here till I return. I am going to be a fakír." His wives gave him some rice and some money, and he went back to Goraknáth.

In old days men who intended to become fakírs had to do three tasks set them by one who was already a fakír ; so Goraknáth said to the king, " Now you must go to a jungle that I will show you, and stay there for twelve years." Then King Burtal took the flat pan and the rolling-pin which he used in making his flour cakes, and was quite ready to start for the jungle, but the fakír stopped him. " You must leave your pan and your rolling-pin behind," he said ; " and all these twelve years you must neither eat nor drink, or you can never be a fakír. You must sit quite still on the same spot and never move." " I shall die if I don't eat," said the king ; " but I don't care if I do die, so I will do all you tell me." Then the fakír took him to a jungle, and made him sit down on the grass, and instantly all the grass round him grew up so tall and thick that King Burtal was quite hidden by it, and no one could see him. Here he lived for twelve years, and never moved, and he ate nothing, and drank nothing, and nobody knew he was there.

At the end of that time Goraknáth came and took him

away and said, "Now go home to your wives." "Why should I go to my wives? I do not wish to see my wives, for they have given me no children," said King Burtal. But Goraknáth said, "Go and see them." So King Burtal went; and he begged for rice from them; and they entreated him to stay with them, but he would not. "I will return to the fakír Goraknáth," he said. "Why should I stay with you? You have never given me a child. What use is all my wealth to me? I have no son to take it when I am dead. I will become a fakír." And they threw themselves on the ground and wrung their hands, and said, "Oh, why will you leave us?" He answered, "Because it pleases me to do so." And he called them all "Mamma," and told them to stay in his palace and take all he possessed for their own use. Then he returned to Goraknáth.

"Now," said Goraknáth, "you must learn to be sweeper to all the beasts of the jungle, and you must serve them for twelve years." So for twelve years King Burtal cleared the grass and kept the jungle clean for all the creatures in it — cows, sheeps, goats, tiger, cats, bears. Sometimes he stayed in one part of the jungle, and sometimes in another.

When the twelve years were over he went to Goraknáth, who said to him, "Good; you have learnt to serve the wild beasts; now you must learn to serve men." Then the fakír took the king to a village, and bade him sweep it and keep it clean for twelve years. Here King Burtal stayed for another twelve years, and all that time he was the village-sweeper and kept the village clean, and he swept all the dust and dirt into a great heap till the heap was as high and as big as a hut.

When the twelve years were over he returned to Goraknáth and stood before him, and as he stood there came a man who was an angel sent by God, and he threw some dirt on King Burtal's head; but the king never moved nor spoke. "Now," cried Goraknáth, "I see you are a true fakír: go and cleanse yourself by bathing in the river."

The river in which he was sent to bathe was the Jámná. In this river lived water-nymphs, and the nymph Gangá was playing in it when her sister Jámná [1] came to her and said, "Come quickly; our father is dying and wants to see you;" and off Jámná went to her father. Gangá was hurrying after her when King Burtal saw her, and stopped her, and asked her where she was going so fast. "To my father, who is very ill and dying," said Gangá; "let me go." "I will not let you go," said King Burtal. Then Gangá began to run, and said, "You cannot keep me, you cannot catch me; no man can catch me, no man can keep me." This provoked King Burtal, and he said, "I can catch you, and I can keep you." "No, no," she answered; "no one can catch me, no one can hold me." Then King Burtal got quite vexed, and he ran till he caught her, and then he said, "Now, I will not let you go; I will keep you." Then he held her in his hands and rubbed her between his palms, and when he opened his hands she had turned into a little round ball. He tried to hide the ball in his hair, but could not, for his hair was too short, and he found he could not hold Gangá, as she was too strong for him; so he thought he would take her to Mahádeo,[2] who had long thick hair, and make him keep her, for King Burtal was dreadfully frightened and did not dare let the ball go, for fear Gangá, who he knew was very angry, should take her own form and bring a great flood to drown him. So he went quickly to Mahádeo, and gave the ball to him. Mahádeo said, "Why not keep her yourself?" "I cannot," said King Burtal, "for my hair is too short to tie her into; and I cannot hold her, for she is too strong for

---

[1] Yamuná.   [2] Mahadeva, i. e. Siva.

me ; but your hair is long, and so you can hide her in it."
Then Mahádeo had a round box made of bamboo, and in
this box was a hole into which he dropped the ball. And
he let down his long hair, and it reached to the ground, and
was thick—so thick ; he put the box in his hair on the top
of his head, and rolled his long hair all round his head and
over the box just like a turban.

Jamná finding her sister did not follow her, came up from
the bottom of the river to look for her, and she asked
whether any one had seen her, and at last some one said,
" King Burtal has taken her away." Jamná set off to King
Burtal and said, " Give me my sister Gangá, for our father
is dying and wants to see her." " It is true that I took her
away," said King Burtal, " but I have not got her now ; she
is with Mahádeo." So Jamná went to Mahádeo,—" Give
me my sister quickly, for our father is dying and wants to see
her." (Now Gangá was in a great passion inside her box.)
" I cannot give you Gangá," said Mahádeo, " for she is so
angry that if I let her loose she will flood the country with
water." " No, she will not ; indeed, she will not," said Jamná.
" If I give her to you, you will not be able to keep her," said
Mahádeo. " Yes, yes, I shall," said Jamná. " I do not
think you will," said Mahádeo ; " but here is the box in which
said is. Hold it tight, and be careful that neither you nor
any one else mentions her name on the journey." Jamná
said she would be very careful, and took the box ; but she
had to pass through a jungle in which were a number of
cowherds and holy men, one of whom was called Gangá.
Just as Jamná passed by, one of these men called to this
man by his name, Gangá, and instantly Gangá burst the box
and flooded the country with water. The holy men and the
cowherd called to her to have pity on them, and so did
Jamná ; but Gangá was too angry to listen to them or speak
to them, so she drowned all the holy men and the cowherds,

and when she got to her father's house and found he was
dead, she was in such a rage that she declared she would
send a still greater flood to ruin the country; and so she
did.

After this, King Burtal went to Goraknáth and stayed
with him some years, till Goraknáth said, " Now go to your
own kingdom," But King Burtal refused, saying, "I wish
to stay with you; my wives have never given me a child. I
have no son. I do not care to return to my kingdom."
However, Goraknáth would not allow him to stay. Go
to your own kingdom," he said again ; " but first tell me how
many wives you have." "A hundred and sixty," answered
the King. " Here are a hundred and sixty lichí fruits for
you," said the fakir. " Give one to each of your wives to
eat, and they will each have a son, and I will go with
you." So King Burtal obeyed, and Goraknáth went with
him.

Seventy years had passed since King Burtal had left his
kingdom. When he and Goraknáth reached it, they went
to an open plain and made a fire and sat down beside it.
Everybody who passed them said, " Who are these fakirs?"
Some servants of King Burtal's Ránís passed too, and when
they got home they told the Ránís that their husband had
returned to his kingdom. But the Ránís said, "What nonsense you talk ! King Burtal went away with the fakír
Goraknáth." The servants answered, " We are quite sure
that King Burtal is here, for Goraknáth is here, and with him
is another man, and we are sure this man is King Burtal."
So all the Ránís went to see for themselves, and when they
saw the fakír that was with Goraknáth they knew he was their
husband. Then the first Rání, who was very angry with him
for having left them, said a spell over him : " God is very
angry with you for leaving us, and he will send you a bad
illness." But King Burtal answered, " Do not be angry with

me. I am your husband, and have come back to you after
an absence of seventy years." At this the youngest Rání
was very glad, and she ordered drums to be beaten and she
beat a drum herself, and they sang songs, and all went to
the palace together, and Goraknáth with them.

Then Goraknáth said he must now go away, but first he
asked King Burtal to show him a grand feat as a proof of his
skill. So King Burtal sent to the smith for a great iron
chain. Then he lit a big fire. This alarmed the palace
servants, who wondered if he were going to burn his palace
and his wives. King Burtal next sent for some ghee. "What
is he going to do with the ghee?" said the palace servants.
Then he drove a nail into the wall, rubbed his hands with the
ghee, put the iron chain into the fire and drew it out red-hot;
flames came from the iron. Then King Burtal hung it on
the nail and pulled and pulled at the chain till he drew it off
the nail, and his hands were not in the least burnt. The
Ránís and palace servants were greatly astonished and Goraknáth much pleased. "You know how to do your work well,"
said he to the king. • Then Goraknáth bade him good bye,
telling him to look after his kingdom and his wives; but
they all said he must not leave them, and they built him a
grand house in the compound, and gave him a great many
servants to wait on him, and plenty of money; so Goraknáth
agreed to live in this house; only, as he was a fakír, he often
went away by himself to spend some time in his jungle,
always returning to his house in King Burtal's compound.
Meanwhile King Burtal gave each of his wives a lichí to eat,
and after a little while each wife had a little son. They
were all such beautiful children; but the biggest and hand-
somest of all was the eldest Ráni's little son. His name was
Sazádá, and his father and mother loved him dearly.

When Prince Sazádá was about six or seven years old, the
fakír Goraknáth came to King Burtal and said, "Now

ou must give me your son Sazádá, for I want to take
aim away with me for some years." The Rání, his mother,
refused to let him go, but at last she had to do so, and then
she became mad and very sick for grief.

Goraknáth took the little prince to Indrásan to be taught
by the fairies, and on arriving he. married him to Jahúr
Rání, who was the daughter of the greatest of the fairy queens.
Goraknáth made a grand wedding for the little prince, and
all the fairies were delighted that he should be the little
Jahúr Rání's husband, for he was such a beautiful child they
all fell in love with him the moment they saw him, and they
taught him to play on all kinds of instruments, and to sing
beautifully, and to read and write, and he grew handsomer
and handsomer every day in the fairy kingdom. Goraknáth
came often to see him, and the fairies took great care of him.

When Prince Sazádá had grown a fine strong young man,
Goraknáth took him and his wife, the Jahúr Rání, and brought
them in great state to King Burtal's kingdom. First he took
the young prince and presented him to his father and said,
" See, here is your son. Now he can read and write, sing and
play on all kinds of instruments, for I have had him taught
all these things." But they, when they saw him, fell on their
faces, for they could not look at him on account of his great
beauty. He had grown so handsome in Indrásan, and his
cheeks were red. " How can this beautiful boy be our son ? "
they said, and they did not recognize him. " Stand up,"
said Goraknáth. " This is your son Sazádá; do not fall
down before your son." So they stood up, and the fakír
said, " I have married your son to the fairy princess Jahúr
Rání, and I will bring her to you." So then he brought
the little Rání, and when they saw her they fell down again,
for they could not look at her beauty. Her hair was like
red gold, her eyes were dark, and her eyelashes black. But
Goraknáth made them stand up; and when they really

understood it was their son and his wife that he had brought them, they took Prince Sazádá into their arms, and kissed him and loved him, and his Rání too. Goraknáth made a grand wedding-feast for them all, and they were all very happy.

Told by Dunkní.

XVI

SOME OF THE DOINGS OF SHEKH FARÍD.

NCE there was a Rájá called Hámánsá Rájá. He had a son, named Gursan Rájá, who married Khelápari Rání, the daughter of Gulábsá Rájá. After the wedding Gursan Rájá brought her home to his father's house.

One day Gursan Rájá came home from hunting, very very tired and thirsty. It was about twelve or one o'clock in the day. He asked Khelápari Rání to fetch him some water, and while she went for it he fell asleep. When she came back she found him still sleeping, and because he was so tired he slept all the afternoon and all night, and never woke till the next morning. His wife stood by him all the time holding the water in a brass cup. When he woke and found she had stood there all the afternoon and all night he was very sorry, and asked God to forgive him, and to give his wife whatever she wished for, no matter what it might be. So Khelápari wished that whatever happened in any country, she might know of it at once of herself without any one telling her, no matter how far away the country might be.

One day Khelápari Rání went to draw water from the tank, and by the tank sat an old man, the fakír Shekh Faríd. He said to the Rání, "Give me a little water to drink." "I will," she said, "only drink it quickly, for my father's house is on fire, and I am going to put it out." "How far off is your father's country?" asked Shekh Faríd. "About twenty miles," answered Khelápari. "Then how can you know his house is on fire ! " said Shekh Faríd; " I have been a fakír for twelve years, and for twelve years neither ate nor drank, and yet I do not know what happens twenty miles away." " But I know," she answered. " Leave your water-jar here," he said, " and go and see if the house really is on fire, and I will not drink till you return to me."

So off went Khelápari Ráni to her father's country, and when she got there his house was burning, and she stayed till the fire was put out, and then returned to the tank where she left the fakír. " Is it true," he asked, "that your father's house was on fire?" " Quite true," she answered. The fakír wondered. " How could she know it when the fire was twenty miles off?" he said to himself, and he determined to go to Gulábsá Rájá's country to see if the Ráni had told him the truth.

He went by a roundabout road, as he did not know the way, so it took him three or four days to get there. When he did, he asked some villagers if there had been a fire at their Rájá's house. " Yes, a few days ago there was," they answered. So the fakír, still more astonished, decided he would go back to Hámánsá Rájá's palace and ask Khelpari Ráni how it came to pass that she was wiser than Shekh Faríd.

As he was returning, he met a bullock-cart laden with bags of sugar, and he asked the driver what the bags contained. The driver was put out because his bullocks would not go on quickly, and he was tired with beating and goading them, so he said crossly, " It's ashes." " Good," said Shekh Faríd, "let it be ashes." When the cartman got to the bazar, and went to make over the sugar to the merchant who had sent him for it, he found all his bags full of ashes, nothing but ashes. He was in a great state of mind, for a good deal of money had been paid for the sugar, and he was a poor man. So he went back to Shekh Faríd and fell downat his

feet, saying, " I am a poor, poor man. My sugar is turned
to ashes. Do make the ashes sugar again." "Good," said
the fakír; "go home, and you will find sugar, and next time
you are asked what you have in your cart, tell the truth and
not lies." The cart-man went home, and when he saw his
sugar was sugar once more, and no longer ashes, he was
very, very glad.

One of his brother-villagers thought, "How pleasant it
would be to become a fakír and do such things myself! I
will go to this fakír and learn from him to be a fakír too."
So he went after Shekh Faríd and found him walking along
the road, and he followed him. Now Shekh Faríd knew at
once what this man wanted, so as they passed a heap of
clay bricks, he said, " O God, let it be thy pleasure to give
me power to turn these clay bricks into gold." Instantly
they became gold, and Shekh Faríd walked on; but the
villager took up two of the bricks and put one under each
arm, and then followed the fakír. Suddenly Shekh Faríd
turned round, and said to him, "You have two clay bricks
under your arms." The man looked, saw it was true, and
threw them away. Then Shekh Faríd said to him, "You
steal bricks, and yet wish to be a fakír?" The man was
ashamed, and went back to his village.

Shekh Faríd continued his journey **and** got to Hámánsá
Rájá's country; but when he got there he found Kheláparí
had gone to another country for a little while, so he never
saw her, nor found out how it was that she knew what happened twenty miles off.

In a jungle in Hámánsá Rájá's country he met a man,
called Fakír-achand, and his wife, who were very poor.
They were going to bury their only son, and were crying
bitterly. Shekh Faríd asked them, "Would you like your
son to be alive again?" "Yes," they said. "Will you give
him to me, and I will bring him to life, and then he shall

H

return to you ? " said Shekh Faríd. " Yes," they answered,
and gave him their dead son, and went to their home.

The fakír carried the dead boy, who was called Mohandás,
a little further on, and then laid him on the ground, and
struck him with a long thin bamboo wand he carried in
his hand. The boy stood up. Shekh Faríd asked him,
"Would you like to go home to your father and mother, or
to stay with me ? " " To stay with you," said Mohandás.
(Had he wished to go home, the fakír would have been very
angry.) " Then," said Shekh Farid, " I will call your mother
here." He did so, and when she came, he said to her,
" See, here is your son alive. Will you give him to me for
twelve years ? " The woman said, " Yes," and went home.
The fakír gave her and her husband a quantity of rupees and
built them a beautiful house. Then he and Mohandás set
out on their travels, and wandered about the jungles for
one whole year, till they came to a country full of large
splendid gardens belonging to a very rich Rájá, called
Dumkás Rájá.

This Rájá had a beautiful daughter, Champákálí Rani.
She had lovely golden hair, golden eyebrows, golden eyelashes, blue eyes, and her skin was transparent. In Dumkás
Rájá's country they had never seen a fakír, so when Shekh
Faríd and Mohandás arrived, the Rájá sent to them, and
asked Shekh Faríd to come to talk to him. " No," said the
fakír, " I will not go to the Rájá : if the Rájá wants me, he
must come to me."

Dumkás Rájá was very angry when his messengers returned with this answer, and he ordered Shekh Farid to leave
his country immediately ; but the fakír said he would not go
until he had married his adopted son, Mohandás, to Cham-
pakálí Ráni. The people all laughed at him for saying this,
and declared such a marriage would never take place.
However, the fakír and Mohandás walked about and saw the

town, and looked at everything, and everybody stared at them. Then they went to live on the border of Dumkás Rájá's country, and lived there for some time.

One day Shekh Faríd bought Mohandás a beautiful horse and fine clothes such as Rájás wear, and told the boy to ride about the fields and high roads. He also told him not to speak to any one unless they spoke to him. Mohandás promised to do as he was bid. As he was riding along, he met the Princess Champákálí, who was also riding. She asked him who he was. " A Rájá's son," he said. " What Rájá ? " asked Champákálí. " Never mind what Rájá," said Mohandás. The princess then went home, and so did Mohandás ; but every day after this they met and talked together, and the princess fell very much in love with Mohandás.

At last she said to her father, " I wish to marry a young man who rides about on the border-land every day, and is very handsome." The Rájá consented, for it was time his daughter was married, and now no Rájá from another country would come to marry her, as the demons who guarded the princess swallowed all her suitors at one gulp, and had already swallowed many Rájás who had come on this errand.

Shekh Faríd said to Mohandás, " Now go up to the palace, and claim the princess for your wife." " If I do," said Mohandás, "the demons will swallow me." " I will not let them swallow you," said Shekh Faríd. So Mohandás consented and set off for the palace, Shekh Faríd following him When Mohandás came to the demons, they were going to swallow him ; but the fakír, who had his sword in his hand, killed them all, and as he did so, the Rájás and princes who had come as suitors to the Princess Champákálí, and had therefore been swallowed by the demons, all came jumping out of the demons' stomachs and ran off in all directions as

H 2

hard as they could, from fear not knowing where they went.

Mohandás was greatly frightened at all this; but Shekh Faríd explained everything to him, so he went on to the palace, and the fakír went too. There Mohandás asked Dumkás Rájá to give him his daughter as his wife, and the Rájá consented. So he was married to Champákalí Rání, and her father gave them a great many elephants, and horses, and camels, and a great deal of money and many jewels. And Mohandás and his wife set off with the fakír to his father Fakír-achand's house, and they took all the elephants, camels, horses, money and jewels with them. On the way Mohandás told Champákalí Rání that he was not a great Rájá's son, but the son of poor people. Champákalí's heart was very sad at this; however, she was not angry, only sorry.

When they reached Hámánsá Rájá's country, and had come to Fakír-achand's house, the fakír said to Mohandás's mother, "See, you lent me one child, and I have brought you back two children. Does this please you?" "Indeed it does please me," she answered; "I am very happy."

They built a beautiful palace and all lived in it together. The mother begged Shekh Faríd to stay with them, saying, "Only stay with us; I will give you a bungalow, and you shall have everything you want." But Shekh Faríd said, "I am a fakír, and so cannot stay with you, as I may never stay in one place, and must, instead, wander from country to country and from jungle to jungle. So he said good-bye to them and went on his wanderings, and never returned to them.

Mohandás, his wife, and his father and mother, all lived happily together.

Told by Dunkní.

XVII.

THE MOUSE.

HERE was a mouse who wanted something to eat; so he went to a garden, where many kinds of grain, and fruit, and cabbages, and other vegetables were growing. All round the garden the people to whom it belonged had planted a hedge of thorns, that nothing might get in. The mouse scrambled through the hedge, but great thorns pierced his tail, and he began to cry. He came out of the garden again through the hedge, and on his way home he met a barber.

"You must take out these thorns," said he to the barber.

"I cannot," said the barber, "without cutting off your tail with my razor."

"Never mind cutting off my tail," said the mouse.

The barber cut off the mouse's tail. But the mouse was in a rage. He seized the razor and ran away with it. At this the poor barber was very unhappy and began to cry, for he had no pice wherewith to buy another.

The mouse ran on and on until at last he came to another country, in which there were no knives or sickles to cut the grass with. There the mouse saw a man pulling the grass out of the ground with his hands.

"You will cut your hands," said the mouse.

"There are no knives here," said the man, "so I must pull up the grass in this way."

"You must take my razor then," said the mouse.

"Suppose your razor should break? I could not buy you another," said the man.

"Never mind if it does break," said the mouse, "I give it to you as a present."

So the man took the razor and began cutting the grass, and as he was cutting, the razor broke.

"Oh, why have you broken my razor?" exclaimed the mouse.

"Did not I tell you it would break?" answered the man.

The mouse snatched up the man's blanket and ran off with it. The grass-cutter began to cry. "What shall I do?" said he. "The mouse has carried away my blanket, and I have not money wherewith to buy another." And he went home very sad.

Meanwhile the mouse ran on and on until he arrived at another country, where he saw a grain merchant chopping up sugar-canes; only as he had no blanket or cloth to lay the canes on, he chopped them up on the ground, and so they got dirty.

"Why do you chop up your canes on the ground?" said the mouse; "they all get dirty."

"What can I do?" answered the man. "I have no pice wherewith to buy a blanket to chop them on."

"Then why don't you take mine?" said the mouse.

"If I took yours it would get cut, and I have no money to buy you another," said the grain merchant.

"Never mind; I don't want another," said the mouse.

So the man took the blanket, and of course he cut it. When he had finished chopping up his sugar-canes, he gave it back to the mouse.

When the mouse saw the blanket was full of holes, he was very angry indeed with the man, and seizing all the sugar-canes he ran away with them as fast as he could. The grain merchant began to cry. "What shall I do?" said he; "I have no more sugar-canes." And he went home very sorrowful.

Then the mouse ran on and on till he came to another country, where he stopped at a sweetmeat-seller's shop. Now in this country there was no salt and no sugar. And the sweetmeat-seller made his sweetmeats of flour and ghee without either sugar or salt, so that they were very nasty.

" Will you give me some sweetmeats for a pice ? " said the mouse to the sweetmeat-seller. " Yes," answered the man, and he gave one. The mouse began to eat it and thought it very nasty indeed.

" Why, there is no sugar in it ! " exclaimed the mouse.

" No," said the man ; " we have no sugar in this country. The few sugar-canes we have are so dear, that poor people like myself cannot buy them."

" Then take my sugar-canes," cried the mouse.

" No," said the man. " Where should I find the money to pay you for them ? They would be all used in making sweetmeats."

" Take them," said the mouse ; " I give them to you."

The sweetmeat-seller took them and began making sweet-meats of all kinds, so that he used all the sugar-canes.

" Why have you used all my sugar-canes?" cried the mouse.

" Did not I tell you I should do so ? " said the man.

" You are a thief ! " cried the mouse, and he knocked down the sweetmeat-seller, seized all his sweetmeats, and ran off with them.

" What shall I do now ? " cried the sweetmeat-seller. " I have no money to buy flour and ghee to make more sweet-meats with ; and if I quarrel with the mouse, he will doubt-less kill me."

Meanwhile the mouse ran on and on till he reached a country, the Rájá of which had a great many cows—hun-dreds of cows. The mouse stopped at the pasture-ground of these cows. Now, the cowherds were so poor they could not buy bread every day, and sometimes they ate bread which was twelve days old. When the mouse arrived, the cowherds were eating their bread, and it was very stale and mouldy.

"Why do you eat that stale bread?" said the mouse.

"Because we have no money to buy any other with," answered the cowherds.

"Look at all these sweetmeats," said the mouse. "Take them and eat them instead of that stale bread."

"But if we eat them, we must pay you for them, and where shall we get the money?" said the cowherds.

"Oh, never mind the money," said the mouse.

So the cowherds took the sweetmeats and ate them all up. At this the mouse was furious. He stuck a pole into the ground, and ran and fetched ropes, and tied the cowherds hand and foot to the pole. Then he took all the cows and ran off with them.

He ran on and on till he got to a country where there were no fowls, no cows, no buffaloes, no meat of any kind; and the people in it did not even know what milk and meat were. The day the mouse arrived was the day the Rájá's daughter was to be married, and a great many people were assembled together. The Rájá's cooks were cooking, but they had neither meat nor ghee.

"Why are all these people assembled together?" said the mouse.

"To-day is our Rájá's daughter's wedding-day, and we are cooking the dinner," answered the cooks.

"But you have no meat," said the mouse.

"No," said the cooks. "There is no meat of any kind in our country."

"Take my cows," said the mouse.

"No," said the cooks; "our Rájá could not pay for them; he is too poor." (He was only a petty Rájá.)

"It does not matter," said the mouse. "I don't want money."

So the cooks took the cows and the sheep and killed them, and dressed their flesh in different ways; made pilaus and curries; they roasted some and boiled some, and gave it to the people to eat. In this way they made an end of all the cows.

"Why have you made an end of all my cows?" cried the mouse.

"Did not we tell you we should make use of them all?" said the cooks.

"Give me my cows," said the mouse.

"We can't. The people have eaten them all up," said the cooks.

The mouse was in a great rage. He ran off to the bridegroom, who was walking near the kitchen, saying to himself, "Now I will go and fetch my bride."

"Give me the money for my cows," cried the mouse to him. "Your people have eaten them all up, and your cooks won't pay me, so you must."

"What have I to do with your cows?" said the bridegroom. "I won't pay you for them."

"Then if you won't pay me, your wife's father must," said the mouse.

"Oh, *he* is too poor to pay for your cows," said the bridegroom, "and I won't."

"Then if I am not paid, I will take away your bride," said the mouse; and he ran off and carried away the bride.

The Rájá was very angry at this; but the mouse ran on and on with his wife (so he called the Rájá's daughter) till he came to another country.

Now, on the day he arrived in it there were going to be grand sights and fun to please its Rájá. Some jugglers and rope-dancers were going to perform.

" Take my wife and let her walk on the rope ; she is young, and your wives are old," said the mouse to the rope-dancers.

" No," they answered, " for she does not know how to walk on a rope and carry at the same time a wooden plate on her head. She would fall and break her neck."

" But you must take my wife," said the mouse. " She won't fall ; she is young, and your wives are old. You really must take her."

So the rope-dancers took her, much against their will, and when she began to walk on the rope with the wooden plate on her head, she fell and died.

" Oh, why have you killed my wife ? " cried the mouse.

" Did we not tell you she would fall and kill herself ? " answered the rope-dancers.

The mouse seized all the jugglers' and rope-dancers' wives, and the things they used in dancing and juggling, and ran off with them. Then the rope-dancers and jugglers began to cry, and said, " What shall we do ? Our wives and our property are all gone ! "

Meanwhile the mouse ran on and on until he came to another country, where he got a house to live in. And he ate a great deal, and grew so fat that he could not get through the door of his house.

" Send for a carpenter," said he to the rope-dancers' and jugglers' wives, " and tell him to cut off some of my flesh. Then I shall be able to get into my house."

The women sent for a carpenter, and when he came the mouse said to him, " cut off some of my flesh, then I shall be able to go into my house."

" If I do," said the carpenter, " you will die."

" No, I shan't die," said the mouse. " Do as I bid you."

So the carpenter took his knife, and cut off some of the mouse's flesh.

" Oh, dear ! oh, dear ! " cried the mouse ; " how it does hurt ! What can I do to make it stop paining me ? "

" You must go to a certain place, where a particular kind of grain grows, and rub the grain on your wounds. Then they will get quite well," said the carpenter.

So the mouse ran off to the place to which the carpenter had told him to go, and rubbed his wounds with the grain. This gave him such pain that he fell down and died.

The rope-dancers' and jugglers' wives went home to their husbands with all the things the mouse had carried away, and they all lived happily ever after.

Told by Karím.

XVIII.

A WONDERFUL STORY.

ONCE there lived two wrestlers, who were both very very strong. The stronger of the two had a daughter called Ajít; the other had no daughter at all. These wrestlers did not live in the same country, but their two villages were not far apart.

One day the wrestler that had no daughter heard of the wrestler that had a daughter, and he determined to go and find him and wrestle with him, to see who was the stronger. He went therefore to Ajít's father's country, and when he arrived at his house, he knocked at the door and said, "Is any one here?" Ajít answered, "Yes, I am here;" and she came out. "Where is the wrestler who lives in this house?" he asked. "My father," answered Ajít, "has taken three hundred carts to the jungle, and he is drawing them himself, as he could not get enough bullocks and horses to pull them along. He is gone to get wood." This astonished the wrestler very much. "Your father must indeed be very strong," he said.

Then he set off to the jungle, and in the jungle he found two dead elephants. He tied them to the two ends of a pole, took the pole on his shoulder, and returned to Ajít's house. There he knocked at the door, crying, "Is any one here?" "Yes, I am here," said Ajít. "Has your father come back?" asked the wrestler. "Not yet," said Ajít, who was busy sweeping the soom. Now, her father had twelve elephants. Eleven were in the stables, but one was lying dead in the room Ajít was sweeping; and as she swept, she swept the dead elephant without any trouble out of the door. This frightened the wrestler, "What a strong girl this is!" he said to himself. When Ajít had swept all the dust out of the room, she came and gathered it and the dead elephant up, and threw dust and elephant away. The wrestler was more and more astonished.

He set off again to find Ajít's father, and met him pulling the three hundred carts along. At this he was still more alarmed, but he said to him, "Will you wrestle with me now?" "No," said Ajít's father, "I won't; for here there is no one to see us." The other again begged him to wrestle at once, and at that moment an old woman bent with age came by. She was carrying bread to her son, who had taken his mother's three or four thousand camels to browse.

The first wrestler called to her at once, "Come and see us wrestle." "No," said the old woman, "for I must take my son his dinner. He is very hungry." "No, no; you must stay and see us wrestle," cried both the wrestlers. "I cannot stay," she said; "but do one of you stand on one of my hands, and the other on the other, and then you can wrestle as we go along." "You carry us!" cried the men. "You are so old, you will never be able to carry us." "Indeed I shall," said the old woman. So they got up on her hands, and she rested her hands, with the wrestlers standing on them, on her shoulders; and her son's flour-cakes she put on her head. Thus they went on their way, and the men wrestled as they went.

Now the old woman had told her son that if he did not do his work well, she would bring men to kill him; so he was dreadfully frightened when he saw his mother coming with the wrestlers. "Here is my mother coming to kill me, he said : and he tied up the three or four thousand camels in his cloth, put them all on his head, and ran off with them as fast as he could. " Stop, stop ! " cried his mother, when she saw him running away. But he only ran on still faster, and the old woman and the wrestlers ran after him.

Just then a kite was flying about, and the kite said to itself, " There must be some meat in that man's cloth," so it swept down and carried off the bundle of camels. The old woman's son at this sat down and cried.

The wrestlers soon came up to him and said, " What are you crying for ? " " Oh," answered the boy, " my mother said that if I did not do my work, she would bring men to kill me. So, when I saw you coming with her, I tied all the camels up in my cloth, put them on my head, and ran off. A kite came down and carried them all away. That is why I am crying." The wrestlers were much astonished at the boy's strength and at the kite's strength, and they all three set off in the direction in which the kite had flown.

Meanwhile the kite had flown on and on till it had reached another country, and the daughter of the Rájá of this country was sitting on the roof of the palace, combing her long black hair. The princess looked up at the kite and the bundle, and said, " There must be meat in that bundle." At that moment the kite let the bundle of camels fall, and it fell into the princess's eye, and went deep into it; but her eye was so large that it did not hurt her much. "Oh, mother ! mother ! " she cried, " something has fallen into my eye ! come and take it out." Her mother rushed up, took the bundle of camels out of the princess's eye, and shoved the bundle into her pocket.

The wrestlers and the old woman's son now came up, having seen all that had happened. " Where is the bundle of camels ? " said they, " and why do you cry ? " they asked the princess. " Oh," said her mother, " she is crying because something fell into her eye." "It was the bundle of camels that fell into her eye, and the bundle is in your pocket," said the old woman's son to the Ráni : and he put his hand into her pocket and pulled out the bundle. Then he and the wrestlers went back to Ajít's father's house, and on the way they met his old mother, who went with them.

They invited a great many people to dinner, and Ajít took a large quantity of flour and made it into flat cakes. Then she handed a cake to the wrestler who had come to see her father, and gave one to everybody else. "I can't eat such a big cake as this," said the wrestler. "Can't you?" said Ajít. "I can't indeed," he answered; "it is much too big." "Then I will eat it myself," said Ajít, and taking it and all the other cakes she popped them into her mouth together. "That is not half enough for me," she said. Then she offered him a can of water. "I cannot drink all that water," he said. "Can't you?" said Ajít; "I can drink much more than that." So she filled a large tub with water, lifted it to her mouth, and drank it all up at a draught,

The wrestler was very much astonished, and said to her, "Will you come to my house? I will give you a dinner." "You will never be able to give me enough to eat and drink." said Ajít. "Yes, I shall," he said. "You will not be able to give me enough, I am sure," said Ajít; "I cannot come." "Do come," he said. "Very well," she answered, "I will come; but I know you will never be able to give me enough food."

So they set off to his house. But when they had gone a little way, she said, "I must have my house with me." "I cannot carry your house," said the wrestler. "You must," said Ajít! "if you don't, I cannot go with you." "But I cannot carry your house," said the wrestler. "Well, then," said Ajít, "I will carry it myself." So she went back, dug up her house, and hoisted it on her head. This frightened the wrestler. " What a strong woman she must be ! " he thought. " I will not wrestle with her father ; for if I do, he will kill me."

Then they all went on till they came to his house. When they got to it, Ajít set her house down on the ground, and the wrestler went to get the dinner he had promised her. He brought quantities of things—all sorts of things—everything he could think of. Three kinds of flour, milk, dhall, rice, curries, and meat. Then he showed then all to Ajít. "That is not enough for my dinner," she said. " Why, that would be hardly enough for my mice ! "

The wrestler wondered very much at this, and asked, "Are your mice so very big ? " " Yes, they are very big," she answered ; "come and see." So he took up all the food he had brought, and laid it on the floor of Ajít's house. Then at once all the mice came and ate it up every bit. The wrestler was greatly surprised ; and Ajít said, "Did I not tell you true ? and did I not tell you, you would never be able to get me enough to eat ? " " Come to the Nabha Rájá's country," said the wrestler. "There you will surely get enough to eat."

To this she agreed ; so she, her father, and the wrestler went off to the Nabha Rájá's country. "I have brought a very strong girl," said the wrestler to the Nabha Rájá. " I will try her strength," said the Rájá. " Give me three elephants," said Ajít, "and I will carry them for you." Then the Rájá sent for three elephants, and said to her, " Now, carry these." "Give me a rope," said Ajít. So they gave her a rope, and she tied the three elephants together, and flung them over her shoulder. "Now, where shall I throw, them ? " she said to the astonished Rájá. "Shall I throw them on to the roof of your palace ? or on to the ground ? or away out there ? " " I don't know," said the Rájá. " Throw them upon my roof." She threw the elephants up on to the roof with such force that it broke, and the elephants fell through into the palace.

"What have you done?" cried the Rájá. "It is not my fault," answered Ajít. "You told me to throw the elephants on to your roof, and so I did." Then the Rájá sent for a great many men and bullocks and horses to pull the elephants out of his palace. But they could not the first time they pulled; then they tried a second time and succeeded, and they threw the elephants away.

Then Ajít went home. "What shall I do with this dreadful woman?" said the Nabha Rájá. "She is sure to kill me, and take all my country. I will try to kill her." So he got his sepoys and guns into order, and went out to kill Ajít. She was looking out of her window, and saw them coming. "Oh," she said, "here is the Nabha Rájá coming to kill me." Then she went out of her house and asked him why he had come. "To kill you," said the Rájá. "Is that what you want to do?" she said; and with one hand she took up the Rájá, his guns, and his sepoys, and put them all under her arm: and she carried them all off to the Nabha Rájá's country. There she put the Rájá into prison, and made herself Rání of his kingdom. She was very much pleased at being Rání of the Nabha country; for it was a rich country, and there were quantities of fruits and of corn in it. And she lived happily for a long, long time.

Told by Karím, 13th January, 1877.

XIX.

THE FAKÍR NÁNAKSÁ SAVES THE MERCHANT'S LIFE.

IN a country there was a grain merchant who was a very good man. Now a fakír named Nánaksá, who was also a very good man, came constantly to talk with him.

One day he came as usual, and the merchant and his wife were very glad to see him. As they were all sitting together, they saw a goat led away to be killed. The goat escaped from the man who was leading him and hid behind the merchant, but he was caught and marched off to death.

At this the merchant said nothing, but the fakír laughed.

A little later they saw an old woman who had done something wrong, and, therefore, the king had ordered her to be taken to the jungle and there put to death. The old woman escaped from the men who were leading her and took refuge behind the merchant, but she was seized and led away to die.

The merchant said nothing; the fakír laughed, and the merchant's wife saw him laugh.

At this moment the merchant's little daughter woke and began to scream. Her mother took her in her arms; the child was cross and pulled her mother's clothes all awry.

The fakír laughed.

The mother put her dress straight and held her child in her arms and stopped her crying. She then took a knife and went up to the fakír, saying, "Why did you laugh three times? Tell me the truth. What made you laugh three times?" Nánaksá answered, "What does it signify whether I cry or laugh? Ask me no questions, for I am a fakír, and it does not matter in the least whether I laugh or cry." However, the merchant's wife insisted on knowing why he laughed, and she said, "If you do not tell me, I will kill you with my knife." "Good," said Nánaksá; "if you really do wish to know, I will tell you." "I really do wish to know," she answered.

"Well," said Nánaksá, "you remember the goat took refuge behind your husband? That goat in his former life was your husband's father, and your husband would have saved him from death had he given the man who was taking him to be killed four rupees, for the man would then have gone away contentedly without the goat."

"Good," said the woman. "Why did you laugh the second time?"

"Well," said Nánaksá, "that old woman who hid herself behind your husband was his grandmother in her former life. Had your husband given the men who were taking her to the jungle twenty rupees, they would have given her up to him, and he would have saved her from death. Should a wild beast or a man ever take refuge behind us, it is our duty to save his life."

"Well," said the merchant's wife, "you have told me why you laughed the first two times. Now tell me why you laughed the third time."

"Listen," said Nánaksá. "You remember your husband's sister whom you tormented so much? She died, but then God caused her to be born again as your daughter, that she might torment you and punish you for having been so unkind to her in her former life when she was your sister-in-law."

"Is that true?" said the woman.

"Quite true," answered the fakír, "and that is why I laughed the third time. But now would you like to hear something I wish to tell you? If you promise not to cry, I will tell it you."

"I promise not to cry, so tell me," she said.

"Then listen," said Nánaksá. "God has decreed that your husband shall die to-morrow morning at ten o'clock. He will send four angels to fetch him."

At this the poor woman began to cry bitterly.

"Do not cry," said the fakír. "I will tell you something more. Listen to me. To-morrow morning at four o'clock you must get up, and make your house quite clean and neat. Then buy new dishes and make all the nicest and most delicious sweetmeats you can."

"I will do so," she answered.

When it was yet night she rose, and did all the fakír had bidden her. Then she went to him and said, "The sweetmeats are ready." "Now," said Nánaksá, "go and get a fine, clean cloth; take it and the sweetmeats with you, and set out and walk on and on till you come to a plain which is a long way from this. But you must go on till you reach it, and on it you will see a tank and a tree. By the tank and the tree you must spread your cloth and lay out your sweetmeats on it. At nine o'clock you will see four men, who will come and bathe in the tank. When they have bathed they will come towards you, and you must say to them, 'See! you are four angels, therefore you must eat some of my sweetmeats.'"

The woman set out for the plain and did all Nánaksá had told her to do; and everything happened as he had foretold. When the four men had bathed, they came towards the woman, and she said to them, "See! you are four angels, and therefore you must eat some of my sweetmeats."

The chief of the four angels, who was called Jabrá'íl, and the three other angels answered, "We have no money, wherewith to buy your sweetmeats, so how can we eat any of them?" "Never mind the money," said the woman; "you can pay me another day. Come now and eat some." So the four angels sat down and ate a great many of her sweetmeats.

When they had finished they stood up and said to each other, "Now we must go to the village and fetch the merchant." Then the woman made them a great many salaams and said, "That merchant is my husband. Still, if it is your pleasure to take him away, take him away."

At this the angels were sad, and said to her, "How can we take your husband's life now that we have eaten your food? But stay under this tree till we return, and then we' will pay you for your sweetmeats."

So the angels left her, and the wife waited under the tree. She was very sad; and after some time she thought, "Now I will go home: perhaps these angels are gone to take his life;" and then she cried bitterly and remained under the tree.

Meanwhile the four angels had gone back to God, who asked them, "Have you brought the merchant?" They were sorry not to have brought him, and told God all that had happened. And God was very angry; but he said to them, "Never mind. I know the fakír Nánaksá is with the merchant and his wife just now, and it is he who has played you this trick."

Then God wrote a letter in which he promised the merchant twenty years more life, only at the end of the twenty years he was really to die and not to be allowed to live any longer. This letter he gave to the angels, and bade them take it to the merchant's wife and tell her to have a silver box made, into which she was to put the letter, and then hang it round her husband's neck, so that he should live for twenty years more.

The four angels came down to earth again, and went to the tree under which they had left the woman. They found her waiting for them, and gave her the letter saying, "You must get a silver box made and put this letter in it; then hang it round your husband's neck, so that he may live for twenty years more."

The woman thanked them, and was very happy. She took the letter and went home. There she found her husband quite well, and with him was Nánaksá. She gave Nánaksá the letter and told him what the angels had bidden her do with it. Nánaksá read the letter, and was very much pleased. Then he said to her, "Call a silversmith here, and let him make you the silver box. Then you must get a great dinner ready, and ask all your friends, rich and poor, to come and eat it."

All this she did, and when the dinner was ready and all their friends had come, the fakír said, " None who are here, men, women, or children, must eat, till they have put their hands before their faces and worshipped God." Everybody hid his face in his hands at once and worshipped God : while they did this the fakír stole away from them, so when they uncovered their faces he was nowhere to be seen. No one knew where he had gone, and no one had seen him go. Some of the men went to look for him, but they could not find him, and none of them ever saw him again.

But the merchant and his wife lived happily together.

Told by Múniyá.

XX

THE BOY WHO HAD A MOON ON HIS FORE-HEAD AND A STAR ON HIS CHIN.

IN a country were seven daughters of poor parents, who used to come daily to play under the shady trees in the King's garden with the gardener's daughter; and daily she used to say to them, "When I am married I shall have a son. Such a beautiful boy as he will be has never been seen. He will have a moon on his forehead, and a star on his chin." Then her playfellows used to laugh at her and mock her.

But one day the King heard her telling them about the beautiful boy she would have when she was married, and he said to himself he should like very much to have such a son; the more so that though he had already four wives he had no child. He went, therefore, to the gardener and told him he wished to marry his daughter. This delighted the gardener and his wife, who thought it would indeed be grand for their daughter to become a princess. So they said "Yes" to the King, and invited all their friends to the wedding. The King invited all his, and he gave the gardener as much money as he wanted. Then the wedding was held with great feasting and rejoicing.

A year later the day drew near on which the gardener's daughter was to have her son; and the King's four other wives came constantly to see her. One day they said to her, "The King hunts every day; and the time is soon coming when you will have your child. Suppose you fell ill whilst he was out hunting and could therefore know nothing of your illness, what would you do then?"

When the King came home that evening, the gardener's daughter said to him, "Every day you go out hunting. Should I ever be in trouble or sick while you are away, how could I send for you?" The King gave her a kettle-drum which he placed near the door for her, and he said to her, "Whenever you want me, beat this kettle-drum. No matter how far away I may be, I shall hear it, and will come at once to you."

Next morning, when the King had gone out to hunt, his four other wives came to see the gardener's daughter. She told them all about her kettle-drum. "Oh," they said, "do drum on it just to see if the King really will come to you." "No, I will not," she said; "for why should I call him from his hunting when I do not want him?" "Don't mind interrupting his hunting," they answered. "Do try if he really will come to you when you beat your kettle-drum." So at last, just to please them, she beat it, and the King stood before her.

"Why have you called me?" he said. "See, I have left my hunting to come to you." "I want nothing," she answered; "I only wished to know if you really would come to me when I beat my drum." "Very well," answered the King; "but do not call me again unless you really need me." Then he returned to his hunting.

The next day, when the King had gone out hunting as usual, the four wives again came to see the gardener's daughter. They begged and begged her to beat her drum once more, "just to see if the King will really come to see you this time." At first she refused, but at last she consented. So she beat her drum, and the King came to her. But when he found she was neither ill nor in trouble, he was angry, and said to her, "Twice I have left my hunting and lost my game to come to you when you did not need me. Now you may call me as much as you like, but I will not come to you," and then he went away in a rage.

The third day the gardener's daughter fell ill, and she beat and beat her kettle-drum; but the King never came. He heard her kettle-drum, but he thought, "She does not really want me; she is only trying to see if I will go to her."

Meanwhile the four other wives came to her, and they said, "Here it is the custom before a child is born to bind its mother's eyes with a handkerchief that she may not see it just at first. So let us bind your eyes." She answered, "Very well, bind my eyes." The four wives then tied a handkerchief over them.

Soon after, the gardener's daughter had a beautiful little son, with a moon on his forehead and a star on his chin; and before the poor mother had seen him, the four wicked wives took the boy to the nurse and said to her, "Now you must not let this child make the least sound for fear his mother should hear him; and in the night you must either kill him, or else take him away, so that his mother may never see him. If you obey our orders, we will give you a great many rupees." All this they did out of spite. The nurse took the little child and put him into a box, and the four wives went back to the gardener's daughter.

First they put a stone into her boy's little bed, and then they took the handkerchief off her eyes and showed it her, saying, "Look! this is your son!" The poor girl cried bitterly, and thought, "What will the King say when he finds no child?" But she could do nothing.

When the King came home, he was furious at hearing his youngest wife, the gardener's daughter, had given him a stone instead of the beautiful little son she had promised him. He made her one of the palace servants, and never spoke to her.

In the middle of the night the nurse took the box in which was the beautiful little prince, and went out to a broad plain in the jungle.   There she dug a hole, made the fastenings of the box sure, and put the box into the hole, although the child in it was still alive.   The King's dog, whose name was Shankar, had followed her to see what she did with the box.   As soon as she had gone back to the four wives (who gave her a great many rupees), the dog went to the hole in which she had put the box, took the box out, and opened it. When he saw the beautiful little boy, he was very much delighted and said, "If it pleases God that this child should live, I will not hurt him; I will not eat him, but I will swallow him whole and hide him in my stomach."   This he did.

After six months had passed, the dog went by night to the jungle, and thought, "I wonder whether the boy is alive or dead."   Then he brought the child out of his stomach and rejoiced over his beauty.   The boy was now six months old. When Shankar had caressed and loved him, he swallowed him again for another six months.   At the end of that time he went once more by night to the broad jungle-plain.   There he brought up the child out of his stomach (the child was now a year old), and caressed and petted him a great deal, and was made very happy by his great beauty.

But this time the dog's keeper had followed and watched the dog; and he saw all that Shankar did, and the beautiful little child, so he ran to the four wives and said to them, "Inside the King's dog there is a child! the loveliest child! He has a moon on his forehead and a star on his chin. Such a child has never been seen!"   At this the four wives were very much frightened, and as soon as the King came home from hunting they said to him, "While you were away your dog came to our rooms, and tore our clothes and knocked about all our things.   We are afraid he will kill us."   "Do not be afraid," said the King.   "Eat your dinner and be happy. I will have the dog shot to-morrow morning."

Then he ordered his servants to shoot the dog at dawn, but the dog heard him, and said to himself, " What shall I do ? The King intends to kill me. I don't care about that, but what will become of the child if I am killed ? He will die. But I will see if I cannot save him."

So when it was night, the dog ran to the King's cow, who was called Surí, and said to her, " Surí, I want to give you something, for the King has ordered me to be shot to-morrow. Will you take great care of whatever I give you ? " " Let me see what it is," said Surí ; " I will take care of it if I can." Then they both went together to the wide plain, and there the dog brought up the boy. Surí was enchanted with him. "I never saw such a beautiful child in this country," she said. " See, he has a moon on his forehead and a star on his chin. I will take the greatest care of him.' So saying she swallowed the little prince. The dog made her a great many salaams, and said, " To-morrow I shall die ; " and the cow then went back to her stable.

Next morning at dawn the dog was taken to the jungle and shot.

The child now lived in Surí's stomach ; and when one whole year had passed, and he was two years old, the cow went out to the plain, and said to herself, " I do not know whether the child is alive or dead. But I have never hurt it, so I will see." Then she brought up the boy; and he played about, and Surí was delighted ; she loved him and caressed him, and talked to him. Then she swallowed him, and returned to her stable.

At the end of another year she went again to the plain and brought up the child. He played and ran about for an hour to her great delight, and she talked to him and caressed him. His great beauty made her very happy. Then she swallowed him once more and returned to her stable. The child was now three years old.

But this time the cowherd had followed Surí, and had seen the wonderful child and all she did to it. So he ran and told the four wives, " The King's cow has a beautiful boy inside her. He has a moon on his forehead and a star on his chin. Such a child has never been seen before ! "

At this the wives were terrified. They tore their clothes and their hair and cried. When the King came home at evening, he asked them why they were so agitated. " Oh," they said, " your cow came and tried to kill us ; but we ran away. She tore our hair and our clothes." " Never mind," said the King. " Eat your dinner and be happy. The cow shall be killed to-morrow morning."

Now Surí heard the King give this order to the servants, so she said to herself, " What shall I do to save the child ? " When it was midnight, she went to the King's horse called Katar, who was very wicked, and quite untameable. No one had ever been able to ride him; indeed no one could go near him with safety, he was so savage. Surí said to this horse, " Katar, will you take care of something that I want to give you, because the King has ordered me to be killed to-morrow ? " " Good," said Katar ; " show me what it is." Then Surí brought up the child, and the horse was delighted with him. " Yes," he said, " I will take the greatest care of him. Till now no one has been able to ride me, but this child shall ride me." Then he swallowed the boy, and when he had done so, the cow made him many salaams, saying, " It is for this boy's sake that I am to die." The next morning she was taken to the jungle and there killed.

The beautiful boy now lived in the horse's stomach, and he stayed in it for one whole year. At the end of that time the horse thought, " I will see if this child is alive or dead." So he brought him up ; and then he loved him, and petted him, and the little prince played all about the stable, out of which the horse was never allowed to go. Katar was very glad to see the child, who was now four years old. After he had played for some time, the horse swallowed him again. At the end of another year, when the boy was five years old, Katar brought him up again, caressed him, loved him, and let him play about the stable as he had done a year before. Then the horse swallowed him again.

But this time the groom had seen all that happened, and when it was morning, and the King had gone away to his hunting, he went to the four wicked wives, and told them all he had seen, and all about the wonderful, beautiful child that lived inside the King's horse Katar. On hearing the groom's story the four wives cried, and tore their hair and clothes, and refused to eat. When the King returned at evening and asked them why they were so miserable, they said, "Your horse Katar came and tore our clothes, and upset all our things, and we ran away for fear he should kill us." "Never mind," said the King. "Only eat your dinner and be happy. I will have Katar shot to-morrow." Then he thought that two men unaided could not kill such a wicked horse, so he ordered his servants to bid his troop of sepoys shoot him.

So the next day the King placed his sepoys all round the stable, and he took up his stand with them; and he said he would himself shoot any one who let his horse escape.

Meanwhile the horse had overheard all these orders. So he brought up the child and said to him, "Go into that little room that leads out of the stable, and you will find in it a saddle and bridle which you must put on me. Then you will find in the room some beautiful clothes such as princes wear; these you must put on yourself; and you must take the sword and gun you will find there too. Then you must mount on my back." Now Katar was a fairy-horse, and came from the fairies' country, so he could get anything he wanted ; but neither the King nor any of his people knew this. When all was ready, Kaṭár burst out of his stable, with the prince on his back, rushed past the King himself before the King had time to shoot him, galloped away to the great jungle-plain, and galloped about all over it. The King saw his horse had a boy on his back, though he could not see the boy distinctly. The sepoys tried in vain to shoot the horse; he galloped much too fast ; and at last they were all scattered over the plain. Then the King had to give it up and go home; and his sepoys went to their homes. The King could not shoot any of his sepoys for letting his horse escape, for he himself had let him do so.

Then Kaṭar galloped away, on, and on, and on ; and when night came they stayed under a tree, he and the King's son. The horse ate grass, and the boy wild fruits which he found in the jungle. Next morning they started afresh, and went far, and far, till they came to a jungle in another country, which did not belong to the little prince's father, but to another king. Here Kaṭar said to the boy, " Now get off my back." Off jumped the prince. " Unsaddle me and take off my bridle ; take off your beautiful clothes and tie them all up in a bundle with your sword and gun." This the boy did. Then the horse gave him some poor, common clothes, which he told him to put on. As soon as he was dressed in them the horse said, " Hide your bundle in this grass, and I will take care of it for you. I will always stay in this jungle-plain, so that when you want me you will always find me. You must now go away and find service with some one in this country." This made the boy very sad. " I know nothing about anything," he said. " What shall I do all alone in this country ? " " Do not be afraid," answered Kaṭar. " You will find service, and I will always stay here to help you when you want me. So go, only before you go, twist my right ear." The boy did so, and his horse instantly became a donkey.

"Now twist your right ear," said Katar. And when the boy
had twisted it, he was no longer a handsome prince, but a
poor, common-looking, ugly man ; and his moon and star
were hidden.

Then he went away further into the country, until he came
to a grain merchant of the country, who asked him who he was.
"I am a poor man," answered the boy, "and I want service."
"Good," said the grain merchant, "you shall be my servant."

Now the grain merchant lived near the King's palace, and
one night at twelve o'clock the boy was very hot ; so he
went out into the King's cool garden, and began to sing a
lovely song. The seventh and youngest daughter of the
King heard him, and she wondered who it was who could
sing so deliciously. Then she put on her clothes, rolled up
her hair, and came down to where the seemingly poor common man was lying singing, "Who are you? where do you
come from?" she asked. But he answered nothing. "Who
is this man who does not answer when I speak to him?"
thought the little princess, and she went away. On the
second night the same thing happened, and on the third
night too. But on the third night, when she found she could
not make him answer her, she said to him, "What a strange
man you are not to answer me when I speak to you." But
still he remained silent, so she went away.

The next day when he had finished his work, the young
prince went to the jungle to see his horse, who asked him,
"Are you quite well and happy?" "Yes, I am," answered
the boy. "I am servant to a grain merchant. The last three
nights I have gone into the King's garden and sung a song.
And each night the youngest princess has come to me and
asked me who I am, and whence I came, and I have answered
nothing. What shall I do now?" The horse said, "Next
time she asks you who you are, tell her you are a very poor
man, and came from your own country to find service here."

The boy then went home to the grain merchant, and at night, when every one had gone to bed, he went to the King's garden and sang his sweet song again. The youngest princess heard him, got up, dressed, and came to him. "Who are you? Whence do you come?" she asked. "I am a very poor man," he answered. "I came from my own country to seek service here, and I am now one of the grain merchant's servants." Then she went away. For three more nights the boy sang in the King's garden, and each night the princess came and asked him the same questions as before, and the boy gave her the same answers.

Then she went to her father, and said to him, "Father, I wish to be married; but I must choose my husband myself." Her father consented to this, and he wrote and invited all the Kings and Rájás in the land, saying, "My youngest daughter wishes to be married, but she insists on choosing her husband herself. As I do not know who it is she wishes to marry, I beg you will all come on a certain day, for her to see you and make her choice."

A great many Kings, Rájás, and their sons accepted this invitation and came. When they had all arrived, the little princess's father said to them, "To-morrow morning you must all sit together in my garden" (the King's garden was very large), "for then my youngest daughter will come and see you all, and choose her husband. I do not know whom she will choose."

The youngest princess ordered a grand elephant to be ready for her the next morning, and when the morning came, and all was ready, she dressed herself in the most lovely clothes, and put on her beautiful jewels; then she mounted her elephant, which was painted blue. In her hand she took a gold necklace.

Then she went into the garden where the Kings, Rájás, and their sons were seated. The boy, the grain merchant's servant, was also in the garden : not as a suitor, but looking on with the other servants.

The princess rode all round the garden, and looked at all the Kings and Rájás and princes, and then she hung the gold necklace round the neck of the boy, the grain merchant's servant. At this everybody laughed, and the Kings were greatly astonished. But then they and the Rájás said, "What fooling is this?" and they pushed the pretended poor man away, and took the necklace off his neck, and said to him, "Get out of the way, you poor, dirty man. Your clothes are far too dirty for you to come near us!" The boy went far away from them, and stood a long way off to see what would happen.

Then the King's youngest daughter went all round the garden again, holding her gold necklace in her hand, and once more she hung it round the boy's neck. Every one laughed at her and said, "How can the King's daughter think of marrying this poor, common man!" and the Kings and the Rájás, who had come as suitors, all wanted to turn him out of the garden. But the princess said, "Take care! take care!. You must not turn him out. Leave him alone." Then she put him on her elephant, and took him to the palace.

The Kings and Rájás and their sons were very much astonished, and said, "What does this mean? The princess does not care to marry one of us, but chooses that very poor man!" Her father then stood up, and said to them all, "I promised my daughter she should marry any one she pleased, and as she has twice chosen that poor, common man, she shall marry him." And so the princess and the boy were married with great pomp and splendour : her father and mother were quite content with her choice; and the Kings, the Rájás and their sons, all returned to their homes.

Now the princess's six sisters had all married rich princes- and d they laughed at her for choosing such a poor ugly hus,

K

band as hers seemed to be, and said to each other, mock-
ingly, "See! our sister has married this poor, common man!"
Their six husbands used to go out hunting every day, and
every evening they brought home quantities of all kinds of
game to their wives, and the game was cooked for their
dinner and for the King's; but the husband of the youngest
princess always stayed at home in the palace, and never
went out hunting at all. This made her very sad, and she
said to herself, "My sisters' husbands hunt every day, but
my husband never hunts at all."

At last she said to him, "Why do you never go out hunting as my sisters' husbands do every day, and every day they
bring home quantities of all kinds of game? Why do you
always stay at home, instead of doing as they do?"

One day he said to her, "I am going out to-day to eat
the air." "Very good," she answered; "go, and take one
of the horses." "No," said the young prince, "I will not
ride, I will walk." Then he went to the jungle-plain where
he had left Katar, who all this time had seemed to be a
donkey, and he told Katar everything. "Listen," he said;
"I have married the youngest princess; and when we were
married everybody laughed at her for choosing me, and said,
'What a very poor, common man our princess has chosen
for her husband!' Besides, my wife is very sad, for her six
sisters' husbands all hunt every day, and bring home quantities of game, and their wives therefore are very proud of
them. But I stay at home all day, and never hunt. To-day
I should like to hunt very much."

"Well," said Katar, "then twist my left ear;" and as soon
as the boy had twisted it, Katar was a horse again, and
not a donkey any longer. "Now," said Katar, "twist your
left ear, and you will see what a beautiful young prince
you will become." So the boy twisted his own left ear, and
there he stood no longer a poor, common, ugly man, but a

grand young prince with a moon on his forehead and a star on his chin. Then he put on his splendid clothes, saddled and bridled Kaṭar, got on his back with his sword and gun, and rode off to hunt.

He rode very far, and shot a great many birds and a quantity of deer. That day his six brothers-in-law could find no game, for the beautiful young prince had shot it all. Nearly all the day long these six princes wandered about looking in vain for game; till at last they grew hungry and thirsty, and could find no water, and they had no food with them. Meanwhile the beautiful young prince had sat down under a tree, to dine and rest, and there his six brothers-in-law found him. By his side was some delicious water, and also some roast meat.

When they saw him the six princes said to each other, "Look at that handsome prince. He has a moon on his forehead and a star on his chin. We have never seen such a prince in this jungle before; he must come from another country." Then they came up to him, and made him many salaams, and begged him to give them some food and water. "Who are you?" said the young prince. "We are the husbands of the six elder daughters of the King of this conntry," they answered; "and we have hunted all day, and are very hungry and thirsty." They did not recognize their brother-in-law in the least.

"Well," said the young prince, "I will give you something to eat and drink if you will do as I bid you." "We will do all you tell us to do," they answered, "for if we do not get water to drink, we shall die." "Very good," said the young prince. "Now you must let me put a red-hot pice on the back of each of you, and then I will give you food and water. Do you agree to this?" The six princes consented, for they thought, "No one will ever see the mark of the pice, as it will be covered by our clothes; and we shall die if we have no water to drink." Then the young prince took six pice, and made them red-hot in the fire ; he laid one on the back of each of the six princes, and gave them good food and water. They ate and drank ; and when they had finished they made him many salaams and went home.

The young prince stayed under the tree till it was evening ; then he mounted his horse and rode off to the King's palace. All the people looked at him as he came riding along, saying, "What a splendid young prince that is ! He has a moon on his forehead and a star on his chin." But no one recognized him. When he came near the King's palace, all the King's servants asked him who he was ; and as none of them knew him, the gate-keepers would not let him pass in. They all wondered who he could be, and all thought him the most beautiful prince that had ever been seen.

At last they asked him who he was. " I am the husband of your youngest princess," he answered. " No, no, indeed you are not," they said ; "for he is a poor, common-look-ing, and ugly man." " But I am he," answered the prince ; only no one would believe him. "Tell us the truth," said the servants ; "who are you ? " " Perhaps you cannot re-cognize me," said the young prince, "but call the youngest princess here. I wish to speak to her." The servants called her, and she came. "That man is not my husband," she said at once. "My husband is not nearly as handsome as that man. This must be a prince from another country."

Then she said to him, " Who are you ? Why do you say you are my husband ? " " Because I am your husband. I am telling you the truth," answered the young prince. " No you are not, you are not telling me the truth," said the little princess. " My husband is not a handsome man like you. I married a very poor, common-looking man." " That is true," he answered, " but nevertheless I am your husband.

I was the grain merchant's servant; and one hot night I went into your father's garden and sang, and you heard me, and came and asked me who I was and where I came from, and I would not answer you. And the same thing happened the next night, and the next, and on the fourth I told you I was a very poor man, and had come from my country to seek service in yours, and that I was the grain merchant's servant. Then you told your father you wished to marry, but must choose your own husband; and when all the Kings and Rájás were seated in your father's garden, you sat on an elephant and went round and looked at them all; and then twice hung your gold necklace round my neck, and chose me. See, here is your necklace, and here are the ring and the handkerchief you gave me on our wedding day."

Then she believed him, and was very glad that her husband was such a beautiful young prince. "What a strange man you are!" she said to him. "Till now you have been poor, and ugly, and common-looking. Now you are beautiful and look like a prince; I never saw such a handsome man as you are before; and yet I know you must be my husband." Then she worshipped God and thanked him for letting her have such a husband. "I have," she said, "a beautiful husband. There is no one like him in this country. He has a moon on his forehead and a star on his chin." Then she took him into the palace, and showed him to her father and mother and to every one. They all said they had never seen any one like him, and were all very happy. And the young prince lived as before in the King's palace with his wife, and Katar lived in the King's stables.

One day, when the King and his seven sons-in-law were in his court-house, and it was full of people, the young prince said to him, "There are six thieves here in your court-house." "Six thieves!" said the King. "Where are they? Show them to me." "There they are," said the young prince, pointing to his six brothers-in-law. The King and every one else in the court-house were very much astonished, and would not believe the young prince. " Take off their coats," he said, "and then you will see for yourselves that each of them has the mark of a thief on his back." So their coats were taken off the six princes, and the King and everybody in the court-house saw the marks of the red-hot pice. The six princes were very much ashamed, but the young prince was very glad. He had not forgotten how his brothers-in-law had laughed at him and mocked him when he seemed a poor, common man.

Now when Kaṭar was still in the jungle, before the prince was married, he had told the boy the whole story of his birth, and all that had happened to him and his mother. "When you are married," he said to him, " I will take you back to your father's country." So two months after the young prince had revenged himself on his brothers-in-law, Kaṭar said to him, " It is time for you to return to your father. Get the King to let you go to your own country, and I will tell you what to do when we get there."

The prince always did what his horse told him to do; so he went to his wife and said to her, " I wish very much to go to my own country to see my father and mother." " Very well," said his wife ; " I will tell my father and mother, and ask them to let us go." Then she went to them, and told them, and they consented to let her and her husband leave them. The King gave his daughter and the young prince a great many horses, and elephants, and all sorts of presents, and also a great many sepoys to guard them. In this grand state they travelled to the prince's country, which was not a great many miles off. When they reached it they pitched their tents on the same plain in which the prince had been left in his box by the nurse, where Shankar and Surí had swallowed him so often.

When the King, his father, the gardener's daughter's husband, saw the prince's camp, he was very much alarmed, and thought a great King had come to make war on him. He sent one of his servants, therefore, to ask whose camp it was. The young prince then wrote him a letter, in which he said, "You are a great King. Do not fear me. I am not come to make war on you. I am as if I were your son. I am a prince who has come to see your country and to speak with you. I wish to give you a grand feast, to which every one in your country must come—men and women, old and young, rich and poor, of all castes ; all the children, fakírs, and sepoys. You must bring them all here to me for a week, and I will feast them all."

The King was delighted with this letter, and ordered all the men, women, and children of all castes, fakírs and sepoys, in his country to go to the prince's camp to a grand feast the prince would give them. So they all came, and the King brought his four wives too. All came, at least all but the gardener's daughter. No one had told her to go to the feast, for no one had thought of her.

When all the people were assembled, the prince saw his mother was not there, and he asked the King, " Has every one in your country come to my feast ? " " Yes, every one," said the King. " Are you sure of that ? " asked the prince.

" Quite sure," answered the King. " I am sure one woman has not come," said the prince. " She is your gardener's daughter, who was once your wife and is now a servant in your palace." " True," said the King, " I had forgotten her." Then the prince told his servants to take his finest palanquin and to fetch the gardener's daughter. They were to bathe her, dress her in beautiful clothes and handsome jewels, and then bring her to him in the palanquin.

While the servants were bringing the gardener's daughter, the King thought how handsome the young prince was ; and he noticed particularly the moon on his forehead and the star on his chin, and he wondered in what country the young prince was born.

And now the palanquin arrived bringing the gardener's daughter, and the young prince went himself and took her out of it, and brought her into the tent. He made her a great many salaams. The four wicked wives looked on and were very much surprised and very angry. They remembered that, when they arrived, the prince had made them no salaams, and since then had not taken the least notice of them; whereas he could not do enough for the gardener's daughter, and seemed very glad to see her.

When they were all at dinner, the prince again made the gardener's daughter a great many salaams, and gave her food from all the nicest dishes. She wondered at his kindness to her, and thought, "Who is this handsome prince, with a moon on his forehead and a star on his chin? I never saw any one so beautiful. What country does he come from?"

Two or three days were thus passed in feasting, and all that time the King and his people were talking about the prince's beauty, and wondering who he was.

One day the prince asked the King if he had any children. "None," he answered. "Do you know who I am?" asked the prince. "No," said the King. "Tell me who you are." "I am your son," answered the prince, "and the gardener's daughter is my mother." The King shook his head sadly. "How can you be my son," he said, "when I have never had any children?" "But I am your son," answered the prince. "Your four wicked wives told you the gardener's daughter had given you a stone and not a son; but it was they who put the stone in my little bed, and then they tried to kill me." The King did not believe him. "I wish you were my son," he said; "but as I never had a child, you cannot be my son." " Do you remember your dog Shankar, and how you had him killed? And do you remember your cow Suri, and how you had her killed too? Your wives made you kill them because of me. And," he said, taking the King to Katar, "do you know whose horse that is?"

The King looked at Katar, and then said, "That is my horse Katar." ".Yes," said the Prince. " Do you not remember how he rushed past you out of his stable with me on his back?" Then Katar told the King the prince was really his son, and told him all the story of his birth, and of his life up to that moment; and when the King found the beautiful prince was indeed his son, he was so glad, so glad. He put his arms round him and kissed him and cried for joy.

" Now," said the King, "you must come with me to my palace, and live with me always." " No," said the prince, "that I cannot do. I cannot go to your palace. I only came here to fetch my mother; and now that I have found her, I will take her with me to my father-in-law's palace. I have married a King's daughter, and we live with her father." " But now that I have found you, I cannot let you go," said his father. "You and your wife must come and live with your mother and me in my palace." "That we will never do," said the prince, " unless you will kill your four wicked wives with your own hand. If you will do that, we will come and live with you."

So the King killed his wives, and then he and his wife, the gardener's daughter, and the prince and his wife, all went to live in the King's palace, and lived there happily together for ever after; and the King thanked God for giving him such a beautiful son, and for ridding him of his four wicked wives.

Katar did not return to the fairies' country, but stayed always with the young prince, and never left him.

Told by Múniyá.

XXI.

THE BÉL-PRINCESS.

IN a country lived a King who had seven sons. Six of these sons married, but the seventh and youngest son would not marry ; and, moreover, he disliked his six sisters-in-law, and could not bear to take food from their hands. One day, they got very angry with him for disliking them, and they said to him, taunting him, "We think that you will marry a Bél-Princess."

"A Bél-Princess," said the young prince to himself. "What is a Bél-Princess? and where is one to be found? I will go and look for one." But the next day he thought, "How can I find a Bél-Princess? I don't know where to seek for her."

At last one day he saddled and bridled one of his father's beautiful horses. Then he put on his grand clothes, took his sword and gun, and said good-bye to his father and mother, and set out on his search. They cried very much at parting with him.

He rode from his father's country for a long, long way. At length, when he had journeyed for six months, he found himself in a great jungle, through which he went for many nights and days, until he at last came to where a fakír lay sleeping. The young prince thought, "I will watch by this fakír till he wakes. Perhaps he can help me." So he stayed with the fakír for one whole month; and all that time he took care of him and watched by him, and kept his hut clean.

This fakír used to sleep for six whole months at a time, and then he would remain awake for six months.

When the prince had watched over him for one month the fakír woke, for his six months' sleep had come to an end; and when he saw what care the young prince had taken of him, and how clean his hut was, he was very much pleased with the King's son, and said to him, " How have you been able to reach this jungle, to which no man can come? and who are you? and whence do you come?"

"I am a King's son," answered the prince. "My father's country is a six months' journey away from this; and I am come to look for a Bél-Princess. I hear there is a Bél-Princess, and I want to find her. Can you tell me where she is?"

"It is true that there is one," answered the fakír, "and I know where she is. She is in the fairies' country, whither no man can go."

This made the young prince very sad. "What shall I do?" he said. "I have left my father and mother, and have travelled a long, long way to find the Bél-Princess. And now you tell me I cannot go where she lives."

"I will help you," said the fakír, "and if you do exactly what I tell you, you will find her. But, first, stay here with me for a little while."

So the King's son stayed for another month with the fakír, and took care of him, and did everything for him, as he did for his own father.

At the end of the month, the fakír gave him his stick, and said to him, "Now you must go to the fairies' country. It is one week's journey distant from this jungle. When you get there, you will see a number of demons and fairies who live in it." Then the fakír took a little earth from the ground, and put it in the prince's hand. "When you have come to the fairies' country, in order that they and the

demons may not see you, you must blow all this earth away
from the palm of your hand, and then you will be invisible.
You must ride on till you come to a great plain in the
middle of their garden, and on this plain you will see a
large bél-tree and on it one big bél-fruit. In this fruit is the
Bél-Princess. You must throw my stick at it, and it will
fall; but you must take care to catch the fruit in your
shawl, and not let it fall to the ground. Then ride quickly
back to me, for as soon as the fruit falls you will cease to
be invisible, and the fairies and demons who guard the fruit
will all come running after you, and they will all call to you.
But take care, take care not to look behind you when they
call you. Ride straight on to me with the fruit, and do
not look behind you. If you do, you will become stone, and
your horse too, and they will take the bél-fruit back to its
tree."

The prince promised to do all the fakír bade him. He
rode for a week, and then he came to the fairies' country. He blew the earth the fakír had given him away from
his palm all along his fingers, just as he had been told,
and then he became invisible. He rode through the great
garden to the plain. There he saw the bél-tree, and the
one fruit hanging all alone. He threw the fakír's stick at
it, and caught it in a corner of his shawl as it fell, but
then he was no longer invisible. All the fairies and demons could see him, and they came running after him as
he rode quickly away, and called to him. He looked
behind at them, and instantly he and his horse became
stone; and the bél-fruit went back to its tree and hung itself
up.

For one week the fakír sat in his jungle, waiting for the
King's son. But the moment he was turned into stone, the
fakír knew of it, and he set off at once for the fairies' country. He walked all through it, but neither the fairies nor

demons could touch him. He went straight to the great
plain, and there he saw the King's son sitting on his horse,
and both he and the horse were stone.

This made the fakír very sad ; and he said to God,
"What will the father and mother do, now that their son is
changed into a stone?" And he prayed to God and said,
"If it be God's pleasure, may this King's son be alive once
more." Then he cut his little finger on the inside from the tip
to the palm, and smeared the prince's forehead with the blood
that came from it. He rubbed some blood on the horse too,
all the time praying to God to give the prince his life again.
The King's son and his horse were alive once more. The
fakír took the prince back to his jungle, and said to him,
"Listen. I told you not to look behind you, and you dis-
obeyed me and so were turned to stone. Had I not come
to save you, you would always have remained stone."

The fakír kept the prince with him in the jungle for one
whole week. Then he gave him his stick and some earth
he picked up from the ground on which they were standing,
and said, "Now you must go to the fairies' country again,
and throw my stick at the bĕl-fruit, and catch it in a corner
of your shawl as you did before. But mind, mind you do
not look behind you this time. If you do you will be
turned to stone, and you will for ever remain stone. Ride
straight back to me with the fruit, and take care never to
look behind you once till you get to me."

So the King's son went again to the fairies' country, and
all happened as before, till he had caught the fruit in his
shawl. But then he rode straight back to the fakír without
looking behind him, although the fairies and demons ran
after him and called to him the whole way.

He rode so fast they could not catch him, and when he
came to the fakír, the fakír turned him into a fly and thus
hid him. Up came all the fairies and demons and said to

the fakír, " There is a thief in your hut." " A thief ! Where is the thief? " said the fakír.   Look everywhere for him, and take him away if you can find him."   Then they searched and searched everywhere, but could not find the prince ; so at last they went away.

When they had all gone, the fakír took the little fly and turned it back into a King's son.   A few days afterwards he said to the prince, " Now you have found what you wanted ; you have the Bél-Princess you came to seek.   So go back to your father and mother."   " Very well," said the prince.   Then he got his horse all ready for the journey, took the bél-fruit, and made many salaams to the fakír, who said to him, " Now, listen.   Take care not to open the fruit on the road.   Wait till you are in your father's house with your father and mother, and then open it.   If you do not do exactly as I tell you, evil will happen to you ; so mind you only open the fruit in your father's house.   Out of it will come the Bél-Princess."

The prince set out on his journey, and rode on and on for six months till he came to his father's country, and then to his father's garden.   There he sat down to rest by a well under a clump of great trees.   He said to himself, " Now that I am in my father's country, and in my father's garden, I will sit and rest in this cool shade ; and when I am rested I will go up to the palace."   He bathed his face and his hands in the well, and drank some of its water.   Then he thought, " Surely, now that I am in my father's country and in his garden, I need not wait till I get to his palace to open my bél-fruit.   What harm can happen if I do open it here ? "

So he broke it open, in spite of all the fakír had told him, and out of it came such a beautiful girl.   She was more beautiful than any princess that ever was seen—so beautiful that the King's son fainted when he saw her.   The princess fanned him, and poured water on his face, and presently he recovered, and said to her, "Princess, I should like to sleep for a little while, for I have travelled for six months, and am very tired. After I have slept we will go together to my father's palace." So he went to sleep, and the princess sat by him.

Presently a woman came to the well for water, and she said to herself, "See, here is the King's youngest son. What a lovely princess that is sitting by him! What fine clothes and jewels she has on!" And the wicked woman determined to kill the princess and to take her place. Then she came up to the beautiful girl, and sat down beside her, and talked to her. "Listen to me, princess," she said at last. "Let us change clothes with each other. Give me yours, and I will give you mine." The princess, thinking no harm, did as the woman suggested. "And now," said the woman, "let me put on your beautiful jewels." The princess gave them to her, and then the wicked, wicked woman, said to her, "Let us walk about this pretty garden, and look at the flowers, and amuse ourselves." By and by she said, "Princess, let us go and look at ourselves in the well, and see what we look like, you in my clothes, and I in yours." The young girl consented, and they went to the well. As they bent over the side to look in, the wicked woman gave the princess a push, and pushed her straight over the edge into the water.

Then she went and sat down by the sleeping prince, just as the princess had done. When he awoke and saw this ugly, wicked woman, instead of his Bél-Princess, he was very much surprised, and said to himself, "A little while ago I had a beautiful girl by me, and now there is such an ugly woman. It is true she has on the clothes and jewels my Bél-Princess wore; but she is so ugly, and there is something wrong with one of her eyes. What has happened to her?" Then he said to this wicked woman, whom he took for his Bél-Princess, "What is the matter with you? Has anything happened to you? Why have you become so ugly?" She answered, "Till now I have always lived in a bél-fruit. It is the bad air of your country that has made me ugly, and hurt one of my eyes."

The prince was ashamed of her, and very, very sorry. "How shall I take her to my father's palace now?" he thought. "My mother and all my brothers' wives will see her, and what will they say?" However, never mind; I must take her to my house, and marry her. I cannot think what can have happened to her." Then he got a palanquin, and took her up to the palace.

His father and mother were very glad that their youngest son had come back to them; but when they saw the wicked woman, and heard she was his Bél-Princess, they, and every one else in the palace, said, "Can she be a Bél-Princess? She is not at all pretty, and she is not at all pleasant." "She was lovely when she came out of the fruit," said the prince. "No one ever saw such a beautiful girl before. I cannot think what has happened to her. It must be the bad air of this country that has made her so ugly." Then he told them all about his journey to the jungle where he had met the fakir, and how, with the fakir's help, he had found his Bél-Princess, and how he had opened the fruit in his father's garden, and then fallen asleep.

The King made a great wedding-feast for his son, and he and the wicked woman were married, and all the time the King's youngest son thought he was marrying the Bél-Princess.

Meanwhile, the beautiful girl had not been drowned in the well, but had changed into a most lovely pink lotus-flower. This flower was first seen by a man from the village who came to the well for water. "What a lovely lotus-flower!" said the man; "I must gather it." But when he tried to reach it the flower floated away from him. Then he went and told all the people in the village of the beautiful flower, and then the palace servants heard of it. They all tried to gather it, but could not, for the flower always went just out of their reach. Then the King and his six elder sons heard of it, and they came to the well; but the King tried in vain to gather it, and his six sons too. The lotus-flower always floated away from them.

Last of all, the youngest prince heard of the lotus, and he grew very curious to see it, and said, " I will try if I cannot gather this wonderful flower that no one can touch." So he, too, came to the well, and stooped, and stretched out his hand, and the minute he did so the flower floated of itself into his hand.

Then he was very happy and proud, and he took the flower up to his wife and showed it to her. " Just see," he said, " every one in the village and the palace were talking of this lotus-flower; and every one tried to gather it; and no one could, for the flower would not let any one touch it. My father tried, and my brothers all tried, and they, too, could not gather it; but as soon as I stretched out my hand the flower floated into it of itself."

When his wicked wife saw the flower, she said nothing; but her heart told her it was the beautiful girl she had pushed into the well. The prince laid the flower on his pillow, and was very glad and happy. As soon as he had gone out, his wife seized the lotus-flower, tore it to bits, and threw them far away into the garden.

In a few days a bél-tree was growing on the spot where she had thrown the pieces of the lotus-flower. On it grew one big bél-fruit, and it was so fine and large that every one in the village and the palace tried to gather it; but no one could touch it, for the fruit always went just out of reach. The King and his six elder sons also tried, but they could not touch it. The youngest prince heard of this fruit, so he said to his wife, " I will go and see if I can gather this bél-fruit that no one can even touch." The wicked woman's heart said to her, " In the bél-fruit is the Bél-Princess ;" but she said nothing.

The prince went to the bél-tree ; the bél-fruit came into his hand, and he broke it off the tree, and brought it home to his wife. " See," he said, " here is the bél-fruit; it let me gather it at once." And he was very proud and happy. Then he laid the fruit on a table in his room.

When he had gone out the wicked wife came, and took the fruit, and flung it away in the garden. In the night the fruit burst in two, and in it lay a lovely, tiny girl baby. The gardener, as he went round the garden early in the morning, found the little baby; and he wondered who had thrown away the beautiful fruit, and who the lovely baby girl could be. She was so tiny and so pretty, and the gardener was delighted when he saw her, for he had no children, and thought God had sent him a little child at last.

He took her in his arms and carried her to his wife.

"See," he said, " we have never had any children, and now God has sent us this beautiful little girl." His wife looked at the child, and she was as delighted with her as her husband was. " Yes," she said, " God has sent us this child, and she is certainly most beautiful. I am very happy. But I have no milk for her; if only I had milk for her, I could nurse her and she would live." And the gardener's wife was very sad to think she had no milk in her breasts for the little child.

Then her husband said, "Let us ask God to send you milk for her." So they prayed to God and worshipped him. And God was pleased with them both, and sent the gardener's wife a great deal of milk.

The little girl now lived in the gardener's house, and he and his wife took the greatest care of her, and were very happy to think they had now a child. She grew very fast, and became lovelier every day. She was more beautiful than any girl that had ever been seen, and all the people in the King's country used to say, " How lovely the gardener's daughter is ! She is more beautiful than any princess."

The King's youngest son's wicked wife heard of the child, and her heart told her, " She is the Bél-Princess." She said nothing, but she often thought of how she could contrive to have her killed.

One day, when the gardener's daughter was seven years old, she was out in her father's garden, making a little garden of her own near the house-door. While she was busy over her flowers, the wicked woman's cow strayed into the garden and began eating the plants in it. The little girl would not let it make its dinner off her father's flowers and grass, but pushed it out of the garden.

The wicked woman was told how the gardener's daughter had treated her cow; so she cried all day long, and pretended to be ill. When her husband asked her what was the matter, she answered, " I am sick because the gardener's daughter has ill-treated my cow. She beat it, and turned it out of her father's garden, and said many wicked things. If you will have the girl killed, I shall live ; but if you do not kill her, I shall die." The prince at once ordered his servants to take the gardener's daughter the next morning to the jungle, and there kill her.

So the next morning early the servants went to the gardener's house to take away his daughter. He and his wife cried bitterly, and begged the servants to leave the girl with them. They offered them a great many rupees, saying, " Take these rupees, aud leave us our daughter." How can we leave you your daughter," said the servants, " when the King's youngest son has ordered us to take her to the jungle and kill her, that his wife may get well ? "

So they led the girl away; and as they went to the jungle, they said to each other, " How beautiful this girl is ! " They found her so beautiful that they grew very sorrowful at the thought of killing her.

They took the girl to a great plain, which was about ten miles distant from the King's country; but when they got there they said they could not kill her. She was so beautiful that they really could not kill her. She said to them, " You were ordered to kill me, so kill me." " No," they answered, " we cannot kill you, we cannot kill you."

Then the girl took the knife in her own hand and cut out her two eyes ; and one eye became a parrot, and the other a *maind.* Then she cut out her heart and it became a great tank. Her body became a splendid palace and garden—a far grander palace than was the King's palace ; her arms and legs became the pillars that supported the verandah roof ; and her head the dome on the top of the palace.

The prince's servants looked on all the time these changes were taking place, and they were so frightened by them, that when they got home they would not tell the prince or any one else what they had seen. No one lived in this wonderful house. It stood empty in its garden by its tank, and the parrot and *maind* lived in the garden trees.

Some time afterwards the youngest prince went out hunting, and towards evening he found himself on the great plain where stood the wonderful palace. He rode up to it and said to himself, "I never saw any house here before. I wonder who lives here?" He went through the great gate into the garden, and then he saw the large tank, and how beautiful the garden was. He went all through the garden and was delighted with it, and he saw that it was beautifully kept, and was in perfect order. Then he went into the palace, and went through all the rooms, and wondered more and more to whom this beautiful house could belong. He was very much surprised, too, at finding no one in the palace, though the rooms were all splendidly furnished, and very clean and neat.

"My father is a great king," he said to himself, "and yet he has not got a palace like this." It was now deep night, so the prince knew he could not go home till the next day. "Never mind," he said, "I will sleep in the verandah. I am not afraid, though I shall be quite alone."

So he lay down to sleep in the verandah, and while he lay there, the parrot and *mainá* flew in, and they perched near him, for they knew he was there, and they wanted him to hear what they said to each other. Then they began chattering together and the parrot told the *mainá* how the prince's father was king of the neighbouring country, and how he had seven sons, and how six of the sons had married six princesses, "but this prince, who was the youngest son, would not marry; and what is more, he did not like his brother's wives at all." Then the birds stopped talking and did not chatter any more that night. The prince was very much surprised at the birds knowing who he was, and all about his dislike to his brothers' wives.

The next morning he rode home; and there he stayed all day, and would not talk. His wife asked him, "What is the matter with you? Why are you so silent?" "My head aches," he answered : "I am ill." But towards evening he felt he must go back to the empty palace on the great plain, so he said to his wife, "I am going out to eat the air for a little while." Then he got on his horse and rode off to the palace.

As soon as he had laid himself down in the verandah, the parrot and the *mainá* perched near him; and the parrot told the *mainá* how the prince had heard of the Béll-Princess ; and all about his long journey in search of her, and how he found the bél-fruit, and how he was turned to stone. Then he stopped chattering, and the birds said nothing more to each other that night.

In the morning the King's son rode home, and was as silent and grave as he had been before. He told his wife his head ached when she asked him whether he was ill.

That night he again slept in the verandah of the strange palace, and heard a little more of his story from the birds.

The next day he was still silent and grave, and his wife was very uneasy. " I am sure the Bél-Princess is alive," she said to herself, " and that he goes every night to see her." Then she asked him, " Why do you go out every evening? Why do you not stay at home ? " " I am not well," he answered, " so I go to my mother's house " (the prince had a little house of his own in his father's compound). " I will not sleep at home again till I am well."

That night he lay down to sleep again in the verandah of the great empty palace, and heard the parrot tell the *mainá* all that happened to the prince up to the time that he fell asleep in his father's garden with the beautiful Bél-Princess sitting beside him.

On the fifth night the prince lay down to sleep again in the verandah of the palace on the great plain, and watched eagerly for the little birds to begin their talk. This night the parrot told how the wicked woman had come and taken the Bél-Princess's clothes, and thrown her down the well ; how the princess became a lotus-flower which the wicked wife broke to bits ; how the bits of the lotus-flower turned into a bél-fruit which she threw away ; how out of the fruit came a tiny girl-baby that the gardener adopted ; how the wicked woman persuaded the prince to have this girl killed when she was seven years old ; how he and the *mainá* had once been this girl's eyes ; how the tank was once her heart, and how her body had changed into this palace and garden, while her head became the dome on the top of the palace.

Then the *mainá* asked the parrot where the Bél-Princess was. " Cannot she be found ? " said the *mainá*. " Yes," said the parrot, "she can be found; but the King's youngest son alone can find her, and he is so foolish! He believes that his ugly, wicked wife is the beautiful Bél-Princess!" "And where is the princess?" asked the *mainá*. "She is here," said the parrot. "If the prince would come one day and go through all the rooms of this palace till he came to the centre room, he would see a trap-door in the middle of that room. If he lifted the trap-door he would see a staircase which leads to an underground palace, and in this palace is the Bél-princess." "And can no one but the prince lift the trap-door?" asked the *mainá*. "No one," answered the parrot. "It is God's order that only the King's youngest son can lift the trap-door and find the Bel-Princess."

The next day the young prince went through all the rooms of the palace, instead of going home. When he came to the centre room, he looked for the trap-door, and when he had lifted it he saw the staircase. He went down it, and found himself in the under-ground palace, which was far more beautiful than the one above-ground. It was full of servants; and in one room a grand dinner was standing ready. In another room he saw a gold bed, all covered with pearls and diamonds, and on the bed lay the Bél-Princess.

Day and night she prayed to God and read a holy book. She did nothing else.

When the prince went into her room and she saw him, she was very sad, not happy, for she thought, "He is so foolish; he knows nothing of what has happened to me." Then she said to him, "Why did you come here? Go home again to your father's palace."

The prince burst out crying. "See, princess," he said, "I knew nothing of your palace? I only found it by chance five nights ago. I have slept here in the verandah for the last five nights, and only last night did I learn what had happened to you, and how to find you." " I know it is true," she said, " that you knew nothing of what happened to me. But now that you have found me, what will you do?"

" I will go home to my father's palace," he answered, " and make everything ready for you, and then I will come and marry you and take you home."

So it was all settled, and he ate some food, and returned to his father. He told his father and mother all that had happened to the Bél-Princess, and how her body had turned into the beautiful garden and palace that stood on the big plain; and of the little birds; and of the underground palace in which she now lived. So his father said that he and the prince's mother, and his six brothers and their wives, would all take him in great state to the palace and marry him to the beautiful Bél-Princess; and that then they would all return to their own palace, and all live together. " But first the wicked woman must be killed," said the King.

So he ordered his servants to take her to the jungle and kill her, and throw her body away. So they took her away at four o'clock in the afternoon and killed her.

One morning two or three days later, the prince and his father and mother, and brothers and sisters-in-law, went to the great palace on the wide plain; and there, in the evening, the king's youngest son was married to the Bél-Princess. And when his father and mother and brothers, and his brothers' wives, saw her, they all said, " It is quite true. She is indeed a Bél-Princess!"

After the wedding they all returned to the King's palace, and there they lived together. But the King and his sons used often to go to the palace on the great plain to eat the air; and they used to lend it sometimes to other rájás and kings.

Told by Múniyá.

XXII.

HOW THE RÁJÁ'S SON WON THE PRINCESS LABÁM.

N a country there was a Rájá who had an only son who every day went out to hunt. One day the Rání, his mother, said to him, "You can hunt wherever you like on these three sides ; but you must never go to the fourth side." This she said because she knew if he went on the fourth side he would hear of the beautiful Princess Labám, and that then he would leave his father and mother and seek for the princess.

The young prince listened to his mother, and obeyed her for some time ; but one day, when he was hunting on the three sides where he was allowed to go, he remembered what she had said to him about the fourth side, and he determined to go and see why she had forbidden him to hunt on that side. When he got there, he found himself in a jungle, and nothing in the jungle but a quantity of parrots, who lived in it. The young Rájá shot at some of them, and at once they all flew away up to the sky. All, that is, but one, and this was their Rájá, who was called Híráman parrot.

When Híráman parrot found himself left alone, he called out to the other parrots, " Don't fly away and leave me alone when the Rájá's son shoots. If you desert me like this, I will tell the Princess Labám."

Then the parrots all flew back to their Rája, chattering. The prince was greatly surprised, and said, "Why, these birds can talk !" Then he said to the parrots, " Who is the Princess Labám ? Where does she live ? " But the parrots would not tell him where she lived. "You can never get to the Princess Labám's country." That is all they would say.

The prince grew very sad when they would not tell him anything more; and he threw his gun away, and went home. When he got home, he would not speak or eat, but lay on his bed for four or five days, and seemed very ill.

At last he told his father and mother that he wanted to go and see the Princess Labám. "I must go," he said; "I must see what she is like. Tell me where her country is." "We do not know where it is," answered his father and mother. "Then I must go and look for it," said the prince. "No, no," they said, "you must not leave us. You are our only son. Stay with us. You will never find the Princess Labám." "I must try and find her," said the prince. "Perhaps God will show me the way. If I live and I find her, I will come back to you; but perhaps I shall die, and then I shall never see you again. Still I must go."

So they had to let him go, though they cried very much at parting with him. His father gave him fine clothes to wear, and a fine horse. And he took his gun, and his bow and arrows, and a great many other weapons, "for," he said, "I may want them." His father, too, gave him plenty of rupees.

Then he himself got his horse all ready for the journey, and he said good-bye to his father and mother; and his mother took her handkerchief and wrapped some sweetmeats in it, and gave it to her son. "My child," she said to him, "when you are hungry eat some of these sweetmeats."

He then set out on his journey, and rode on and on till he came to a jungle in which were a tank and shady trees. He bathed himself and his horse in the tank, and then sat down under a tree. "Now," he said to himself, "I will eat some of the sweetmeats my mother gave me, and I will drink some water, and then I will continue my journey." He opened his handkerchief, and took out a sweetmeat. He found an ant in it. He took out another. There was an ant in that one too. So he laid the two sweetmeats on the ground, and he took out another, and another, and another, until he had taken them all out ; but in each he found an ant. "Never mind," he said, "I won't eat the sweetmeats ; the ants shall eat them." Then the Ant-Rájá came and stood before him and said, "You have been good to us. If ever you are in trouble, think of me and we will come to you."

The Rájá's son thanked him, mounted his horse and continued his journey. He rode on and on till he came to another jungle, and there he saw a tiger who had a thorn in his foot, and was roaring loudly from the pain.

"Why do you roar like that ? " said the young Rájá. " What is the matter with you ? " " I have had a thorn in my foot for twelve years," answered the tiger, "and it hurts me so ; that is why I roar." "Well," said the Rájá's son, "I will take it out for you. But, perhaps, as you are a tiger, when I have made you well, you will eat me ? " " Oh, no," said the tiger, " I won't eat you. Do make me well."

Then the prince took a little knife from his pocket, and cut the thorn out of the tiger's foot ; but when he cut, the tiger roared louder than ever, so loud that his wife heard him in the next jungle, and came bounding along to see what was the matter. The tiger saw her coming, and hid the prince in the jungle, so that she should not see him.

"What man hurt you that you roared so loud ? " said the wife. " No one hurt me," answered her husband; " but a Rájá's son came and took the thorn out of my foot." " Where is he ? Show him to me," said his wife. " If you promise not to kill him, I will call him," said the tiger. " I won't kill him ; only let me see him," answered his wife.

Then the tiger called the Rájá's son, and when he came the tiger and his wife made him a great many salaams.

Then they gave him a good dinner, and he stayed with them for three days. Every day he looked at the tiger's foot, and the third day it was quite healed. Then he said good-bye to the tigers, and the tiger said to him, " If ever you are in trouble, think of me, and we will come to you."

The Rájá's son rode on and on till he came to a third jungle. Here he found four fakírs whose teacher and master had died, and had left four things,—a bed, which carried whoever sat on it whithersoever he wished to go ; a bag, that gave its owner whatever he wanted, jewels, food, or clothes ; a stone bowl that gave its owner as much water as he wanted, no matter how far he might be from a tank ; and a stick and rope, to which its owner had only to say, if any one came to make war on him, " Stick, beat as many men and soldiers as are here," and the stick would beat them and the rope would tie them up.

The four fakírs were quarrelling over these four things. One said, " I want this ; " another said, " You cannot have it, for I want it ; " and so on.

The Rájá's son said to them, " Do not quarrel for these things. I will shoot four arrows in four different directions. Whichever of you gets to my first arrow, shall have the first thing—the bed. Whosoever gets to the second arrow, shall have the second thing—the bag. He who gets to the third arrow, shall have the third thing—the bowl. And he who gets to the fourth arrow, shall have the last things—the stick and rope." To this they agreed, and the prince shot off his first arrow. Away raced the fakírs to get it. When they brought it back to him he shot off the second, and when they had found and brought it to him he shot off his third, and when they had brought him the third he shot off the fourth.

While they were away looking for the fourth arrow, the Rájá's son let his horse loose in the jungle, and sat on the bed, taking the bowl, the stick and rope, and the bag with him. Then he said, "Bed, I wish to go to the Princess Labám's country." The little bed instantly rose up into the air and began to fly, and it flew and flew till it came to the Princess Labám's country, where it settled on the ground. The Rájá's son asked some men he saw, "Whose country is this?" "The Princess Labám's country," they answered. Then the prince went on till he came to a house where he saw an old woman. "Who are you?" she said. "Where do you come from?" "I come from a far country," he said; "do let me stay with you to-night." "No," she answered, "I cannot let you stay with me; for our king has ordered that men from other countries may not stay in his country. You cannot stay in my house." "You are my aunty," said the prince; "let me remain with you for this one night. You see it is evening, and if I go into the jungle, then the wild beasts will eat me." "Well," said the old woman, "you may stay here to-night; but to-morrow morning you must go away, for if the king hears you have passed the night in my house, he will have me seized and put into prison."

Then she took him into her house, and the Rájá's son was very glad. The old woman began preparing dinner, but he stopped her, "Aunty," he said, "I will give you food." He put his hand into his bag, saying, "Bag, I want some dinner," and the bag gave him instantly a delicious dinner, served upon two gold plates. The old woman and the Rájá's son then dined together.

When they had finished eating, the old woman said, "Now I will fetch some water." "Don't go," said the prince. "You shall have plenty of water directly." So he took his bowl and said to it, "Bowl, I want some water," and then it filled with water. When it was full, the prince cried out, "Stop, bowl," and the bowl stopped filling. "See, aunty," he said, "with this bowl I can always get as much water as I want."

By this time night had come. "Aunty," said the Rájá's son, "why don't you light a lamp?" "There is no need," she said. "Our king has forbidden the people in his country to light any lamps; for, as soon as it is dark, his daughter, the Princess Labám, comes and sits on her roof, and she shines so, that she lights up all the country and our houses, and we can see to do our work as if it were day."

When it was quite black night, the princess got up. She dressed herself in her rich clothes and jewels, and rolled up her hair, and across her head she put a band of diamonds and pearls. Then she shone like the moon, and her beauty made night day. She came out of her room, and sat on the roof of her palace. In the daytime she never came out of her house; she only came out at night. All the people in her father's country then went about their work and finished it.

The Rájá's son watched the princess quietly, and was very happy. He said to himself, "How lovely she is!"

At midnight, when everybody had gone to bed, the princess came down from her roof, and went to her room; and when she was in bed and asleep, the Rájá's son got up softly, and sat on his bed. "Bed," he said to it, "I want to go to the Princess Labám's bed-room." So the little bed carried him to the room where she lay fast asleep.

The young Rájá took his bag and said, "I want a great deal of betel-leaf," and it at once gave him quantities of betel-leaf. This he laid near the princess's bed, and then his little bed carried him back to the old woman's house.

Next morning all the princess's servants found the betel-leaf, and began to eat it. "Where did you get all that betel-leaf?" asked the princess. "We found it near your bed," answered the servants. Nobody knew the prince had come in the night and put it all there.

In the morning the old woman came to the Rájá's son. "Now it is morning," she said, "and you must go; for if the king finds out all I have done for you, he will seize me." " I am ill to-day, dear aunty," said the prince; "do let me stay till to-morrow morning." " Good," said the old woman. So he stayed, and they took their dinner out of the bag, and the bowl gave them water.

When night came the princess got up and sat on her roof, and at twelve o'clock, when every one was in bed, she went to her bed-room, and was soon fast asleep. Then the Rájá's son sat on his bed, and it carried him to the princess. He took his bag and said, " Bag, I want a most lovely shawl." It gave him a splendid shawl, and he spread it over the princess as she lay asleep. Then he went back to the old woman's house and slept till morning.

In the morning, when the princess saw the shawl, she was delighted. "See, mother," she said; " God must have given me this shawl, it is so beautiful." Her mother was very glad too. " Yes, my child," she said; "God must have given you this splendid shawl."

When it was morning the old woman said to the Rájá's son, " Now you must really go." " Aunty," he answered, " I am not well enough yet. Let me stay a few days longer. I will remain hidden in your house, so that no one may see me." So the old woman let him stay.

When it was black night, the princess put on her lovely clothes and jewels, and sat on her roof. At midnight she went to her room and went to sleep. Then the Rájá's son sat on his bed and flew to her bed-room. There he said to his bag, " Bag, I want a very, very beautiful ring." The bag gave him a glorious ring. Then he took the Princess Labám's hand gently to put on the ring, and she started up very much frightened.

" Who are you ? " she said to the prince. "Where do you come from ? Why do you come to my room ? " " Do not be afraid, princess," he said; "I am no thief. I am a great Rájá's son. Híráman parrot, who lives in the jungle where I went to hunt, told me your name, and then I left my father and mother, and came to see you."

"Well," said the princess, "as you are the son of such a great Rájá, I will not have you killed, and I will tell my father and mother that I wish to marry you."

The prince then returned to the old woman's house; and when morning came, the princess said to her mother, "The son of a great Rájá has come to this country, and I wish to marry him." Her mother told this to the king. "Good," said the king; "but if this Rájá's son wishes to marry my daughter, he must first do whatever I bid him. If he fails I will kill him. I will give him eighty pounds weight of mustard seed, and out of this he must crush the oil in one day. If he cannot do this he shall die."

In the morning the Rájá's son told the old woman that he intended to marry the princess. "Oh," said the old woman, "go away from this country, and do not think of marrying her. A great many Rájás and Rájás' sons have come here to marry her, and her father has had them all killed. He says whoever wishes to marry his daughter must first do whatever he bids him. If he can, then he shall marry the princess; if he cannot, the king will have him killed. But no one can do the things the king tells him to do; so all the Rájás and Rájás' sons who have tried have been put to death. You will be killed too, if you try. Do go away." But the prince would not listen to anything she said.

The king sent for the prince to the old woman's house, and his servants brought the Rájá's son to the king's court-house to the king. There the king gave him eighty pounds of mustard seed, and told him to crush all the oil out of it that day, and bring it next morning to him to the court-house. "Whoever wishes to marry my daughter," he said to the prince, "must first do all I tell him. If he cannot, then I have him killed. So if you cannot crush all the oil out of this mustard seed, you will die."

The prince was very sorry when he heard this. "How can I crush the oil out of all this mustard seed in one day?" he said to himself; "and if I do not, the king will kill me." He took the mustard seed to the old woman's house, and did not know what to do. At last he remembered the Ant-Rájá, and the moment he did so, the Ant-Rájá and his ants came to him. "Why do you look so sad?" said the Ant-Rájà. The prince showed him the mustard seed, and said to him, "How can I crush the oil out of all this mustard seed in one day? And if I do not take the oil to the king to-morrow morning, he will kill me." "Be happy," said the Ant-Rájá; "lie down and sleep: we will crush all the oil out for you during the day, and to-morrow morning you shall take it to the king." The Rájá's son lay down and slept, and the ants crushed out the oil for him. The prince was very glad when he saw the oil.

The next morning he took it to the court-house to the king. But the king said, "You cannot yet marry my daughter. If you wish to do so, you must first fight with my two demons and kill them." The king a long time ago had caught two demons, and then, as he did not know what to do with them, he had shut them up in a cage. He was afraid to let them loose for fear they would eat up all the people in his country; and he did not know how to kill them. So all the kings and kings' sons who wanted to marry the Princess Labám had to fight with these demons; "for," said the king to himself, "perhaps the demons may be killed, and then I shall be rid of them."

When he heard of the demons the Rájá's son was very sad. "What can I do?" he said to himself. "How can I fight with these two demons?" Then he thought of his

M

tiger : and the tiger and his wife came to him and said, "Why are you so sad?" The Rájá's son answered, "The king has ordered me to fight with his two demons and kill them. How can I do this?" "Do not be frightened," said the tiger. "Be happy. I and my wife will fight with them for you."

Then the Rájá's son took out of his bag two splendid coats. They were all gold and silver, and covered with pearls and diamonds. These he put on the tigers to make them beautiful, and he took them to the king, and said to him, "May these tigers fight your demons for me?" "Yes," said the king, who did not care in the least who killed his demons, provided they were killed. "Then call your demons," said the Rájá's son, "and these tigers will fight them." The king did so, and the tigers and the demons fought and fought until the tigers had killed the demons.

"That is good," said the king. But you must do something else before I give you my daughter. Up in the sky I have a kettle drum. You must go and beat it. If you cannot do this, I will kill you."

The Rájá's son thought of his little bed ; so he went to the old woman's house and sat on his bed. "Little bed," he said, "up in the sky is the king's kettle-drum. I want to go to it." The bed flew up with him, and the Rájá's son beat the drum, and the king heard him. Still, when he came down, the king would not give him his daughter. "You have," he said to the prince, "done the three things I told you to do ; but you must do one thing more." "If I can, I will," said the Rájá's son.

Then the king showed him the trunk of a tree that was lying near his court-house. It was a very, very thick trunk. He gave the prince a wax hatchet, and said, "To-morrow morning you must cut this trunk in two with this wax hatchet."

The Rájá's son went back to the old woman's house. He was very sad, and thought that now the Rájá would certainly

kill him. "I had his oil crushed out by the ants," he said
to himself. "I had his demons killed by the tigers. My
bed helped me to beat his kettle-drum. But now what can
I do? How can I cut that thick tree trunk in two with a
wax hatchet?"

At night he went on his bed to see the princess. "To-
morrow," he said to her, "your father will kill me." "Why?"
asked the princess.

"He has told me to cut a thick tree-trunk in two with a
wax hatchet. How can I ever do that?" said the Rájá's son.
"Do not be afraid, said the princess; "do as I bid you, and
you will cut it in two quite easily."

Then she pulled out a hair from her head, and gave it to
the prince. "To-morrow," she said, "when no one is near
you, you must say to the tree-trunk, "The Princess Labám
commands you to let yourself be cut in two by this hair.
Then stretch the hair down the edge of the wax hatchet's
blade."

The prince next day did exactly as the princess had told
him; and the minute the hair that was stretched down the
edge of the hatchet-blade touched the tree-trunk, it split into
two pieces.

The king said, "Now you can marry my daughter." Then
the wedding took place. All the Rájás and kings of the
countries round were asked to come to it, and there were
great rejoicings. After a few days the prince's son said to
his wife, "Let us go to my father's country." The Princess
Labám's father gave them a quantity of camels and horses
and rupees and servants; and they travelled in great state to
the prince's country, where they lived happily.

The prince always kept his bag, bowl, bed, and stick; only
as no one ever came to make war on him, he never needed
to use the stick.

Told by Múniyá.

M 2

XXIII.

THE PRINCESS WHO LOVED HER FATHER LIKE SALT.

IN a country there lived a king who had seven daughters. One day he called them all to him and said to them, "My daughters, how much do you love me?" The six eldest answered, "Father, we love you as much as sweetmeats and sugar;" but the seventh and youngest daughter said, "Father, I love you as much as salt." The king was much pleased with his six eldest daughters, but very angry with his youngest daughter. "What is this?" he said; "my daughter only loves me as much as she does salt!" Then he called some of his servants, and said to them, "Get a palanquin ready, and carry my youngest daughter away to the jungle."

The servants did as they were bid; and when they got to the jungle, they put the palanquin down under a tree and went away. The princess called to them, "Where are you going? Stay here; my father did not tell you to leave me alone in the jungle." "We will come back," said the servants; "we are only going to drink some water." But they returned to her father's palace.

The princess waited in the palanquin under the tree, and it was now evening, and the servants had not come back. She was very much frightened and cried bitterly. "The tigers and wild beasts will eat me," she said to herself. At last she went to sleep, and slept for a little while. When she awoke she found in her palanquin some food on a plate, and a little water, that God had sent her while she slept. She ate the food and drank the water, and then she felt happier, for she thought, " God must have sent me this food and water." She decided that as it was now night she had better stay in her palanquin, and go to sleep. " Perhaps the tigers and wild beasts will come and eat me," she thought ; "but if they don't, I will try to-morrow to get out of this jungle, and go to another country."

The next morning she left her palanquin and set out. She walked on, till, deep in the jungle, she came to a beautiful palace, which did not belong to her father, but to another king. The gate was shut, but she opened it, and went in. She looked all about, and thought, " What a beautiful house this is, and what a pretty garden and tank ! "

Everything was beautiful, only there were no servants nor anybody else to be seen. She went into the house, and through all the rooms. In one room she saw a dinner ready to be eaten, but there was no one to eat it. At last she came to a room in which was a splendid bed, and on it lay a king's son covered with a shawl. She took the shawl off, and then she saw he was very beautiful, and that he was dead. His body was stuck full of needles.

She sat down on the bed, and there she sat for one week, without eating, or drinking, or sleeping, pulling out the needles. Then a man came by who said to her, " I have here a girl I wish to sell." " I have no rupees," said the princess ; " but if you will sell her to me for my gold bangles, I will buy her." The man took the bangles, and left the girl with the princess, who was very glad to have her. " Now," she thought, " I shall be no longer alone."

All day and all night long the princess sat and pulled out the needles, while the girl went about the palace doing other work. At the end of other two weeks the princess had pulled out all the needles from the king's body, except those in his eyes.

Then the king's daughter said to her servant-girl, "For three weeks I have not bathed. Get a bath ready for me, and while I am bathing sit by the king, but do not take the needles out of his eyes. I will pull them out myself." The servant-girl promised not to pull out the needles. Then she got the bath ready; but when the king's daughter had gone to bathe, she sat down on the bed, and pulled the needles out of the king's eyes.

As soon as she had done so, he opened his eyes, and sat up. He thanked God for bringing him to life again. Then he looked about, and saw the servant-girl, and said to her, "Who has made me well and pulled all the needles out of my body?" "I have," she answered. Then he thanked her and said she should be his wife.

When the princess came from her bath, she found the king alive, and sitting on his bed talking to her servant. When she saw this she was very sad, but she said nothing. The king said to the servant-maid, "Who is this girl?" She answered, "She is one of my servants." And from that moment the princess became a servant-girl, and her servant-girl married the king. Every day the king said, "Can this lovely girl be really a servant? She is far more beautiful than my wife.

One day the king thought, "I will go to another country to eat the air." So he called the pretended princess, his wife, and told her he was going to eat the air in another country. "What would you like me to bring you when I come back?" She answered, "I should like beautiful sárís and clothes, and gold and silver jewels." Then the king said, "Call the servant-girl, and ask her what she would like me to bring her." The real princess came, and the king said to her,

"See, I am going to another country to eat the air. What would you like me to bring for you when I return?"

"King," she answered, "if you can bring me what I want I will tell you what it is; but if you cannot get it, I will not tell you." "Tell me what it is," said the king. "Whatever it may be I will bring it you." "Good," said the princess. "I want a sun-jewel box." Now the princess knew all about the sun-jewel boxes, and that only fairies had such boxes. And she knew, too, what would be in hers if the king could get one for her, although these boxes contain sometimes one thing and sometimes another.

The king had never heard of such a box, and did not know what it was like; so he went to every country asking all the people he met what sort of box was a sun-jewel box, and where he could get it. At last one day, after a fruitless search, he was very sad, for he thought, "I have promised the servant to bring her a sun-jewel box, and now I cannot get one for her; what shall I do?"

Then he went to sleep, and had a dream. In it he saw a jungle, and in the jungle a fakír who, when he slept, slept for twelve years, and then was awake for twelve years. The king felt sure this man could give him what he wanted, so when he woke he said to his sepoys and servants, "Stay here in this spot till I return to you; then we will go back to my country."

He mounted his horse and set out for the jungle he had seen in his dream. He went on and on till he came to it, and there he saw the fakír lying asleep. He had been asleep for twelve years all but two weeks: over him were a quantity of leaves, and grass, and a great deal of mud. The king began taking off all the grass, and leaves, and mud, and every day for a fortnight when he got up he cleared them all away from off the fakír. When the fakír awoke at the end of the two weeks, and saw that no mud, or grass, or leaves were upon him, but that he was quite clean, he was very much pleased, and said to the king, " I have slept for twelve years, and yet I am as clean as I was when I went to sleep. When I awoke after my last sleep, I was all covered with dirt and mud, grass and leaves ; but this time I am quite clean."

The king stayed with the fakír for a week, and waited on him and did everything for him. The fakír was very much pleased with the king, and he told this to him : "You are a very good man." He added, " Why did you come to this jungle? You are such a great king, what can you want from me ? " " I want a sun-jewel box," answered the king. " You are such a good man," said the fakír, " that I will give you one."

Then the fakír went to a beautiful well, down which he went right to the bottom. There, there was a house in which lived the red fairy. She was called the red fairy not because her skin was red, for it was quite white, but because everything about her was red—her house, her clothes, and her country. She was very glad to see the fakír, and asked him why he had come to see her. " I want you to give me a sun-jewel box," he answered. " Very good," said the fairy, and she brought him one in which were seven small dolls and a little flute. " No one but she who wants this box must open it," said the fairy to the fakír. " She must open it when she is quite alone and at night." Then she told him what was in the box.

The fakír thanked her, and took the box to the king, who was delighted and made many salaams to the fakír. The fakír told him none but the person who wished for the box was to open it ; but he did not tell him what more the fairy had said.

The king set off on his journey now, and when he came to his servants and sepoys, he said to them he would now return to his country, as he had found the box he wanted.

When he reached his palace he called the false princess, his wife, and gave her her silks and shawls, and sárís, and gold and silver jewels. Then he called the servant-girl—the true princess—and gave her her sun-jewel box. She took it, and was delighted to have it. She made him many salaams and went away with her box, but did not open it then, for she knew what was in it, and that she must open it at night and alone.

That night she took her box and went out all by herself to a wide plain in the jungle, and there opened it. She took the little flute, put it to her lips, and began to play, and instantly out flew the seven little dolls, who were all little fairies, and they took chairs and carpets from the box, and arranged them all in a large tent which appeared at that moment. Then the fairies bathed her, combed and rolled up her hair, put on her grand clothes and lovely slippers. But all the time the princess did nothing but cry. They brought a chair and placed it before the tent, and made her sit in it. One of them took the flute and played on it, and all the others danced before the princess, and they sang songs for her. Still she cried and cried. At last, at four o'clock in the morning, one of the fairies said, " Princess, why do you cry ? " " I took all the needles out of the king, all but those in his eyes," said the princess, " and while I was bathing, my servant-girl, whom I had bought with my gold bangles, pulled these out. She told the king it was she who had pulled out all the other needles and brought him to life, and that I was her servant, and she has taken my place and is treated as the princess, and the king has married her, while I am made to do a servant's work and treated as the servant." " Do not cry," said the fairies. " Everything will be well for you by and by."

When it was close on morning, the princess played on the flute, and all the chairs, sofas, and fairies became quite tiny, and went into the box, and the tent disappeared. She shut it up, and took it back to the king's palace. The next night she again went out to the jungle-plain, and all happened as on the night before.

A wood-cutter was coming home late from his work, and had to pass by the plain. He wondered when he saw the tent. "I went by some time ago," he said to himself, "and I saw no tent here." He climbed up a big tree to see what was going on, and saw the fairies dancing before the princess, who sat outside the tent, and he saw how she cried though the fairies did all they could to amuse her. Then he heard the fairies say, "Princess, why do you cry?" And he heard her tell them how she had cured the king, and how her servant-girl had taken her place and made her a servant. "Never mind, don't cry," said the fairies. "All will be well by and by." Near morning the princess played on her flute, and the fairies went into the box, and the tent disappeared, and the princess went back to the palace.

The third night passed as the other two had done. The wood-cutter came to look on, and climbed into the tree to see the fairies and the princess. Again the fairies asked her why she cried, and she gave the same answer.

The next day the wood-cutter went to the king. "Last night and the night before," he said, "as I came home from work, I saw a large tent in the jungle, and before the tent there sat a princess who did nothing but cry, while seven fairies danced before her, or played on different instruments, and sang songs to her." The king was very much astonished, and said to the wood-cutter, "To-night I will go with you, and see the tent, and the princess, and the fairies."

When it was night the princess went out softly and opened her box on the plain. The wood-cutter fetched the king, and the two men climbed into a tree, and watched the fairies as they danced and sang. The king saw that the princess who sat and cried was his own servant-girl. He heard her tell the fairies all she had done for him, and all that had happened to her ; so he came suddenly down from the tree, and went up to her, and took her hand. "I always thought you were a princess, and no servant-girl," he said. "Will you marry me ?"

She left off crying, and said, "Yes, I will marry you." She played on her flute, and the tent disappeared, and all the fairies, and sofas, and chairs went into the box. She put her flute in it, as she always did before shutting down the lid, and went home with the king.

The servant-girl was very vexed and angry when she found the king knew all that had happened. However, the princess was most good to her, and never treated her unkindly.

The princess then sent a letter to her mother, in which she wrote, "I am going to be married to a great king. You and my father must come to my wedding, and must bring my sisters with you."

They all came, and her father and mother liked the king very much, and were glad their daughter should marry him. The wedding took place, and they stayed with her for some time. For a whole week she gave their servants and sepoys nice food cooked with salt, but to her father and mother and sisters she only gave food cooked with sugar. At last they got so tired of this sweet food that they could eat it no longer. At the end of the week she gave them a dinner cooked with salt. Then her father said, "My daughter is wise though she is so young, and is the youngest of my daughters. I know now how much she loved me when she said she loved me like salt. People cannot eat their food without salt. If their food is cooked with sugar one day, it must be cooked with salt the next, or they cannot eat it."

After this her father and mother and sisters went home, but they often came to see their little daughter and her husband.

The princess, the king, and the servant-maid all lived happily together.

Told by Múniyá.

XXIV.

THE DEMON IS AT LAST CONQUERED BY THE KING'S SON.

IN a country there were seven men, no two of whom belonged to the same family, or were of the same trade. One was a grain merchant's son, one a baker's, and so on ; each had a different trade.

These seven men determined they would go to seek for service in another country. They said good-bye to their fathers and mothers, and set off.

They travelled every day, and walked through many jungles. At last, a long way from their homes, they came to a wide plain in the midst of a jungle, and on it they saw a goat which seemed to be a very good milch-goat. The seven men said to each other, "If this goat belonged to any one, it would not be left all alone in the jungle. Let us take it with us." They did so, and no one they met asked them any questions about the goat.

In the evening they arrived at a village where they stayed for the night. They cooked and ate their dinners, and gave the goat grass and grain. At midnight, when they were all asleep, the goat became a great she-demon, with a great mouth, and swallowed one of the seven men. Then she became a goat again, and went back to the place where she had been stabled.

The men got up in the morning, and were very much surprised to find they were only six, not seven. "Where is the seventh gone? " they said. " Well, when he returns we will all go on together." They sat waiting and waiting for him, till, as it was getting late and he had not come, they all thought they had better start without him. So they continued their journey, taking the goat with them. Before they went they said to the villagers, " If our seventh man comes back to you, send him after us."

At evening they came to another village, where they stayed for the night. They cooked and ate their dinners, and gave grain and grass to the goat. At midnight, when they were fast asleep, the goat became a demon and swallowed another man, and then took her goat's shape again.

In this way she ate five men. The two that were left were very sad at finding themselves alone. " We were seven men," they said, " now we are but two." The grain merchant's son was one of the two, and he was very quick and sharp. He determined he would not say anything to his companion, but that he would watch by him that night, and find out, if he could, what had happened to his other friends. To keep himself awake he cut a piece out of his finger, and rubbed a little salt into the wound, so that when his companion went to sleep, he should not be able to sleep because of the pain. At midnight the goat came and turned into a huge demon. She went quickly up to the sleeping man to swallow him ; but the merchant's son rushed at her, beat her, and snatched his companion from her mouth. The demon turned instantly into a goat, and went back to the place where it had been stabled.

The two men next morning set out from the village where they had passed the night. They would have killed the goat had they been able. As they could not do so, they took it with them till they came to a plain in the jungle, where they tied it up to a tree, and left it. Then they continued their journey, and were very sorry they had not known how wicked the goat was before it had swallowed their five companions.

The goat meanwhile turned itself into a most beautiful young girl, dressed in grand clothes and rich jewels, and she sat down in the jungle and began to cry. Just then the king of another country was hunting in this jungle; and when he heard the noise of the crying, he called his servants and told them to go and see who was crying. The servants looked about until they saw the beautiful girl. They asked her a great many questions, but she only cried, and would not answer. The servants returned to the king, and told him it was a most beautiful young girl who was crying; but she would do nothing but cry, and would not speak.

The king left his hunting and went himself to the girl, and asked her why she cried. " My husband married me." she said, " and was taking me to his home. He went to get some water to drink, and left me here. He has never come back, and I don't know where he is ; perhaps some tiger has killed him, and now I am all alone, and do not know where to go. This is why I cry." The king was so delighted with her beauty, that he asked her to go with him. He sent his servants for a fine palanquin, and when it came he put the girl into it, and took her to his palace, and there she stayed.

At midnight she turned into a demon, and went to the place where the king's sheep and goats were kept. She tore open all their stomachs, and ate all their hearts. Then she dipped seven knives in their blood, and laid the knives on the beds of the seven queens.

Next morning the king heard that all his sheep and goats were lying dead; and when his seven wives woke, they saw that their clothes were all bloody, and that bloody knives lay on their beds. They wondered who had done this wicked thing to them.

The next night at twelve o'clock the beautiful girl turned into a demon again, and went to the cow-house. There she tore open the cows and ate their hearts. Then she smeared the queens' clothes, and laid knives dipped in blood on their beds ; but she washed her own hands and clothes, so that no blood should show on them. For a long time the same thing happened every night, till she had eaten all the elephants, horses, camels,—every animal, indeed, belonging to the king. The king wondered very much at his animals all being killed in this way, and he could not understand either why every morning his wives' clothes were bloody, and bloody knives found on their beds.

When she had eaten all the animals, the demon said to the king, " I am afraid your wives are very wicked women. They must have killed all your cows and sheep, goats, horses, elephants, and camels. I am afraid one day they will eat me up." " I have been married to them for many years," answered the king, " and anything like this has never happened before." " I am very much afraid of them," said the demon, who all this time looked a most beautiful girl. " I am very much afraid ; but if you cut out their eyes, then they cannot kill me "

The king called his servants and said to them, " Get ready seven palanquins, and carry my seven wives into the jungle. There you must leave them ; only first take out their eyes, which you must bring to me." The servants took the queens to a jungle a long way from the king's country. There they took out their eyes, and left them, and brought the eyes to the king, who gave them into the demon's hands. She pounded them to bits with a stone, and threw the bits away.

The seven queens in the jungle did not know which way to go ; so they walked straight on, and fell into a dry well which lay just before them. In this well they stayed ; and the day when they thought they must die of hunger and thirst was drawing near. But before it came the eldest queen had a little son. She and the five next wives were so hungry, that they agreed to kill the child, and divide it into seven pieces. They each ate a piece, and gave one to the seventh and youngest wife. She said nothing, and hid the piece. These five wives each had a son one after the other, and they killèd and divided their children as the eldest wife had done with hers. But the youngest wife hid all the six pieces that were given her, and would eat none. Her son was born last of all. Then the six eldest wives said, " Let us kill and divide your child." " No," she said, " I will never kill or divide my boy ; I would rather die of hunger. Here are the six pieces you gave me. I would not eat them. Take them and eat them, but you must not touch my son." God was so pleased with her for not killing her child, that he made the boy grow bigger and bigger every day ; and the little queen was very happy.

They all lived in the dry well without any food till the little prince was five years old. By that time he was very quick and clever. One day he said to his mother, " Why have we lived all this while in the well ? " His mother and all the other wives told him about the wicked demon who lived in his father's palace, and how the king believed her to be a beautiful girl and had married her, and of all the evil things that she had done to them, and how she had made the king send them to the jungle and have their eyes cut out and given to her, and how from not being able to see they had fallen into this well, and how they had eaten all his brothers, because they were so very hungry they thought they should die—all but his mother at least, for she would not eat the other wives' children and would not kill her own little son. " Let me climb out of this well," said the boy, who determined in his heart that he would kill this wicked

N

demon one day. His mother said, " No, stay here ; you are too young to leave the well."

The boy did not listen to her, but scrambled out. Then he saw they were in a wide plain in the jungle. He ran after a few birds, caught and killed them. Then he roasted the birds and brought them with some water to his seven mothers in the well. When they had eaten them and drunk the water, they were happy and worshipped God. The six mothers who had eaten their children were full of sorrow, and said, "If our six sons were now living, how good it would be for us : how happy we should be." The young prince went out hunting for little birds every day, and in the evening he cooked those he caught and brought them, with water, to his mothers.

Now the demon, because she was a demon and was therefore wiser than men and women, knew that the seven queens lived in the well, and that the son of the youngest queen was still alive. She determined to kill him ; so she pretended her eyes hurt her, and began crying, and making a great to-do. The king asked her, "What is the matter?" "See, king, see my eyes," she said. "They ache and hurt me so much." "What medicine will make them well again?" said the king. "If I could only bathe them with a tigress's milk, they would be well," she answered.

The king called two of his servants and said to them, "Can either of you get me a tigress's milk? Here are two thousand rupees for whichever of you brings me the milk." Then he gave them the rupees, and told them to get it at once.

The servants took the rupees, and said nothing to the king, but they said to each other, "How can we get a tigress's milk?" And they were very sad. They left the king's country, and wandered on till they came to the jungle-plain, where lived the young prince and his mothers. There they saw him sitting by a dry well and roasting birds. "Do you live in this jungle?" they said to him. "Yes," answered the boy. Then the servants talked together. "See," they said, "this boy lives in the jungle, so he will surely be able to get us the milk. Let us tell him to get it, and give him the two thousand rupees."

So they came back to the boy, who asked them where they were going. "Our queen is very ill with pain in her eyes, and our king has sent us for some tigress's milk for her to bathe them with, that they may get well. He has given us two thousand rupees, for whichever of us to keep who gets the milk. But we do not know where or how to get it."

"Good," said the boy; "give me the two thousand rupees and I will get it for you. Come here for it in a week's time."

The king's servants were very much pleased at not having to try and get it themselves, so they gave him the rupees and went home. The demon knew quite well when she asked for the milk that none of the king's servants would dare to go for it, but that his son would be brave enough to go. This is why she asked for it, for she meant the tigers to kill him.

The little prince now took his seven mothers out of the well, and they all went together to his father's country. There he got a small house for them, and good clothes and food. He got a servant, too, for them, to cook their dinner and take care of them. "Be very tender to them," he said to the servant, "for they cannot see." For himself he bought a little horse, and good clothes, and a gun, and a sword. Then he made his mothers many salaams, and told them he was going to get a tigress's milk. They all cried and begged him not to go.

But he set off and rode for three or four days through the jungles. Then he came to a large jungle which was in a great blaze, and two tiger-cubs were running about in the jungle trying to get out of the fire. He jumped off his horse, and took them in his hands; then he mounted his horse

again and rode out of the jungle. He rode on till he came
to another which was not on fire. He let the cubs loose in
it that they might run away ; but they placed themselves in
front of his horse, and said, " We will not let you go till you
have seen our father and mother."

Meanwhile the tiger and tigress saw the boy coming with
their cubs, and they came running to meet them. Till then
they had thought their cubs were burned in the jungle-fire.
Now they knew at once this boy had saved them. The
cubs said to their father and mother, " We should have died
had it not been for this boy. Give him food ; and when he
has eaten some food, we will drink milk." The tigers were
very happy at having their children safe. They went to a
garden and got food and good water for the boy, who ate
and drank. Then the little cubs drank their mother's
milk.

The tiger said to the prince, " You are such a little child,
how is it your mother let you come alone to this jungle ? "

" My mother's eyes are sore and pain her ; and the doctor
says that if she bathes them in a tigress's milk they will get
well. So I came to see if I could get a little for her."

" I will give you some," said the tigress, and she gave him
a little jar full of her milk. The cubs said, " One of us will go
with you, and the other will stay with our father and mother."
" No," said the little prince, " do you both stay with your
father and mother. I will not take either of you away.
What should I do with you ? " " No," said one of the cubs ;
" I will go with you. I will do all you tell me. Wherever
you bid me stay, there I will stay ; and I will eat any food
you give me." " Take him with you," said the old tiger ;
" one day you will find him of use." So the boy took the
cub and the milk, and made his salaam to the old tigers
and went home. His mothers were delighted at his return,
though, as they had no eyes, they could not see him.

He tied up the tiger's cub and fed him. Then he took a little of the milk, and went to the dry well in the jungle and sat down by it. The king's servants came when the week had passed, and the boy gave them the milk. The servants took it to the king, who gave it to the demon. She was very angry when she found the tigers had not eaten the boy; but she bathed her eyes with the milk, and said nothing.

At the end of another week she would not eat or drink, and did nothing but cry. "What is the matter?" said the king. "See how my eyes pain me," she answered. "If I could only get an eagle's feather to lay on them they would be well. Oh, how they hurt me!"

The king called his servants and gave them four thousand rupees. "Go and get me an eagle's feather," he said, "and he who gets it is to take the four thousand rupees." Let us go to the jungle well," they said, "and find the boy who got us the tigress's milk. We could never get an eagle's feather, but this child certainly can get one for us."

So they went to the well where they found the boy. The little prince was very wise, though he was such a little child; and he knew the demon would try to send him on some other errand that she might get rid of him. He was quite willing to go on her errands, for he thought he might thus learn how to kill her. He was not a bit afraid of being killed himself, for he knew that God loved him, and that no one but God could kill him.

He at once asked the king's servants, "What do you want now?" "Our king has sent us for an eagle's feather to lay on the queen's eyes, which pain her again. Here are four thousand rupees for you if you will get it for us." "Give me the rupees," said the king's son. "Come here in two weeks, and I will give you the feather."

He took the rupees to his mothers, and told them he was going to fetch an eagle's feather. "Where will you find one?"

they said. " I don't know," he answered, " but I am going
to look for one." He hired some more servants, and told
them to take care of his mothers and the tiger-cub.

He rode straight on for two or three days, and at last
came to a very dense jungle, through which he rode for
another three or four days. When he got out of it he
found himself on a beautiful smooth plain in which was
a tank. There, too, was a large fig-tree, and under the tree
cool shade, and cool, thick grass. He was very much
pleased when he saw the tank and the tree. He got off his
horse, bathed in the tank, and sat down under the fig-tree,
thinking, " Here I will sleep a little while before I go
further."

While he lay asleep in the grass, a great snake crawled up
the tree, at the top of which were two young eagles. They
began screaming very loud. Their cries awakened the little
prince. He looked about and saw the great snake in the
tree. Then he took his gun and fired at it, and the snake
fell dead to the ground. He cut it into five pieces, and hid
them in the long grass. Then he lay down again and went
to sleep.

The baby eagles were alone in the tree, as their father and
mother had gone to another country. But now the old
birds came home, and found the king's son sleeping in the
grass. " See," they said, " here is the thief who every year
robs us of our children! But now he cannot get away.
We will kill him." However, they thought it better to go
and look first at their children, to see if they were safe or not.
They flew up to the top of the tree, and when they found
their children safe, they wished to give them food. All the
time they kept saying, " Eat ; then we will kill the thief
who steals away our children every year." The young eagles
thought, " Oh, if God would only give us the power to
speak, then we would tell our father and mother that this

boy is no thief." Then God gave them the power to speak, and they said to the old eagles, " Listen ; if that boy had not been here, we should have died, for he killed a huge snake that was going to swallow us : only go and look, and you will see it dead and cut into pieces." And the eaglets refused to eat till the boy had been fed.

The big eagles flew down and found the bits of the snake : so they flew away to a beautiful garden, where they got delicious fruits and water. These they brought to the boy, and awoke him and fed him. Then they said to him, " It is indeed good to find our children alive. Hitherto our children have always been eaten by that snake. How are your father and mother? Why did they let you come to this jungle ? What have you come here for ? " The little prince said, " My mother's eyes are very sore ; but they would be cured if she could have an eagle's feather to lay on them. So I came to look for one." Then the mother gave him one of her feathers.

When the boy was going home, the eaglets said they would go with him. " No," he said, " I will not take you with me." But the old birds said, " Take one of them, it will help you one day." The little prince made his salaam to the big eagles, and took one of their young ones, mounted his horse, and rode off. The eaglet flew over his head to shade him from the sun.

When he got home to his seven mothers, he took the feather and went and sat by the dry well. The king's servants came there to him, and he gave them the feather, and said, " Take it to your king." This they did, and the king gave it to the demon, who flew into a great rage. She said to herself, " The tigers did not kill him, and now the eagles have not killed him."

At the end of two weeks she began to cry and would not eat. The king asked her, " What is the matter with you ?

what has happened to you?" "My eyes pain me so much," she said. "What will cure them?" said the king. "If I had only some night-growing rice," she said, "I would boil it, and make rice-water, which I would drink. Then I should get well." Now this night-growing rice was a wonderful rice that no men, and only one demon, possessed. This was the demon-queen's brother. He used to put a grain of this rice into his huge cavern of a mouth at night when he went to sleep, and when he woke in the morning this grain would have become a tree. Then the demon used to take the rice-tree out of his mouth.

The demon, who seemed such a lovely girl, now wrote a letter to her brother, in which she said, "The bearer of this letter goes to you for some night-growing rice. You must kill him at once; you must not let him live." The king gave this letter to his servants, with six thousand rupees. "Take this letter," he said, "and fetch some of the night-growing rice. Here are six thousand rupees for whichever of you finds it." The king had no idea that it was not these men who had gone for the tigress's milk and the eagle's feather.

The servants said, "Let us go to the well, to the boy who has helped us before. We don't know where to get this night-growing rice, but that boy is sure to know."

The boy was sitting by the well, and asked what they wanted. They answered, "See, the king has given us six thousand rupees and a letter, and told us to fetch him some night growing rice." "Very good," said the king's son. "Come here in three weeks' time, and I will give you some." The servants gave him the rupees and returned home.

He took the rupees to his mothers, and told them he was going on a fresh errand, and they were to keep the money. Then he made them salaams, took his letter, and rode off. The eaglet went too, and flew above his head. The tiger's cub he left at home.

He rode on and on through a very large jungle, and he rode a long, long way : at last in a jungle he saw a fakír, who was living in it. He made him salaams, and the fakír was delighted to see him, "because," he said, "for many years I have been in this country, and all that time have never seen any man." The prince sat down by the fakír, and the fakír was very much pleased. He asked the boy who had sent him to the jungle, and why he had come to it. " My mother has sore eyes," he answered, "and wants some night-growing rice. She has given me a letter to the man who owns it."

The fakír took and read the letter, and was very sorry. He tore it up and threw it away. Then he wrote another, in which he said, " Your sister is very ill, and her son has come for some night-growing rice for her." This he gave to the boy, and told him to continue his journey. He also told him that the man who had the rice was a huge demon, and that he lived in the country by the great sea. Then he told him the way.

The boy rode on and on, and after a week's journeying he came to the demon's country. There he saw the huge demon sitting on the ground, with his great, big mouth, that was just like a cavern. As soon as the demon saw him he stood up and said, " It is many days since a man came here. Now I will eat this one." He went towards the prince to seize him, and a great rushing wind came blowing from the demon, as it always did when he was angry. But the boy, who had begun to walk towards him when he stood up, threw the letter to him with all his might, so that it fell on him ; at the same time he made many salaams. The demon read the letter, and found his sister was very ill, and this was her son ; so he stopped the wind, and came up to the boy, who he thought was his sister's son. " You have come for the rice for my sister who is ill," he said to him ; " you shall have it."

The demon had a splendid house full of beautiful things, and a great many servants. He took the little prince home with him, and told his servants to get water ready and gave the child a bath. They were also to cook a good dinner for him. Then the demon showed the boy all his gardens, and all his beautiful things, and took him through all the rooms of his house. One room he did not show to the prince. He told him he was never to go into it, though he might go everywhere else that he liked. In this room lived the demon's daughter, who was very beautiful, just like a fairy. She was ten years old. Every day before her father went out, he used to make the girl lie on her bed, and cover her with a sheet, and he placed a thick stick at her head, and another at her feet ; then she died till he came home in the evening and changed the sticks, putting the one at her head at her feet, and the one at her feet at her head. This brought her to life again.

The next day, when the demon had gone out, the boy went to this room, and opened the door, for he wanted to see what was in it. He went in, and saw the beautiful girl lying on the bed. " How lovely she is !" he said ; " but she is dead." Then he saw the sticks, and, to amuse himself, he put the one at her head at her feet, and the one at her feet at her head, just as the demon did every evening. The girl at once came to life, and opened her eyes and got up. "Who is this?" she said to herself, when she saw the king's son. "This is not my father." She asked him, " Who are you ? Why do you come here ? If my father sees you he will eat you." " No, he won't," said the prince, " for I am your aunt's son, and your father himself brought me to his house. But why is it that you are dead all day, and alive all night ?" The girl had told him that her father brought her to life every evening, and made her dead every morning. " Such is my father's pleasure," she answered.

So they talked together all day, and he said to her, "Suppose one day your father made you dead as usual, and that he was killed before he had brought you to life, what would you do? You would always be dead then." "Listen," she said; "no one can kill my father." "Why not?" said the boy. "Listen," she answered; "on the other side of the sea there is a great tree, in that tree is a nest, in the nest is a *mainá*. If any one kills that *mainá*, then only will my father die. And if, when the *mainá* is killed, its blood falls to the ground, a hundred demons would be born from this blood. This is why my father cannot be killed."

At evening, before the demon came home, the prince made the girl dead. Then he went softly into another room.

The fakír had said to the boy, when they were in the jungle together, "If ever you are in trouble, come to me and I will help you. It will take you now one week to ride to the demon's country; but if ever you need me, you shall be able to come to me here in this jungle, and to return to the demon's house in one day." The fakír was such a holy man that everything he said should happen did happen. So now the prince determined he would go to the fakír and ask him what he should do to kill this *mainá*. In the morning, therefore, as soon as the demon had gone out, he set off for the fakír's jungle, and, thanks to the holy man's power, he got there very quickly. He told him everything, and the fakír made a paper boat which he gave him. "This boat will take you over the sea," he said to the prince. "This paper boat!" said the boy. "How can a paper boat go over the sea? It will get soaked and sink." "No, it will not," said the fakír. "Launch it on the sea, and get into it. The boat will of itself carry you to the tree where the *mainá's* nest is."

The prince took the boat, and went back to the demon's house. He got there before the demon came home, so that he did not know the boy had been to the fakír. When the demon returned that evening, the king's son said, "To-morrow I will go home, as my mother is very ill. Will you give me the rice?" "Good," said the demon, "you shall have it to-morrow." Next morning he gave the rice, and went off to the jungle.

Then the boy took his paper boat down to the sea, launched it, and got into it; and of itself the boat went straight over the sea to the opposite shore. The eaglet flew above his head; but he left his horse on land. When he got to the other side, he saw the great tree, with the nest and the *mainá*. He climbed the tree, and took down the nest, and the demon, who was far away, knew it at once, and said to himself, "Some one has come to catch and kill me." He set out at once for the tree. The prince saw him coming, so he wrapped the *mainá* up in his handkerchief, that no blood should fall to the ground. Then he broke off one of its legs, and one of the demon's legs fell off. Still the demon came on. Then he broke off the other leg, but the demon walked on his hands. The boy saw him coming nearer and nearer, so he wrung the bird's head off, and the demon fell dead.

The prince jumped into his paper boat, and of itself the boat went straight back to the other shore, to the demon's country. Then he went up to the demon's house, and made his daughter alive.

She was frightened, and said to him, "Oh, take care. If my father comes back, and finds us together, he will eat us both." "He will not come back," said the prince. "I have killed him."

Then he dressed her in boy's clothes, that no one might know she was a girl, and he found a horse, and had it made ready for her. Her father had collected a quantity of rupees. Some of these the prince gave to the servants as a present, and said to them, "Stay here and be happy; do not be afraid, for there is no demon now to come and eat you."

Then he took the rice and mounted his horse, and made the girl mount also, and went off to the fakír. The paper boat he left, as he did not want it any more. He and the demon's daughter made the fakír many salaams, and they stayed with him for a day before they rode to the prince's country. Here they went to his seven mothers, who were very, very glad to see them, and thanked God that their son had come back safe.

He took a little of the rice, and went and sat by the well till the king's two servants came. Then he gave them the rice for their king, and the king gave it to the demon. She said nothing while the king was with her; but when she was alone she cried, for she knew the boy must have killed her brother, as he had brought her the rice.

She waited a week, and then she began to cry again, and would not eat. The king was very sorry, and thought, "What can I do to make her well and happy?" Then he said, "What will cure your eyes?" "See, king," she answered, "if I could only bathe my eyes with water from the Glittering Well, they would not pain me any more." This well was in the fairies' country, and was guarded by the demon's sister, whose name was Jangkatar. She lived in the well; and when any one came to draw water from it, she used to drag him down and eat him.

The king called his servants, gave them eight thousand rupees, and said, "Go and fetch me water from the Glittering Well." The servants went at once to the dry well in the jungle. There they found the prince, who asked them what they wanted. "Here are eight thousand rupees," they said; "and the king has ordered us to bring him water from the Glittering Well." "Come in three weeks, and I will give it to

you," said the king's son.   He took to his mothers the eight
thousand rupees which the servants had given him, and said
to them, "Take care of these rupees, for I am going away
for a little while."   Then he got his horse ready and mounted
it, and made many salaams to his mothers.   The tiger-cub
said to him, "Take me with you this time.   Last time you
only took the eagle.   Now we will both go with you."

So he rode off; and the eaglet flew above his head and
the young tiger ran by his side.   It took him a week to get
to the fairies' country, and then he came to a beautiful
smooth plain, in which was a garden, but no house.   In
the middle of this garden was the Glittering Well.   It was
a deep well, and the water sprang up out of it like a fountain,
and then fell back into the well, and the water shone and
sparkled as if it were gold, and silver, and diamonds.   This
is why it was called the Glittering Well.

The prince dipped his jar in the well, and Jangkatar put
up her hand and caught him.   She dragged him into the
water and swallowed him whole.   Then the young eagle
flew down into the well, seized Jangkatar in his talons, and
took her out and threw her on the ground.   The tiger-cub
rushed at her instantly, tore her open, and pulled the king's
son out of her.   But he was half dead.   The cub and the
eaglet lay down on him to warm him, and when they had
warmed him, he was better.

"We have saved you," they said to him.   "But for us
you would have died."   The young prince thanked them
and caressed them.   "It is quite true," he said; "without
you I should have died."   Then he filled his jar with water,
and mounted his horse and rode home.   He made salaams
to his seven mothers, with whom all this time the demon's
daughter had stayed.   He bathed his mothers' eyes with the
water from the Glittering Well, and then they saw perfectly
once more.

He took a little of the water, and went to wait for the king's servants by the dry jungle well, and he was very happy thinking that now his mothers could see. He gave the water to the king's servants, who took it to the king, and the king gave it to his demon-wife, and she was very sad and angry, for she knew the boy must have killed her sister, the guardian of the Glittering Well.

When a whole month had passed, and he had not been sent on any more errands, the king's son said to himself, " Good; now nothing more is going to happen to me. I am not to be sent anywhere else." So he bought a fine horse and grand clothes, and rode to the king's court-house. He went in, and seated himself at the king's right hand; but he made no salaam to the king, and spoke to no one. This he did every day for three days. Everybody was wondering who this boy was, and why he never made any salaam to the king.

On the fourth day, as he sat at the king's right hand, the king asked him, " Whose child are you? Where do you come from? Where are you going? " The young prince answered, " See, king, I am a merchant's son; my ship has been wrecked, and I want to find service with some one." " What can you do? " asked the king. " I don't know any trade," said his son; " but I can tell you a story." " What wages do you want? " said the king. " One thousand rupees a day," answered the boy. " I shall only stay a short time in your country." " Good," said the king; " I will give you one thousand rupees a day, and a servant to wait on you besides. So come every day to my court ·house, and tell me your story."

The prince told the king his own story. He began from where the king found the beautiful demon-girl crying in the jungle, and ended it where his demon-wife cried and cried for her sister Jangkatar. It took him three weeks to tell the story; and when he had finished it, the king knew that he himself was the king in the story, and that this boy was his own son. "How can I find my seven queens again?" he said. "If you will kill this wicked demon-woman they will come back to you," said his son. The king was very sad, and thought, "My seven wives and my boy must have suffered very much." Then he loved his son, and was very happy that he had found him. He ordered his servants to dig a deep pit in the jungle, so deep that should his demon-wife take her demon form when put into it, only her head would be above it. He thought that if her body were buried in the ground she would not be able to do them much harm while they were shooting her. Then he, and his son, and his servants took their guns and bows and arrows, and took the demon with them to the deep pit. She went quite quietly, though she knew they were going to kill her. Since Jangkatar's death she had been very quiet and sad. And now she thought, "That boy will most certainly kill me as he has killed my sister and brother. He is stronger than I am. I have no one else to send him to; and if I had, he could not be killed. What is the use of my trying to save myself?" So she went along quite quietly, looking like a beautiful girl. She let them put her into the pit, and shoot her to death with their guns and bows and arrows. Then they filled the pit up with earth.

The king went to his seven wives, and begged them to forgive him. He brought them, his son, and the demon's daughter home to his palace. Later the king married his son to the demon's daughter, and every one was glad.

But the king grieved that his six other sons were dead.

Told by Múniyá.

XXV.

THE FAN PRINCE.

N a country there lived a king who had a wife and seven daughters. One day he called all his daughters to him, and said to them, " My children, who gives you food ? and by whose permission do you eat it ? " Six of them answered, " Father, you give us food ; and by your permission we eat it." But the seventh and youngest said, " Father, God gives me my food ; and by my own permission I eat it." This answer made her father and mother very angry with their youngest daughter. They said, " We will not let our youngest child stay with us any longer." And her father called some servants and said to them, " Get a palanquin ready, and put my youngest daughter into it ; then carry her away to the jungle, and there leave her.

The servants got the palanquin ready, put the youngest princess into it, and carried her into the jungle. There they put the palanquin down and said to her, " We are going to drink some water." " Go home now," said the girl, " as my father ordered you to do." They left her, therefore, in the jungle alone, and went back to the king's palace.

The girl prayed to God and worshipped him ; then she went to sleep for a little while in her palanquin. When she awoke, it was evening, and she found in her palanquin a jar of water and some food on a plate which God had sent her while she slept. She knew that God had sent her this nice dinner, and thanked him and worshipped him. Then she bathed her face and hands in a little of the water, and ate and drank, and went to sleep quietly in her palanquin as night had come.

This little princess had always been a very gentle girl, and had always done what was right, and been very good, so God loved her dearly. While she slept, therefore, he made a beautiful palace for her on the jungle-plain where. she was lying in her palanquin. God made a garden and tank for her, too. When the princess woke in the morning, and got out of her palanquin, she saw the palace standing by its tank in a beautiful garden. " I never saw that palace before," she said. " It was not here last night." She went into the garden, and servants met her and made her salaams. The palace was far finer than her father's ; and when she went into it she found it full of servants. " To whom does this palace belong ? " she asked " To you," they answered. " God made all this for you last night, and he sent us to wait on you and be your servants." (Now, they were all men, not angels, that God had sent to take care of her.) The princess thanked God, and worshipped him.

A few days later, her father heard that in the jungle to which he had sent her a beautiful palace and garden and tank had suddenly appeared, and that in this palace she was living ; and he said, " Yes ; my daughter told me the truth : it is God who gives us everything. I know it is he who gave her this beautiful house." So some time passed, and the princess lived in her palace in the jungle ; but her father did not go to see her.

One day he said to himself, " To-day I will go and eat the air in another country, and I will go by water." So he ordered a boat to be got ready, and he went to his six daughters, and told them he was going away for a little while. " What would you like me to bring you from this other country ? " he said. " I will bring you anything you would like to have." Some of them wanted jewels, a necklace, a pair of earrings, and so on ; and some wanted silk stuffs for sárís and other clothes. Then the king remembered his youngest child, and thought, " I must send to her, and see what she would like." He called one of his servants, and told him to go to the jungle to his youngest daughter and say, "Your father is going to eat the air of another country. He wishes to know what you would like him to bring back for you."

The servant found the little princess reading her prayer-book. He gave her the king's message. "She said, "Sabr" (that is *wait*), for she meant him to wait for her answer till she had finished reading her prayers. The servant, however, did not understand, but went away at once to the king and told him, "Your daughter wants you to bring her Sabr." "Sabr?" said the king ; "what is Sabr? Never, mind, I will see if I can find any Sabr ; and if I do, I will bring it for her."

The king then went in his boat to another country. There he stayed for a little while and bought the jewels and silks for his six elder daughters. When he thought he should like to go home again, he went down to his boat and got into it. But the boat would not move, because he had forgotten one thing ; the thing his youngest daughter had asked for.

Suddenly he remembered he had not got any Sabr. So he gave one of his servants four thousand rupees, and told him to go on shore, and go through the bazar, and try and find the Sabr, and he was to give the four thousand rupees for it.

The man went to the bazar and asked every one if they, had Sabr to sell. Then he asked if they could tell him what it was. "No," they said, "but our king's son is called Sabr ; you had better speak to him."

The servant went to Prince Sabr. "Our king's youngest daughter," he said, "has asked her father to bring her Sabr, and the king has given me four thousand rupees to buy it for her; but I cannot get any, and no one knows what it is." The prince said, "Very good. Give this little box to your king, and tell him to give it to his youngest daughter. But it is only the princess who has asked for Sabr who is to open the box." Then he told the man to keep the four thousand rupees as a present from him.

The servant went back to the boat to the king and gave him the box, saying, "In this is the Sabr," and he told him Prince Sabr said no one but the youngest princess was to open it. And now the boat moved quite easily, and the king journeyed home safely.

He gave his six eldest daughters the presents he had brought for them, and sent the little box to his youngest daughter. She said, "My father has sent me this. I will look at it by and by." Then she put it away and forgot it. At the end of a month she found the little box, and thought, "I will see what my father has sent me," and opened the box. In it was a most lovely little fan. She was very much pleased, and fanned herself with it, and at once a beautiful prince stood before her.

The princess was delighted. "Who are you? Where did you come from?" she said. "My name is Prince Sabr," he answered. "Your father came to my father's country, and he said you had asked him to bring you Sabr, so I gave him this little fan for you. I am obliged to come to whoever uses this little fan with the right side turned outwards. And when you want me to go away, you must turn the right side of the fan towards you and then fan yourself with it." The little princess said, "Very good. And so your name is Prince Sabr?" They talked together for some time. Then she turned her fan, so that the wrong side was outside, and fanned herself with it, and the prince disappeared.

This went on for a month. The princess used to fan herself with the right side turned outwards, and then Prince Sabr came to her. When she turned her fan wrong side outwards and fanned herself, then he vanished.

One day the prince said to her, "I should like to marry you. Will you marry me?" "Yes," she answered. Then she wrote a letter to her father and mother and six sisters, in which she said, "Come to my wedding. I am going to marry Prince Sabr." They all came. Her father was very glad that she married Prince Sabr, and said, "I see it is true that God loves my youngest daughter."

The day of the wedding her six sisters said to her, "To-day we will not let the servants make your bed. We will make it ourselves for you." "I have plenty of servants to make it," she said; "but you can do so if you like." Her sisters went to make the bed. They took a glass bottle and ground it into a powder, and they spread the powder all over the side where Prince Sabr was to lie. This they did because they were angry at their youngest sister being married, while they, who were older, were not married, and they thought, being her elders, they should have married first, especially as they had lived in their father's palace, and been cared for, while she was cast out in the jungle.

When the wedding was over, and Prince Sabr and his wife had gone to bed, the prince became very ill, from the glass powder going into his flesh. "Turn your fan the wrong way and fan yourself quickly, that I may go home to my father's country," he said to her, "for I am very ill, and dare not remain here." So she fanned herself at once with the fan turned the wrong way. Then he went home to his father, and was very ill for a long while. The poor princess knew nothing of the glass powder.

Her father and mother and sisters went home after the wedding, and left the princess alone in her palace. Every day she turned her fan the right side outwards and fanned and fanned herself; but Prince Sabr never came. He was far too ill. One day she cried a great deal, and was very, very sad. "Why does my prince not come to me?" she said. "I don't know where he is, or what has become of him." That night she had a dream, and in her dream she saw Prince Sabr lying very ill on his bed.

When she got up in the morning she thought she must go and try to find her prince. So she took off all her beautiful clothes and jewels, and put on a yogí's dress. Then she mounted a horse and set out in the jungle. No one knew she was a woman, or that she was a king's daughter; every one thought she was a man.

She rode on till night, and then she had come to another jungle. Here she got off her horse, and took it under a tree. She lay down under the tree and went to sleep. At midnight she was awakened by the chattering of a parrot and a *mainá*, who came and sat on the tree knowing she was lying underneath.

The *mainá* said to the parrot, "Parrot, tell me something." The parrot said, "Prince Sabr is very, very ill in his own country. The day he was married, the bride's six sisters took a glass bottle and ground it to powder. Then they spread the powder all over the prince's bed, so that when he lay down it got into his flesh. The glass powder has made him very ill." "What will make him well?" said the *mainá*; "what will cure him?" "No doctors can cure him," said the parrot; "no medicine will do him any good : but if any one slept under this tree, and took some of the earth from under it, and mixed it with cold water, and rubbed it all over Prince Sabr, he would get well."

All this the princess heard. She got up and longed for morning to come. When it was day she took some of the

earth, mounted her horse, and rode off. She went on till she
came to Prince Sabr's country. Then she asked to whom
the country belonged ; she was told it was Prince Sabr's
father's country, "but Prince Sabr is very ill."

" I am a yogí," said the princess, "and I can cure him."
This was told to the king, Prince Sabr's father. "That
is very good," he said. "Send the yogí to me." So the
little princess went to the king, who said to her, "My son
is very, very ill; make him well." "Yes," she said, " I will
make him well. Bring me some cold water."

They brought her the cold water, and she mixed it with
the earth she had got from under the tree. This she rubbed
all over the prince. For three days and nights she rubbed
him with it. After that he got better, and in a week he
was quite well. He was able to talk, and could walk about
as usual.

Then the yogí said, " Now I will go back to my own
country." But the king said to her, " First you must let me
give you a present. You shall have anything that you like.
As many horses, or sepoys, or rupees)as you want you shall
have ; for you have made my son well." " I want nothing
at all," said the princess, "but Prince Sabr's ring, and the
handkerchief he has with his name worked on it." She
had given him both these things on their wedding day.
Prince Sabr's father and mother went to their son and begged
him to give the handkerchief and ring to the yogí ; and he
did so quite willingly. " For," he thought, "were it not for
that yogí, I should never see my dear princess again."

The yogí took the ring and handkerchief and went home.
When she got there, she took off her yogí's dress and put
on her own beautiful clothes. Then she turned her fan
right side outwards, and fanned herself with it, and immediately her Prince Sabr stood by her. "Why did you not
come to me before ? " she said. " I have been fanning and

fanning myself." "I was very ill, and could not come," said Prince Sabr. "At last a yogí came and made me well, and as a reward I gave him my ring and handkerchief." "It was no yogí," said the princess. "It was I who came to you and made you well." "You !" said the prince. "Oh, no ; it was a yogí. You were sitting here in your palace while the yogí came and cured me." "No, indeed," she said; "I was the yogí. See, is not this your ring? is not this your handkerchief with your name worked on it?" Then he believed her, and she told him of her dream, and her journey in the yogí's dress, and the birds' talk, and all that had happened.

And Prince Sabr was very happy that his wife had done so much for him, and they lived happily together.

Told by Múniyá.

XXVI.

THE BED.

IN a country there was a grain merchant's son, whose father and mother loved him so dearly that they did not let him do anything but play and amuse himself while they worked for him. They never taught him any trade, or anything at all; for they never reflected that they might die, and that then he would have to work for himself. When he was old enough to be married, they found a wife for him, and married him to her. Then they all lived happily together for some years till the father and mother both died.

Their son and his wife lived for awhile on the pice his father and mother had left him. But the wife grew sadder and sadder every day, for the pice grew fewer and fewer. She thought, "What shall we do when they are all gone? My husband knows no trade, and can do no work." One day when she was looking very sorrowful, her husband asked her, "What is the matter? Why are you so unhappy?" "We have hardly any pice left," she answered, "and what shall we do when we have eaten the few we have? You know no trade, and can do no work." "Never mind," said her husband, "I can do some work."

So one day when there were hardly any pice left, he took an axe, and said to his wife, "I am going out to-day to work. Give me my dinner to take with me, and I will eat it out of doors." She gave him some food, wondering what work he had; but she did not ask him.

He went to a jungle, where he stayed all day, and where he ate his dinner. All day long he wandered from tree to tree, saying to each, "May I cut you down?" But not a tree in the jungle gave him any answer: so he cut none down, and went home in the evening. His wife did not ask where he had been, or what he had done, and he said nothing to her.

The next day he again asked her for food to take with him to eat out of doors, "for," he said, "I am going to work all day." She did not like to ask him any questions, but gave him the food. And he took his axe, and went out to a jungle which was on a different side to the one he had been to yesterday. In this jungle also he went to every tree, and said to it, "May I cut you down?" No tree answered him; so he ate his dinner and came home.

The next day he went to a third jungle on the third side. There, too, he asked each tree, "May I cut you down?" But none gave him any answer. He came home therefore very sorrowful.

On the fourth day he went to a jungle on the fourth side. All day long he went from tree to tree, asking each, "May I cut you down?" None answered. At last, towards evening, he went and stood under a mango-tree. "May I cut you down?" he said to it. "Yes, cut me down," answered the tree. God loved the merchant's son and wished him to grow a great man, so he ordered the mango-tree to let itself be cut down.

Now the grain merchant's son was happy, for he was quite sure he could make a bed, if he only had some wood; so he hewed down the mango-tree, put it on his head, and carried it home. His wife saw him coming, and said to herself, "He is bringing home a tree! What can he be going to do with a tree?"

Next morning he took the tree into one of the rooms of his house. He told his wife to put food and water to last him for a week in this room, and to make a fire in it. Then he went up to the room, and said to her, " You are not to come in here for a whole week. You are not to came near me till I call you." Then he went into the room and shut the door. The whole week long his wife wondered what he could be doing all alone in that room. " I cannot see into it," she said to herself," and I dare not open the door. I wonder what he is about."

By the end of the week the grain merchant's son had carved a most beautiful bed out of the mango-tree. Such a beautiful bed had never been seen. Then he called his wife, and when she came he told her to open the door, and when she opened it he said, " See what a beautiful bed I have made." " Did *you* make that bed ? " she said. " Oh, what a beautiful bed it is ! I never saw such a lovely bed ! "

He rested that day, and on the day following he took the bed to the king's palace, and sat down with it before the palace gate. The king's servants all came to look at the bed. " What a bed it is ! " they said. " Did any one ever see such a bed ! It is a beautiful bed. Is it yours ? " they asked the merchant's son. " Is it for sale ? Who made it ? Did you make it ? " But he said, " I will not answer any of your questions. I will not speak to any of you. I will only speak to the king." So the servants went to the king and said to him, " There is a man at your gate with a most beautiful bed. But he will not speak to any of us, and says he will only speak to you." " Very good," said the king ; " bring him to me."

When the grain merchant's son came before the king with his bed, the king asked him, " Is your bed for sale ? " " Yes," he said. " What a beautiful bed it is ! " said the king. " Who made it ? " " I did," he said. " I made it myself." " How much do you want for it?" said the king. "One thousand rupees," answered the merchant's son. "That is a great deal for the bed," said the king. "I will not take less," said the merchant's son. "Good,"said the king, "I will give you the thousand rupees." So he took the bed, and the merchant's son said to him, "The first night you pass on it, do not go to sleep. Take care to keep awake, and you will hear and see something." Then he took the rupees home to his wife, who was frightened when she saw them. "Are those your rupees?" she said. "Where did you find such a quantity of rupees?" "The king gave them to me for my bed," he said. "I am not a thief; I did not steal them." Then she was happy.

That night the king lay down on his bed, and at ten o'clock he heard one of the bed's legs say to the other legs, "Listen, you three. I am going out to see the king's country. Do you all stand firm while I am away, and take care not to let the king fall." "Good," the three legs answered; "go and eat the air, and we will all stand fast, so that the king does not fall while you are away."

Then the king saw the leg leave the bed, and go out of his room door. The leg went out to a great plain, and there it saw two snakes quarrelling together. One snake said, "I will bite the king." The other said, "I will bite him." The first said, "No, you won't; I will climb on to his bed and bite him." "That you will never do," said the second. "You cannot climb on to his bed; but I will get into his shoe, and then when he puts it on to-morrow morning, I will bite his foot."

The bed-leg came back and told the other legs what it had seen and heard. "If the king will shake his shoe before he puts it on to-morrow morning," it said, "he will see a snake drop out of it." The king heard all that was said.

" Now," said the second bed-leg, " I will go out and eat the air of the king's country. Do you all stand firm while I am away." "Go," the others answered; "we will take care the king does not fall." The second bed-leg then went out, and went to another plain on which stood a very old palace belonging to the king, and the wind told it the palace was so ruinous that it would fall and kill the king the first time he went into it : the king had never once had it repaired. So it came back and told the three other legs all about the palace and what the wind had said. "If I were the king," said the second bed-leg, "I would have that palace pulled down. It is quite ready to fall ; and the first time the king goes into it, it will fall on him and kill him." The king lay, and listened to everything. As it happened, he had forgotten all about his old palace, and had not gone near it for a long time.

Then the third bed-leg said, "Now I will go out and see all the fun I can. Stand firm, you three, while I am away." He went to a jungle-plain on which lived a yogí. Now there was a sarai[1] not far off in which lived a woman, the wife of a sepoy, whose husband had gone a year ago to another country, leaving her in the sarai. She was so fond of the yogí, that she used to come and talk to him every night. That very day her husband came back to her, and therefore it was later than usual when she got to the yogí ; so he was very vexed with her. "How late you are to-night," he said. "It is not my fault," she answered. "My husband came home to-day after having been away a year, and he kept me." "Which of us do you love best ?" asked the yogí ; "your husband or me ?" "I love you best," said the woman. "Then," said the yogí, "go home and cut off your husband's head, and bring it here for me to see."

---

[1] That is, a resting-place for travellers, composed of a number of small houses in a walled enclosure.

The sepoy's wife went straight to the sarai, cut off her husband's head, and brought it to the yogí. "What a wicked woman you are to do such a thing at my bidding!" he said. "Go away at once. You are a wicked woman, and I do not want to see you." She took the head home, · set it again on the body and began to cry. All the people in the sarai came to see what was the matter. "Thieves have been here," she said, "and have killed my husband, and cut off his head," and then she cried again. The third bed-leg now went back to the palace, and told the others all it had seen and heard. The king lay still and listened.

The fourth bed-leg next went out to see all it could, and it came to a plain on which were seven thieves, who had just been into the king's palace, and had carried off his daughter on her bed fast asleep; and there she lay still sleeping. They had, too, been into the king's treasury and had taken all his rupees. The fourth bed-leg came quickly back to the palace, and said to the other three legs, "Now, if the king were wise he would get up instantly and go to the plain. For some thieves are there with his daughter and all his rupees which they have just stolen out of his palace. If he only made haste and went at once, he would get them again."

The king got up that minute, and called his servants and some sepoys, and set off to the plain. He shook his shoe before he put it on, and out tumbled the snake (the other had quietly gone into the jungle, and not come to the palace); so he saw that the first bed-leg had spoken the truth.

When he reached the plain he found his daughter and his rupees, and brought them back to his palace. The princess slept all the time, and did not know what had happened to her. The king saw the fourth leg had told the truth. The thieves he could not catch, for they all ran away when they saw him coming with his sepoys.

The king sent men to the old palace to pull it down. They found it was just going to fall, and would have fallen on any one who had entered it, and crushed him. So the second bed-leg had told the truth.

When the king was sitting in his court-house he heard how during the night thieves had gone into the sarai and killed a sepoy there and cut off his head. Then he sent for the sepoy's wife, and asked her who had killed her husband. "Thieves," she said. The king was very angry, for he was sure the third bed-leg had told the truth as the other three legs had done. So he ordered the man to be buried ; and bade his servants make a great wooden pile on the plain, and take the woman and burn her on it. They were not to leave her as long as she was alive, but to wait till she was dead.

He next sent for the grain merchant's son, and said to him, "Had it not been for your bed, I should this morning have been bitten by a snake ; and, perhaps, killed by my old palace falling on me, as I did not know it was ready to fall, and so might have gone into it. My daughter would certainly have been stolen from me ; and a wicked woman been still alive. So now, to-morrow, bring as many carts as you like, and I will give you as a present as many rupees as you can take away on them in half a day."

Early the next morning the merchant's son brought his cart and took away on them as many rupees as he could in half a day. His wife was delighted when she saw the money, and said, "My husband only worked for one week, and yet he earned all these rupees !" And they lived always happily.

Told by Múniyá, February 23rd, 1879.

XXVII.

PÁNWPATTÍ RÁNÍ.

I N a country a big fair was held, to which came a great many people and Rájás from all the countries round. Among them was a Rájá who brought his daughter with him. Opposite their tent another tent was pitched, in which lived a Rájá's son. He was very beautiful; so was the little Rání, the other Rájá's daughter.

Now, the Rájá's son and the Rájá's daughter did not even know each other's names, but they looked at each other a great deal, and each thought the other very beautiful. "How lovely the Rájá's daughter is!" thought the prince. "How beautiful the Rájá's son is!" thought the princess.

They lived opposite each other for a whole month, and all that time they never spoke to each other nor did they speak of each other to any one. But they thought of each other a great deal.

When the month was over, the little Rání's father said he would go back to his own country. The Rájá's son sat in his tent and watched the servants getting ready the little Rání's palanquin. As soon as the princess herself was dressed and ready for the journey, she came out of her tent, and took a rose in her hand. She first put the rose to her teeth; then she stuck it behind her ear; and lastly, she laid it at her feet. All this time the Rájá's son sat in his tent and looked at her. Then she got into her palanquin and was carried away

The Rájá's son was now very sad. "How lovely the princess is!" he thought. "And I do not know her name, or her father's name, or the name of her country. So how can I ever find her? I shall never see her again." He was very sorrowful, and determined he would go home to his country. When he got home he laid himself down on his bed, and night and day he lay there. He would not eat, or drink, or bathe, or change his clothes. This made his father and mother very unhappy. They went to him often, and asked him, "What is the matter with you? Are you ill?" "I want nothing," he would answer. "I don't want any doctor, or any medicine." Not one word did he say to them, or to any one else, about the lovely little Ráni.

The son of the Rájá's kotwál [1] was the prince's great friend. The two had always gone to school together, and had there read in the same book; they had always bathed, eaten, and played together. So when the prince had been at home for two days, and yet had not been to school or seen his friend, the kotwál's son grew very anxious. "Why does the prince not come to school?" he said to himself. "He has been here for two days, and yet I have not seen him. I will go and find out if anything is the matter. Perhaps he is ill."

He went, therefore, to see the prince, who was lying very miserable on his bed. "Why do you not come to school? Are you ill?" asked his friend. "Oh, it is nothing," said the prince. "Tell me what is the matter," said the kotwál's son; but the Rájá's son would not answer. "Have you told any one what is the matter with you?" said the kotwál's son. "No," answered the prince. "Then tell me," said his friend; "tell me the truth: what is it that troubles you?"

"Well," said the prince, "at the fair there was a Rájá who had a most beautiful daughter. They lived in a tent opposite

---

[1] The chief police officer in a town.

mine, and I used to see her every day. She is so beautiful ! But I do not know her name, or her father's name, or her country's name; so how can I ever find her ? " " I will take you to her," said his friend; " only get up and bathe, and eat." " How can you take me to her ? " said the prince. "You do not even know where she is; so how can you take me to her ? " " Did she never speak to you ? " said the kotwál's son. " Never," said the prince. " But when she was going away, just before she got into her palanquin, she took a rose in her hand ; and first she put this rose to her teeth ; then she stuck it behind her ear ; and then she laid it at her feet." " Now I know all about her," said his friend. "When she put the rose to her teeth, she meant to tell you her father's name was Rájá Dánt [Rájá Tooth]; when she put it behind her ear she meant you to know her country's name was Karnátak [on the ear]; and when she laid the rose at her feet, she meant that her name was Pánwpatti [Foot-leaf]. Get up; bathe and dress, eat and drink, and we will go and find her."

The prince got up directly, and told his father and mother he was going for a few days to eat the air of another country. At first they forbad his going ; but then they reflected that he had been very ill, and that perhaps the air of another country might make him well; so at last they consented. The prince and his friend had two horses saddled and bridled, and set off together.

At the end of a month they arrived in a country where they asked (as they had asked in every other country through which they had ridden), " What is the name of this country ? " " Karnátak " [the Carnatic]. " What is your Rájá's name ?" "Rájá Dánt." Then the two friends were glad. They stopped at an old woman's house, and said to her, " Let us stay with you for a few days. We are men from another country and do not know where to go in this place." The old woman said, "You may stay with me if you like. I live all alone, and there is plenty of room for you."

After two or three days the kotwál's son said to the old woman, "Has your Rájá a daughter?" "Yes," she answered; "he has a daughter; her name is Pánwpattí Rání." "Can you go to see her?" asked the kotwál's son. "Yes," she said, "I can go to see her. I was her nurse, and she drank my milk. It is the Rájá who gives me my house, and my food, and clothes—everything that I have." "Then go and see her," said the kotwál's son, "and tell her that the prince whom she called to her at the fair has come."

The old woman went up to the palace, and saw the princess. After they had talked together for some time, she said to the little Rání, "The prince you called to you at the fair is come." "Good," she said; "tell him to come to see me to-night at twelve o'clock. He is not to come in through the door, but through the window." (This she said because she did not want her father to know that the prince had come, until she had made up her mind whether she would marry him.)

The old woman went home and told the kotwál's son what the Princess Pánwpattí said. That night the prince went to see her, and every night for three or four nights he went to talk with her for an hour. Then she told her mother she wished to be married, and her mother told her father. Her father asked whom she wished to marry, and she said, "The Rájá's son who lives in my nurse's house." Her father said she might marry him if she liked; so the wedding was held. The kotwál's son went to the wedding, and then returned to the old woman's house; but the prince lived in the Rájá's palace.

Here he stayed for a month, and all that time he never saw his friend. At last he began to fret for him, and was very unhappy. "What makes you so said?" said Pánwpattí Rání.

P 2

" I am sad because I have not seen my friend for a whole month," answered her husband. " I must go and see him." " Yes, go and see him," said his wife. The Rájá's son went to the old woman's house, and there he stayed a week, for he was so glad to see the kotwál's son. Then he returned to his wife. Now she thought he would only have been away a day, and was very angry at his having stayed so long from her. " How could you leave me for a whole week?" she said to him. " I had not seen my friend for a month," he answered. Pánwpattí Rání did not let her husband see how angry she was; but in her heart she thought, " I am sure he loves his friend best."

The prince remained with her for a month. Then he said, " I must go and see my friend." This made her very angry indeed. However, she said, " Good; go and see your friend, and I will make you some delicious sweetmeats to take him from me." She set to work, and made the most tempting sweetmeats she could; only in each she put a strong poison. Then she wrapped them in a beautiful handkerchief, and her husband took them to the kotwál's son. " My Rání has made you these herself," he said to his friend, "and she sends you a great many salaams." The Rájá's son knew nothing of the poison.

The kotwál's son put the sweetmeats on one side, and said, " Let us talk, and I will eat them by and by." So they sat and talked for a long time. Then the kotwál's son said, " Your Rání herself made these sweetmeats for me?" "Yes," said the Rájá's son. His friend was very wise, and he thought, " Pánwpattíi Rání does not like me. Of that I am sure." So he took some of the sweetmeats, and broke them into bits and threw them to the crows. The crows came flying down, and all the crows who ate the sweetmeats died instantly. Then the kotwál's son threw a sweetmeat to a dog that was passing. The dog devoured it and fell dead. This put the Rájá's son into great rage. "I will never see my Rání again!" he exclaimed. "What a wicked woman she is to try and poison my friend—my friend whom I love so dearly ; but for whom I should never have married her!" He would not go back to his wife, and stayed in the old woman's house. The kotwál's son often told him he ought to return to his wife, but the prince would not do so. "No," he said, "she is a wicked woman. You never did her any evil or hurt ; yet she has tried to poison you. I will never see her again."

When a month had 'passed, the kotwál's son said to the prince, "You really must go back to Pánwpattí Rání ; she is your wife, and you must go to her, and take her away to your own country." Still the Rájá's son declared he would never see her again. "If you would like to see something that will please you," said his friend, "go back to your wife for one day ; and to-night 'when she is asleep' you must take off all her jewels, and tie them up in a handkerchief, and bring them to me. But before you leave her you must wound her in the leg with this trident." So saying, he gave him a small iron trident.

The prince went back to the palace. His wife was very angry with him, though she did not show her anger. At night 'when she was fast asleep' he took off all her jewels and tied them in a handkerchief, and he gave her a thrust in the leg with his trident. Then he went quickly back to his friend. The princess awoke and found herself badly hurt and alone ; and she saw that her jewels were all gone. In the morning she told her father and mother that her jewels had been stolen ; but she said nothing about the wound in her leg. The king called his servants, and told them a thief had come in the night and stolen his daughter's jewels, and he sent them to look for the thief and seize him.

That morning the kotwál's son got up and dressed himself like a yogí. He made the prince put on common clothes such as every one wears, so that he could not be recognized, and sent him to the bazar to sell his wife's jewels. He told'him, too, all he was to say. The pretended yogí went to the river and sat down by it, and the Rájá's son went through the bazar and tried to sell the jewels. The Rájá's servants seized him immediately. "You thief!" they said to him, "what made you steal our Rájá's daughter's jewels?" "I know nothing about the jewels," said the prince. "I am no thief; I did not steal them. The holy man, who is my teacher, gave them to me to sell in the bazar for him. If you want to know anything more about them, you must ask him." "Where is this holy man?" said the servants. "He is sitting by the river," said the Rájá's son. "Let us go to him. I will show you where he is."

They all went down to the river, and there sat the yogí. "What is all this?" said the servants to him. "Are you a yogí, and yet a thief? Why did you steal the little Rání's jewels?" "Are those the little Rání's jewels?" said the yogí. "I did not steal them; I did not know to whom they belonged. Listen, and I will tell you. Last night at twelve o'clock I was sitting by this river when a woman came down to it—a woman I did not know. She took a dead body out of the river, and began to eat it. This made me so angry, that I took all her jewels from her, and she ran away. I ran after her and wounded her in the leg with my trident. I don't know if she were your Raja's daughter, or who she was; but whoever she may be, she has the mark of the trident's teeth in her leg."

The servants took the jewels up to the palace, and told the Rájá all the yogí had said. The Rájá asked his wife whether the Princess Pánwpattí had any hurt in her leg, and told her all the yogí's story. The Rání went to see her daughter, and found her lying on her bed and unable to get up from the pain she was in, and when she looked at her leg she saw the wound. She returned to the Rájá and said to him, "Our daughter has the mark of the trident's teeth in her leg."

The Rájá got very angry, and called his servants and said to them, "Bring a palanquin, and take my daughter at once to the jungle, and there leave her. She is a wicked woman, who goes to the river at night to eat dead people. I will not have her in my house any more. Cast her out in the jungle." The servants did as they were bid, and left Pánwpattí Ráni, crying and sobbing in the jungle, partly from the pain in her leg, and partly because she did not know where to go, and had no food or water.

Meanwhile her husband and the kotwál's son heard of her being sent into the jungle, so they returned to the old woman's house and put on their own clothes. Then they went to the jungle to find her. She was still crying, and her husband asked her why she cried. She told him, and he said, "Why did you try to poison my friend? You were very wicked to do so." "Yes," said the kotwál's son; "Why did you try to kill me? I have never done you any wrong or hurt you. It was I who told your husband what you meant by putting the rose to your teeth, behind your ear, and at your feet. Without me he would never have found you, never have married you." Then she knew at once who had brought all this trouble to her, and she was very sorry she had tried to kill her husband's friend.

They all three now went home to her husband's country; and his father and mother were very glad indeed that their son had married a Rájá's daughter, and the Rájá gave the kotwál's son a very grand present.

The young Rájá and his wife lived with his father and mother, and were always very happy together.

Told by Múniyá, February, 1879.

XXVIII.

THE CLEVER WIFE.

IN a country there was a merchant who traded in all kinds of merchandise, and used to make journeys from country to country in his boat to buy and sell his goods. He one day said to his wife, " I cannot stay at home any more, for I must go on a year's journey to carry on my business. And he added, laughing, " When I return I expect to find you have built me a grand well; and also, as you are such a clever wife, to see a little son." Then he got into his boat and went away.

When he was gone his wife set to work, and she spun four hanks of beautiful thread with her own hands. Then she dressed herself in her prettiest clothes, and put on her finest jewels. " I am going to the bazar," she said to her ayahs, " to sell this thread." " That is not right," said one of the ayahs. " You must not sell your thread yourself, but let me sell it for you. What will your husband say if he hears you have been selling thread in the bazar ? " " I will sell my thread myself," answered the merchant's wife. " You could never sell it for me."

So off she set to the bazar, and every one in it said, " What a beautiful woman that is ! " At last the kotwál saw her, and came to her at once.

" What beautiful thread ! " he said. " Is it for sale ? " " Yes," she said. " How much a hank ? " said the kotwál. " Fifty rupees," she answered. " Fifty rupees ! Who will ever give you fifty rupees for it?" "I will not sell it for less," said the woman. "I shall get fifty rupees for it." "Well," said the kotwál, "I will give you the fifty rupees. Can I dine with you at your house?" "Yes," she answered, "to-night at ten o'clock." Then he took the thread and gave her fifty rupees.

Then she went away to another bazar, and there the king's wazír saw her trying to sell her thread. "What lovely thread! Is it for sale?" he said. "Yes, at one hundred rupees the hank," she answered. "Well, I will give you one hundred rupees. Can I dine with you at your house?" said the wazír. "Yes," she answered, "to-night at eleven o'clock." "Good," said the wazír; "here are the hundred rupees." And he took the thread and went away.

The merchant's wife now went to a third bazar, and there the king's kází saw her. "Is that beautiful thread for sale?" he asked. "Yes," she answered, "for one hundred and fifty rupees." "I will give you the hundred and fifty rupees. Can I dine with you at your house?" "Yes," she said, "to-night at twelve o'clock." "I will come," said the kází. "Here are one hundred and fifty rupees." So she took the rupees and gave him the thread.

She set off with the fourth hank to the fourth bazar, and in this bazar was the king's palace. The king saw her, and asked if the thread was for sale. "Yes," she said, "for five hundred rupees." "Give me the thread," said the king; "here are your five hundred rupees. Can I dine with you at your house?" "Yes," she said, "to-night at two o'clock."

Then she went home and sent one of her servants to the bazar to buy her four large chests; and she told her other servants that they were to get ready four very good dinners for her. Each dinner was to be served in a different room;

and one was to be ready at ten o'clock that night, one at
eleven, one at twelve, and one at two in the morning. The
servant brought her four large chests, and she had them
placed in four different rooms.

At ten o'clock the kotwál arrived. The merchant's wife
greeted him graciously, and they sat down and dined. After
dinner she said to him, " Can you play at cards ? " " Yes,"
he answered. She brought some cards, and they sat and
played till the clock struck eleven, when the doorkeeper
came in to say, " The wazír is here, and wishes to see you."
The kotwál was in a dreadful fright. " Do hide me somewhere," he said to her. " I have no place where you can
hide in this room," she answered ; " but in another room I
have a big chest. I will shut you up in that if you like, and
when the wazír is gone, I will let you out of it." So she
took him into the next room, and he got into one of the four
big chests, and she shut down the lid and locked it.

Then she bade the doorkeeper bring in the wazír, and
they dined together. After dinner she said, " Can you play
at cards ? " " Yes," said the wazír. She took out the cards,
and they played till twelve o'clock, when the doorkeeper
came to say the kází had come to see her. " Oh, hide me !
hide me ! " cried the wazír in a great fright. " If you come
to another room," she said, " I will hide you in a big chest
I have. I can let you out when he is gone." So she
locked the wazír up in the second chest.

She and the kází now dined. Then she said, " Can you
play at cards ? " " Yes," said the kází. So they sat playing
at cards till two o'clock, when the doorkeeper said the king
had come to see her. " Oh, what shall I do ? " said the
kází, terribly frightened. " Do hide me. Do not let me be
seen by the king." " You can hide in a big chest I have in
another room, if you like," she answered, " till he is gone."
And she locked up the kází in her third chest.

˙ The king now came in, and they dined. " Will you play
a little game at cards ? " she asked. " Yes," said the king.
So they played till three o'clock, when the doorkeeper came
running in (just as she had told him to do) to say, " My
master's boat has arrived, and he is coming up to the house.
He will be here directly." " Now what shall I do ? "
said the king, who was as frightened as the others had
been. " Here is your husband. He must not see me.
You must hide me somewhere." " I have no place to
hide you in," she said, " but a big chest. You can get into
that if you like, and I will let you out to-morrow morning."
So she shut the lid of the fourth chest down on the king
and locked him up. Then she went to bed, and to sleep,
and slept till morning.

The next day, after she had bathed and dressed, and
eaten her breakfast, and done all her household work, she
said to her servants, " I want four coolies." So the servants
went for the coolies ; and when they came she showed them
the four chests, and said, " Each of you must take one of
these chests on your head and come with me." Then they
set out with her, each carrying a chest.

Meanwhile the kotwál's son, the wazír's son, the kází's
son, and the king's son, had been roaming about looking
everywhere for their fathers, and asking every one if they
had seen them, but no one knew anything about them.

The merchant's wife went first to the kotwál's house, and
there she saw the kotwál's son. She had the kotwál's chest
set down on the ground before his door. " Will you buy
this chest ? " she said to his son. " What is in it ? " he asked.
" A most precious thing," she answered. " How much do
you want for it ? " said his son. " One thousand rupees,"
she said ; " and when you open the chest, you will see the
contents are worth two thousand. But you must not open
it till you are in your father's house." " Well," said the

kotwál's son, "here are a thousand rupees." The woman and the other three chests went on their way, while he took his into the house. "What a heavy chest!" he said. "What can be inside?" Then he lifted the lid. "Why, there's my father!" he cried. "Father, how came you to be in this chest?" The kotwál was very much ashamed of himself. "I never thought she was the woman to play me such a trick," he said; and then he had to tell his son the whole story.

The merchant's wife next stopped at the wazír's house, and there she saw the wazír's son. The wazír's chest was put down before his door, and she said to his son, "Will you buy this chest?" "What is inside of it?" he asked. "A most precious thing," she answered. "Will you buy it?" "How much do you want for it?" asked the son. "Only two thousand rupees, and it is worth three thousand. So the wazír's son bought his father, without knowing it, for two thousand rupees. "You must not open the chest till you are in the house," said the merchant's wife. The wazír's son opened the chest in the house at once, wondering what could be in it; and the wazír's wife stood by all the time. When they saw the wazír himself, looking very much ashamed, they were greatly astonished. "How came you there?" they cried. "Where have you been?" said his wife. "Oh," said the wazír, "I never thought she was a woman to treat me like this;" and he, too, had to tell all his story.

Now the merchant's wife stopped at the kázi's door, and there stood the kázi's son. "Will you buy this chest?" she said to him, and had the kázi's chest put on the ground. "What is in it?" said the kázi's son. "Silver and gold," she answered. "You shall have it for three thousand rupees. The contents are worth four." "Well, I will take it, said the son. "Don't open it till you are in your house," she said, and took her three thousand rupees and went away. Great was the excitement when the kází stepped out of the chest. "Oh!" he groaned, "I never thought she could behave like this to me."

The merchant's wife now went to the palace, and set the king's chest down at the palace gates. There she saw the king's son. "Will you buy this chest?" she said. "What is in it?" asked the prince. "Diamonds, pearls, and all kinds of precious stones," said the merchant's wife. "You shall have the chest for five thousand rupees, but its contents are worth a great deal more." "Well," said the king's son, "here are your five thousand rupees; give me the chest." "Don't open it out here," she said. "Take it into the palace and open it there." And away she went home.

The king's son opened the chest, and there was his father. "What's all this?" cried the prince. "How came *you* to be in the chest?" The king was very much ashamed, and did not tell much about his adventure; but when he was sitting in his court-house, he had the merchant's wife brought to him, and gave her a quantity of rupees, saying, "You are a wise and clever woman."

Now the kotwál knew the wazír had gone to see the merchant's wife; and the wazír knew the kází had gone; and the kází, that the king had gone; but this was all that any of them knew.

The merchant's wife had now plenty of rupees, so she had a most beautiful well built and roofed over. Then she locked the door of the well, and told the servants no one was to drink any of its water, or bathe in it, till her husband came home : he was to be the first to drink its water, and bathe in the well.

Then she sent her ayah to the bazar to buy her clothes and ornaments such as cowherd's wives and daughter's wear; and when the ayah had brought her these, she packed them up in a box. Then she dressed herself in men's clothes, so that no one could tell she was a woman, and ordered a horse to be got ready for her. "I am going to eat the air of another country for a little while," she said. "You must all take great care of the house while I am away." The servants did not like her going away at all; they were afraid her husband might return during her absence, and that he would be angry with them for having let her go. "Don't be afraid," she said. "There is nothing to be frightened about. I shall come back all right."

So she set out, taking the key of the well, the box with the clothes her ayah had bought for her in the bazar, and plenty of rupees. She also took two of her servants. She travelled a long, long way, asking everywhere for her husband's boat. At last at the end of a month she came to where it was. Here she hired a little house, and dressed herself like a cowherd's daughter. Then she got some very good milk, and went down to the banks of the river to sell it. Everybody said, "Do look what a beautiful woman that is selling milk!" She sold her milk very quickly, it was so good. This she did for several days, till her husband, the merchant, saw her. He thought her so beautiful, that he asked her to bring him some milk to his boat. So every day for a little while she sold him milk. One day he said to her, "Will you marry me?" "How can I marry you?" she said. "You are a merchant, and I am a cowherd's daughter. Soon you will be leaving this country, and will travel to another in your boat; you will want me to go with you. Then I shall have to leave my father and mother, and who will take care of them?" "Let us be married," said the merchant. "I am going to stay here for three months. When I go, you shall return to your father and mother, and later I will come back to you." To this she agreed, and they were married, and she went to live in the boat. At the end of three months, the merchant said to her, " My business here is done, and I must go to another country. Would you like to go home to your father and mother while I am away ? " " Yes," she said. " Here are some rupees for you to live on in my absence," he said. " I do not want any rupees," said his wife. " I only want you to give me two things : your old cap, and your picture." These he gave her, and then he went to his boat, and she went back to her own home.

Some time afterwards she had a little son. The servants were greatly frightened, for they thought their master would not be pleased when he came home ; and he was not pleased when he did come two months later. He was so cross that he would not look at the baby-boy, and he would hardly look at his beautiful well.

One night he lay awake thinking, and he thought he would kill his wife and her little son. But the next day she came to him : " Tell me the truth," she said; " you are angry with me ? Don't be angry, for I want to show you a picture I like very much—the picture of my boy's father." Then she showed him his own picture, and the old cap he had given her on board his boat ; and she told him how she had been the cowherd's daughter ; and also how she had gained the money to build his well. " You see," she said, " I have done all you bade me. Here is your well, and here is your 'son." Then the merchant was very happy. He kissed and loved his little son, and thought his well was beautiful; and he said to his wife, "What a clever woman you are ! "

Told by Múniyá, Calcutta, March 3rd, 1879.

XXIX.

RÁJÁ HARICHAND'S PUNISHMENT.

THERE was once a great Rájá, Rájá Harichand, who every morning before he bathed and breakfasted used to give away one hundred pounds weight of gold to the fakírs, his poor ryots, and other poor people. This he did in the name of God, "For," he said, "God loves me and gives me everything that I have ; so daily I will give him this gold."

Now God heard what a good man Rájá Harichand was, and how much the Rájá loved him, and he thought he would go and see for himself if all that was said of the Rájá were true. He therefore went as a fakír to Rájá Harichand's palace and stood at his gate. The Rájá had already given away his hundred pounds' weight of gold, and gone into his palace and bathed and breakfasted ; so when his servants came to tell him that another fakír stood at his gate, the Rájá said, "Bid him come to-morrow, for I have bathed, and have eaten my breakfast, and therefore cannot attend to him now." The servants returned to the fakír, and told him, "The Rájá says you must come to-morrow, for he cannot see you now, as he has bathed and breakfasted." God went away, and the next day he again came, after all the fakírs and poor people had received their gold and the Rájá had gone into his palace. So the Rájá told his servants, "Bid the fakír come to-morrow. He has again come too late for me to see him now."

On the third day God was once more too late, for the
Rájá had gone into his palace. The Rájá was vexed with
him for being a third time too late, and said to his servants,
" What sort of a fakír is this that he always comes too late?
Go and ask him what he wants." So the servants went to
the fakír and said, " Rájá Harichand says, ' What do you
want from him?'" " I want no rupees," answered God, "nor
anything else ; but I want him to give me his wife." The
servants told this to the Rájá, and it made him very angry.
He went to his wife, the Rání Báhan, and said to her,
" There is a fakír at the gate who asks me to give you to
him ! As if I should ever do such a thing ! Fancy my
giving him my wife ! "

The Rání was very wise and clever, for she had a book,
which she read continually, called the kop shástra ; and this
book told her everything. So she knew that the fakír at the
gate was no fakír, but God himself. (In old days about two
people in a thousand, though not more, could read this
book ; now-a-days hardly any one can read it, for it is far
too difficult.) So the Rání said to the Rájá, " Go to this
fakír, and say to him, ' You shall have my wife.' You need
not really give me to him ; only give me to him in your
thoughts." " I will do no such thing," said the Rájá in a
rage ; and in spite of all her entreaties, he would not say to
the fakír, " I will give you my wife." He ordered his servants
to beat the fakír, and send him away ; and so they did.

God returned to his place, and called to him two angels.
" Take the form of men," he said to them, " and go to Rájá
Harichand. Say to him, ' God has sent us to you. He
says, Which will you have—a twelve years' famine throughout your land during which no rain will fall? or a great
rain for twelve hours?'"

The angels came to the Rájá and said as God had bidden
them. The Rájá thought for a long while which he should

Q

choose. "If a great rain pours down for twelve hours," he said to himself, "my whole country will be washed away. But I have a great quantity of gold. I have enough to send to other countries and buy food for myself and my ryots during the twelve years' famine." So he said to the angels, "I will choose the famine." Then the angels came into his palace ; and the moment they entered it, all the Rájá's servants that were in the palace, and all his cows, horses, elephants, and other animals became stone. So did every single thing in the palace, excepting his gold and silver, and these turned to charcoal. The Rájá and Rání did not become stone.

The angels said to them, " For three weeks you will not be able to eat anything; you will not be able to eat any food you may find or may have given you. But you will not die, you will live." Then the angels went away.

The Rájá was very sad when he looked round his palace and saw everything in it, and all the people in it, stone, and saw all his gold and silver turned to charcoal. He said to his wife, " I cannot stay here. I must go to some other country. I was a great Rájá ; how can I ask my ryots to give me food ? We will dress ourselves like fakírs, and go to another country."

They put on fakírs' clothes and went out of their palace. They wandered in the jungle till they saw a plum-tree covered with fruit. " Do gather some of those plums for me," said the Rání, who was very hungry. The Rájá went to the tree and put out his hand to gather the plums ; but when he did this, they at once all left the tree and went a little way up into the air. When he drew back his hand, the plums returned to the tree. The Rájá tried three times to gather the plums, but never could do so.

He and the Rání then went on till they came to a plain in another country, where was a large tank in which men were fishing. The Rání said to her husband, "Go and ask those men to give us a little of their fish, for I am very hungry. The Rájá went to the men and said, "I am a fakír, and have no pice. Will you give me some of your fish, for I have not eaten for four days and am hungry?" The men gave him some fish, and he and his wife carried it to a tank on another plain. The Rání cleaned and prepared the fish for cooking, and said to her husband, "I have nothing in which to cook this fish. Go up to the town (there was a town close by) and ask some one to give you an earthen pot with a lid, and some salt."

The Rájá went up to the town, and some one in the bazar gave him the earthern pot, and a grain merchant put a little salt into it. Then he returned to the Rání, and they made a fire under a tree, put the fish into the pot, and set the pot on the fire. "I have not bathed for some days," said the Rájá. "I will go and bathe while you cook the fish, and when I come back we will eat it." So he went to bathe, and the Rání sat watching the fish. Presently she thought, "If I leave the lid on the pot, the fish will dry up and burn." Then she took off the lid, and the fish instantly jumped out of the pot into the tank and swam away. This made the Rání sad; but she sat there quiet and silent. When the Rájá had bathed, he returned to his wife, and said, "Now we will eat our fish." The Rání answered, "I had not eaten for four days, and was very hungry, so I ate all the fish." "Never mind," said the Rájá, "it does not matter."

They wandered on, and the next day came to another jungle where they saw two pigeons. The Rájá took some grass and sticks, and made a bow and arrow. He shot the pigeons with these, and the Rání plucked and cleaned them. Her husband and she made a little fire, put the pigeons in their pot, and set them on it. There was a tank near. "Now I will go and bathe," said the Rání; "I have not bathed for some days. When I come back, we will eat the pigeons." So she went to bathe, and the Rájá sat down to watch the pigeons. Presently he thought, " If I leave the pot shut, the birds will dry up and burn." So he took off the lid, and instantly away flew the pigeons out of the pot. He guessed at once what the fish had done yesterday, and sat still and silent till the Rání came back. "I have eaten the pigeons in the same way that you ate the fish yesterday," he said to her. The Rání understood what had happened, and saw the Rájá knew how the fish had escaped.

So they wandered on ; and as they went the Rání remembered an oil merchant, called Gangá Télí, a friend of theirs, and a great man, just like a Rájá. " Let us go to Gangá Télí, if we can walk as far as his house," she said. " He will be good to us." He lived a long way off. When they got to him, Gangá Télí knew them at once. " What has happened ? " he said. " You were a great Rájá ; why are you and the Rání so poor and dressed like fakírs ? " " It is God's will," they answered. Gangá Télí did not think it worth while to notice them much now they were poor ; so, though he did not send them away, he gave them a wretched room to live in, a wretched bed to lie on, and such bad food to eat that, hungry as they were, they could not touch it. " When we were rich," they said to each other, " and came to stay with Gangá Télí, he received us like friends ; he gave us beautiful rooms to live in, beautiful beds to lie on, and delicious food to eat. We cannot stay here."

So they went away very sorrowful, and wandered for a whole week, and all the time they had no food, till they came to another country whose Rájá, Rájá Bhoj, was one of their friends. Rájá Bhoj received them very kindly. " What has brought you to this state ? How is it you are so poor ? " he said. " What has happened to you ? " " It is God's will," they answered. Rájá Bhoj gave them a beautiful room to live in, and told his servants to cook for them the very nicest dinner they could. This the servants did, and they brought the dinner into Rájá Harichand's room, and set it before him and left him. Then he and the Rání put some of the food on their plates; but before they could eat anything, the food both in the dishes and on their plates became full of maggots. So they could not eat it. They felt greatly humbled. However, they said nothing, but worshipped God; and they buried all the food in a hole they dug in the floor of their room.

Now the daughter of Rájá Bhoj had left her gold necklace hanging on the wall of the room in which were Rájá Harichand and the Rání Báhan. At night when Rájá Harichand was asleep, the Rání saw a crack come in the wall and the necklace go of itself into the crack; then the wall joined together as before. She at once woke her husband, and told him what she had seen. "We had better go away quickly," she said. "The necklace will not be found to-morrow, and Rájá Bhoj will think we are thieves. It will be useless breaking the wall open to find it." The Rájá got up at once, and they set out again. Rájá Bhoj, when the necklace was not found, thought Rájá Harichand and the Rání Báhan had stolen it.

They wandered on till they came to a country belonging to another friend, called Rájá Nal, but they were ashamed to go to his palace. The three weeks were now nearly over, only two more days were left. So the Rání said, "In two days we shall be able to eat. Go into the jungle and cut grass, and sell it in the bazar. We shall thus get a few pice and be able to buy a little food." The Rájá went out to the jungle, but he had to break and pull up the grass with his hands. He worked half the day, and then sold the grass in the bazar for a few pice. They were able to buy food, and worshipped God and cooked it; and as the three weeks were now over they were allowed to eat it.

They stayed in Rájá Nal's country, and lived in a little house they hired in the bazar. Rájá Harichand went out every day to the jungle for grass, which he pulled up or broke off with his hands, and then sold in the bazar for a few pice. The Rání saved a pice or two whenever she could, and at the end of two years they were rich enough to buy a hook such as grass-cutters use. The Rájá could now cut more grass, and soon the Rání was able to buy some pretty-coloured silks in the bazar.

Her husband went daily to cut grass, and she sat at home making head-collars with the silks for horses. Four years after they had bought the hook, she had four of these head-collars ready, and she took them up to Rájá Nal's palace to sell. It was the first time she had gone there, for she and her husband were ashamed to see Rájá Nal. Their fakírs' dresses had become rags, and they had only been able to get wretched common clothes in their place, for they were miserably poor.

"What beautiful head-collars these are !" said Rájá Nal's coachmen and grooms ; and they took them to show to their Rájá. As soon as he saw them he said, "Where did you get these head-collars ? Who is it that wishes to sell them ? " for he knew that only one woman could make such head-collars, and that woman was the Rání Báhan. "A very poor woman brought them here just now," they answered. "Bring her to me," said Rájá Nal. So the servants brought him Rání Báhan, and when she saw the Rájá she burst into tears. "What has brought you to this state ? Why are you so poor ? " said Rájá Nal. "It is God's will," she answered. "Where is your husband ? " he asked. "He is cutting grass in the jungle," she said. Rájá Nal called his servants and said, "Go into the jungle, and there you will see a man cutting grass. Bring him to me." When Rájá Harichand saw Rájá Nal's servants coming to him, he was very much frightened; but the servants took him and brought him to the palace. As soon as Rájá Nal saw his old friend, he seized his hands, and burst out crying. "Rájá," he said, "what has brought you to this state?" "It is God's will," said Rájá Harichand.

Rájá Nal was very good to them. He gave them a palace to live in, and servants to wait on them; beautiful clothes to wear, and good food to eat. He went with them to the palace to see that everything was as it should be for them. "To-day," he said to the Rání, "I shall dine with your husband, and you must give me a dinner cooked just as you used to cook one for me when I went to see you in your own country." "Good, I will give it you," said the Rání; but she was quite frightened, for she thought, "The Rájá is so kind, and everything is so comfortable for us, that I am sure something dreadful will happen." However, she prepared the dinner, and told the servants how to cook it and serve it; but first she worshipped God, and entreated him to have mercy on her and her husband. The dinner was very good, and nothing evil happened to any one. They lived in the palace Rájá Nal gave them for four and a half years.

Meanwhile the farmers in Rájá Harichand's country had all these years gone on ploughing and turning up the land, although not a drop of rain had fallen all that time, and the earth was hard and dry. Now just when the Rájá and Rání had lived in Rájá Nal's palace for four and a half years Mahádeo was walking through Rájá Harichand's country. He saw the farmers digging up the ground, and said, "What is the good of your digging and turning up the ground? Not a drop of rain is going to fall." "No," said the farmers, "but if we did not go on ploughing and digging, we should forget how to do our work." They did not know they were talking to Mahádeo, for he looked like a man. " That is true," said Mahádeo, and he thought, " The farmers speak the truth; and if I go on neglecting to blow on my horn, I shall forget how to blow on it at all." So he took his deer's horn, which was just like those some yogís use, and blew on it. Now when Rájá Harichand had chosen the twelve years' famine, God had said, " Rain shall not fall on Rájá Harichand's country till Mahádeo blows his horn in it." Mahádeo had quite forgotten this decree; so he blew on his horn, although only ten and a half years' famine had gone by. The moment he blew, down came the rain, and the whole country at once became as it had been before the famine began; and moreover, the moment it rained, everything in Rájá Harichand's palace became what it was before the angels entered it. All the men and women came to life again; so did all the animals; and the gold and silver were no longer charcoal, but once more gold and silver. God was not angry with Mahádeo for forgetting that he said the famine should last for twelve years, and that the rain should fall when Mahádeo blew on his horn in Rájá Harichand's country. " If it pleased Mahádeo to blow on his horn," said God, " it does not matter that eighteen months of famine were still to last." As soon as they heard the rain had fallen, all the ryots who had gone to other countries on account of the famine returned to Rájá Harichand's country.

Among the Rájá's servants was the kotwál, and very anxious he was, when he came to life again, to find the Rájá and Rání; only he did not know how to do so, and wondered where he had best seek for them.

Meanwhile the Rání Báhan had a dream that God sent her, in which an angel said to her, " It is good that you and your husband should return to your country." She told this dream to her husband; and Rájá Nal gave them horses, elephants, and camels, that they might travel like Rájás to their home, and he went with them. They found everything in order in their own palace and all through their country, and after this lived very happily in it. But the Rání said to Rájá Harichand, "If you had only done what I told you, and said you would give me to the fakír, all this misery would not have come on us."

Later they went to stay again with Rájá Bhoj, and slept in the same room as they had had when they came to him poor and wretched. In the night they saw the wall open, and the necklace came out of the crack and hung itself up as before, and the wall closed again. The next day they showed the necklace to Rájá Bhoj, saying, "It was on account of this necklace that we ran away from you the last time we were here," and they told him all that had happened to it.

As for Gangá Téli, they never went near him again.

Told by Múniyá, March 4th, 1879.

XXX.

THE KING'S SON AND THE WAZÍR'S DAUGHTER.

IN a country there was a great king who had a wazír. One day he thought he should like to play at cards with this wazír, and he told him to go and get some for him, and then play a game with him. So the wazír brought the cards, and he and the king sat down to play. Now neither the king nor the wazír had any children; and as they were playing, the king said, "Wazír, if I have a son and you have a daughter, or if I have a daughter and you have a son, let us marry our children to each other." To this the wazír agreed. A year after the king had a son; and when the boy was two years old, the wazír had a daughter. Some years passed, and the king's son was twelve years old, and the wazír's daughter ten. Then the king said to the wazír, "Do you remember how one day, when we were playing at cards, we agreed to marry our children to each other?" "I remember," said the wazír. "Let us marry them now," said the king. So they held the wedding feast; but the wazír's little daughter remained in her father's house because she was still so young.

As the king's son grew older he became very wicked, and took to gambling and drinking till his father and mother died of grief. After their death he went on in the same way, gambling and drinking, until he had no money left, and had to leave the palace, and live anywhere he

could in the town, wandering from house to house in a
fakír's dress, begging his bread, and sleeping wherever he
found a spot on which to lie down.

Meanwhile the wazír's daughter was living alone, for her
husband had never come to fetch her as he should have done
when she was old enough. Her father and mother were
dead too. She had given half of the money they left her
to the poor, and she lived on the other half. She spent
her days in praying to God, and in reading in a holy book ;
and though she was so young, she was very wise and good.

One day, as the prince was roaming about in his fakír's
rags, not knowing where to find food or shelter, he remembered his wife, and thought he would go and see her. She
ordered her servants to give him good food, a bath, and
good clothes ; "for," she said, "we were married when we
were children, though he never fetched me to his palace."
The servants did as she bade them. The prince bathed and
dressed, and ate food, and he wished to stay with his wife.
But she said, " No ; before you stay with me you must
see four sights. Go out in the jungle and walk for a whole
week. Then you will come to a plain where you will see
them." So the next day he set out for the plain, and reached
it in one week.

There he saw a large tank. At one corner of the tank he
saw a man and a woman who had good clothes, good food,
good beds, and servants to wait on them, and seemed very
happy. At the second corner he saw a wretchedly poor
man and his wife, who did nothing but cry and sob because
they had no food to eat, no water to drink, no bed to lie on,
no one to take care of them. At the third corner he saw
two little fishes that were always going up and down in the
air. They would shoot down close to the water, but they
could not go into it or stay in it ; then they would make
a salaam to God, and would shoot up again into the air, but

before they got very high, they had to drop down again. At the fourth corner he saw a huge demon who was heating sand in an enormous iron pot, under which he kept up a big fire.

The prince returned to his wife, and told her all he had seen. "Do you know who the happy man and woman are?" she said. "No," he answered. "They are my father and mother," she said. "When they were alive, I was good to them, and since their death I gave half their money to the poor; and on the other half I have lived quietly, and tried to be good. So God is pleased with them, and makes them happy. "Is that true?" said her husband. "Quite true," she said. "And the miserable man and woman who did nothing but cry, do you know who they are?" "No," said the prince. "They are your father and mother. When they were alive, you gambled and drank; and they died of grief. Then you went on gambling and drinking till you had spent all their money. So now God is angry with them, and will not make them happy. "Is that true?" said the prince. "Quite true," she said. "And the fishes you saw were the two little children we should have had if you had taken me to your home as your wife. Now they cannot be born, for they can find no bodies in which to be born; so God has ordered them to rise and sink in the air in these fishes' forms." "Is that true?" asked the prince. "Quite true," she answered. "And by God's order the demon you saw is heating that sand in the big iron pot for you, because you are such a wicked man."

The moment she had told all this to her husband, she died. But he did not get any better. He gambled and drank all her money away, and lived a wretched life, wandering about like a fakír till his death.

Told by Múniyá, March 8th, 1879.

NOTES.

INTRODUCTORY.

IN these stories the word translated God, is *Khudá*. Excepting in "How king Burtal became a Fakír" (p. 85), and in "Rájá Harichand's Punishment" (p. 224), in which Mahádeo plays a part, the tellers of these tales would never specify by name the god they spoke of. He was always *Khudá*, "the great *Khudá* who lives up there in the sky." In this they differed from the narrator of the *Old Deccan Days* stories, who almost always gives her gods and goddesses their Hindú names—probably because, from being a Christian, she had no religious scruples to deter her from so doing.

When the heroes of these stories are called Rájás, the word Rájá has been kept : when they are called Bádsháhs, we have called them kings. The Ayahs say, " A Bádsháh is a much greater man than a Rájá." When *bádsháh* (the Persian *pádisháh*) in its corrupted form of *básá* is tacked on to a proper name, such as *Anár* (*Anárbásá*), *Hírálál* (*Hírálálbásá*), the *básá* has been preserved, because, Dunkní says, in these cases *básá* is no longer a title, but part of the proper name.

Old Múniyá tells her stories with the solemn, authoritative air of a professor. She sits quite still on the floor, and uses no gestures. Dunkní gets thoroughly excited over her tales, marches up and down the room, acting her stories, as it were. For instance, in describing the thickness of Mahádeo's hair in King Burtal's story, she put her two thumbs to her ears, and spread out all her fingers from her head saying, " His hair stood out like this," and in " Loving Lailí," after moving her hand as if she were pulling the magic knife from her pocket and unfolding it, she swung her arm out at full length with great energy, and then she said, " Lailí made one ' touch ' " (here she brought back the edge of her hand to her own throat), " and the head fell off." Dunkní sometimes used an English word, such as the " touch " in the present case.

All these stories were read back in Hindústání by my little girl to the tellers at the time of telling, and nearly all a second time by me this winter before printing. I never saw people more anxious to have their tales retold exactly than are Dunkí and Múniya. Not till each tale was pronounced by them to be *thik* (exact) was it sent to the press.

It is strange in these Indian tales to meet golden-haired, fair-complexioned heroes and heroines. Mr. Thornton tells me that in the Panjáb when one native speaks of another with contempt, he says, "he is a black man," *ek kálá ádmi hai.* Sir Neville Chamberlain tells me that if you wish to praise a native for his valour and brave conduct, you say to him, " Your countenance is red," or " your cheeks are red," and that nothing is worse than to tell him his " face is black." And this is what Mr. Boxwell says about the expression " kálá ádmí " and our fairy tales :—

" The stories are of the Aryan conquerors from beyond the Indus ; distinguished by their fair skin from the dark aborigines of India. In Vedic times Varṇa, ' colour,' is used for stock or blood, as the Latins used Nomen. It is in India ' Yas Dásam varṇam adharam guhákar.' ' Who sank in darkness the Barbarian colour.' R. V. II. 4.

" Indra, again, ' Hatvé Dasyún pra Áryam varṇam ávat.' ' Having slain the Barbarians, helped the Aryan colour.' R. V. III. 34.

"Again, in K. V. I. 104. They pray—

"' Te nas ávaksa suvitáya varṇam.' "' May they bring our colour to success.'

" In later times ' varṇa ' is the regular word for caste ; and the Brahmins and the rest of the twice-born who still represent the Aryan varṇa are much fairer than the Çúdras and Hill people.

" In the Ikhwán ussafa the black skin is one of the results of the Fall to Adam and Hawa.

"' Áftáb ki garmí se rang mutaghaiyar aur siáh ho gayá.' ' From the heat of the sun their colour became changed and black.' "

But I think the fact that the conquering races that invaded India from the north were fair and ruddier than the aborigines, and that their descendants, the high-caste natives, are to this day fairer than the aborigines, though it explains the phrases, " he is only a black man," and " your cheeks are red," does not account for the golden hair and fair skin of so many of our princes and princesses. I believe that they all owe their characteristics to the fact that such are the characteristics of the solar hero, although they cannot all lay claim to a solar origin for themselves. For this golden hair and white skin, at first the property of the shining sun-hero alone, would naturally in the course of time be given to other Indian folk-lore heroes on whose beauty and brightness it was necessary to lay a stress. Prince Majnún, for instance, certainly has nothing solar about him, yet his hair is described as red. Dunkní, in answer to a half incredulous, half inquiring exclamation of mine when I heard this, asserted, " Red ! yes, it was red : red like gold."

The black-haired Maoris give their sea-nymphs yellow hair (*Old New Zealand*, p. 19) ; and Sir George Grey in his *Polynesian Mythology*, p. 295, writes thus of the Maori fairies : " Their appearance is that of human beings, nearly resembling an European's ; their hair being very fair, and so is their skin. They are very different from the Maoris, and do not resemble them at all." But as the Maoris do not seem to have any myths of golden-haired solar heroes, these peculiarities of hair and complexion cannot be referred to the same cause as those of my little daughter's Indian princes and princesses.

I.—PHÚLMATI RÁNI.

1. Phúlmati is a garden rose, not a wild rose. It must be a local name for the flower. I can find it in no dictionary. Dunkní says her heroine was named after a pink rose.

2. She has hair of pure gold. Compare in this book : Princess Jaháran, p. 43, the Monkey Prince, p. 50, Sonahrí Rání, p. 54, Jahár Rání, p. 93, Prince Dímá-ahmad and Princess Atása, Notes, p. 253. Also, Híra Bai, the cobra's daughter in *Old Deccan Days*, p. 35. So many princely heroes and heroines in European fairy tales are noteworthy for their dazzling golden hair that I will only mention one of them, Princess Golden-Hair, one of whose hairs rings if it falls to the ground—see Naake's *Slavonic Fairy Tales*, p. 100. And devils being fallen heroes or angels, the following references may be made to them. In Haltrich's *Sieben-buergische Maerchen*, p. 171, in "Die beiden Fleischhauer in der Hoelle," the devil's grandmother gives the good brother a hair that had fallen from the devil's head while he slept. The man carries it home and the hair suddenly becomes as big as a "Heubaum" and is "of pure gold." Also in one of Grimm's stories the hero is sent to fetch three golden hairs from the devil's head—see *Kinder und Hausmaerchen*, vol. I. p. 175, "Der Teufel mit den drei goldenen Haaren."

3. Her beauty lights up a dark room. In this shining quality she resembles many Asiatic and European fairy-tale heroes and heroines. See in this book Hírálí, whose face shone like a diamond, p. 69 ; and the Princess Labám, who shone like the moon, and her beauty made night day, p. 158. In *Old Deccan Days*, p. 156, the prince's dead body on the hedge of spears

dazzles those who look at it till they can hardly see. Pánch Phúl
Rání, p. 140, shines in the dark jungle like a star. So does the
princess in Chundun Rájá's dark tomb, p. 229. In a Dinájpur
story published by Mr. G. H. Damant in the *Indian Antiquary* for February 1875, vol. IV. p. 54, the dream-nymph,
Tillottama, whenever she appears, lights up the whole place
with her beauty. "At every breath she drew when she slept, a
flame like a flower issued from her nostril, and when she drew in
her breath the flower of flame was again withdrawn." Her
beauty lit up her house "as if by lightning." See Appen-
dix *A*. In Naake's *Slavonic Fairy Tales*, p. 96, is the Bohemian
tale quoted above of Princess Golden-Hair. "Every morning
at break of day she [the princess] combs her golden locks ;
its brightness is reflected in the sea, and up among the
clouds," p. 102. When she let it down "it was bright as
the rising sun," and almost blinded Irik with its radiance,
p. 107. The golden children (Schott's *Wallachische Maerchen*,
p. 125) shine in the darkened room "like the morning sun in
May." Gubernatis in the 2nd vol. of his *Zoological Mythology*, mentions at p. 31 a golden boy who figures in one of
Afanassieff's stories ; when this child's body is uncovered on his
restoration to his father, "all the room shines with light." And
at p. 57 of the same volume he quotes another of Afanassieff's
stories, in which the persecuted princess has three sons "who
light up whatever is near them with their splendour." Of Gerd
in Jötunheim, the beautiful giant maiden with the bright shining arms, Thorpe says (*Northern Mythology*, vol. I. p. 47), when
she raised "her arms to open the door, both air and water gave
such a reflection that the whole world was illumined." The
boar Trwyth (who was once a king, but because of his sons was
turned into a boar) after his fall preserves some of his old kingly
splendour ; for "his bristles were like silver wire, and whether he
went through the wood or through the plain he was to be traced
by the glittering of his bristles " (*Mabinogion*, vol. II. p. 310). In
the same work (vol. III. p. 279), in "The Dream of Maxen
Wledig," is a maiden, of whom it is told : "Not more easy than
to gaze upon the sun when brightest was it to look upon her by
reason of her beauty." And in "Goldhaar" (Haltrich's *Sieben-*

buergische Maerchen, p. 61) when the hero's cap fell off he stood there " in all splendour and his golden locks fell round his head, and he shone like the sun."

In a Santhali tale published by the Rev. F. T. Cole in the *Indian Antiquary* for January 1875, p. 10, called " Toria the Goatherd and the Daughter of the Sun," a beggar's eyes are as dazzled by the Sun's daughter's beauty "as if he had stared at the sun."

4. Phúlmati Ráni has on her head the sun, on her hands moons, and her face is covered with stars. Compare in these stories " The Indrásan Rájá," p. 1, " The boy who had a moon on his forehead and a star on his chin," p. 119, and " Prince Dímá-ahmad and Princess Atása," Notes, p. 253. In Fräulein Gonzenbach's *Sicilian Fairy Tales*, No. 5 (vol. I. p. 21), the king's son's children are born, the boy with a golden apple in his hand, the girl with a star on her forehead. In the Notes to this story (vol. II. p. 207) Herr Köhler mentions a Tyrolean fairy tale, " Zingerle, II. p. 112," where the king's son's daughter has a golden apple in her hand, and her brother a golden star on his forehead. In Milenowsky's *Bohemian Fairy Tales*, p. 1, is the story " Von den Sternprinzen " in which the king's son by the queen has a gold star on his forehead, and his son by the old woman has a silver star, p. 2. These princes' children also are born with gold and silver stars on their foreheads, p. 30. In a Hungarian tale, " Die verwandelten Kinder," the old man's youngest daughter promises, and keeps her promise, to give the king, if he marries her, twin sons, who will be most beautiful, will have golden hair, and each a golden ring on his arm ; further, one is to have a planet, the other a sun on his forehead— Stier's *Ungarische Volksmaerchen*, p. 57. Also in the same author's *Ungarische Sagen und Maerchen* in " Die beiden juengsten Koenigskinder," the hero wins a bride (p. 77) who has a sun on her forehead, a moon on her right, and three stars on her left, breast. In " Eisenlaci " in the same collection the snake-king's daughter has a star on her forehead (p. 109). Gubernatis (*Zoological Mythology*, vol. I. p. 412) says, " In the seventh story of the third book of Afanassieff, the queen bears two sons ; one has a moon on his forehead and the other a star

on the nape of his neck. Her wicked {sister buries them ; a golden and a silver sprout spring up which a sheep eats and then has two lambs, one with a moon on its head, the other with a star on its neck. The wicked sister who has married the king orders them to be torn in pieces, and their intestines to be thrown into the road. The good, lawful queen eats them and again gives birth to her sons." Gubernatis in the 2nd volume of the same work, p. 31, quotes another of Afanassieff's stories, the thirteenth of the third book, in which a merchant's wife has a son "whose body is all of gold, effigies of stars, moon, and sun covered it." This is the gold boy mentioned in the preceding paragraph as lighting up the room when his body was uncovered. In "Das Schwarze Lamm," the empress bears a son with a golden star on his forehead (Karadschitsch, *Volksmaerchen der Serben*, p. 177).

5. Phúlmati Rání weighs but one flower : compare Pánch Phúl Rání in *Old Deccan Days*, p. 133.

6. Indrásan (= Indra + Ásana, Indra's throne or home), says Dunkní, is the name of the underground fairy country. Its inhabitants, the fairies (parí) are called the Indrásan people ; they delight in all lovely things ; everything about them is beautiful ; they play exquisitely on all kinds of musical instruments ; they dance and sing a great deal ; they have wings and can fly. They taught the little Monkey Prince (p. 42), and King Burtal's eldest son was taken to them as a pupil by the fakír Goraknáth, p. 93. In Indrásan grows a tree of which no man can ever see the flowers or fruit, as the fairies gather them in the night and take them away. The Irish "good people" who live in clefts of rocks, caves, and mounds, and the Irish fairies who live in the beautiful land of youth under the sea, have many points in common with the Indian fairies. They, too, dance beautifully, are wonderful musicians, and have everything about them lovely and splendid. The "good people" also sometimes impart their knowledge to mortals. See pp. x, xii, and xviii of the Introduction to the *Irische Elfenmaerchen* translated into German by the brothers Grimm. Some of the Cornish fairies, the Small People, like the Indrásan people, live underground (Hunt's *Romances and Drolls of the West of Eng-*

land, pp. 116, 118, 125), aid those to whom they take a fancy and are very playful among themselves (*ib.* p. 81); they have the most ravishing music (*ib.* pp. 86, 98); their singing is clear and delicate as silver bells (*ib.* p. 100); everything about them is joyous and beautiful (*ib.* pp. 86, 99, 100); they are a tiny race (*ib.* p. 81), but can at pleasure take the size of human beings (*ib.* pp. 115, 122, 123); and their queen has hair "like gold threads" (*ib.* p. 102). The fair-haired New Zealand fairies are, too, a kindly happy race. See Grey's *Polynesian Mythology*, pp. 287 to 295. Nothing is said about their dancing, but they are described as "merry, cheerful, and always singing like a cricket" (*ib.* p. 295), and from one of their fishing-nets left on the sea shore, when its fairy owners were surprised by the rising of the sun, the Maories learnt the stitch for netting a net. Like the Indian fairies they appear to be as big as human beings.

7. Phúlmati Rání is drowned in a tank and becomes a flower; she is killed and brought to life several times : compare in this collection the story of the "Pomegranate Children" and note to that story. In one of Ralston's *Russian Folk-Tales*, "The Fiend," p. 15, the heroine is killed through witchcraft : from her grave springs a flower which is herself transformed : she afterwards regains her human shape.

8. With Phúlmati's last transformation compare the last that the Bél-Princess goes through (p. 148 of this collection), and that of a woman, who figures in a Dinájpur story published by Mr. G. H. Damant in the *Indian Antiquary* of April 5th, 1872, vol. I. p. 115. She, though living in the Rakshas country, is not a Rakshas, but does not appear to be an ordinary mortal, and when cut to bits by a certain magic knife becomes a tree. "Her feet became a silver stem, her two hands golden branches, her head ornaments were diamond leaves, all her bracelets and bangles were pearly fruits, and her head was a peacock dancing and playing in the branches." As soon as the magic knife is thrown to the ground she regains her human form.

Eisenlaci in Stier's *Ungarische Sagen und Maerchen* (pp. 107—109) comes in the form of a horse to the twelve-headed dragon's house. He is killed ; the first two drops of his blood are thrown into the garden and from them springs a tree with golden apples : the tree is cut down, but the first two chips (which are flung into the pond) become a gold fish : the gold fish turns into Eisenlaci himself in human form.

9. Winning a wife by seizing her dress while she bathes is an incident common to fairy tales of many countries.

II.—THE POMEGRANATE KING.

1. Such is the story as told by Dunkní in 1876 ; at that time, when it was read over to her, she said it was correct. On my asking her in 1878, when the story was going through the press, to explain some points in it, such as why the children said they had been brought to life *three* times, the boy having only died twice, and the girl once, she told me the following variation : After the attempt to get rid of the boy by making him into a curry had failed, the Rání Sunkásí sent for a sepoy and bade him carry the two children to the jungle and there kill them ; and as a proof of their death he was to bring her their livers. Once in the jungle with the children, the sepoy had not the heart to kill them ; so he left them in it, and brought the livers of two goats to Sunkásí Rání. She buried the livers in the garden and was content ; but some months later as she was walking (literally "eating the air") in the jungle she saw her step-children playing about ; she returned to the palace, sent for the sepoy, and asked him why he had not killed the children. " I did kill them," said the sepoy, " and brought you their livers." " Those livers were not the children's livers," answered the Rání ; " I have just seen the children alive and playing in the jungle." " They must have been other people's children that you saw," said the sepoy, " yours I killed." " Do not tell me lies," said the Rání. " Now you must at once go to the jungle, kill the children, and bring me their eyes." The sepoy went to find the children, but when he found them he could not kill them, so he took them to some people who lived in a hut, and said to these people, " Take great care of the two children. Be very kind to them." He then killed two goats and took their eyes to the Rání, who was now satisfied for some time. But

one day another of the Pomegranate Rájá's sepoys passed near the hut, and saw the children playing about. So he went to Sunkásí Rání and told her the children were alive and well. At this the Rání was very angry, and she thought, " It is of no use my sending the first sepoy again to kill them. I will send this man." She said, therefore, to the second sepoy, " If you will kill these children for me, you shall have a great reward." The sepoy agreed, went to the little hut, and seized the children. The poor people who took care of the children begged and prayed him to have pity on them ; but the sepoy said, " No." He had the Rání's orders to kill them, and they must and should be killed. And so he killed them and brought their livers to the Rání as she had bidden him. Sunkási Rání was very happy when she saw the livers, and she buried them close to a large tank that was in her garden.

Some three months later her servants came to her and told her a beautiful large bél-fruit was floating on the water of the tank. Sunkásí Rání went at once with them to the tank, and when she saw the fruit she was seized with a great longing to have it. So she sent all her servants, one after the other, into the tank to fetch it ; but all to no purpose, for as soon as any one of them got close to the fruit it floated away from him. Then the Rání herself went into the tank. She, however, was not a whit more able to get it : when she thought she had only to put out her hand to take it, the fruit rose up into the air, and fell into the water again as soon as she had come up out of the tank. She went to the Mahárájá and told him of this lovely bél-fruit, and then went to her room while he came down to the tank. He said, " I should like to catch the fruit : I wonder if I can do so. What a lovely fruit ! " As soon as he put his hand into the water the fruit came floating towards him, and floated into it. " I think this fruit is quite ripe," said the Mahárájá. " Quite ripe," said the servants, and they struck it with a stone to break it open. " Oh, you hurt us ! you hurt us ! " cried little voices from inside the bél-fruit. " Gently, gently ; don't hurt us." The Mahárájá and all the servants were greatly surprised, and the Mahárájá went to Sunkásí Rání, and told her all about the little voices. She at once guessed her step-children were in the fruit,

so she said to the Mahárájá, "You had better take the fruit to
the jungle and there break it open with a big stone, so that anything inside it may be crushed to bits." "I will not do that,"
said the Mahárájá. Then he went back to his servants and
made them cut the fruit's rind very carefully cross-ways and
the fruit broke into halves : in one half sat his little son, in
the other his little daughter. As soon as the halves were laid
on the ground the children stepped out, and at once grew to
their natural size. Their father was very angry when he saw
them. "Why, I thought you were at school," said he. "The
Maháráni told me you were at school. Why are you not there?
What funny (Dunkni's own word) children you are to get into
this bél-fruit ! What made you like to live in a fruit ?" But to
all his questionings and scoldings the children said not one word.
At last he sent them up to the palace, and there they stayed
with him for some three months. But the Mahárání said to
him, "These are not your children. Yours are at school."
"They *are* my children," he answered.

All this time the Mahárání hated them more and more, and
at last she went to them and said, "Now I really will kill you."
"Just as you please," answered the children ; "we don't mind
being killed. You may kill us three times, four times, as often
as you like : it does not matter in the least ; for God will always
bring us to life again."

At this Sunkásí Rání flew into a rage and she called her servants and said, "Kill these children, cut them into mince-meat
and throw them to the crows and kites. When the crows and
kites have eaten them, they cannot come to life any more." So
the servants killed the children, and chopped them up very fine
and fed the crows and kites with their flesh ; and now the Mahárání was very happy.

Some months later, as she was walking in her garden, she
saw two beautiful flower-buds on a large bél-tree that grew in it.
She showed them to the gardener, and asked if he had seen
them before. "Never," said the man. "On this tree there
have never been either flowers or fruit till now." "Gather the
flowers for me," said the Rání, "I do so wish to have them."
The gardener said to her, "Wait till the buds are fully blown

and then I will gather them for you." At the end of three or
four days the Rání Sunkásí asked if the buds had grown into
large flowers, and the gardener said, " Yes, to-day I will gather
them for you." He got a long, long bamboo cane, and tied a
piece of wood cross-ways on one of its ends so as to make a sort
of hook wherewith to catch hold of and break off the flowers.
He tried and tried to get them, but all in vain. Then he made
all the servants try. It was of no use, no one could make the
hook touch the flowers. They always bent themselves just out
of its reach. Then Sunkásí Rání tried, but with no better success.
She told the Mahárájá, who said, " I will try to-morrow to
gather these wonderful flowers."

That night as the Rání lay in her bed she suddenly thought,
" Those children are in the flowers," and she determined to be
with her husband when he gathered them, to get them into her
own hands some way or other.

The next morning Anárbásá Mahárájá and his wife went to
the bél-tree, and as soon as he held out his hand towards the
flowers, they dropped into it. " What lovely flowers ! What
beautiful flowers ! Do give them to me," said Sunkásí Rání.
" No," said the Mahárájá, " I will keep them myself." Then he
carried them to his room and laid them on the table while he
shut the door and the venetians. Then he came and sat down
before them : he took them in his hand, and looked at them
and laid them again on the table ; then he took them and smelt
them, and they smelt, oh ! so sweet. This he did many times.
At last he held them to his ears, for the adventure of the bél-fruit
had made him wise (*hushyár*), and he heard little tiny voices,
saying, " Papa " (Dunkní's own word), " we want to stay with
you ; we should like to be with you." The Mahárájá looked
very carefully at the flowers, and at last, in one of them he saw
a little splinter of wood like a thorn sticking : he pulled this out,
and his own little son stood before him. Then he looked at the
other flower, and in that, too, was a little splinter of wood sticking. When he pulled it out his little girl stood there.

The Mahárájá was vexed with his children, and asked them
why they were so naughty, and why they liked to live in fruits
and flowers instead of staying in the palace or going to school.

The children answered, " We go to school sometimes, and then we come back and live in our flowers, and then we return to school, and then we come back to our flower-homes again." " This is a lie you are telling me," said their father. " You know quite well you have not been at school at all." The Maháráni came in to hear what all this talking meant, and when she saw the children she said to Anárbásá Mahárájá, " These are not your children, yours are at school." " They are my children," he answered, " and they have never been at school at all, and they are very naughty." He then sent them away to play, and the Ráni returned to her room. But he sat alone in his room, for he was angry and cross. As he sat there one of his chaprásís came to him and said, " Maháráj, you do not know how ill the Maháráni treats your children, or you would not be angry with them. She has killed them several times, and sent them away into the jungle ; and after they came out of the bél-fruit she killed them and chopped them into small pieces, and fed the kites and crows with their flesh." When the Mahárájá heard all this, he said to the chaprásí, " You must have a beautiful little house built for me ; you must take care that it is chiefly made of wood ; the flooring must be very thin and of wood ; and the hollow place under the flooring must be filled with dry wood. Then you must put plenty of flowers inside the house, and plenty outside so as to make it very pretty."

As soon as the house was ready the Mahárájá went to his wife and asked her if she would go out with him to eat the air. " I should like to show you a new house I have had built for you," he said. So she went with him and thought her new house lovely. While she was inside looking at the pretty flowers in the rooms, the Mahárájá slipped out, and bolted the door so that she could not escape, and he told his servants to set fire to the wood under the flooring. When the flames began to rise the Ráni got very frightened. She rushed to the window and called to the Mahárájá and his servants, who were standing there looking on, to save her. No one said anything to her. " Save me," she cried, " or I shall be burnt to death." " If you are burnt, what does it matter ? " said the Mahárájá.

"You ill-treated my children; you killed them; so, now burn."

As soon as she was burnt to death the Mahárájá had all her bones collected and put into four dishes, and he gave them to one of his servants to take to Sunkási Rání's mother. When her mother uncovered dish after dish and found nothing but bones, she asked the servant, "Of what use are bones?" "These are your daughter's bones," said he: "therefore Anárbásá Mahárájá sent them to you. Sunkási Rání ill-treated and killed his children, and so he burnt her."

The rest of the story she pronounced exact (*thík*).

2. The bél-tree is the *Ægle Marmelós* of botanists.

3. With the different deaths and transformations of the children compare in this book : Phúlmati Rání, pp. 3 and 4: the Kite's Children, p. 22 : the Bél-Princess, pp. 144, 145, 148 : and in *Old Deccan Days* Surya Bai, pp. 85, 86. In "Die goldenen Kinder" (Schott's *Wallachische Maerchen*) the golden children are killed and buried (p. 122). From their hearts spring two apple-trees having golden leaves and apples. The trees are destroyed; but a sheep has eaten an apple and then has two golden lambs. The step-mother kills them at once and sends the maid to wash the entrails in the stream, intending to cook them for her husband to eat (compare the curry in the "Pomegranate King," p. 8 ; the broth (*Suhr*) in Grimm's "von dem Machandelboom," *Kinder und Hausmaerchen*, vol. I. p. 271 ; and the stew in the Devonshire story, "The Rose-Tree," told in Henderson's *Folk-lore of the Northern Counties of England*, p. 314). A piece of the entrail escapes, and as it floats away it swells and swells. On reaching the opposite bank it bursts, and out of it step the golden children. In a Hungarian story the children, one with a planet and one with a sun on his forehead, and each with a ring on his arm, are killed by a wicked woman who wants her daughter to take their mother's place as queen. They turn first into two golden pear-trees. These are destroyed by fire, but one glowing coal from the fire is eaten by an old she-goat. The old goat then has two little golden-fleeced kids. They are killed, an old crow swallows a piece of the entrails as they are being washed in the brook ; she flies to the seventy-seventh

island in the ocean, builds a nest and lays two golden eggs. Out of the eggs come the golden-haired children with their planet, sun and golden rings. The old crow sends them for seven years to school to a hermit (here is the holy man again, see p. 283 of these notes), and then flies home with them to their father. The pillar of salt, into which their mother was changed, answers all the king's questions. It is not said that she regained her human form ("Die verwandelten Kinder," Stier's *Ungarische Volks-maerchen*, p. 58). In a Siebenburg story, " Die beiden goldenen Kinder," the children are killed by an envious woman who becomes queen in their mother's place. From their remains spring two golden pine-trees which are burnt ; a sheep eats two of the sparks and has two golden lambs that are killed ; from two pieces of the entrails step forth the golden-haired children (Haltrich's *Siebenbuergische Maerchen*, pp. 2, 3). In this tale the children are restored to their father, the king, by the intervention of God himself (p. 4), who in these *Siebenbuergische Maerchen* plays a part just as often as " Khudá " does in the Indian tales, taking for the purpose the form of a " good old man," and often wearing a grey mantle that reminds one of Odin. In the Netherlandish story of " The knight with the swan " (Thorpe's *Northern Mythology*, vol. III. p. 302), King Oriant's mother persuades the king his wife gave him seven puppies instead of seven children (each born with a silver chain round its neck in " proof of their mother's nobility "). She sends the children to the forest to be destroyed. They are left there alive, and are fostered by an old man. When the queen-mother learns this, she sends servants to kill them. These are content with depriving six of the children of their silver chains, on which the children instantly become swans. (The seventh child is absent and so is saved.) A goldsmith makes two beakers out of one of the chains, and keeps the others intact. When the chains are hung again round the five swans' necks, and the beaker shown to the sixth, they regain their human forms. See also paragraph 8 of the notes to Phúlmati Rání.

4. With the children in the fruit and flowers compare in these stories, Phúlmati Rání, p. 3 : Loving Lailí, p. 81 : the Bél-Princess, p. 146, and paragraph 5 of the notes to that story,

p. 283 : and in *Old Deccan Days*, " Surya Bai," p. 86 : and " Anár Ráni and her two maids," p. 95. With these may be compared the Polish Madey (Naake's *Slavonic Fairy Tales*, p. 220). Madey is a robber who commits fearful crimes ; he repents, and sticks his " murderous club " upright in the ground, swearing to kneel before it till the boy who has caused his repentance returns as a bishop. Years go by : the boy, now a bishop, passes through Madey's forest. The club has become an apple-tree full of apples and he discovers Madey through their sweet odour. At Madey's request the bishop confesses him ; and as Madey confesses his crimes, the apples on the tree, one after another, become white doves and fly to heaven. They were the souls of those he had murdered.

In an unpublished story told by Dunkní, the incidents of the children being in the fruit, and the fruit not letting itself be gathered by any but the rightful owner of its contents (as is the case also with the Bél-Princess), again occur. In this story there is a prince called Aisab, who, as he wished very much to have children, married. At the same time he took an oath that if his child, when he had one, cried, he would kill it, and then if his wife cried he would kill her too. His first wife gave him a child who died ; she cried and was killed by her husband. The same thing happened to the second wife. He then married a third wife, called Gulfanár. She had a little son, Dímá-ahmad, and two or three years later another son, called Kará-mat. The first boy died, but Gulfanár did not cry—she only grieved for him in her heart. Karámat was unhappy from seeing other children playing with their brothers and sisters, and asked his mother " why he had no brother or sister to play with ? " She said, " Once you had a little brother and he died." Then Karámat began to cry, and his father killed him immediately with his sword because of his oath, though he loved Karámat dearly. The " mother was still sadder than before, but she never wept." Then God took pity on her and sent down into Prince Aisab's garden a big bél-tree, and on this bél-tree was a fruit. Every one tried to gather this fruit, even Prince Aisab tried, but each time their hands approached it the fruit rose into the air and returned again when the hands were withdrawn. Then Gulfanár stretched

out her hand "and the fruit fell into it." She took it into the
house and tried to break it open with a stone, and a voice called
out, "Mother, mother, not so hard ; you hurt us," She was
very much frightened, thinking a Rakshas or a demon was in
the fruit. Prince Aisab was equally alarmed, but his wazir,
Mamatsa, broke the fruit open gently in obedience to the little
voice that called out, " Don't knock so hard, Mamatsa ; you
hurt us ;" and out of it stepped the two little children Dímá-
ahmad and Karámat. Dímá-ahmad was very beautiful. On
his head was the sun, on his face the moon, and on his hands
stars, and he had long golden hair. He married a princess,
Atásá, who also had the sun on her head, the moon on her face,
stars on her hands, and "her hair was of pure gold and reached
down to the ground." The idea that none but the rightful owner
can catch the child is found too in Grey's *Polynesian Mythology*
at pp. 116, 117, in the story of Whakatau, who was fashioned in
the sea from his mother Apakura's apron by the god Rongota-
kawiu. This child lived at the bottom of the sea ; but one day
he came on shore after his kite, and all who saw him tried in
vain to catch him. Then said Whakatau, " You had better go
and bring Apakura here ; she is the only person who can catch
me and hold me fast." His mother then comes and catches him.

5. Sunkásí's bones are sent to her mother. In the *Sicilianische Maerchen* collected by Laura Gonzenbach, it is a
common practice for husbands to punish their second wives'
treachery with death, and then to send their remains to their
mothers, who feast on them, thinking they are eating tunny-
fish, and die of grief on learning what they have really
swallowed.

6. With Guliánar's change into a bird compare Laura Gonzenbach's 13th *Sicilianisches Maerchen*, vol. I. p. 82, where the
real bride is transformed into a dove by a black-headed pin
being driven into her head, and regains her human form when
the pin is pulled out. Schott has a similar incident in his *Wallachische Maerchen*, p. 251. So has Gubernatis (*Zoological Mythology*, vol. II. p. 242) in a story from near Leghorn, where
the woman is changed into a swallow (in all these stories it is
the husband who pulls out the pin) ; and he says similar stories

wfth a transformation into a dove are told in Piedmont, in other parts of Tuscany, in Calabria, and are to be found in the *Tutiname.* Ralston's Princess Mariya (*Russian Folk Tales*, p. 183), and Thorpe's second story of " The Princess that came out of the water " (*Yule Tide Stories*, p. 41), may also be compared.

7. The golden bird in the Siebenburg story drops pearls from its beak whenever it sings (" Der goldne Vogel," Haltrich's *Siebenbuergische Maerchen*, pp. 31, 35). The princess, its mistress, wears (p. 39) a golden mantle "adorned with *carbuncles* and pearls from the golden bird."

III.—THE CAT AND THE DOG.

1. The Tiger promises not to eat the man who helps him and then tries to break his promise. Compare " The Brahman, the Tiger, and the six Judges," *Old Deccan Days*, p. 159 ; and " Ananzi and the Lion " in Dasent's *Ananzi Stories*, p. 490.

2. In a Slavonic story mentioned by Gubernatis (*Zoological Mythology*, vol. II. p. 111), a bear is about to kill a peasant in revenge. A fox appears, " shakes its tail and says to the peasant, ' Man, thou hast ingenuity in thy head and a stick in thy hand.' The peasant immediately understands the stratagem," and persuades the bear to get into a sack he has with him that he may carry the bear three times round the field instead of doing penance, after which the bear is to do what he likes with him. The bear gets into the sack, the man " binds it strongly" together, and then beats the bear to death with his stick. Gubernatis at p. 132 of the same volume tells a similar story from Russia in which a wolf plays the part of the bear and of our tiger.

IV.—THE CAT THAT COULD NOT BE KILLED.

1. In an unpublished story told us by Gangiyá, a hill-man from near Simla, a cat saves herself from being eaten by a

jackal very much in the same way that this cat saved herself from the leopard. The jackal (in Gangiyá's story) ate anything it came across, whether it were dead or alive. One day he met a tiger and said to him, " I will eat you. I will not let you go." "Very good," said the tiger, " eat me." So the jackal ate him up. He went a little further and met a leopard ; he said to the leopard, " I will eat you." "Very good," said the leopard. So he ate the leopard. He went a little further and met a tiny mouse. " Mouse," he said, " I have eaten a tiger and a leopard, and now I will eat you." "Very good," said the mouse. He ate the mouse. He went a little further and met a cat. " I will eat you," said the jackal. The cat answered, " What will it profit you to eat me, who am so small ? A little further on you will see a dead buffalo : eat that." So the jackal left the cat and went to eat the buffalo. He walked on and on, but could find no buffalo ; and the cat, meanwhile ran away. The jackal was very angry, and set off to seek the cat, but could not find her. He was furious.

VI.—THE RAT AND THE FROG.

Compare the Bohemian " Long-desired child," Naake's *Slavonic Fairy Tales*, p. 226. This child is carved out of a tree-root by a woodman, who brings him home to his wife. They delight in having a child at last. The child eats all the food in the house ; his father and mother ; a girl with a wheelbarrow full of clover ; a peasant, his hay-laden cart, and his cart-horses ; a man and his pigs ; a shepherd, his flock and dog ; lastly, cabbages belonging to an old woman who cuts him in two with her mattock just as he tries to eat her. Out of him jump unhurt every thing and every one he has swallowed. In a story from the south of Siberia (Gubernatis' *Zoological Mythology*, vol. I. p. 140) the hero vanquishes a demon, who tells him that in his stomach he will find a silver casket. He cuts the monster open and out of him come " innumerable animals, men, treasures, and other objects. Some of the men say, ' What noble youth has delivered us from the black night?'" In two of the caskets the hero finds the eyes of an old woman who has befriended him, and money, "and from the last casket came forth more men, animals, and valuables of every kind." In a Russian story quoted by Gubernatis (*Zoological Mythology*, vol. I. pp. 406, 407) the wolf eats the kids all but one. The mother goat persuades him to jump over a fire. The fire splits his belly open, out tumble all the little kids, lively as ever. There is a very similar story with fox, goat, and kid for actors in Campbell's *Popular Tales of the West Highlands*, vol. III. p. 93; and Grimm has one also, "Der Wolf und die sieben jungen Geislein," in his *Kinder und Hausmaerchen*, vol. I. p. 29. In the notes to this story, vol. III. p. 15, Grimm says, " In Pomerania this is told of a child who when his mother had gone out was swallowed by the child-spectre, resembling the varlet Ruprecht. But the stones which he swallows with the child make the spectre so heavy that he falls to the earth, and the child unhurt springs out of him." See, too, the demons at p. 99 of these stories, who swallow the Princess Chámpákalí's suitors.

Tylor in his *Primitive Culture*, vol. I. p. 341, classes Little Red Riding Hood among these Day and Night myths. It is, he says, "mutilated in the English Nursery version, but known more perfectly by old wives in Germany, who can tell that the lovely little maid in her shining red satin cloak was swallowed with her grandmother by the wolf, but they both came out safe and sound when the hunter cut open the sleeping beast." He also quotes among these myths (*ib.* p. 338) a story of the Ojibwas in which the hero is swallowed by a great fish and cut out again by his sister ; and another belonging to the Basutos in which all mankind save the hero and his mother were devoured by a monster. The hero "attacked the creature and was swallowed whole, but cutting his way out he set free all the inhabitants of the world." At the same page is the story of the Zulu Princess Untombinde who was carried off by a dreadful beast. "The king gathered his army and attacked it, but it swallowed up men, and dogs, and cattle, all but one warrior ; he slew the monster, and there came out cattle, and horses, and men, and last of all the princess herself." Mr. Tylor quotes, too (*ib.* p. 336), in connexion with this class of myths, the story of the death of the New Zealand sun-hero, Maui, which he tells more fully than does Sir George Grey in his *Polynesian Mythology;* and he goes on at pp. 338, 339, 340, to connect these myths with those of Perseus and Andromeda ; Heracles and Hesione ; the story of Jonah and his fish ; the Greenland angakok swallowed by bear and walrus and thrown up again ; and the legend of Hades.

Besides the angakok mentioned by Mr. Tylor, Dr. Rink, in his *Tales and Traditions of the Eskimo,* has two other stories of escapes from the stomach of a dead animal when it is cut open. In the first, at p. 260, the boy is devoured by a gull ; his sister kills the bird, takes her brother's bones from its pouch and carries them home : on the way the boy comes to life again. The other tale, p. 438, tells how Nakasungnak jumped out of the hole his friends had made in the dead "ice-covered" bear's side ; but his hair as well as the skin of his face had come off, and he shivered from cold and ague. And in Ralston's *Songs of the Russian People,* p. 177, is a story of a snake who steals "the luminaries of the night. A hero cuts off his head, and out of the slain monster issue the Bright Moon and the Morning Star."

VII.—FOOLISH SACHÚLÍ.

1. Foolish Sachúlí lives in many lands. In his Russian dress he figures in "The Fool and the Birch-tree," Ralston's *Russian Folk Tales,* p. 52. In the Sicilian "Giufá" we find him again (Gonzenbach's *Sicilianische Maerchen,* vol. I. p. 249). In England he appears in an out-of-the-way village in the south (see *Pall Mall Budget,* July 12, 1878, p. 11, *Wild Life in a Southern Country,* No. XIV.) with, to use his mother's words, "no more sense than God had given him." She wishing to have his testimony discredited when he bears witness against her, as she knows he will, goes upstairs and rains raisins on

him from the window. So when asked to specify the time he speaks of, he says, "When it rained raisins," and is of course disbelieved.

Note by Mr. J. F. Campbell : "This story of a stupid boy has a parallel in a Gaelic tale in my collection, where the boy dated an event which was true by a fall of pancakes or something of the kind which was not true, and was not believed though he told the truth." [At p. 385, vol. II. of the *Tales of the West Highlands* a "half booby" is inveigled by his mother into dating his theft of some planks by a "shower of milk-porridge."]

2. The magic gifts given by the fairies are a common incident in fairy tales : so is the adventure with the jar of ghee.

VIII.—BARBER HÍM AND THE TIGERS.

1. Forbes in his Hindústání Dictionary says *Kans* or *Kansa* was the name of a wicked tyrant whom Krishna was born to destroy, and that the word now means a wicked tyrant. But Rájá Káns is an historical character. All that is known of him is told by the late Professor Blochmann in the Bengal Asiatic Society's Journal for 1873, Pt. I. p. 264.

2. In the note (p. 380) to the XIXth Tale in the *Sagas from the Far East*, is a story in which Barber Hím's part is played by a he-goat, and that of his tigers by a lion. See, too, "How the three clever men outwitted the demons" in *Old Deccan Days*, pp. 273—278. In a Santálí tale, "Kanran and Guja," sent by the Rev. F. T. Cole to the *Indian Antiquary*, vol. IV. September 1875, p. 257, two brothers, Kanran and Guja, climb into a tál tree. Here they are discovered by a tiger whom they have deprived of his tail, and who has brought a number of his friends to help him revenge himself on the brothers. The tailless tiger proposes they shall all stand one the top of the other, to reach the men in the tree. His friends agree provided he takes his stand at the bottom, and they climb as proposed till they almost reach the brothers. Then Kanran calls out to

Guja, " Give me your axe. I will kill the tailless tiger." The tigers in terror all tumble to the ground, crushing their tailless friend in their fall, and flee to their homes. In " The Leopard and the Ram " (Bleek's *Hottentot Fables and Tales*, p. 24) the ram and the leopard play the parts of the barber and his tigers. See, too, " The Lion and the Bushman," p. 59 of the same collection.

Note by Mr. J. F. Campbell: " Compare the Irish story of two hunchbacks in Keightley. A version is in Mitford's Japanese book ; and far better versions are common in Japan."

IX.—THE BULBUL AND THE COTTON-TREE.

1. Cotton-tree, in Hindústání *Semal.*
2. Koel, Indian cuckoo.

X.—THE MONKEY PRINCE.

1. Bandarsá means like a monkey ; Dunkní in telling this husk-story just as often called the monkey-skin a husk (*chhilka*) as she called it a skin (*chamrá*).
2. Princess Jahúran throws mattresses to her drowning husband. In a Manípurí tale published by Mr. G. H. Damant in the *Indian Antiquary*, vol. IV. September 1875, p. 260, Basanta's wife throws him a pillow that he may save himself when the envious merchant, on board whose boat they are, pitches the prince into the river that he may secure the princess for himself.

XI.—BRAVE HÍRÁLÁBÁSÁ.

1. With this story all through compare " The Demon is at last conquered by the King's Son," p. 173 of this collection.
2. Rakshas means protector, and is, probably, an euphemistic term. The chapter on Mystic Animals in Swedish traditions

(Thorpe's *Northern Mythology*, vol. II. p. 83) gives a list of certain creatures that are not to be mentioned by their own but by euphemistic names for fear of incurring their wrath. This belief, Thorpe in the same chapter, p. 84, says, extends to certain inanimate things : water used for brewing, for instance, must not be called *vatn* (water) or the beer will not be so good ; and fire occasionally is to be spoken of as *hetta* (heat). The girl in an Esthonian tale quoted by Gubernatis at p. 151 of the 1st vol. of his *Zoological Mythology* addresses a crow whose help she needs as "Bird of light." Fiske says (*Myths and Mythmakers*, p. 223), "A Dayak will not allude by name to the small-pox, but will call it "The chief" or "Jungle leaves;" the Laplander speaks of the bear as "the old man with the fur coat;" in Annam the tiger is called "Grandfather," or "Lord." The Finnish hunters called the bear "the Apple of the Forest, the beautiful Honey-claw, the Pride of the thicket" ("The Mythology of Finnland," *Fraser's Magazine*, May 1857). The Furies, as every one knows, were called the Eumenides, or the gracious ones.

The Rakshases are a kind of huge demons who delight in devouring men and beasts. They can take any shape they please. The female Rakshas often assumes that of a beautiful woman. Compare the demon Mara as described by Fiske at p. 93 of his book above quoted.

The Rakshases do not travel in the way mortals do. See a Dinájpur story told by Mr. G. H. Damant in the *Indian Antiquary* (February 1875, vol. IV. p. 54), where the hero, who has married both the Rakshas-king's daughter and his niece, asks his father-in-law's leave to return home with his Rakshas-wives. The King consents (p. 58), but says, "We Rakshases do not travel in pálkís (palanquins), but in the air." Accordingly the prince, his two Rakshas wives and his mortal wife, all travel towards his father's country through the air "along the sky." One kind of jinn travel in the same way (Lane's *Arabian Nights*, vol. I., "Notes to Introduction," p. 29). So do the drakes and kobolds in Northern Germany. The drake is as big as a cauldron, "a person may sit in him," and travel with him to any spot he pleases. Both drakes and kobolds look like fiery stripes. The kobolds appear sometimes as a blue, sometimes as a red, stripe passing through the air (Thorpe's *Northern Mythology,*) vol. III. pp. 155, 156).

3. Dunkní says, "All Rakshases keep their souls in birds." Those that do so resemble in this respect some of the Indian demons, and the giants, trolls, and such like noxious actors in the Norse, Scotch, and other popular tales.

Tylor (*Primitive Culture*, vol. II. pp. 152, 153) mentions the Tatar story of the giant who could not be killed till the twelve-headed snake in which he kept his soul was destroyed. This tale, he says, "illustrates the idea of soul-embodiment," and "very likely" indicates the sense of the myths where giants, &c., keep their souls out of their own bodies. The civilized notion of soul-embodiment, he adds (quoting from "Grose's bantering description of the art of laying ghosts in the last century,") is that of conjuring ghosts into different objects: "one of the many good instances of articles of savage belief serving as jests among civilized men." Possibly these giants, trolls, rakshases, demons, once belonged to that class of spirits who could, in popular belief, enter at pleasure into stocks and stones and other objects of idolatrous veneration.

But all Rakshases do not keep their souls in birds. Some have their souls in bees (see a Dinájpur tale published by Mr. G. H. Damant in the *Indian Antiquary* for April 6, 1872, p. 115): and in another Dinájpur story printed by Mr. Damant in the *Indian Antiquary* for June 7, 1872, p. 120, a whole, tribe of Rakshases dwelling in Ceylon kept theirs in one and the same lemon.

4. In the first quoted of these stories collected by Mr. Damant, that where the Rakshases keep their life in bees, the hero is a prince who starts in search of the wonderful tree mentioned in paragraph 8 of the note to Phúlmati Rání (p. 244). In his wanderings he finds himself in the Rakshas country. There he meets with the woman who when cut up turns into the tree he seeks. When he first sees her she lies dead on a bed with a golden wand on one side of her, and a silver wand on the other. He accidently touches her with the golden wand and

she wakes. She tells him the Rakshases, every morning when they go out in search of food, make her dead by touching her with the silver wand, and wake her with the golden wand when they return at night. Mr. Damant has another story in the *Indian Antiquary* (July 5, 1872, vol. I. p. 219), from Dinájpur, in which there is a prince Dalim who dies and is laid in a tomb above ground, not buried. Daily the Apsarases, the dancing-girls in the court of Indra, wake him from death by touching his face with a golden wand, and make him dead again by touching him with a silver wand. These wands they always leave lying beside him. His wife comes one day to mourn over him and accidentally discovers the secret of bringing him to life. He is, finally, restored to her by the Apsarases.

5. According to Gubernatis, "three and seven are sacred numbers in Aryan faith" (*Zoological Mythology*, vol. I. p. 6).

6. Hírálábásá addresses the Rakshas as "uncle." The two brothers Kanran and Guja (in a Santálí fairy tale bearing their name printed by the Rev. F. T. Cole in the *Indian Antiquary*, September 1875, vol. IV. p. 257), address a tiger by the same propitiatory title. The tiger in return addresses them as nephews, and gives them the fire they want.

"Uncle" and "aunt" are used in a propitiatory sense over a great part of the world. Hunt at p. 6 of his introduction to the *Romances and Drolls of the West of England* says, "Uncle is a term of respect, which was very commonly applied to aged men by their juniors in Cornwall. Aunt . . . was used in the same manner when addressing aged women." "Mon oncle" and "ma tante" are sometimes used in the same way in France. Fiske in his *Myths and Mythmakers*, pp. 166, 167, tells how the Zulu solar hero Uthlakanyana outwits a cannibal : in this story the hero addresses the cannibal as "uncle," and the cannibal in return calls him "child of my sister." Fiske, quoting from Dr. Callaway, at p. 166, says, "It is perfectly clear that the cannibals of the Zulu legends are not common men ; they are magnified into giants and magicians ; they are remarkably swift and enduring ; fierce and terrible warriors." In the Hottentot story of the "Lion who took a woman's shape," the lion and the woman address each other as "my aunt," and "my uncle" (Bleek's *Hottentot Fables and Tales*, pp. 51, 52). In Siberia the Yakuts worship the bear under the name of their "beloved uncle" (Tylor's *Primitive Culture*, vol. II. p. 231); and when the Russian peasant calls on the dreaded Lyeshy to appear he cries, "Uncle Lyeshy" (Ralston's *Songs of the Russian people*, p. 159).

"Grannie" is the word used by Dunkní herself.

7. The Rakshas queen is tricked to her death in the same way as the wicked step-mother in the "Pomegranate King," p. 12 of this collection.

XII.—THE MAN WHO WENT TO SEEK HIS FATE.

1. Compare a Servian story, "Das Schicksal" (Karadschitsch, *Volksmaerchen der Serben*, p. 106), in which a man sets out to seek his fate, and on the road is commissioned by a rich householder to ask the fate why, though he gives abundance of food to his servants, he can never satisfy their hunger, and why his aged, miserable father and mother do not die: by another man, to ask why his cattle diminish instead of thriving: and, thirdly, by a river whose waters bear him safely across it, to ask why no living thing lives in it. His fate answers all these questions, and instructs him how to thrive himself. In Fräulein Gonzenbach's *Sicilian Fairy Tales*, "Die Geschichte von Caterina und ihrem Schicksal," vol. I. p. 130, Caterina is persecuted by her fate, who wears the form of a lovely woman. At last she begs her mistress's fate, to whom she daily carries a propitiatory offering, to intercede for her with her own fate. She is told in answer that her own fate is wrapped in seven veils and so cannot hear her prayer. Finally her mistress's fate leads her to her own. In the same collection, in "Feledico und Epomata" (vol. I. p. 350), Feledico's fate plays a personal part.

This Indian story looks like a relic of stock and stone worship (see Tylor's *Primitive Culture*, vol. II. chapters XIV.

and XV.). Compare the man's beating his fate-stone with the treatment the Ostyak gives his puppet. If it is good to him he clothes and feeds it with broth ; "if it brings him no sport he will try the effect of a good thrashing on it, after which he will clothe and feed it again" (*ib.* p. 170). Other examples are given at the same page. These spirits and gods, for whose dwelling-place stocks and stones and other objects had been supplied, were not supposed always to inhabit these abodes ; but they did so at pleasure. Compare Elijah's address to the priests of Baal, "Cry aloud : for he is a god ; either he is talking, or he is pursuing, or he is in a journey, or per-adventure he sleepeth" (1 Kings xviii. 27), with Caterina's seven-veiled fate, and the prostrate fate-stone in our story whose spirit-owner was evidently absent on some expedition. These fates may be compared with the patron or guardian spirits of whom Mr. Tylor speaks at pp. 199—203 of the same volume. He says (p. 202), "The Egyptian astrologer warned Antonius to keep far from the young Octavius, 'for thy demon,' said he, 'is in fear of his.'" If one man's demon or genius were at enmity with that of another man, it would probably be friendly to that of a third man, and would therefore be acquainted with its secrets and with its motives of behaviour to the man it guarded. Hence the advice given by her mistress to Caterina to inquire of her own fate from her mistress's fate, and the questions to be put to their fates when found given to the men in the Indian and Servian stories. These questions remind one of those entrusted to the youths in European tales as they journey to the dragon or devil to whom they are sent for destruction. Like the fates in the Indian and Servian stories, these dragons and devils live at the end of a long and difficult journey. Caterina has to climb a mountain to visit her mistress's fate.

2. Gubernatis (*Zoological Mythology*, vol. I. p. 22), speaking of the three *Ribhavas*, says, "During the twelve days (the twelve hours of the night or the twelve months in the year) in which they are the guests of Agohyas," &c. So possibly the twelve years in this and other stories in this collection may be the twelve hours of the night. In an unpublished story told by Dunkní, "Prince Húsainsá's journey," the prince journeys for

twelve years. When he returns home he finds his parents as he had left them—fast asleep in bed. To them the twelve years had only been as one night."

XIII.—THE UPRIGHT KING.

1. The Boar is an avatár of Vishnu.

2. A ḍom (the d is lingual) is a Hindú of a very low caste.

3. Possibly this king is the same as the king Harichand in the last story but one in the collection, p. 224, and he may also be the Hariçchandra of the following letter from Mr. C. H. Tawney :—

"I have been looking up the story of 'Hariçchandra.' It is to be found in Muir, vol. I. He gives a summary of it from the *Markaṇḍeya Puráṇa.* It is also found in the 'Chanda Kauçikam,' and in Mutu Coomara Swamy's 'Martyr of Truth.' The following is Muir's summary summarized. Hariçchandra was a king who lived in the Tretá age, and was renowned for his virtue, and for the universal prosperity, moral and physical, which prevailed during his reign. One day he heard a sound of female lamentation which proceeded from the Sciences who were becoming mastered by the austere Sage, Viçvamitra, in a way they had never been before. He rushed to their assistance as a Kshatriya bound to succour the oppressed. By a haughty speech he provoked Viçvamitra, and in consequence of his wrath the Sciences instantly perished. (In the 'Chanda Kauçikam,' as far as I remember, we are told that the anger of Viçvamitra interfered with the success of his austerity.) The king says he had only done his duty as a king, which involves the bestowal of gifts on Bráhmans and the succour of the weak. Viçvamitra thereupon demands from the king as a gift the whole earth, everything but himself, his son, and his wife. The king gives it him. Then Viçvamitra demands his sacrificial fee ; the king goes to Benares, followed by the relentless Sage, the ruler of Çiva, and is compelled to sell his wife. She is bought by a rich old Bráhman. The son cries and the Bráhman buys him too. But Hariçchandra has not enough, even now, to satisfy Viçvamitra, so he sells himself to a Chándála, who is really Dharma, the god of righteousness. The Chándála (man of the lowest caste), carries off the king, bound, beaten, and confused. The Chándála sends him to steal clothes in a cemetery. There he lives twelve months. His wife comes to the cemetery to perform the obsequies of her son, who had died from the bite of a serpent. The two determine to burn themselves with the corpse of their son. When Hariçchandra, after placing his son on the funeral pyre, is meditating on the Supreme Spirit, the lord Hari Náráyaṇa Kṛishṇa, all the gods arrive headed by Dharma (righteousness) and accompanied by Viçvamitra. Dharma entreats the king to desist from his rash enterprise, and Indra announces to him that he, his wife, and his son have gained heaven by their good works. Ambrosia and flowers are rained by the god from the sky, and the king's son is restored to the bloom of youth. The king, adorned with celestial clothing and garments, and the queen, embrace their son. Hariçchandra, however, declares that he cannot go to heaven till he has received his master the Chándála's permission, and paid him a ransom. Dharma, the god of righteousness, then says that he had miraculously assumed the form of a Chándála. The king requests that his subjects may accompany him to heaven, at least for one day. This request is granted by Indra ; and after Viçvamitra has inaugurated the king's son, Rohitaçva, as his successor, Hariçchandra, his friends and followers, all ascend to heaven."

XIV.—LOVING LAILÍ.

1. Majnún is a celebrated lover, whose love for Lailí or Lailá is the subject of many Eastern poems. In this story he does not play a brilliant part.

2. Lailí's knife is like the sun-hero's weapon (the sun's ray), which lengthens at its owner's pleasure (Gubernatis, *Zoological Mythology*, vol. II. p. 147).

3. She cuts her little finger. See "the Bél Princess," p. 141, and paragraph 2 of the note to "Shekh Faríd." "The little

finger, though the smallest, is the most privileged of the five. It is the one that knows eyerything." A Piedmontese mother says, " My little finger tells me everything" (Gubernatis, *Zoological Mythology*, vol. I. p. 166). We have a somewhat similar saying in England. In a Russian story quoted by the same author in the same work (vol. II. p. 151), an old woman while baking a cake, cuts off her little finger and throws it into the fire. From the little finger in the fire is born a strong dwarf who afterwards does many wonderful things. In the tale of the five fingers (" Die Maehr von den fuenf Fingern," Haltrich's *Siebenbuergische Maerchen*, p. 325), where each finger decides what it will do, the little one says, " I will help with wise counsel." In consequence of this assistance, to this day, " when any one has a wise idea (Einfall), he says 'that his little finger told him that'" (p. 327). In Finnish mythology we again find the little finger. " The Para, also originated in the Swedish Bjaeren or Bare, a magical three-legged being, manufactured in various ways, and which, says Castrén, attained life and motion when its possessor, cutting the little finger of his left hand, let three drops of blood fall on it, at the same time pronouncing the proper spell." (" The Mythology of Finnland," *Fraser's Magazine* for May 1857, p. 532.)

In Rink's *Tales and Traditions of the Eskimo*, p. 441, there is an account of Kanak's visit to the man of the moon, where he meets a woman who, he is warned, will take out his entrails if she can only make him laugh. He follows the moon-man's advice, which is to rub his leg with the nail of his little finger when he can no longer keep from smiling, and so saves himself from the old hag. Rishya Sriṅga (to return to the land of our fairy tales) threw a drop of water from the nail of his little finger on a Rakshas who, in the form of a tiger, was rushing to devour him. The demon instantly quitted the tiger's body, and asked the Rishi what he should do. He followed the holy man's instructions and obtained môksha (salvation)—see *Indian Antiquary* for May 1873, p. 142, "The Legend of Rishya Sriṅga," told by V. N. Narasimmiyengar of Bangalor.

XV.—HOW KING BURTAL BECAME A FAKÍR.

1. The Fakír strikes the dead antelope with his wand (*chábuk*), as in "Shekh Faríd," p. 98. In both cases Dunkní says the wand used was a long, slender piece of bamboo. I do not know whether the bamboo is a lightning-plant. Possibly it is, being a grass (some grasses are lightning-plants, see Fiske's *Myths and Myth-makers*, pp. 56, 61), and also because its long slender stems are lance-shaped. If it does belong to this class, naturally a blow from a bamboo (or lightning) wand would give life, for, says Fiske (*ib.* p. 60), "the association of the thunder-storm with the approach of summer has produced many myths in which the lightning is symbolized as the life-renewing wand of the victorious sun-god."

2. The king tries to hide the ball in his hair. The wonderful power and strength of hair appears in tales from all lands : Signor de Gubernatis suggests that, in the case of solar heroes, their hair is the sun's rays (*Zoological Mythology*, vol. I. p. 117, vol. II. p. 154); and it seems to me possible that, just as the *colour* of the solar hero's hair has been appropriated by Indian fairy-tale princes who are not solar, the *qualities* of his hair may have been attributed to that of folk-lore heroes who are not solar, and may also have been the origin of some of the strange superstitions prevalent about human hair. This theory, if correct, would account for most of the strange things that I have hitherto met about hair. It must be remembered that the sun's rays are also his weapons ; they turn to thunderbolts when the sun is hidden in the rain-clouds (Gubernatis, *ib.* vol. I. pp. 9, 17), and also to lightning (see *ib.* vol. II. p. 10, where the sun under the form of a bull is spoken of as the fire which sends forth lightning).

First there is Samson, whose name, according to Gesenius, means "solar," "like the sun." Of the hero Firud, it is told "that a single hair of his head has more strength in it than many warriors" (Gubernatis, *Zoological Mythology*, vol. I. p. 117). Conan was the weakest man of the Féinn, because they used to keep him cropped. "He had but the strength of a man ; but if the hair should get leave to grow, there was the

strength of a man in him for every hair that was in his head ;
but he was so cross that if the hair should grow he would kill
them all " (Campbell's *Popular Tales of the West Highlands*,
vol. III. p. 396). At p. 91 of Schmidt's *Griechische Maerchen,
Sagen, und Volkslieder*, is the story of a king, " Der Capitaen
Dreizehn," who is "the strongest of his time," and who has
three long hairs, so long that they could be twisted twice round
the hand on his breast. When these are cut off he becomes the
weakest of men. When these grow again he regains his
strength. The sun's rays have most power when they are
longest, *i. e.* when the sun is in apogee.

Possibly from this old forgotten myth about the solar hero's
hair came some superstition to which was due the Merovingian
decree that only princes of the blood-royal should wear their
hair long ; cutting their long hair made them incapable of becoming kings. Their slaves were shaved. The barbarians
ruled that only their free men should wear long hair, and that
the slaves should be shaved. Professor Monier Williams, in the
Contemporary Review for January 1879, p. 265, says that Govind,
the 10th Guru and founder of the Sikh nationality, ordered the
Sikhs to wear their hair long to distinguish themselves from
other nations.

In the Slavonic story, " Leben, Abenteuer und Schwaenke des
kleinen Kerza," is a dwarf magician with a long white beard.
With a hair from this beard Kerza binds the magician's wicked
wife, who has taken the form of a wooden pillar the better to carry
out her evil ends. From that moment it was impossible for her
to take again her own shape or to use her former magic powers
(Vogl's *Volksmaerchen*, p. 227). One of the tasks set by Yspadda-
den Penkawr to Kilhwch before he will give him his daughter
Olwen to wife, is to get him "a leash made from the beard
of Dissull Varvawc, for that is the only one that can hold
the two cubs. And the leash will be of no avail unless it be
plucked from his beard while he is alive, and twitched out
with wooden tweezers . . . . and the leash will be of no use
should he be dead because it will be brittle,"—that is, when the
sun is set (dead) his rays have no power (*Mabinogion*,
vol. II. p. 288). The same idea lies at the bottom of the

English superstition that "if a person's hair burn brightly when thrown into the fire, it is a sign of longevity ; the brighter the flame, the longer the life. On the other hand, if it smoulder away, and refuse to burn, it is a sign of approaching death" (Henderson's *Folk-lore of the Northern Counties of England,* p. 84).

The Malays have a story of a woman, called Utahigi, in whose head grew a single white hair endowed with magic power. When her husband pulled it out a great storm arose and Utahigi went up to heaven. She was a bird (or cloud) maiden, and this hair must have been the lightning drawn from the cloud. The Servian Atalanta, when nearly overtaken by her lover, takes a hair from the top of her head and throws it behind her. It becomes a mighty wood (clouds are the forests and mountains of the sky, Gubernatis, *Zoological Mythology,* vol. I. p. 11), Karadschitsch, *Volksmaerchen der Serben,* p. 25, in the story "von dem Maedchen das behender als das Pferd ist." In Schmidt's *Griechische Maerchen, Sagen und Volkslieder,* p. 79, the king's daughter as she flies with her lover from the Lamnissa throws some of her own hairs behind her, and they become a great lake (thunderbolts and lightning bring rain). At p. 98 of the same work is the story "Der Riese vom Berge." When this giant wishes to enter his great high mountain, he takes a hair from his head and touches the mountain with it. The mountain at once splits in two (p. 101). The king's daughter in her encounter with the Efreet, "plucked a hair from her head and muttered with her lips, whereupon the hair became converted into a piercing sword with which she struck the lion [the Efreet], and he was cleft in twain by her blow; but his head became changed into a scorpion" (Lane's *Arabian Nights,* vol. I. p. 156). A Baba Yaga, in Ralston's *Russian Folk Tales,* p. 147, plucks one of her hairs, ties three knots in it, and blows, and thus petrifies her victims. She is a personification of the spirit of the storm, *ib.* p. 164. In *Old Deccan Days,* at p. 62, the old Rakshas says to Ramchundra, "You must not touch my hair ;" "the least fragment of my hair thrown in the direction of the jungle would instantly set it in a blaze." Ramchundra steals two or three of the hairs, and when escaping from the

Rakshas, flings them to the winds and fires the jungle. Chan-
dra (p. 266 of the same book) avenges the death of her husband by tearing her hair, which burns and instantly sets fire
to the land ; all the people in it but herself and a few who had
been kind to her and are therefore saved, were burnt in this great
fire.

In these tales a single hair from the head of the Princess
Labám (the lunar ray can pierce the cloud as well as a solar
ray) cuts a thick tree-trunk in two, p. 163.

Hair has another property ; it can tell things to its owners.
See the three hairs the Queen gives Coachman Toms, saying,
" They will always tell you the truth when you question them."
(Stier's *Ungarische Volksmaerchen*, p. 176), and which, later in
the story (p. 186) adjudge the king worthy of death. (See
Grimm's story *Kinder und Hausmaerchen*, vol. II. p. 174, " The
clear sun brings day".) Also " Das wunderbare Haar "
(Karadschitsch *Volksmaerchen der Serben*, p. 180), which is
blood-red, and in which when split open were found written a
multitude of noteworthy events from the beginning of the world.
(The sun's rays have existed since the early ages of the world.)
The girl from whose head the hair is taken threads a needle
with the sun's rays and embroiders a net made of the hair of
heroes.

See, too, the Eskimo account of the removal of Disco Island
in Rink's *Tales and Traditions of the Eskimo*, p. 464, where one
old man vainly tries to keep back the island by means of a
seal-skin thong which snaps, while two other old men haul it
away triumphantly by the hair from the head of a little child,
chanting their spells all the time. Their success was, perhaps,
due to the spells, not to the hair. In the notes to Der Capitän
Dreizehn in Schmidt's *Griechische Maerchen, Sagen und
Volkslieder*, there are some instances of the strength given by
hair to those on whom it grows.

2. The lichi is Nephelium Lichi.

3. King Burtal's eldest son's name *Sázáda* is perhaps the
boy's title Shahzádá (born of a king), prince. Dunkní says it is
his name.

XVI.—SOME OF THE DOINGS OF SHEKH FARÍD.

1. Khelápari means "playful fairy:" Gulábsá, "like a rose."

2. In another version told to me this year by Dunkní, when Gursan Rájá wakes and learns how long his wife has stood by him, he is horrified, and refuses the water, saying he does not want it. He tells her that as a reward for her patience and goodness, she shall know of herself everything that happens in other countries—floods, fires, and other troubles ; that she shall be able to bring help ; and should any one die from having his throat cut she shall be able to restore him to life, by smearing the wound with some blood taken from an incision in her little finger. Keláparí's acquaintance with Shekh Faríd begins in this version as follows :—She was standing at the door of her house looking down the road, when she saw coming towards her Shekh Faríd, the cartman, and the bullock-cart laden with what once was sugar, but now, thanks to the fakír, is ashes. Through her gift Khelápari knows all that has happened, though the miracle was not performed in her sight ; and Shekh Faríd being a fakír, though his all-knowing talent does not equal hers, knows that she knows. The cartman is in despair when he discovers the ashes, and implores Shekh Faríd to help him. The fakír sends him to Keláparí, saying he must appeal to her as her power of doing good excels his (the fakír's) ; that though he could turn sugar to ashes, he could not turn the ashes to sugar. Keláparí at the cartman's prayer performs this miracle. Their next encounter is by a tank in the jungle by which the holy man is resting. She is hurrying along to put out the fire at her father's palace. The Shekh cannot understand how it is possible for any woman to know of herself what is happening twenty miles off, when he, a fakír, can only know what passes at a short distance, so he follows the Rání to test her truthfulness, and arrives in time to see her helping to put out the fire. The rest of the story is the same as the version printed in this collection.

3. This Shekh Faríd was a famous Súfí saint. He was a contemporary of Nának, and many of his sayings are embodied

in the Granth. In Central India, there is a holy hill of his called Girur. The Gazetteer of the Central Provinces edited by C. Grant, 2nd edition, Nágpur, 1870, says that articles of merchandise belonging to two travelling traders who mocked the saint passed before him, on which he turned the whole stock-in-trade into stones as a punishment. They implored his pardon, and he created a fresh stock for them from dry leaves, on which they were so struck by his power that they attached themselves permanently to his service, and two graves on the hill are said to be theirs. In the *Pioneer* for 5th August 1878, Pekin has a poem on a similar legend about the saint. Standing on his holy hill, one day Shekh Faríd saw a packman pass and he begged for alms. The packman mocked him. Then the saint asked what his sacks contained. "Stones," was the answer. The Shekh said, "Sooth—they are but worthless stones." Whereupon all the sacks burst, and the contents, at one time different kinds of spices, fell stones to the ground. The owner implored the saint's mercy. Shekh Faríd told him to fill his sacks with leaves from the trees, which was done, and then the leaves became gold mohurs. The packman turned saint too and left his bones on Girur. A similar miracle is told of the Irish Saint, Brigit. Once upon a time Brigit beheld a man with salt on his back. "What is that on thy back?" saith Brigit; "Stones," saith the man. "They shall be stones then," saith Brigit, and of the salt stones were made. "The same man again cometh to (or past) Brigit. "What is that on thy back?" saith Brigit. "Salt," saith the man. "It shall be salt then," saith Brigit. Salt was made again thereof through Brigit's word." (*Three Middle Irish Homilies*, p. 81.)

4. Fakírchand means the moon of fakírs. Mohandás, the servant of the Mohan (Krishna). Champákali is a necklace made in imitation of the closed buds of the champa or champak flowers.

5. The demons, in Hindústání *dew* (pronounced deo), god, are something like the Rakshases. They have wings, and have exceedingly long lips, one of which sticks up in the air, while the other hangs down. One of King Arthur's warriors, " Gwevyl, the son of Gwestad, on the day that he was sad, he

T

would let one of his lips drop below his waist while he turned up the other like a cap upon upon his head" (*Mabinogion*, vol. II. p. 266, "Kilhwch and Olwen").

XVII.—THE MOUSE.

1. Unluckily, when Karím was with us, I neglected to write down the name of the grain that kills the mouse, and all the wonderful things he told us of the properties of this grain. His explanations were a kind of note given after he had finished the story.

2. The only parallel I can find to this story is one in Bleek's *Hottentot Fables and Tales*, p. 90, called "The unreasonable child to whom the dog gave its deserts ; or a receipt for putting any one to sleep," in which the child indulges in the uncalled for generosity and unreasonable rage of the mouse.

XVIII.—A WONDERFUL STORY.

1. Ajít means unsubdued, invincible.

2. The wrestler's mode of announcing his arrival at Ajit's house is, probably, the solitary result of many efforts to induce Karím himself to knock at the nursery door before he marched into the nursery. I never heard of natives knocking at each other's house-doors.

3. With these wrestlers compare Grimm's " Der junge Riese," *Kinder und Hausmaerchen*, vol. II. p. 23, and " Eisenhans" in Haltrich's *Siebenbuergische Maerchen*, p. 77.

4. Ajít carries her house. Note by Mr. J. F. Campbell : " Compare an Irish story about Fionn and a giant who was told that the hero turned the house when the wind blew open the door." [See, too, Campbell's *Tales of the Western Highlands*, vol. III. p. 184.]

5. When Karím was here I forgot to ask him how big were Ajít's cakes, can, and mice. Mr. Campbell of Islay, who read this story in manuscript, wrote in the margin where the mice

were mentioned : " The fleas in the island of Java are so big that they come out from under the bed and steal potatoes. They do many such things. Compare [with Ajit's can] a Gaelic story about a man who found the Fenians in an island, and was offered a drink in a can so large that he could not move it."

6. Mr. G. H. Damant, in the *Indian Antiquary* for September 1873, vol. II. p. 271, has a Dinájpur story called "Two gánja-eaters" which is very like our Wonderful Story. In it a gánja-eater who can eat six maunds of gánja [1] hears of another gánja-eater who can eat nine maunds ; so he takes his six maunds of gánja, and sets off for his rival's country with the intention of fighting him. On the road he is thirsty and drinks a whole pond dry, but this fails to quench his thirst. Arrived at the nine-maund gánja-eater's house, he learns from the wife that her husband has gone to cut sugar-cane, and decides to go and meet him. He finds him in the jungle, and wishes to fight there and then ; but his rival does not agree to this, saying he has eaten nothing for seven days. The other answers he has eaten nothing for nine ; whereupon the nine-maund gánja-eater suggests they shall wait till they get back to his country, as in the jungle they will have no spectators. The six-maund gánja-eater consents. So the nine-maund gánja-eater takes up all the sugar-cane he has cut during the last seven days and sets off for his country with his rival. On the way they meet a fish-wife, and call her to stop and see them fight ; she answers she must carry her fish without delay to market, being already late, and proposes they should stand on her arm and fight, and that then she could see them as they go along. While they are fighting on her arm, down sweeps a kite which carries off " the gánja-eaters ; fish and all." They are thrown by a storm in front of a Rájá's daughter, who has them swept away thinking they are bits of straw.

[1] An intoxicating preparation of the hemp-plant (*Cannabis sativa* or *C. indica*).

XIX.—THE FAKÍR NÁNAKSÁ SAVES THE MERCHANT'S LIFE.

1. Nánaksá, *i.e.* Nának Sháh, is doubtless the first guru of the Sikhs (about A.D. 1460—1530).

2. With the transmigration of the souls of the merchant's father, grandmother, and sister into the goat, the old woman and his liittle daughter, compare a Dinájpur story published by Mr. G. H. Damant in the *Indian Antiquary* for June 7, 1872, vol. I. p. 172, in which a king threatens to kill a Bráhman if he does not explain what he means by saying to the king every day, " As thy liberality, so thy virtue." By his new-born daughter's advice the Bráhman tells the king this child would explain it to him. Accordingly the king comes to the Bráhman's house and is received smilingly " by the two-and-a-half-days-old daughter. She sends the king for the desired information to a certain red ox, who in his turn " sends him to a clump of Shahara (*Trophis aspera*) trees. The trees tell him he has been made king in this state of existence, because in a former state of existence he was liberal and full of charity ; that in this former state the child just born as the Bráhman's daughter was his wife : that the red ox was then his son, and that this son's wife, as a punishment for her hardness and uncharitableness, had " become the genius of this grove of trees."

3. Jabrá'il is the Archangel Gabriel.

XX.—THE BOY WHO HAD A MOON ON HIS FORE-HEAD AND A STAR ON HIS CHIN.

1. For these marks see paragraph 4 of the notes to Phúlmati Rání. I think the silver chains with which King Oriant's children are born (see the Netherlandish story, the Knight of the Swan, quoted in paragraph 3 of the notes to the Pomegranate King) are identical with the suns, moons, and stars that the hero in this and in many other tales possesses. They are his princely insignia and proofs of his royalty. When the boy in this tale twists his right ear his insignia are hidden, and so long as they

remain concealed no one can guess he is a king's son, unless he chooses to reveal himself, as he does, partially, through his sweet singing to the youngest princess. (With this partial revelation compare the Sicilian "Stupid Peppe" revealing himself in part by means of the ring he gave to his youngest princess. This ring has the property of flashing brightly whenever he is near. (See the story "Von dem muthigen Königssohn, der viele Abenteuer erlebte" quoted in paragraph 6 of the notes to this story, p. 280.) The shape of the insignia may have been destroyed, as in the case of the sixth swan's chain, in the Netherlandish story, but its substance remains, and as soon as it reappears the hero clothes himself with his own royal form. Chundun Raja's necklace (*Old Deccan Days*, p. 230) and Sodewa Bai's necklace (*ib.* p. 236), in which lay their life, belong, perhaps, to these insignia. Their princely owners' existence depends on their keeping these proofs of their royalty in their own possession, and is suspended whenever the proofs pass into the hands of others.

2. The gardener's daughter promises to bear her husband a son with the moon on his forehead and a star on his chin. Compare "Die verstossene Königin und ihre beiden ausgesetzten Kinder," Gonzenbach's *Sicilianische Maerchen*, vol. I. p. 19, where the girl (p. 21) promises to give the king, if he marries her, a son with a golden apple in his hand, and a daughter with a silver star on her forehead. Also compare with our story "Truth's Triumph" in *Old Deccan Days*, p. 50. In Indian stories, as in European tales, the gardener and his family often play an important part, the hero being frequently the son of the gardener's daughter, or else protected by the gardener and his wife.

3. With the kettledrum compare the golden bell given by the Rájá to Guzra Bai in "Truth's Triumph" (*Old Deccan Days*, p. 53); and the flute given by the nymph Tillottama to her husband in the "Finding of the Dream,' a Dinájpur story published by Mr. G. H. Damant in the *Indian Antiquary*, February 1875, vol. IV. p. 54. See also paragraph 7, p. 287, of notes to "How the Rájá's son won the Princess Labám."

4. *Kaṭar* (the *t* is lingual) means cruel, relentless. With this

fairy-horse compare the Russian hero-horses in Dietrich's collection of Russian tales, who remain shut up behind twelve iron doors, and often loaded with chains as well, till the advent of heroes great enough to ride them. They generally speak with human voices, are their masters' devoted servants, fight for him, often slaughtering more of his enemies than he does himself, and when turned loose in the free fields, as Kaṭar was in his jungle, till they are needed, always staying in them and coming at once to their master when he calls. See in the collection by Dietrich (*Russische Volksmaerchen*) No. 1, "Von Ljubim Zarewitsch," &c., p. 3; No. 2, "Von der selbstspielenden Harfe," p. 17; No. 4, "Von Ritter Iwan, dem Bauersohne," p. 43; No. 10, "Von Bulat dem braven Burschen," p. 133; Jeruslan Lasarewitsch in the story that bears his name (No. 17, p. 208) catches and tames a wonderful horse near which even lions and eagles do not dare to go, p. 214. And the Hungarian fairy horses (Zauberpferde) who, like the Servian hero-horses, become ugly and lame at pleasure, and speak with human voice, must also be compared to Kaṭar. One in particular plays a leading part in the story of "Weissnittle" (Stier's *Ungarische Volksmaerchen*, p. 61). He saves the king's son twice from death and then flies with him to another land. He speaks with human voice, advises him in all his doings, and marries him to a king's daughter; Weissnittle obeying his horse as implicitly as our hero does Kaṭar. The heroes' horses in Haltrich's *Siebenbuergische Maerchen* also speak with human voice and give their masters good counsel. See p. 35 of "Der goldne Vogel;" p. 49 of "Der Zauberross;" p. 101 of "Der Knabe und der Schlange." These last two horses have more than four legs: like Odin's Sleipnir, they each have eight. See, too, the dragon's horse and this horse's brother in "Der goldne Apfelbaum und die neun Pfauinnen" (Karadschitsch, *Volksmaerchen der Serben*, pp. 33 —40). The "steed" in the "Rider of Grianaig," pp. 14 and 15 of vol. III. of Campbell's *Tales of the Western Highlands*, and the "Shaggy dun filly" in "The young king of Easaidh Ruadh," at p. 4 of vol. I. of the same work, may also be compared; and, lastly, in a list of hero-horses Cúchulainn's Gray of Macha deserves a place. On the morning of the day which was to see his last fight, Cúchulainn ordered his charioteer, Loeg, to harness the Gray to his chariot. "' I swear to God what my people swears,' said Loeg, 'though the men of Conchobar's fifth (Ulster) were around the Gray of Macha, they could not bring him to the chariot. . . . If thou wilt, come thou, and speak with the Gray himself.' Cúchulainn went to him. And thrice did the horse turn his left side to his master. . . . Then Cúchulainn reproached his horse, saying that he was not wont to deal thus with his master. Thereat the Gray of Macha came and let his big round tears of blood fall on Cúchulainn's feet." The hero then leaps into his chariot, and goes to battle. At last the Gray is sore wounded, and he and Cúchulainn bid each other farewell. The Gray leaves his master; but when Cúchulainn, wounded to death, has tied himself to a stone pillar to die standing, "then came the Gray of Macha to Cúchulainn to protect him so long as his soul abode in him, and the 'hero's light' out of his forehead remained. Then the Gray of Macha wrought the three red routs all around him. And fifty fell by his teeth and thirty by each of his hooves. This is what he slew of the host. And hence is (the saying) 'Not keener were the victorious courses of the Gray of Macha after Cúchulainn's slaughter.'" Then Lugaid and his men cut off the hero's head and right hand and set off, driving the Gray before them. They met Conall the Victorious, who knew what had happened when he saw his friend's horse. "And he and the Gray of Macha sought Cúchulainn's body. They saw Cúchulainn at the pillar-stone. Then went the Gray of Macha and laid his head on Cúchulainn's breast. And Conall said, 'A heavy care to the Gray of Macha is that corpse.'" Conall himself, in the fight he has with Lugaid, to avenge his friend's slaughter, is helped by his own horse, the Dewy-Red. "When Conall found that he prevailed not, he saw his steed, the Dewy-Red, by Lugaid. And the steed came to Lugaid and tore a piece out of his side." ("Cúchulainn's Death, abridged from the Book of Leinster," *Revue celtique*, Juin 1877, pp. 175, 176, 180, 182, 183, 185.)

5. The prince makes his escape at five years old. Jeruslan Jeruslanowitsch at the same age sets out in search of his father,

Jeruslan Lasarewitsch, equipped as a knight, at p. 250 of the 17th Russian Maerchen in the collection by Dietrich quoted àbove. He meets and fights bravely with his father, proving himself worthy of him (p. 251). Sohrab, Rustam's famous son, gives proof of a lion's courage at five, and at ten years old vanquishes all his companions (Gubernatis, *Zoological Mythology*, vol. I. p. 115).

6. The princess chooses the ugly common-looking man. In *Old Deccan Days*, p. 119, so does the Princess Buccoulee. In the episode of Nala and Damayantí we have the assemblage of suitors, and the public choice of a husband by a princess (*svayamvara*). Damayantí recognizes the mortal Nala among the gods, (each of whom has made himself resemble Nala) from the fact that the flowers of which Nala's garlands were composed had faded while the garlands of the gods were blooming freshly. In a story from Manípúrí told by Mr. G. H. Damant in the *Indian Antiquary*, September 1875, vol. IV. p. 260, Prince Basanta, effectually disguised by misery, and travel-stained, arrives with the merchant at a certain place where the king's daughter that day is to choose her husband. The merchant takes his seat among the princely suitors; Basanta a little way off. There is a general storm of scoffings when the princess hangs her garland of flowers round Basanta's neck. In one of Laura Gonzenbach's Sicilian stories, "Von einem muthigen Königssohn, der viele Abenteuer erlebte," vol. II. p. 21, we have three kings' sons (brothers) and three princesses (sisters.) The two elder brothers marry the two elder sisters. At a tournament held on purpose that she may choose her husband, the youngest sister, to the general disgust, chooses the youngest prince (disguised as the dirty, ill-dressed servant of the court tailor), and who is not even present as a suitor. Her suitors, princes, have passed before her for three days. After the marriage the prince keeps up the disguise. His brothers by way of amusing themselves at his expense take "Stupid Peppe," as they call him, to the wood to shoot birds; he shoots a great number, while they run here and there and cannot find one. They agree to let him brand them with black spots on their shoulders, on condition he gives them his birds. In the notes to this story,

vol. II. p. 240. Herr Köhler gives Spanish, Russian, South Siberian, and others parallels. And in Stier's *Ungarische Volksmaerchen*, p. 61, in the story of " Weissnittle," we have not only the hero-horse mentioned in paragraph 4 of these notes, but also the assemblage of suitors for the princess to choose her husband : her choice of a seemingly stupid gardener's boy, who has partially revealed himself to her ; the prince retaining his disguise, after his marriage, towards every one, even his wife : two brothers-in-law, who are kings' sons and the wife's elder sisters' husbands ; their hunting on three different days, each time meeting a handsome prince in whom they do not recognize their despised brother-in-law, Weissnittle, who sells them his game the first day for their wedding-rings, the second for leave to brand them with these rings on their foreheads, the third for permission to brand them with a gallows on their backs : lastly, we have Weissnittle, as a splendid young prince, publicly shaming his brothers-in-law by exposing their branding marks. In India this branding with red-hot pice was the punishment for stealing. Compare in Taylor's *Confessions of a Thug*, p. 411, Amír Ali's horror at being so branded by the Rájá of Jhalone. It was, he says years later, a punishment worse than death, as the world would think him a thief, and he would carry to his grave " a mark only set on the vile and the outcasts from society."

7. Múniyá tells me that, in a variation of this story, the dog, cow, and horse each swallow the child three times, but for shorter periods, as he is only five years old when he escapes on Katar. Then when the princess chooses her husband she rides three times round the assemblage of Rájás, who all sit on a great plain, and each time she chooses the pretended *old* man ; for in this version the boy loses his youth as well as his good looks. Instead of taking service with the grain merchant, the boy is told by his horse to go boldly to the king's palace and ask for service there. The shaming of the brothers-in-law happens thus. The boy invites these princes, the king, all the king's servants, and all the people in the king's country, to a grand entertainment in the king's court-house. When they are all assembled he has the six princes stripped and every one

mocks at the pice-marks on their backs. These are the only variations in the other version.

Sir George Grey, in his *Polynesian Mythology*, p. 73, tells how the hero Tawhaki when he climbed into heaven in search of his lost wife "disguised himself, and changed his handsome and noble appearance, and assumed the likeness of a very ugly old man." If fact, he looks such a thoroughly common old man that in the heavens he is taken for a slave instead of a great chief, and treated as such.

XXI.—THE BÉL-PRINCESS.

1. Múniyá says that telling the prince he would marry a Bél-Princess was equivalent to saying he would not marry at all, for these brothers' wives knew she lived in the fairy-country, and that it would be very difficult, if not impossible, for the prince to find her, and take her from it.

2. With the fakír's sleep compare that of the dragon who sleeps for a year at a time in the Transylvanian story "Das Rosenmaerchen" (*Siebenbuergische Maerchen*, pp. 124, 126).

3. In a Greek story, "Das Schloss des Helios" (Schmidt's *Griechische Maerchen, Sagen und Volkslieder*, p. 106), the heroine is warned by a monk that as she approaches the magic castle voices like her brothers' voices will call her ; but if, consequently, she looks behind she will become stone. Her two elder brothers go to seek her, and, as they meet no monk to warn them, they become stone. The third brother meets the monk, obeys his warning, and thus, like his sister, escapes the evil fate. To save him from Helios, the sister turns him into a thimble till she has Helios's promise to do him no harm. (Compare the Tiger and Tigress, p. 155 of this collection.) Helios gives him some water in a flask with which he sprinkles the stone brothers, whereupon they and all the other stone princes come to life. In these Indian tales the healing blood from the little finger plays the part of the waters of life and death, found in so many Russian and other European stories.

When reading of the fate of all these princes, it is impossible
not to think of Lot's wife.

The danger of looking back, when engaged on any
dealings with supernatural powers, is insisted on in the tales
and practices of the Russians, Eskimos, Zulus, and the
Khonds of Orissa. In Russia the watcher for the golden fern-
flower must seize it the instant it blossoms and run home,
taking care not to look behind him : whether through fear of
giving the demons, who also watch for it, power over him, or
whether through a dread of the flower losing its magic powers
if this precaution is neglected, Mr. Ralston does not say
(*Songs of the Russian People*, p. 99). When "the Revived
who came to the under-world people" (Dr. Rink tells us in his
Tales and Traditions of the Eskimo, p. 299) took the old couple
to visit the ingnersuit (supernatural beings "who have their
abodes beneath the surface of the earth, in the cliffs along the
sea-shore, where the ordinarily invisible entrances to them are
found" *ib.* p. 46), he warned "them not to look back when
they approached the rock which enclosed the abode of the
ingnersuit, lest the entrance should remain shut for them....
When they had reached the cliff, and were rowing up to it,
it forthwith opened ; and inside was seen a beautiful country,
with many houses, and a beach covered with pebbles and large
heaps of fish and matak (edible skin). Perceiving this the old
people for joy forgot the warning and turned round, and
instantly all disappeared : the prow of the boat knocked right
against the steep rock and was smashed in, so that they all
were thrown down by the shock. The son [the revived] said,
' Now we must remain apart for ever.'" Mr. Tylor, in the 2nd
volume of his *Primitive Culture*, at p. 147 mentions a Zulu
remedy for preventing a dead man from tormenting his widow
in her dreams ; the sorcerer goes with her to lay the ghost,
and when this is done " charges her not to look back till she gets
home :" and he says the Khonds of Orissa, when offering human
sacrifices to the earth-goddess bury their portions of the offering
in holes in the ground behind their backs without looking round
(*ib.* p. 377).

4. In most of the stories of this kind the command is to open

the fruit or casket only near water, for if the beautiful maiden inside cannot get water immediately she dies. Such is the case in the " Drei Pomeranzen " (Stier's *Ungarische Maerchen und Sagen*, p. 83), in " Die Schoene mit dem sieben Schleier " (*Sicilianische Maerchen*, vol. I. p. 73), and in " Die drei Citronen " (Schmidt's *Griechische Maerchen, Sagen und Volkslieder*, p. 71). " Die Ungeborene Niegesehene " (Schott's *Wallachische Maerchen*, p. 248) must be compared with these, though the beautiful maiden does not come out of the golden fairy-apple. She appears suddenly and the prince must give her water to drink and the apple to eat, before he can take her and keep her. In all these stories the hero has a long journey, and encounters many dangers, in seeking his bride. In the Sicilian story he is helped by hermits ; in the Greek story, by a monk—monks in Greek and hermits in Sicilian and Servian stories playing the part of the fakírs in these Indian tales. In all these stories, too, the maiden is killed or transformed by a wicked woman who takes her place. In the Wallachian and Sicilian fairy tales the rightful bride becomes a dove only. But in the Hungarian tale she is drowned in a well and becomes a gold fish ; the wicked gipsy has no rest till she has eaten the fish's liver : from one of its scales springs a tree ; she has the tree cut down and burnt. The woodcutter who hews down the tree makes a cover for his wife's milk-pot from a piece of the wood, and they find their house kept in beautiful order from this moment. So to discover the secret, they peep through the keyhole one day and see a lovely fairy come out of the milk-jar. Then they enter their house suddenly and the girl tells her story : the woodcutter's wife burns the wooden lid to force her to keep her own form, and goes to the king's son to tell him where he will find his Pomegranate-bride again. In the Greek story a Lamnissa eats the citron-girl, but a tiny bone falls unnoticed into the water and becomes a gold-fish. The prince not only takes the Lamnissa home with him, but he takes the gold-fish too, and keeps it in his room, " for he loved it dearly." The Lamnissa never rests till he gives her the fish to eat. Its bones are thrown into a garden and from them springs a rose bush on which blooms a rose which the king's old washerwoman wishes to break off to sell it at the castle. From out of the bush springs the beautiful citron-maiden, and tells the old woman her story. She also gives her the rose for the king's son, and in the basket with the rose she lays a ring he had given her, but charges the old woman to say nothing about her to him. The next day he comes to the old woman's cottage and finds his real bride.

5. The youngest prince alone can gather the lotus-flower and bél-fruit. Compare the Pomegranate-king, pp. 10 and 11, and paragraphs 1 and 4, pp. 245, 252, of the notes to that story. In his *Northern Mythology*, vol. I., in the footnotes at p. 290, Thorpe mentions a maiden's grave from which spring " three lilies which no one save her lover may gather." I think he must quote from a Danish ballad.

6. The princess after drowning is first in a lotus-flower ; then in a bél-fruit again ; and, lastly, her body is changed to a garden and palace. Signor de Gubernatis at p. 152 of the 1st volume of his *Zoological Mythology* mentions an Esthonian story where a girl (she who addressed the crow as " bird of light"—see paragraph 2, p. 259 of the notes to " Brave Hírálálbásá ") while fleeing with her lover is thrown into the water by a magic ball sent after them by the old witch, and there becomes " a pond-rose (lotus-flower)." Her lover eats hogs'-flesh and thus learns the language of birds, and then sends swallows to a magician in Finnland to ask what he must do to free his bride. The answer is brought by an eagle ; and the prince following the magician's instructions helps the girl to recover her human form. And just as Surya Bai is born again in her mango (*Old Deccan Days*, p. 87) and the Bél-Princess in her bél-fruit, so is the girl in the Hottentot tale of " The Lion who took a woman's shape " born from her heart in the calabash full of milk in which her mother has put it. The lion had eaten the girl ; but her mother burns the lion and persuades the fire in which she burns him to give her her daughter's heart (Bleek's *Hottentot Fables and Tales*, pp. 55 and 56). With the change into the garden and palace compare the Russian story of a maiden whose servant-girl blinds her and takes her place as the king's wife. After some time the false queen learns her mistress is still living ; so she has her

murdered and cut to pieces. "Where the maiden is buried a garden arises, and a boy shows himself. The boy goes to the palace and runs after the queen, making such a din that she is obliged, in order to silence him, to give him the girl's heart which she had kept hidden. The boy then runs off contented, the king follows him, and finds himself before the resuscitated maiden" (Gubernatis, *Zoological Mythology*, vol. I. pp. 218, 219). See paragraphs 7 and 8 of the notes to "Phúlmati Rání," p. 244, and 1, 3 and 4, pp. 245, 250, 252, of those to "The Pomegranate-king."

7. The commonplace fate of the wonderful palace is deplorable.

XXII.—HOW THE RÁJÁ'S SON WON THE PRINCESS LABÁM.

1. The "four sides" in this story (p. 153), the "four directions" (p. 156) which ought to have been translated four sides and the four sides in "The Bed," p. 202, are the four points of the compass. They appear in a Dinájpur story told by Mr. G. H. Damant in the *Indian Antiquary*, 5th April 1872, p. 115. In the first Russian fairy tale published by Dietrich, the hero's parents give their elder sons permission "to go on the four sides" when they start on their journeys (*Russische Volksmaerchen*, p. 1). In another fairy tale in the same collection (No. 11, p. 144) the Prince Malandrach, when he has lost his way flying in the air and is over the sea, raises himself by a last effort and looks on all the "four sides" in search of a resting-place for his foot, p. 147. Of course, too, like orthodox Russians, the Russian heroes generally bow to all the "four sides," before attempting their journeys and adventures.

2. Hiráman is the name of a kind of parroquet. Irik in the Bohemian tale "Princess Golden-Hair" (Naake's *Slavonic Fairy Tales*, p. 99) first hears of the princess's existence from the chattering of birds.

3. "Aunty" was the word used in English by old Múniya.

4. With the stone bowl compare the pot in Grimm's "Der suesse Brei," *Kinder und Hausmaerchen*, vol. II. p. 104.

5. With the tigers' coats compare the robes of honour where-with the knights in the Mabinogion clothe themselves when they go to combat. "And he (Gwalchmai) went forth to meet the knight (Owain), having over himself and his horse a satin robe of honour sent him by the daughter of the Earl of Rhangyw ; and in this dress he was not known by any of the host" ("The Lady of the Fountain," *Mabinogion,* vol. I. p. 67). Peredur wears "a bright scarlet robe of honour over his armour" given him by the king's daughter (*ib.* p. 363 of "Peredur the son of Evrawc"). And in "The Dream of Rhonabwy" a knight and his horse wear a robe of honour (*ib.* vol. II. p. 413).

6. With the tigers' fight with the demons compare the com-bat of the grateful lion with the giant, in which the lion bears the brunt of the battle. On the giant's saying, "Truly, I should find no difficulty in fighting with thee were it not for the animal that is with thee," Owain shuts the lion up in the castle. "The lion in the castle roared very loud, for he heard that it went hard with Owain," so he climbed to the top of the castle, sprang down and "joined Owain. And the lion gave the giant a stroke with his paw, which tore him from his shoulder to his hip, and his heart was laid bare. And the giant fell down dead" ("The Lady of the Fountain," *Mabinogion*), vol. I. pp. 79, 80).

7. Gubernatis in vol. I. p. 160, of his *Zoological Mythology,* says, "The drum or kettle-drum thunder is a familiar image in Hindu poetry, and the gandharvas, the musician warriors of the Hindu Olympus, have no other instrument than the thunder." "The magic flute is a variation of the same celestial instru-ment," *ib.* p. 161.

8. For the hair, see note to "How King Burtal became a Fakír," paragraph 2, p. 267.

XXIII.—THE PRINCESS WHO LOVED HER FATHER LIKE SALT.

1. With the task of pulling out the needles, the purchase of the maid-servant, the sleep of the princess, the usurping of her

place by the maid who makes the prince believe the princess
is her servant-girl, compare "Der böse Schulmeister und die
wandernde Königstochter," in Laura Gonzenbach's *Sicilianische Maerchen,* vol. I. p. 59.   Here, too, the princess is driven
forth from her home ; she finds a prince lying dead with a tablet
by him on which is written, " If a maiden will rub me seven
years, seven months and seven days long with grass from
Mount Calvary, I shall return to life, and she shall become my
wife" (p. 61).

2. Sun-jewel box. The word thus translated is Rav-ratan-
ke-piṭárá. *Raví,* sun ; *ratan,* jewel ; *piṭárá,* a kind of box.

3. In one of Grimm's stories, " Die Gänsehirtin am Brunnen,"
Kinder und Hausmaerchen, vol. II. p. 419, a king asks his three
daughters how much they love him (p. 425).   The eldest loves
him as much as the "sweetest sugar," the second as much as
her "finest dress," and the third as much as salt.   So her father
in a rage has a sack of salt bound on her back, and makes two
of his servants take her away to the forest.   See also Auerbach's
Barfüssele, Stuttgart, 1873, ss. 236, 237.

XXIV.—THE DEMON IS AT LAST CONQUERED BY
THE KING'S SON.

1. The leading idea of this story is the same as that in " Brave
Hírálálbásá."

2. With this demon as a goat, compare the Rakshas in the
Pig's Head Soothsayer in *Sagas from the Far East,* p. 63,
and the Rakshas in a Bengáli story printed by Mr. G. H. Damant
in the *Indian Antiquary,* 7th June, 1872, p. 120. This last
story opens with seven labourers, brothers, six of whom go
down to the water to drink and never return.   The seventh goes
to see what has happened to them, and finds, instead of his
brothers, a goat which is really a Rakshas.   This goat then turns
into a beautiful woman who marries the king, first making him
give into her hands the eyes of his queen, who is sent blind into
the forest, where she bears a little son.   The Rakshas wife learns

this, and when the boy later takes service with the king she sends him three times to her people in Ceylon, with orders to them to kill him. He has to bring her foam from the sea, a wonderful rice which is sown, ripens, and can be boiled in one day, and a singular cow. With the help of a Sannyásí (a Bráhman of the fourth order, a religious mendicant), he does these errands safely. The Rakshases in Ceylon receive him as their sister's son, show him his own mother's eyes and the clay with which they can be set again in any human sockets, a lemon which contains the life of the tribe, and a bird in which is that of the Rakshas-queen. The boy cuts up the lemon, and thereby kills them all, carries her eyes to his mother, and kills the Rakshas-queen by killing the bird. In this story, as in " Brave Hírálálbásá," the Rakshas-queen takes her own fearful form on seeing her danger.

3. The *Bargat*, fig-tree, is the *Ficus Bengalensis* of Linnæus.

4. Múniyá sends her hero for a *Garpank's* feather ; *Garpank* I can find in no dictionary, but have ventured to translate it by eagle, as she says it is like a kite, only very much bigger ; she sent us to see a statue of a garpank that stood over a gateway in a street in Calcutta, which might be that of an eagle or of a huge hawk. She said such birds did not exist in Bengal, and that it was not the Garuḍa (the sovran of the feathered race and vehicle of Vishṇu, Benfey). Gubernatis, in the 2nd volume of his *Zoological Mythology*, p. 189, tells a story from Monferrat where a king is blind, and can only be cured by " bathing his eyes in oil with a feather " of a griffin that lives on a high mountain. His third and youngest son catches and brings him one of the griffins and the king regains his sight.

5. Winning the gratitude of a bird by killing the snake or dragon that year after year devours its young birds is such a common incident in fairy tales, that I will only mention two instances. One occurs in a Dinájpur tale published by Mr. G. H. Damant in the *Indian Antiquary* for 5th April, 1872, p. 145, where the hero saves the young birds from the snake. They tell the old birds. He lies under the tree and listens to the old birds relating how he will find the tree with the silver stem and golden branches he has come to seek. The

U

other occurs at pp. 119 110, of a story collected by Vogl (*Volksmaerchen* [Slavonic], p. 79) called Schön-Jela. In this tale the hero is sheltered in the dreadful under-ground wilderness by a hermit. Here there is the gigantic bird, Einja, who every third year has a brood of four young birds which a dragon as regularly devours. The hero, Prince Milan, watches by the nest for the dragon and kills him. The young birds, overjoyed, fly out of the nest and cover the hero with their wings till the old bird on her return asks who has saved them. Then they unfold their wings and she sees Prince Milan. In return she carries him to the upper world.

6. The word translated " night-growing rice " is Rát-vashá-kedhán ; and the ayah's description of this rice is given in the story. In this description she spoke of it as cháwal, the common word for uncooked rice, and said the Rakshas wished to drink its kánjí-pání (rice-water). As, it is a fairy plant I am afraid it is hopeless trying to find its botanical name. Unluckily, Dr. George King says *vashá* is not rice at all. This is what he wrote to me on the subject : " *Vashá* is, I suppose, the same as *vasaka*, and in that case is *Justitia Adhatoda*, a straggling shrub common over the whole of India [very unlike the Rátvashá-ke-dhán] and which was in the Sanscrit as it is in the native pharmacopœias. It is not a kind of rice, but belongs to the natural order of Acanthaceæ (the family to which Acanthus and Thunbergia belong)." This night-growing rice may be compared to the day-growing rice in paragraph 2, p. 288, of the notes to this story.

7. Compare with the paper boat the rolled-up burdock leaf given to the hero by the dwarf in the seventh Esthonian tale quoted by Gubernatis (*Zoological Mythology*, vol. I. p. 155) : whenever this hero wishes to cross water he unrolls his burdockleaf. Gubernatis compares this leaf to the lotus-leaf on which the Hindús represented their god as floating in the midst of the waters (*ibid.*).

8. With the great wind that comes from the demon, compare the following Swedish account of a giant in Thorpe's *Northern Mythology*, vol. II. p. 85. He asks his road of a lad, who directs him : then " he went off as in a whirlwind, and the lad now dis-

covered, to his no small astonishment, that his forefinger with
which he had pointed out the way had followed along with the
giant." In the old Scandinavian belief the Giant Hræsvelgr
sat at the end of heaven in an eagle's garb (arna ham). From
the motion of his wings came the wind which passed over men
(*ib.* vol. I. p. 8). It must be mentioned also that " in the German popular tales the devil is frequently made to step into the
place of the giants " (*ib.* vol. I. p. 234), and that Stöpke or
Stepke is in Lower Saxony an appellation of the devil or of the
whirlwind, from which proceed the fogs which spread over the
land (*ib.* p. 235). The devil sits in the whirlwind and rushes
howling and raging through the air (Mark Sagen, *ib.* p. 377).
The whirlwind is also ascribed to witches. If a knife be cast
into it, the witch will be wounded and become visible (Schrei-
ber's Taschenbuch, 1839, p. 323; *ib.* p. vol. I. p. 235). Mr.
Ralston, in his *Songs of the Russian People*, p. 382, says the
Russian peasant attributes whirlwinds to the mad dances in
which the devil celebrates his marriage with a witch, and at
p. 155 of the same book tells us how the malicious demon Lyeshy
not only makes use of the whirlwind as a travelling conveyance
for himself and a means of turning intruders out of quarters he
had selected for his own refuge, but sends home in it people
to whom he is grateful. In Ireland we find a wind blowing
from hell. King Loegaire tells Patrick, " I perceived the wind
cold, icy, like a two-ridged spear, which almost took our hair
from our heads and passed through us to the ground. I ques-
tioned Benén as to this wind. Said Benén to me, ' This is the
wind of hell which has opened before Cúchulainn.' " *Lebar na
huidre*, p. 113 a. This " wind of hell " makes one think of the
sweet-scented wind from the mid-day regions, and the evil-
scented wind from the north, which in old Persian religious
belief blew to meet pure and wicked souls after death (Tylor's
Primitive Culture, vol. II. pp. 98, 99). Mr. Tylor mentions also
the Fanti negroes' belief that the men and animals they sacrifice
to the local fetish are carried away in a whirlwind imperceptibly
to the worshippers (*ib.* p. 378).

8. Ábjhamjham-ke pání is what has been translated by
" water from the glittering well."

9. The king had a great pit dug in the jungle. This is how Kai and Bedwyr plucked out the beard of Dillus Varwawc, which had to be plucked out during life. They made him eat meat till he slept. " Then Kai made a pit under his feet, the largest in the world, and he struck him a violent blow, and squeezed him into the pit. And there they twcezed out his beard completely with the wooden tweezers ; and after that they slew him altogether " (" Kilhwch and Olwen," *Mabinogion*, vol. II. p. 304).

XXV.—THE FAN PRINCE.

1. The boat would not move because the king had forgotten to get the thing his youngest daughter had asked him to bring her. Signor de Gubernatis (*Zoological Mythology*, vol. II. p. 382) mentions an unpublished story from near Leghorn in which a sailor promises to bring his youngest daughter a rose. The eldest daughter is to have a shawl, and the second a hat. " When the voyage is over, he is about to return, but having forgotten the rose, the ship refuses to move ; he is compelled to go back to look for a rose in a garden ; a magician hands the rose with a little box to the father to give it to one of his daughters, whom the magician is to marry. At midnight, the father, having returned home, relates to his third daughter all that had happened. The little box is opened; it carries off the third daughter to the magician, who happens to be King Pietraverde, and is now a handsome young man."

2. The princess's ring recalls Portia and Nerissa.

3. " A yogí is a Hindú religious mendicant.

XXVI.—THE BED.

The merchant's son possibly was afraid of incurring the wrath either of an original spirit residing in the tree, or of some human soul who had been born again as its genius (see paragraph 1, p. 275, of note to "The fakír Nánaksá saves the merchant's life "). Múniyá could give no reason for his asking each tree's permission to cut it down.

XXVII.—PANWPATTI RÁNÍ.

See another version of this tale in the Baiṭal Pachísi, No. 1. There the heroine is called Padmávatí, and her father King Dantavát.

XXVIII.—THE CLEVER WIFE.

1. The merchant's wife tricks the four men into chests. Upakosâ makes the like appointments, and plays a similar trick: compare her story translated from the Kathápítha by Dr. G. Bühler in the *Indian Antiquary* for 4th October, 1872, pp. 305, 306: and in "The Touchstone," a Dinájpur legend told by Mr. G. H. Damant at p. 337 of the *Indian Antiquary* for December, 1873, the hero-prince's second wife, Pránnásiní, in order to regain the touchstone for her husband (like Upakosá and the Clever Wife) makes appointments with, and then tricks, the kotwál, the king's councillor, the prime minister, and lastly the king himself.

2. She plays cards (*tás*). Forbes in his Hindústání and English Dictionary p. 543, says *tás* is the word used for *Indian* playing cards. The Indian pack, he says, contains eight suits, each suit consisting of a king, wazír, and ten cards having various figures represented on them from one to ten in number.

[A close parallel to this tale is *Adi's Wife*, a Bengáli legend from Dinagepore, told by the late Mr. Damant in the *Indian Antiquary* for January, 1880, p. 2.]

XXXIX.—RÁJÁ HARICHAND'S PUNISHMENT.

1. This king is probably the same as "The Upright King," Harchand Rájá, p. 68 of this collection.

2. The Kop Shástra. Múniyá says *kop* is a Hindústání, not a Bengáli word, and has nothing whatever to do with demons. This is what Mr. Tawney writes on the subject : " It might mean *kapi*, or *kapila* if the woman is a Bengáli. *Kapi* is a name of Vishṇu, possibly it might be the Rámáyana as treating of monkeys, but I really do not know. I see Monier Williams says that there are certain demons called *kapa*. But of course *kôpa* is anger. I suppose you know that the natives of Bengal pronounce the short *a* as *o* in the English word *hop*." Múniyá pronounces *kop* like the English word *cope*. This Shastra seems as hopelessly mythical as the *Rát-vashá-ke-dhán*.

XXX.—THE KING'S SON AND THE WAZÍR'S DAUGHTER.

In a Servian story, "Des Vaters letzter Wille," pp. 134, 135, 136, of the *Volksmaerchen der Serben* collected by Karadschitsch, the youngest brother has to take his brother-in-law's horse over a bridge under which he sees an immense kettle full of boiling water in which men's heads are cooking while eagles peck at them. He then passes through a village where all is song and joyfulness because, so the inhabitants tell him, each year is fruitful with them and they live, therefore, in the midst of plenty. Then he sees two dogs quarrelling which he cannot succeed in separating. He next passes through a village where all is sorrow and tears because each year comes hail, so the inhabitants " have nothing." Next he sees two boars fighting together and cannot separate them any more than he could part the dogs. Lastly, he reaches a beautiful meadow. In the evening his brother-in-law expounds the meaning of all he has seen. The heads in the boiling vessel represent the everlasting torment in the next world. The happy villagers are good, charitable men, with whom God is well pleased. The dogs are his elder brothers' wives. The sorrowing villagers are men who know neither righteousness, concord, nor God. The boars are his two wicked elder brothers. The meadow is paradise.

GLOSSARY.

Bél, a fruit; *Ægle marmelos*.

Bulbul, a kind of nightingale.

Chaprásí, a messenger wearing a badge (*chaprás*).

Cooly (Tamil *kúli*), a labourer in the fields ; also a porter.

Dál, a kind of pulse; *Phaseolus aureus*, according to Wilson·; *Paspalum frumentaceum*, according to Forbes.

Dom (the d is lingual), a low-caste Hindú.

Fakír, a Muhammadan religious mendicant.

Ghee (*ghí*), butter boiled and then set to cool.

Kází, a Muhammadan Judge.

Kotwál, the chief police officer in a town.

Líchí, a fruit ; *Scytalia litchi*, Roxb.

Mahárájá (properly Maháráj), literally great king.

Maháráni, literally great queen.

Mainá, a kind of starling.

Maund (*man*), a measure of weight, about 87 lb.

Mohur (*muhar*), a gold coin worth 16 rupees.

Nautch (*nátya*), a union of song, dance, and instrumental music.

Pálkí, a palanquin.

Pice (*paisa*), a small copper coin.

Pilau, a dish made of either chicken or mutton, and rice.

Rájá, a king.

Rakshas, a kind of demon that eats men and beasts.

Ráni, a queen.

Róhu, a kind of big fish.

Rupee (*rúpíya*), a silver coin, now worth about twenty pence.

Ryot (*ràíyat*), a cultivator.

Sarai, a walled enclosure containing small houses for the use of travellers.

Sárí, a long piece of stuff which Hindú women wind round the body as a petticoat, passing one end over the head.

Sepoy (*sipáhí*), a soldier.

Wazír, prime minister.

Yogí, a Hindú religious mendicant.

LIST OF BOOKS REFERRED TO.

Bleek. *Hottentot Fables and Tales*, London, 1864.

Campbell, J. F. *Popular Tales of the West Highlands*, 4 vols. Edinburgh, 1860.

Dasent, G. *Norse Tales*, Edinburgh, 1859.

Dietrich, Anton. *Russische Volksmaerchen*, Leipzig, 1831.

Fiske. *Myth and Mythmakers*, London, 1873.

Frere, Miss. *Old Deccan Days*, 2nd edition, London, 1870.

Gonzenbach, Laura. *Sicilianische Maerchen*, Leipzig, 1870.

Grant, C. *Gazetteer of India for the Central Provinces*, edited by, 2nd edition, Nágpur, 1870.

Grey. *Polynesian Mythology*, London, 1855,

Grimm. *Kinder und Haunsmaerchen*, 3 vols., Gœttingen, first 2 vols. 1850, 3rd vol. 1856.

Grimm. *Irische Elfenmaerchen, uebersetzt von den Bruedern Grimm*, Leipzig, 1826.

Gubernatis, Angelo de. *Zoological Mythology*, 2 vols., London, 1870.

Guest, Lady Charlotte. *The Mabinogion*, translated by, 3 vols. Llandovery, 1849.

Haltrich, Joseph. *Deutsche Volksmaerchen aus dem Sachsenlande in Siebenbuergen*, Berlin, 1856.

Henderson. *Folklore of the Northern Counties of England and the Border*, London, 1866.

Hunt. *Romances and Drolls of the West of England*, 2nd edition, London, 1871.

Indian Antiquary, vols. I. (1872), II. (1873), and IV. (1875), Bombay.

Karadschitsch, W. S. *Volksmaerchen der Serben*, Berlin, 1854.

Lane. *Arabian Nights*, 3 vols., London, 1859.

Lebar na Huidre. Lithographic facsimile, Dublin, 1870.

Milenowsky. *Maerchen aus Boehmen*, Breslau, 1853.

Naake. *Slavonic Fairy Tales*, London, 1874

Old New Zealand, 1876.

Ralston. *Songs of the Russian People*, London, 1872. *Russian Folk Tales*, London, 1873.

Rink. *Tales and Traditions of the Eskimo,* Edinburgh and London, 1875.

Sagas from the Far East, London, 1873.

Schmidt, G. *Griechische Volksmaerchen, Sagen und Volkslieder,* Leipzig, 1877.

Schott. *Wallachische Maerchen,* Stuttgart und Tuebingen, 1845.

Stier, G. *Ungarische Maerchen und Sagen,* Berlin, 1850. *Ungarische Volksmaerchen,* Pesth (preface is dated 1857).

Taylor, Meadows. *Confessions of a Thug,* London, 1873.

Thorpe. *Yule Tide Stories,* London, 1853.

Three Middle Irish Homilies, Calcutta, 1877.

Tylor. *Primitive Culture,* 2nd edition, London, 1873.

Vogl, Johann, N. *Volksmaerchen* [Slavonic], Wien, 1837.

INDEX.

www.ingramcontent.com/pod-product-compliance
Lightning Source LLC
Chambersburg PA
CBHW020935030726
47496CB00005B/1206